Their passion grew more and more intimate...

"Jim. Jim, we mustn't," she managed weakly, her resistance receding with dismaying speed as hot, pulsing desire surged through her. She trembled against his tall, powerful frame. It was always thus when she was in his arms. Her body swayed beneath the spell of his, rendering her helpless to the dictates of passion. "The guests..." she murmured, even as her fingers curled in his thick, dark-brown hair.

"Damn the guests!"

Books by Jill Gregory

MY TRUE AND TENDER LOVE
PROMISE ME THE DAWN
TO DISTANT SHORES
THE WAYWARD HEART

MY TRUE AND TENDER LOVE

JILL GREGORY

BERKLEY BOOKS, NEW YORK

MY TRUE AND TENDER LOVE

A Berkley Book/published by arrangement with
the author

PRINTING HISTORY
Berkley trade paperback edition/April 1985

ISBN: 0-425-07666-0

Berkley Books are published by The Berkley Publishing Group,
200 Madison Avenue, New York, N.Y. 10016.
The name "BERKLEY" and the stylized "B" with design are
trademarks belonging to Berkley Publishing Corporation.

PRINTED IN THE UNITED STATES OF AMERICA

*To my family, especially Rachel and Larry,
with all my love.*

CHAPTER ONE

IT WAS that quiet hour between sunset and dusk. The air was still and heavy, the graying sky streaked with rose and pink and gold. As Bryony Logan stood at the bedroom window, gazing out at the endless rolling plains of Texas, she almost fancied that she could see the night shadows stealing in, settling silently upon the prairie, clinging like mist to the dying day. A small, eager smile played upon her lips. How mysterious, how seductive nightfall was. It held no terror for Bryony, for her nights were filled with love and tenderness, and a passion as fierce as the Texas sun. She welcomed the night as she welcomed the day: with outstretched arms and a glorious smile. In all of her eighteen years, she had never been happier than she was at this moment. She had never looked toward any evening with the anticipation she felt now, tonight. All of the world seemed cupped in her palm, a precious gift meant especially for her. Her heart sang with a happiness born of love, of love and contentment and a bliss that came from knowing she was needed and cherished. The secret she carried within her warmed her soul. The smile on her lips deep-

1

ened. Her eyes, gazing out at the sunset sky, grew dreamy.

Suddenly, she felt strong hands grip her shoulders and spin her about. She found herself staring up into steely, glinting blue eyes, and her heartbeat quickened.

"Jim." Her voice was low and soft with laughter as her slim arms circled his neck. "I didn't hear you come in. You startled me."

Her husband grinned down at her, holding her close. His gaze fell to her slender form, clad only in a peach-colored satin wrapper. Her thick cloud of silken black hair was still slightly damp, and it smelled of lilacs. So did her skin. His lips brushed her throat, and he inhaled her scent. The familiar, sharp desire he always felt when he held her, or even looked at her, stirred in his loins. "Damn it, Bryony, must you always smell so good? You make it damned difficult for a man to resist you."

Texas Jim Logan, the feared and deadly gunfighter, tightened his arms about her.

"Why should you want to resist?" she laughed, her green eyes saucy in the wide, dusky room, which was lit only by a single oil lamp on an oak table beside the bed. Her finger stroked his temple. Suddenly, though, she stiffened as she noticed how thickly the dust caked his bronzed flesh. Even his face—that lean, bronzed, handsome face—was streaked with grime and glistened slightly with sweat. She drew away. The events of the night ahead loomed before her. Her vivid jade-green eyes widened in dismay. "Jim! I almost forgot! The party!" She squirmed in his embrace, shrinking from his filthy chaps and boots, and from the dirt-laden blue shirt that fit tautly over his muscular chest and wide shoulders. "Let me go, you filthy beast! You've just come in from the range, and I've already bathed! You must do the same, and quickly! Our guests will be arriving in little over an hour, and ... ohhh—"

His mouth, closing hard upon hers, cut off her words. His arms clamped like iron bands around her slender form as his lips claimed hers with cool determination. He kissed her until she stopped squirming and her soft mouth melted beneath the onslaught of his lips. His tongue probed deep into the warm recesses of her mouth, tasting, exploring, as Bryony moaned softly.

"Jim. Jim, we mustn't," she managed weakly, her resistance receding with dismaying speed as hot, pulsing desire surged through her. She trembled against his tall, powerful frame. It was always thus when she was in his arms. Her body swayed beneath the spell of his, rendering her helpless to the dictates of passion. "The guests..." she murmured, even as her fingers curled in his thick, dark-brown hair.

"Damn the guests!" His voice was husky in her ear, and he swept her into his arms. He carried her to the magnificent four-poster brass bed, which was the focal point of the immense room, and lowered her upon the silken coverlet. His eyes glinted into hers. "Let them wait!" he growled, then tossed open the satin folds of her wrapper. Hot fire shot through him as he gazed down at her luminous naked form. He cupped her full breasts with his strong hands and crushed his lips to hers.

Bryony gasped and pulled him closer, reveling in the feel of him. After only three months of marriage, their passion was never far from the surface; in fact, it seemed to intensify as the love between them grew stronger, more intimate and open. Her body moved beneath his, writhing, tangling. She pressed her mouth into his neck as the wildfire licked through her. Her hands flew at his clothes, and soon they were both naked, clutching each other with a desperate need that built like a raging inferno within them. As his thumb teased the nipple of her breast and his mouth seared her flesh, Bryony's senses quivered with almost unbearable delight. Her slender fingers journeyed up and down the rippling muscles of his back, stroking his thighs and, finally, grasping and possessing the core of his manhood. Jim made a low sound deep in his throat, and his arms tightened about her. He took her mouth savagely in his, his tongue thrusting into hers until she was lost in a world of hot, swirling passion, aware of neither time nor space.

"Jim, Jim!" She trembled, and he poised above her, his face glistening with sweat and passion, his dark eyes alight with desire. "I love you so!"

"I know." He grinned, his teeth very white against the grime of his bronzed skin. "Almost as much as I love you."

He entered her then, thrusting deep and with awesome strength, taking her to dizzying heights of pleasure, driving her upward in delicious soaring spirals until her senses exploded like shooting fireworks lighting up the blackest night.

Afterward, he kissed her damp face and stroked her dark, cascading curls. "Sorry to be so quick and rough, little tenderfoot." He smiled and kissed her very gently on the mouth. "But as you said, there isn't much time. And you can't expect me to resist my own wife when she's so damned alluring she'd make a coyote howl."

"I'm so glad you feel that way," Bryony purred. She sat up and put her arms around his neck, letting her luxuriant, coal-black hair swirl around her shoulders and breasts. "After all, I do worry that after three months of respectable married life, you might grow bored." Her eyes and voice teased him, sparkling seductively as she rubbed his powerful chest and lightly stroked the thick mat of brown hair that curled there. Her lips brushed his nipples, biting gently at his warm flesh. "You're not bored, are you, Jim?" she murmured.

He lifted an eyebrow at her, vastly amused. "How could I grow bored when I'm married to you? A woman who throws herself at me in a passionate fury only an hour before a houseful of guests arrive for the biggest party this side of the Brazos?" he drawled. His lips curled as Bryony gave a little screech and jumped, naked, from the bed. "Forget something, little tenderfoot?" he said lazily.

"Yes, you fiend, the party! How could you make me forget all about it—twice! Jim, the guests will be arriving any minute!"

"So they will." He lounged on the bed a moment, watching as she scurried about in agitation. Then he swung his long legs over the side of the four-poster and stood, his tall, muscular frame glistening in the light of the oil lamp. He crossed the huge bedroom in a few quick strides and pulled Bryony into his arms.

"I must order a bath for both of us!" she chattered, her ears straining now for the sounds of approaching wagons and horses in the deepening night. "We're going to be dreadfully late . . ."

"There's one more thing, little tenderfoot," Jim said quietly. She stopped talking and stared up at him with wide, vivid green eyes. "I love you more than anything in this world," he said quite simply, then bent to kiss her.

An hour later they were both downstairs, mingling with the more than one hundred guests who had come from miles around Fort Worth to attend the first party at the Triple Star Ranch in more than a decade.

Jim Logan smoked his thin cigar as he leaned his broad shoulders against the parlor door, watching his wife through cool, narrowed eyes. Despite all the tumult in the festive, candle-lit room, despite the color and whirl of guests and servants moving through the handsomely furnished, flower-filled parlor, despite the rousing sounds of the guitars and fiddles from the musicians who serenaded those in the courtyard, Bryony alone seemed to shine and shimmer, a glowing vision of beauty in the center of this storm. Attired in a daringly décolleté gown of pale-yellow satin, with a velvet sash about her tiny waist and her creamy white shoulders enticingly bare, she looked as beautiful as he had ever seen her. Her midnight-black hair was dressed in clusters of curls that cascaded fetchingly down her back and showed to advantage the delicate, fine bones of her face and throat. Her milky complexion was tinted with pink by the excitement of the night, and her brilliant jade-green eyes, fringed by long, sooty lashes, shone enchantingly in the candlelight. Each feature of her face was lovely and sweet: the small, straight nose; the pink rosebud lips; and the stubborn, proud chin, which she had so many times stuck in the air when Texas Jim Logan had confronted her. Jim's blue eyes frosted as he remembered those first days, when she had hated him so, when he had wanted her with tormenting desire and had thought she could never be his. Even now, he could hardly believe his good fortune, he could hardly believe that those empty, solitary days of roaming and fighting and whore-bedding were over, that he was home at last on his father's ranch—no, *his* ranch—with the woman he loved.

"You're sure a lucky man, brother." Danny Logan clapped him on the shoulder and shook his head. "Bryony is about the purtiest woman I ever laid eyes on. And she knows how to throw a party, too. Look at her: charming, sweet, gay as you please. Everybody's talkin' about her."

Jim glanced down at his younger brother. At nineteen, Danny was a slim, lanky boy with an open face and the eager, friendly disposition of a puppy. He had been overjoyed when Jim had come home at last, bringing with him a brand-new bride. For a time Danny had tried to run the Triple Star himself, a massive and grueling undertaking, one too demanding for his age and temperament. He had needed Jim, needed his brother's strength and guidance and toughness, yet for so long Jim had refused to even think of coming home, letting pride keep him on the move and earning for himself a fearsome reputation with his gun.

The feud with his father that had driven him from the Triple Star when he was only fifteen had kept Jim away for thirteen long years. Danny knew it was Bryony who had changed all that. The slender, green-eyed beauty had won his heart and somehow melted the wall of ice Jim Logan had constructed around himself. Bryony, through her own forgiveness and love, had taught Jim how to forgive himself for the past, had given him the will to begin again. Danny would have loved her for that alone, but when he met her, her warmth and spirit and charm overwhelmed him. He had instantly become her champion, her friend, and her confidant, all to Jim's amusement and pleasure. Now, Jim Logan smiled at his brother's comments.

"I reckon she's the best thing that ever happened to me," he replied, his eyes still following the girl as she warmly grasped a neighbor's hand and bestowed her dazzling smile. "Just so long as she doesn't get *too* friendly with Duke Crenshaw," he added dryly as the neighboring rancher, a tall, burly man in his mid-forties, placed an arm around Bryony's shoulders, still holding her small hand in his large, calloused one. "Or anyone else for that matter."

"What—are you jealous, Jim?" Danny's laughter rang through the noisy parlor. "That girl is loco over you, absolutely loco. If ever I saw a woman in love, it's Bryony Logan. I can't believe the expression on your face!" He chortled again. "You look like you want to gun down poor Duke just for flirting with her."

Jim grinned in spite of himself. His strong fists unclenched as he realized how foolishly he was behaving. It was natural that men would flirt with Bryony, admire her, yes, even desire her. She was a woman who would fascinate any man, for there was about her an inner fire that shone through the outward loveliness, an assured, joyous spirit that was reflected in her glowing green eyes and rapturous smile. When he first met her, he had noted that she possessed the innocent charm of an angel and the striking beauty of a born temptress, and it was true. Especially in this golden gown that hugged her slender waist and showed off so much of her creamy, generous breasts. Suddenly, he stubbed the butt of his cigar in a clay bowl provided for that purpose and nodded at his brother.

"Excuse me, pardner, I've got a lady to see. I reckon my wife needs rescuing from a certain hombre who's already had too much whiskey for his own good."

Jim strode through the parlor, shouldering his way past the throng of guests until he reached Bryony and Duke Crenshaw. The dark-haired girl was still laughing, trying unsuccessfully to draw her small hand out of the man's bearlike paw. Crenshaw was fondling it, grinning down at her with his wide, crooked teeth. Whether the lustful light in his deep-set blue eyes was due more to the liquor he had consumed in the past hour or to the alluring beauty of the girl before him was uncertain, but the fact remained that he appeared bent on ingratiating himself with his delicate hostess, genially imprisoning her as he allowed his bold gaze to rake her in the most brazen manner imaginable.

Jim's voice broke over him like a thunderclap.

"Howdy, Crenshaw," he drawled in the cool, deliberate way that had caused hardened desperadoes to blanch. "Glad you could make it tonight."

The effect of these few polite words was instantaneous. Duke Crenshaw released Bryony's hand as though it were a rattlesnake, and his arm dropped hastily from her shoulders. His big face, already reddened from the liquor he had drunk, flushed even more darkly, and he stared at Texas Jim Logan through slightly dilated pupils.

"Uh, howdy, Texas. I, uh, was just telling your little wife here how glad we all are to have you two here at the Triple Star." He nervously licked his sun-blistered lips, glancing rapidly from Jim's face to Bryony's, and then back to Jim's. "Uh, it seems like a long time since we had any shindigs in this ranch house. It's real nice, real nice to be here."

Jim merely nodded.

Bryony touched her husband's arm. "Jim," she smiled, "Mr. Crenshaw and his wife have kindly invited us to Sunday supper tomorrow at the Bar Y. Isn't that lovely?"

Jim, glancing down at her, nearly burst out laughing at the worried expression in her jade eyes. Bryony, who had spent the past month planning this party for the purpose of meeting and getting to know their neighbors, feared he would spoil the impression she was striving to achieve by fighting with the rancher whose property most closely adjoined the Triple Star's. She had insisted that he hang up his guns for the duration of the evening, stating that he looked formidable enough without them and would surely frighten away half the county if he came downstairs to greet his guests with his Colts in view. He had consented, despite the fact that it was as natural for him to wear his guns as his trousers. Now, though, she thought he might come to blows with Duke Crenshaw over the rancher's bold attentions to her. Her eyes pleaded with him to remain calm. Amused, he responded to the urgent pressure on his arm by politely addressing the uneasy rancher.

"Yes. Thanks, Crenshaw. I reckon we'll be there."

"You do want Danny to come, too, don't you, Mr. Crenshaw?" Bryony inquired with a relieved smile. "We are all a family, you know."

"Sure, honey, sure." The rancher expelled his breath slowly. He took out a bandana from the pocket of his plaid shirt and wiped his sweat-beaded face. "Well, I reckon we'll see you folks tomorrow then, 'bout noon," he boomed heartily. He started inching away, moving awkwardly through the throng of guests. "I'll tell Berta the good news right away. She'll sure be pleased. Yep, pleased as punch."

Bryony turned to Jim as soon as Duke Crenshaw had escaped into the crowd. Now that the danger was over, laughter sprang to her lips. Her eyes danced, even though she struggled to keep her tone reproving. "Jim, you monster, how could you? You shouldn't have frightened him like that! Aren't you ashamed of yourself? He's really very sweet, and he didn't mean anything at all by holding my hand and putting his arm around me. I could have handled it, you know, instead of you marching up and nearly causing him to have a nervous collapse."

Jim put a hand under her chin and tilted her head up gently. "What did I do, Bryony?" he inquired innocently. "I just welcomed the man to the party, said I was glad he could make it."

Her eyes sparkled. "It was the *way* you said it. You know perfectly well that you scare everybody half to death with that cool, lazy drawl of yours and that dead-calm look you get in your eyes. Poor Mr. Crenshaw thought you were going to shoot him then and there!"

"Crenshaw's a fool." He dismissed with a shrug the rancher he had known since boyhood. "If he had any brains or sense, he'd have doubled his herd in the past five years instead of losing three thousand head, as Danny tells me he's done. Most Texans don't scare so easily, little tenderfoot. We're a tough breed."

"I know." She linked her arm through his as a stout, beaming woman in a too-tight red silk dress waddled toward them, accompanied by a moustachioed, gray-haired man. "Oh, no, Jim! It's Mrs. Prescott!" she groaned. Henry Prescott was the president of the Fort Worth Bank, and his wife the town's most determined socialite. She was exactly the kind of overbearing, stuffily pretentious woman Bryony detested, yet she had done nothing but fawn over the girl ever since they had met in town a few weeks ago. Bryony spoke under her breath. "She's been plaguing me for two weeks to help her form some sort of Fort Worth Grand Society, for all the prominent people in the area—the ones *she* considers worthy, of course. Save me!" she implored as the matron bore down upon her with all the fervor of a buzzard swooping down upon its hapless prey. "Jim, do something!"

Her husband gave her a wicked grin. Then he disengaged his arm from hers. "I know you can handle any situation yourself, little tenderfoot. You've told me so often enough," he murmured as he extended his hand to the dignified banker.

"Mr. Prescott . . . it's a pleasure to welcome you,

and your wife, to the Triple Star." He bowed over Mary Prescott's plump, perfumed hand and kissed it, causing the portly, normally chattering woman to blush a deep shade of scarlet and to momentarily forget the stream of words ready to flow from her lips. By the time she had recovered herself, Jim had led the banker away with a careless "Let's find ourselves a drink, and discuss some business. I'm sure the ladies will have plenty to talk about together." They left both Bryony and Mary Prescott staring after them in stunned silence. Mary Prescott, who had never before this moment had the opportunity to meet the renowned gunfighter, found herself tingling to the tips of her toes from the impression this handsome, aloof, and very dangerous man had made on her with one easy gesture. Bryony, meanwhile, fumed inwardly at the husband who had sworn to love and protect her, and then, when she needed him, abandoned her to the clutches of this social-climbing she-moose.

"Well, my dear! Isn't your husband a fine gentleman!" Mary Prescot gasped when her powers of speech finally returned. "Why, he's not at all what I expected." She gazed at Bryony piercingly a moment. "I've only lived in Fort Worth for eight years, so I never knew him as a boy, but I've certainly heard stories, many stories, about the deadly Texas Jim Logan! But I wasn't prepared for *this!*"

"For what?" Bryony inquired innocently.

"Why, for such a handsome, strong figure of a man!" the woman exclaimed. "My dear, you're a very lucky girl, a very lucky girl indeed!" She stared at Jim and her husband for a moment, her dark, close-set eyes fixed in awe upon the gunfighter. "If I were twenty years younger..." she murmured, and then suddenly broke off with an embarrassed laugh. Twin spots of color still

burned her flabby cheeks. "Well! That's enough of *that!*"
she said brusquely. "Now. Where was I? Oh, yes, that's
right. The matter at hand." She turned to Bryony with
a businesslike air. "This is a lovely party, child, a most
creditable affair. It indicates to me that you are a young
woman of great management abilities." She patted the
girl's arm approvingly, her voice dropping. "We need
people like you my dear—intelligent, well-bred, a lady
through and through. Why don't you put some of your
talents to good use? I'm sure your husband would be
proud to have you organizing the Fort Worth Grand
Society, overseeing the formation of a group sure to
enhance the stature of our wonderful town..."

Bryony listened with half an ear while the woman
rattled on, thinking all the while of how she would make
Jim pay for this rogue's trick! She finally managed to
escape Mrs. Prescott after promising to consider the
matter, and then she promptly put it out of her head.
Gliding through the noisy parlor, she hurried to find
Rosita, the Mexican housekeeper who had come with
her from Arizona and who was not only a trusted em-
ployee but a dear friend.

"Rosita!" she called, bursting into the large, im-
maculate kitchen in the rear of the adobe ranch house.
The kitchen was filled with servants bustling around
with platters of food and tableware, and the ovens were
fragrant with the aroma of freshly baked pies and breads.
"It's nearly suppertime. Is everything ready?"

"*Sí, señora.*" Rosita was heaping silver platters with
thick roast beef, slicing the juicy pink meat with an
enormous butcher knife. "Pedro says the spits have finished—all the meat is cooked *perfectamente*—and now
we have only to set everything out in the courtyard.
Soon, señora, the guests will be feasting."

"Excellent." Bryony thought of the menu: tender

beef, barbecued outdoors on spits over the great open-pit fire, black bass grilled with lemon butter, goose with rhubarb sauce, hot, fresh bread, corn tamales, peach tarts and raisin tarts, blueberry pie, coffee, punch, wine, and whiskey. She was proud of her efforts for this party, proud to have planned and executed such an elaborate festivity to formally reinstate Jim Logan, along with his brother Danny, as the masters of the Triple Star. She wanted to make a new life here for herself and for Jim, to become part of Texas, part of this great and spirited land. And she wanted their neighbors to see that the new Mr. And Mrs. Logan were good, responsible people, interested in being part of this community.

With Jim's arrival, there had of course been plenty of rumors, not all of them pleasant. Bryony wanted to show, once and for all, that Texas Jim Logan was not a monster, not a cruel and cold-blooded killer, but a man who had achieved notoriety with a gun, yet wanted to live in peace and prosperity with his neighbors. She believed, by the way the party was proceeding thus far, that she was succeeding.

"*Gracias*, Rosita. You're doing a marvelous job." She smiled, and the plump, brown-skinned woman smiled back. "Did you ever think it would turn out this way, Rosita?" Bryony asked suddenly, her eyes lighting. "I never did."

"*Sí, señora*. From the first time I saw you and the señor together, I knew you belonged with each other." Rosita's dark eyes misted. "It was dangerous, I knew, and I feared for you both, but I believed that you and señor Logan would never be able to live apart."

"You're right," Bryony said softly. "I thought I hated him at first, but now, I don't think I could ever live without him. I don't think I'd want to."

She left the kitchen, threading her way through the

milling guests in their colorful garb, until she had passed through the parlor doors onto the wide porch overlooking the courtyard. All was gay and festive out here, from the colored lanterns strung all about to the swaying, clapping figures of the dancers stirred by the flamenco rhythms of the guitars. The night was ablaze with stars, millions of winking crystal gems set in a black velvet canopy. The October moon was full: a gleaming white orb that appeared close enough to touch with one's fingers, if one but reached out a hand. Bryony smiled, content.

Yes, she was happy it had turned out this way. But her life had not always been so serene. Only a few short months ago she had left Miss Marsh's School for Young Ladies in St. Louis and traveled alone to Arizona, a green schoolgirl, a tenderfoot, determined to run her father's cattle ranch there, determined to hate the gunfighter who had shot and killed her father, Wesley Hill. But Texas Jim Logan had saved her life, and saved her virtue. He had rescued her from the ruthless outlaw band that had kidnapped her from the stagecoach, and from the first moment they met, he had captured her heart.

She had tried to hate him, tried to resist the passion that flared within her whenever she was anywhere near him, but her efforts had been in vain. Every time she had stared into those cool blue eyes and felt the power of his strong arms about her, her resolutions crumbled and the flame leapt into her soul. He had haunted her nights, her dreams, compelling her to look beyond the image of the man, the cold-blooded, vicious reputation, and into his heart. She had come to see the man behind the mask, the gentle and compassionate man who had made such unforgettable love to her in a storm-swept mountain cave. He had fought for her, killed for her.

Three times Jim Logan had saved her life. She had come
to know that her heart belonged to him, only to him,
forever. The future stretched before her, a future filled
with love and sharing. How lucky she was that they
had found each other, had conquered all the obstacles
between them and forged a marriage of love and com-
mitment.

All her life she had been lonely. Her mother had
died when Bryony was only eight years old, and her
father had abandoned her to the care of relatives and
boarding-school administrators. She had never had anyone with whom to share her laughter, her joy, and her
fears. Now she had Jim, a man who held her in his arms
like a fragile china cup, who adored her, protected her,
ignited her with a blazing passion she had never dreamed
possible. He had given her his love, and a home, and
a family, for Danny was as dear to her as though he
truly was her brother. Only one thing remained to make
her life complete. And soon, in a matter of months, that
too would be hers...

Suddenly, her blissful reverie was broken by a crude
voice.

"Well, howdy, little lady," the voice sneered, and
Bryony glanced up to see a tall, wiry cowboy in a red
shirt lounging before her. "I been watching you inside
the parlor there, talkin', smilin' at everyone. Seems to
me you're the lady of the house. Mrs. Logan. That right?"

Bryony summed up his appearance swiftly. The
man was thin but muscular, with a thatch of dirty brown
hair, unshaven stubble on his narrow face, and a dark
moustache over thin, twitching lips. He looked and
smelled as though he hadn't bathed in days. There was
mud on his boots and grime on his neck. His small
brown eyes were red-rimmed, and they drooped, giving
him a wicked appearance. *Drunk,* Bryony thought dis-

gustedly, wrinkling her nose at the stench of alcohol and filth. *And mean, by the looks of him.* She cast about in her mind for his identity, wondering if he was a neighbor or a merchant from Fort Worth, someone Jim might have invited to the party. There was a coiled tension and an ugliness in his stance and expression that she didn't like. When she didn't immediately answer him, the red-shirted cowboy shot out a hand and roughly gripped her wrist.

"I asked you a question, lady," he rasped. "Are you Texas Jim Logan's new little wife?"

"Yes. Now take your hands off me, if you please!" she flashed back, pulling her arm free of him. She glared at him, green eyes ablaze. The cowboy chuckled, his small dark eyes shining in his swarthy face.

"Who are you?" she demanded, her anger growing as his insolence became increasingly apparent. "I don't recognize you as one of our guests."

"You don't, eh?" The seedy-looking stranger stepped closer to her, making Bryony uneasily aware that they were alone now on the porch. Rosita and the other servants had set up the long tables of food at the opposite end of the courtyard, and the hungry guests had congregated near the sumptuous spread prepared for their pleasure. The wide porch was now deserted, except for Bryony and the thin, surly man before her. For the first time, a prickle of fear touched her.

CHAPTER TWO

THE STRANGER stared at her until she felt she could stand his eyes on her no longer.

"I'm a friend of your husband's," he said in a low, unpleasant tone. "A real good friend, you might say. We go back a long way, old Texas and me."

"Indeed?" Bryony's tone was icy. She looked the interloper over with obvious disdain. "Well, in that case, I think we ought to find my husband and let him renew his acquaintance with you. If," she went on, "there really *is* an acquaintance between you."

"Just a minute, Miss Uppity." The stranger caught her arm as she turned away. The expression in his eyes was ugly. "I'd kinda like to get to know you a little better before we find old Jim," he jeered, yanking her up against his hard, sweat-soaked form. "I think Texas has picked himself a real beauty all right, and I jest wonder if—"

He never finished the sentence. Even before Bryony could begin to struggle, an iron arm yanked her backward while at the same time a fist slammed with bone-crunching impact into the cowboy's face. Bryony cried out, startled, and stared up at the face of her husband.

His expression terrified her. She hadn't seen such deadly rage since they'd left Arizona, and she knew that if he were wearing his guns at this moment, the unwelcome guest would be on his way to hell.

"Jim, it's all right," she began hurriedly, clutching his arm, but he shook free of her without sparing her a glance, his gaze riveted to the mangy fellow sprawled on the porch. "Please, don't make a scene..."

"Get off my property, Chester!" Jim ordered, his voice, for all its softness, pelting the October night like bullets. "If you ever come within three feet of my wife again, you're a dead man!"

The brown-haired stranger crawled to his hands and knees. Blood trickled from his mouth, and the side of his face showed a raw purple bruise. His eyes had darkened with savage emotion as he glared into the cold, hard face of Texas Jim Logan. Then, with a jerky, fumbling movement, he snatched out his gun and leveled it.

"I'm goin' to kill you, Logan!" he snarled.

Bryony paled, her heart freezing in terror. "No!" she cried, darting forward in an effort to throw herself between Jim and the stranger. "That would be murder! You'd be shooting an unarmed man!" She wanted to shield Jim, to protect him from this menacing coward, but before she could say or do anything further, Jim seized her arm and thrust her brutally behind him.

"Stay there, damn it! Don't move!" he commanded her. Then he turned to face the stranger, his lean face filled with contempt.

The scraggly cowboy wobbled to his feet, holding the heavy Colt with two shaking hands. He sneered at the towering gunfighter before him.

"I reckon I wouldn't put murder past you for a minute, Chester," Jim remarked coolly. "But in the open, with witnesses? I wouldn't have thought even *you* capable of such stupidity."

The man's eyes narrowed to ugly slits. "Stupidity, eh?" He glanced swiftly out of the corner of his eye at the throng of guests milling about the laden tables. "Well, mebbe you're right. I'd jest be hangin' myself to kill you now," he growled. "But I'll do it yet, Texas, jest you wait and see." At Bryony's cry of dismay, he turned his eyes upon her once again. "Allow me to introduce myself, ma'am," he rasped. "The name's Willie Joe Chester. Remember it. You'll be hearin' it again."

"I hope not!" Bryony retorted, stepping forward to stand beside Jim. She was trembling with fear and anger, regarding the intruder with venomous loathing in her jade-green eyes. "I think you've already overstayed your welcome, Mr. Chester, and it's high time you left. Good night!" Her lovely face was set and cold in the moonlight.

Willie Joe Chester snickered. He glanced at Bryony, standing still and proud, her slender arm linked with Jim Logan's muscular one. For one moment his gaze lingered on the beautiful, delicate girl, taking final note of her lustrous ebony hair, her glimmering green eyes, and her creamy, swelling breasts above the pale-yellow satin of her gown. Lust mixed with hatred as he stared at her. Then he turned his narrowed eyes to Texas Jim Logan, so tall and arrogant and strong. The damned gunfighter looked as cool and nonchalant at this moment as if *he* were the one holding the gun. His light-blue eyes were cold and piercing. There was no fear upon his lean face, only contempt. Willie Joe felt his fury doubling. He wiped his bloodied mouth across the sleeve of his shirt.

"I'm goin' ... fer now," he muttered. "But you'll pay, Logan. Sure as I can spit, you'll pay." The intensity of the hatred in his voice stunned Bryony. She stared at him in horror as he continued to address Jim, his eyes glittering like coals. "I never forgot Tommy, and neither did Frank. One of these days, we'll make you pay."

"You have five seconds to clear off my property, Chester," Jim returned grimly. The whipcord tension Bryony had sensed in him earlier when he had first struck Willie Joe Chester had eased, leaving him cool and in complete control. "And don't forget what I said," he drawled. "I'll send you to hell before you have time to blink if you ever so much as speak to my wife again, or show your face in these parts. And there won't be enough left of you worth burying. Now get out!"

Chester stared into Jim's merciless blue eyes and involuntarily took a step backward. He opened his mouth to speak, then shut it with a snap as he apparently thought better of provoking Jim Logan further. He backed away, still wiping at the blood that streamed from his mouth. Bryony couldn't help staring at him, and the expression on his face sent shivers of fear racing up and down her spine. Willie Joe Chester hated Jim, and hated her, too, from all she could see. But why? She waited motionless while Chester mounted a shaggy mustang tethered to a mesquite tree beyond the courtyard. He galloped off in a flurry of dust. Then Bryony took a deep breath and turned wide, questioning eyes to her husband.

"Jim, that man hates you!" she whispered, her voice shaking. "But why? What did you do to him?"

"Later, Bryony." Jim glanced down at her agitated face, and his own hard features softened. "Don't worry, little tenderfoot. You have nothing to fear from Willie Joe Chester. He's all talk. No guts. I'd never let him get near you."

"I'm not worried about myself," she began, moving

close against him, her eyes searching his face. "It's you
I fear for..."

Suddenly, he laughed, and his arms tightened
around her. "Have no fear, my darling." His eyes
gleamed with amusement. "I can handle men like Willie
Joe Chester. He's a mangy, vicious little dog that needs
kicking once in a while, that's all. Don't give him another
thought." He kissed the tip of her nose lightly, quickly.
"Don't look now, little tenderfoot, but our guests are
approaching. I think we've stirred up some excitement
at this little fiesta."

"I know." Bryony sighed. "It's exactly the kind of
excitement I wished to avoid." Bryony realized in dismay that this violent little exchange with Willie Joe Chester threatened to undo all her efforts. Trying to make
the best of things, she turned with a bright smile as the
Crenshaws, the Prescotts, and a handful of other guests
hurried over to where the couple stood.

"My dear, is everything all right?" Mary Prescott
demanded, scrutinizing Bryony's face shrewdly. "Who
was that man? I do declare, I thought Texas was going
to shoot him on the spot!"

"That would have been somewhat difficult, ma'am,
since I'm not wearing my guns," Jim said in his cool,
quiet way.

"There's nothing at all to be concerned about,"
Bryony spoke quickly, her voice light as silk. "We merely
turned away a drunk and uninvited guest. Please," she
continued with her warm, appealing smile, spreading
her hands as she addressed her guests, "let's get on
with the festivities. Enjoy your supper, and let the music
continue. I, for one, am going to dance with my dear
brother-in-law, that handsome cowpoke, Dan Logan!"

With these words, Bryony turned quickly to Danny,
who stood on the fringes of the little group that had

gathered about. The other guests, grinning, parted so
that she could reach his side, and she firmly grasped
his arm. "Come, Daniel, you can't refuse me now," she
said in an undertone as he glanced up in embarrass-
ment. A slow blush crept up his neck, showing around
the corners of his plaid bandana.

"Aw, Bryony..." he began, with a backward step,
but seeing the imploring expression in her eyes, he took
a deep breath and plopped his wide white sombrero on
his chestnut head. "Oh, hell, why not!" he exclaimed
loudly, and a cheer went up from the watching crowd.
He led his sister-in-law to the center of the courtyard,
and as the musicians plucked out the rousing notes of
a reel, Bryony and Dan began to dance.

Bryony felt Jim's eyes upon her and, turning, saw
the glint of admiration in them. She hoped that this
distraction would make the guests forget about the little
scene on the porch and perhaps save the party from
ruin. So she threw all her energy into the dance, whirling gracefully about the courtyard in her flowing satin
gown, her eyes glowing bewitchingly in the light of the
lanterns. A foot-stomping, hand-clapping crowd formed
around her and Danny, and as she twirled beside him,
a joyous laugh sprang to her lips.

"I'm sorry, Dan," she whispered, knowing that this
public scrutiny was harrowing to her normally shy
brother-in-law, but her eyes sparkled with mischief because she could tell that Dan Logan was enjoying himself every bit as much as she. He grinned at her, sketching
a low bow, then suddenly, with a theatrical flourish of
his hat, he began to back away into the circle of onlookers, leaving Bryony whirling alone in the center of
the courtyard. The applause increased. Bryony, seeing
his desertion, placed her hands on her hips in a gesture
of mock exasperation and moved to rejoin the crowd,
but voices echoed each other, begging her to continue.

"Come on, little lady. Don't stop now!" Big Bob Walker, owner of the Crooked T ranch, called out encouragingly.

"More, boss-lady!" one of the Triple Star's own ranch hands whooped.

Dan cupped his hands around his mouth. "Dance for us, Bryony! You'll do a whole lot better without me stepping on your toes!"

A roar of laughter went up, and hands beat together in rapid thunder until Bryony herself laughed and returned to the center of the courtyard. The guitarists, smiling and nodding, increased their tempo, and the fiddlers played with zest while the girl in the pale-yellow gown, her black curls flying, twirled lightly, expertly to their throbbing music. Her lithe, slender body spun gracefully about, her feet in their delicate satin slippers flying like a bird's wings. She gave herself up to the passion of the dance, to the music that enflamed her blood, and to the beauty of the black October night. Above her, the Texas skies stretched to eternity; she reached out her arms as if to embrace them, whirling, dipping, arching her body and her soul in a celebration of all that was wild and beautiful and free. When she had finished, curtsying low and gracefully to thunderous applause, her heart was racing, pounding against the bodice of her gown. Jim strode forward, raised her, and kissed her hand. The guests cheered. Then he pulled her close and stared down into her flushed face.

"You dance almost as well as you shoot a gun, little tenderfoot," he remarked softly. "Is there anything you *cannot* do?"

Her eyes shone into his like green flames. "I can't stop loving you," she whispered, then lifted her lips for his kiss.

"You'd better not!" he growled in her ear, holding her tightly against his strong frame. "I'd never let you go, Bryony! I'd track you to the ends of the earth!"

Their lips met in a fierce and loving kiss that sent the grinning onlookers back to their supper, leaving the entwined couple alone on the moonlit court. It was some time before the newlyweds roused themselves from the passion of their embrace to rejoin their heartily feasting guests, but eventually they did return.

The party lasted well into the night, with more merriment, singing, and foot-stomping than most of the guests remembered participating in for years. When the last rancher had finished telling the last tall tale about Pecos Bill and his would-be bride Slue-foot Sue, and the final verse of "The Cowboy's Lament" had been sung, the last of the guests drifted out to their wagons and their buggies, most too drunk or too happy to notice that the sky had already begun lightening to dusky lavender in readiness for the dawn. Danny planted a noisy kiss on Bryony's cheek and shook hands vigorously with Jim, then staggered upstairs to his bedroom, all the while warbling the bawdy refrain of a trail song. Jim and Bryony walked slowly through the ranch house, surveying the debris of the party. Rosita was wearily gathering plates and glasses onto a tray in the parlor, but with his customary air of command, Jim interrupted her work.

"Don't bother with all of this tonight, Rosita," he said firmly. "It's nearly morning already. Get some sleep."

"Señor, I hate to leave such a mess..." the housekeeper protested, despite the heavy bags under her eyes and the fact that her square shoulders sagged tiredly. "It will not take me long to finish."

"No." Jim removed the tray from her hands and carried it himself toward the kitchen. "Tomorrow will be soon enough. I'll dismiss the kitchen servants, too." There was no arguing with the authoritative note in his voice.

Rosita shook her head, smiling at Bryony. "The señor is very kind."

"Yes, but *you* have worked very hard and have done a superb job," Bryony retorted. "Now, please, go to sleep. In the morning we'll deal with this mess together."

"*Sí, señora. Buenas noches.*" Rosita stifled a yawn as she lumbered off to her small, cozy room beyond the kitchen.

Bryony smiled as Jim returned to the parlor and took her arm. Together they climbed the wide oaken staircase leading to their bedroom on the upper floor of the ranch house.

A short time later, Bryony sat before her dressing-table mirror, clad in a white satin nightgown trimmed in French lace. Her cloud of black hair spilled becomingly down her back and about her milky shoulders as she brushed it with the silver-handled brush Jim had bought her on their honeymoon in San Francisco. She was gazing at the photograph framed in silver that rested amidst the perfume bottles, lace handkerchief, and the slender crystal vase filled with bluebonnets on her ivory dressing table. It was a photograph of Bryony and Jim in San Francisco, taken the first day of their arrival in that city. They were standing side by side with Jim's arm about her shoulders. They both looked rapturously happy. She was smiling up at him with a saucy, yet adoring look, and he was regarding her with love and the pride that comes with possession. It was a magnetic, appealing portrait. Instead of the wooden image of people so often found in such photographs, the photographer had managed to capture the life and vitality of this newly married pair, to show in that one brief flash the love and passion that flowed between them. Bryony set down her hairbrush and reached out a hand to gently touch the silver frame. As she did so, she felt Jim's hand on her shoulder and glanced up to meet his eyes in the mirror.

"What are you thinking, little tenderfoot?" he asked softly, stroking her satiny hair with his other hand. He was bare-chested, but still wore the elegant black trousers and boots he had worn during the party. The muscles on his sun-bronzed chest rippled as he bent over her, tangling his hands in her long, midnight-black hair.

"I'm thinking about how happy we were on our honeymoon—the two of us, alone together—and how happy we are tonight," she answered, leaning back against him. "I want us always to be this happy. I don't want anything to change between us..." She paused, doubt suddenly clouding her eyes. Then she spoke again, trying to ignore the sudden thudding of her heart. "Jim, I have something to tell you. I...I hope you will be pleased." She hesitated, biting her lip.

Why was this so difficult? She had been in a state of bliss ever since learning the news she was about to impart, but now she was suddenly nervous. Perhaps Jim would be angry, perhaps he would resent this profound change in their lives. This possibility hadn't occurred to her before, but somehow, when she had glanced at the photograph of the two of them so content with just each other on their honeymoon, doubts had arisen. The lovely secret she had been savoring all evening, waiting for just the right moment to share, now hovered on her tongue, yet she hesitated, unsure of its reception. She saw Jim's eyes settle questioningly on her face, their cool blue depths reflecting calm, patient strength.

Suddenly, he lifted her to her feet and turned her slowly to face him. He put a finger beneath her small, proud chin. "What is it, sweetheart?" he asked.

"I'm going to bear our child," she said slowly, then

held her breath waiting for his reaction.

Jim Logan stared into her upturned face for one startled moment. Then he let out a yell. Joy flooded his lean, rugged features and shot through his powerful frame. With an earsplitting whoop, he swept Bryony into his arms and spun her wildly about.

"Jim! Jim!" she shrieked, laughing helplessly as the room tilted about her. "Stop it—please!"

Furious pounding sounded on the bedroom door. Danny's voice brought Jim to a halt.

"What's going on in there? You two all right?" the younger Logan brother shouted.

"We're fine! Come on in!" Jim ordered.

Danny opened the door, clad only in a pair of denim trousers he had donned hastily upon hearing Jim yell. His face was still flushed from the effects of the liquor he had consumed during the evening's festivities. "What is it?" he demanded, running a hand through his hair as he stared at his brother, still holding Bryony in his arms, in the center of the bedroom floor. "What the hell is going on?"

"You're going to be an uncle, Dan!" Jim announced, and after one stunned moment, Dan Logan let out a shout that was an exact duplicate of his brother's.

"Well, congratulations! How 'bout that? When is the little feller going to arrive?"

"In May," Bryony interjected, adding with a toss of her head, "and don't you assume that this baby is going to be a little feller! I just might bear my husband a darling little daughter."

"A daughter! Wouldn't that be something?" Jim spoke in a low, wondering voice. His eyes lit with pleasure, and once again he spun Bryony about the room, impervious to her squealed protests.

"I think I'll leave you two alone to celebrate," Dan chuckled. He departed with a grin, shutting the bedroom door behind him. No sooner had he left than Jim set Bryony on her feet and wrapped his arms around her. He kissed her exuberantly.

"How long have you known, you vixen?" he demanded. "Why didn't you tell me sooner?"

"Doc Webster confirmed my suspicions only this morning. I wanted to surprise you tonight." Her enormous green eyes gazed searchingly into his as she clasped her arms around his neck. "Jim, are you truly pleased? I . . . I was almost frightened to tell you just now. I didn't know how you would react."

"Pleased?" He grinned at her. "Sweetheart, I'm loco about this news. A baby!" He shook his head. "Before I met you, I never cared enough about living to even think of continuing on my name, my family. I didn't give a damn. Now"—he placed one hand on each side of her face and tenderly kissed her—"now I want to put down roots, to raise a family with you. I want to see my children grow, and I damn well intend to get on better with them than I did with my own father." His deep voice was filled with determination. "Don't you see, Bryony? Here's a chance to do something for my father, one last thing. I can bring his grandchild into the world, raise him or her here on this ranch that he worked so damn hard to build. It's a gift, the gift of posterity, which I can pass on to my parents even in their death. Maybe it will make up some little bit for having run off all those years ago and never coming back until after my parents were gone. I don't know. I only know that I want this baby, I want this child we can raise together and share our love with. Oh, Bryony, you've made me the happiest man in the world!"

Tears of joy sparkled on her eyelashes. "And I am the happiest woman! Oh, Jim, I love you so!"

She drew his head down to her mouth and kissed him with all the love that poured from her heart. He clasped her to him with an iron grip, his mouth hungrily devouring hers. Warmth flowed through her as his hands slid up and down her satin nightgown and then deftly slipped the thin straps down her shoulders. The gown drifted to the floor in a filmy cloud. He touched her naked form with warm, strong, yet gentle hands, caressing her breasts as she pressed her hips tightly against him, rocking slowly. Desire flamed in her blood as she unfastened his breeches and cradled his hard manhood in her hands. Naked and trembling, they sank together upon the bed. Jim kissed her slowly and deliciously, nibbling his way from her eyelids, mouth, and throat all the way down the length of her quivering body, driving her to a feverish state of rapture as he probed and tasted the honeyed warmth between her thighs. Bryony moaned in delightful torment. She curled her fingers in his hair, her hips writhing. By the time he poised himself above her, his eyes dark with passion, she was afire with need. When he entered her with a single, powerful thrust, she greeted him with a fervent cry. Locked together, as close as two people could possibly be, they rocked and thrashed, swept up in a storm that shook them to their very bones and left them spent and weary when the fierce whirlwind had at last run its course. They lay together in peaceful silence when it was over, their bodies glistening with sweat in the moonlit bed, arms and legs still intimately entwined. Bryony could feel the pounding of Jim's heart. Her lips moved against his shoulder, tasting the saltiness of his flesh.

"Thank you." He spoke quietly, his voice husky in the deep, silent night, comforting her as always with its strength, its warmth and tenderness.

"For what?" She settled her head against his shoulder, her hair billowing around her like an ebony cloud.

"For loving me." Jim's powerful arms tightened

around her, his lips brushing her hair. "And for giving me this child."

"It's a gift to both of us," Bryony murmured, holding him close. "A precious, beautiful gift of love."

Dawn was approaching. The night shadows had already fled the plains. Jim and Bryony drifted peacefully off to sleep, content and happy with the promise of the future before them. But sometime in the early hours of the dawn, when the sky was an eerie shade of gray tinged with yellow and the night creatures scurried for cover before the rise of the sun, Bryony awoke. She sat up in bed, terror flooding through her. Her flesh was cold and clammy in the gust of wind that swept in through the open window. She gasped, trying to calm her thudding heart, but it raced on, attuned to some secret, horrifying danger. Her tongue was dry, and her hands shook as she raised them to her pale cheeks. She fought the unreasoning fear, staring down at Jim, who slept calmly beside her. What was it? What had awakened her so suddenly, filling her with a panic that made her eyes widen, her blood chill? Then she heard it. The coyote howled again in the night, its melancholy cry piercing the still, heavy air. She had heard that cry before, many times, but for some reason, it now struck fear in her heart. And as she sat in the bed, listening to the animal's wail, a vision appeared unbidden in her mind. Willie Joe Chester's dirty, unshaven face swam into her view. She saw his small, dark eyes shining at her, smelled his rank odor. Indeed, as the coyote wailed again upon the prairie, she almost imagined that she felt Willie Joe's stubby hands upon her, clutching her close, closer, until... She shivered, the terror enveloping her anew. She stuck her small fist in her mouth to keep from screaming aloud.

In the excitement of her announcement tonight, she had forgotten all about Willie Joe Chester and had ne-

glected to question Jim about him. She still had no idea
who he was or why he hated Jim so fiercely. Now, in
the still hour of the dawn, she couldn't stop thinking
of him, worrying about the danger he presented. She
forced herself to lie down again, pulling the coverlet
over Jim and herself, snuggling against him for warmth
and reassurance. Yet her distress did not subside. She
tried to shake it off. After all, she told herself, shivering
beneath the sheets, Jim didn't fear the man. He had
assured her that Willie Joe would do them no harm.
Still, some chord in Bryony throbbed wildly. Perhaps,
she thought, it was because the man's hatred had been
so intense, so violent. It had made a strong impression
on her senses, and for some odd reason, the coyote
howling outside her window had triggered her memory
of that unkempt, mangy outlaw. She was being foolish.
She ought to be ashamed. There was nothing to fear.

She touched Jim's arm, reminding herself that they
were safe together, and happy, that nothing could harm
them. They were going to have a wonderful life, a beautiful, healthy baby...

Gradually, sleep returned. But it was not the deep,
untroubled sleep she had known earlier. It was a restless
slumber, one disturbed by murky dreams in which she
ran alone and terrified through a misty fog. And through
it all, despite Jim's warmth beside her, despite the heavy
coverlet draped across her slender body, Bryony was
cold. She shivered and shook, chilled to her core by a
nameless dread, a ghastly, abominable terror.

CHAPTER THREE

THE WEEKS of October were dry and mild. Bryony, happy as she had never been before, rode out every day upon her magnificent stallion, Shadow, to savor the tall grasses of the prairies, to feast her eyes upon the brilliant wild flowers that carpeted the land. The hills overflowed with mountain pinks, daisies, and bluebonnets, while verbena and primrose flamed brightly in the valleys. The sky blazed sapphire blue, laced by occasional rolling white clouds. When November arrived, however, a subtle change came over the landscape. The air cooled, slapping briskly at her face as she galloped the range, and the ocean of flowers receded, leaving the prairies barren save for the tall, waving grasses and the mesquites and cacti that dotted the land. Winter was coming soon. She could feel it in the wind, sense it in the land. Soon, snow would cap the mountains beyond the Rio Grande and northers would race across the prairies.

Staring out at the countryside from the peak of a low hill some miles from the ranch one crisp November noon, Bryony shivered in happy anticipation. Winter. Then spring. Soon after that, her baby would be born.

This would be Bryony's first winter since she had

35

come west from St. Louis, and she envisioned long cozy nights with Jim before the fire, when she would knit tiny garments for their baby and make plans for the nursery. Her belly had only just begun to swell, and her normally slender frame now boasted a becoming round- ness that seemed to render her even more fascinating in her husband's eyes. Their lives had grown, if pos- sible, even more joyful since the announcement of her pregnancy. Each night their lovemaking was lingering and sweet, and often Jim would meet her at their special rendezvous on the range and they would lay together in the sunshine for interludes of stolen pleasure.

Wrapped in happiness, Bryony had all but forgot- ten the strange, piercing terror that had enveloped her in the aftermath of the Triple Star's party. The following day she had questioned Jim about Willie Joe Chester, and his calm dismissal of the vicious, dirty rider had dissipated her anxiety.

"Willie Joe Chester and his brother Frank are low- down hombres living on the fringes of the law," Jim had told her in his curt, straightforward manner. "They had a younger brother, Tommy, a kid of about Danny's age, eighteen, maybe nineteen years old. Two years ago, over in New Mexico territory, I was playing cards in a hellhole saloon. Tommy Chester was in that game. I caught him cheating, called him on it. He was a kid, Bryony, though a mean, conniving one, and I wouldn't have shot him if he'd have just thrown in his cards and left like I ordered him. But he went for his gun. I had no choice." Jim's face had grown taut at the memory. "I reckoned that was the end of it, but about a month later, two hombres calling themselves Willie Joe and Frank Chester, older brothers to that trigger-happy kid, showed up in my hotel room in Albuquerque. They took me by surprise, bent on beating me to death."

At this point, Bryony had gone white as marble,

gripping the edges of the smooth oak table in the dining room where they were breakfasting. Jim, seeing her alarm, had lifted his brows.

"As you can see, little tenderfoot, they failed. It was a hell of a fight, though. The hotelkeeper heard the ruckus and called the sheriff, and he threw the Chesters in jail. I reckon that's about all there is to the story, except that they both swore their revenge on me." He shrugged. "It's all part of life out West, sweetheart. I've a dozen enemies like that: mangy, no-guts hombres too scared to face me in a fair gunfight. They'd shoot me in the back if I gave them the chance, but," he added drawlingly, "I don't reckon I ever did, or will. I know what it takes to survive in this country, little tenderfoot, and it would take more than the Chesters to finish me. They're low-down, mean as can be, but they don't have the guts or the savvy to get the drop on me. So you just forget about Willie Joe and Frank. They're no more important to us than those pesky little insects that swarm around at dusk. A few good swats, and they're gone."

At first uneasy, Bryony had at last succeeded in accepting Jim's appraisal of the situation. She realized that a man with Jim's past would have enemies, and she also realized that he had always succeeded in outwitting or outdrawing them. Surely now that he had given up the dangerous life of a gunfighter, removing himself from those perilous situations that previously had been an everyday occurence for him, the danger to him was drastically reduced. Here they were, ensconced on this vast, bustling cattle ranch, continuing the empire Jim's father had begun. Where else would they be safer? Nowhere, she concluded, and reflecting with pride exactly how proficient her husband really was with his guns, how keen his intelligence and quick his instincts, she felt the last vestiges of fear drop away, leaving her buoyant and exquisitely confident of the future.

In the weeks following the party, she roamed the wide expanses of the Triple Star range; it stretched for more than seventy-five thousand acres across the prairies, encompassing low, rolling hills, and deep valleys and gorges, through which the Trinity River ran. Each day she felt as though life had grown even sweeter and more precious than before, for she knew that few people on earth were as fortunate as she. She vowed to make the most of the gifts bestowed on her, to savor her life and the love she shared with Jim.

With these thoughts in mind on this particular bracing day in November, she sent Shadow trotting down the hill from where she had been surveying the changing scenery and raced toward the special spot where she and Jim often rendezvoused.

It didn't take long for the long-legged black stallion to reach the secluded clearing in the valley, where two oak trees guarded a grassy knoll on which squirrels and jackrabbits frolicked. The timid animals scampered away when the horse and rider approached, and Bryony pulled the stallion to a halt beside a mesquite tree. Sliding from the saddle, she tethered her mount and strolled forward until she reached the shade of the oaks. Then, setting her small white stetson on the grass beside her, she sank down upon the soft earth.

The sun blazed overhead in an azure sky. She waited, peacefully content, hoping that Jim would find the opportunity to break away and meet her today as he had so often in the past at the noon hour. Suddenly, though, Shadow snorted and reared straight up on his powerful legs. Bryony was on her feet in an instant, her derringer drawn from the pocket of her denim riding skirt. Her eyes strained to see what had caused the horse to panic, noting in alarm that Shadow was straining at his halter. "What is it, boy?" she whispered softly. Then she saw the coral snake slithering through the tall grass.

She recognized the red, black, and yellow rings that completely encircled its body, and noted its small, blunt head with the black snout. A shudder ran through her. The coral was the most dangerous snake in all of Texas, its bite hideously poisonous. She raised her arm, aiming the derringer carefully. Then she fired. The snake convulsed as the bullet tore through its striped body. A moment later it lay dead in the grass. Bryony replaced the derringer and went to Shadow, gently calming the stallion as she stroked his head.

As she soothed the horse, her ears caught the drum of another horse's hooves on the narrow trail. She turned expectantly and saw Jim thundering toward her astride his bay stallion, Pecos.

Jim pulled the bay up seconds later. His face was grim. "What's wrong?" he demanded, swinging his tall frame from the saddle. "I heard your shot." He surveyed her swiftly. With her mass of black hair tied back securely with a red ribbon and her red shirt, blue denim jacket, and matching blue denim riding skirt, she looked the picture of competent cowgirl. She wore a red and blue bandana about her slender throat and soft calf boots upon her feet. There was no sign of alarm or distress on her face, he noted, relaxing somewhat as he strode toward her and the black stallion.

"It was nothing," Bryony assured him as he approached. "A coral snake, there in the grass. I killed him cleanly with one shot."

She appeared quite proud of her feat and flashed a dazzling smile up at him, but Jim didn't return her smile. "You might have been bitten, Bryony," he commented, his eyes darkening. "What would have happened if—"

"If nothing," she interrupted him with a laugh. "Stop worrying so about me. You know I can take care of myself."

"I know you're a damned good shot, and I know you can think on your feet, but accidents still happen." Jim frowned. He studied her small, delicate face. The beautiful green eyes gazed directly up at him in a way that tugged at his heart, and her soft pink mouth seemed to beg for kissing. His gaze traveled irresistibly downward to her belly where he knew a tiny new life was growing. Every muscle in his body tightened protectively. He spoke with decision. "I don't want you to meet me here after today, Bryony. In fact, I don't want you riding out alone anymore at all."

"Jim!" Bryony stared at him in amazement. "Don't be ridiculous! I'm pregnant. I'm not an invalid, and I'm certainly not helpless. Doc Webster told me I can ride until the last months of my pregnancy. I intend to do so!"

"No." Having finished tethering Pecos beside the black stallion, Jim turned to her and gripped her shoulders. "I'm not going to let you take any chances, Bryony. A dozen things could happen to you alone on the range. Snakes, bobcats, Indians. Yes, Indians," he continued, cutting her off as she tried to dispute this last danger. "I know most of the tribes have been sent to the reservation in Indian Territory, but there are still renegade bands of Comanche and Cheyenne who have escaped. They make raids now and then, and I don't want you exposed to that kind of danger. In fact, I reckon I never should have let you get accustomed to riding out so far on your own at all. Gun or no gun, it's just not safe. And now, especially, I don't want you taking any risks."

"I won't stop living simply because I'm going to have a baby!" Bryony retorted. Anger sparked within her. She shook loose of him, staring up at his towering form. "I'll do as I please! I'm hardly a half-wit, Jim! I know what is good for my baby and for me and—"

"Damn your stubborn, pigheaded pride!" Jim's face

darkened with rage. His blue eyes narrowed. "I thought I'd tamed that willful, stubborn streak of yours! Now I can see that I still have my work cut out for me!"

"Tamed..." Bryony's lips parted incredulously. Fury flamed in her as though someone had struck flint to tinder. So he thought he'd tamed her, did he? She gave him a burning look, lifting her chin in the proud gesture he recognized so well. "You may have married me, Jim Logan, but you haven't tamed me. You'll never tame *me!*" she cried.

She started to turn away from him, but he caught her wrist and yanked her back, deadly fury pounding through him. Bryony struggled to pull free, but his fingers were closed about her wrist like steel bands and she could not escape. She winced, biting her lips in frustration. Jim, watching her pain-darkened eyes, released her abruptly. Suddenly, he pulled her into his arms.

"I'm sorry, Bryony," he muttered, his arms nearly crushing the breath out of her. "I didn't want to hurt you. I'm just so damned worried about you and the baby—it makes me loco!"

Her anger vanished. She heard the pain in his voice and felt love surging through her. She clung to him, savoring the feel of his hard-muscled arms around her. "I know, Jim. I know. I understand how important the baby is to you." Her soft voice caressed him as she brought her arms up about his neck. Her eyes were wide and earnest as they searched his face. "Darling, don't you know I would never do anything that would hurt our baby?" she whispered. "I want this child every bit as much as you do! I can scarcely wait until next spring!" Her voice quivered. "But Jim, I must have my freedom!" She emphasized the words, hoping he would realize just how important it was to her. She continued, speaking with heartfelt determination. "I came West because

I didn't want to live a life where I was stifled and confined. I left boarding school and the social whirl of St. Louis because I wanted to know the wildness, the freedom, the beauty of the frontier. You can understand that, can't you, Jim? You need it, too." She leaned against him, holding him close. "I proved myself out West, too. You know I did. I learned to run my father's cattle ranch in Arizona, and I did a damn good job of it. Those range hands who scoffed when I first arrived at the Circle H came to respect me. I took charge of the ranch in a way they never expected. I tamed Shadow, and I learned how to shoot straight and quick. And when Matt Richards tried to scare me into leaving, I stayed. Despite his attempts to murder me, and your warnings that I get out fast, I stayed. Remember?"

"How could I forget?" he drawled, grinning down at her. "You were the most headstrong little spitfire I ever laid eyes on."

"Yes," she replied, a slow, answering smile curving her lips. "I was. And I still am. Because I won't be shut up on a shelf like a china doll who might break. I want to embrace this wild, open land, to master it." She slid her hands to his chest, staring up at him through glimmering jade-green eyes. "Please, don't deny me what my spirit demands," she implored. "I need to learn this Texas range, to be at home with it. I need to be free."

Jim smiled down at her, his muscles relaxing. His hand smoothed a stray wisp of hair from her cheek. "All right, little tenderfoot," he conceded slowly, "you win." He sighed. "Ride, if you must, but don't come so far on your own. Try to stay closer to the ranch house from now on, whenever you can. That's fair, isn't it?"

"I suppose so," Bryony replied reluctantly. She studied his lean, sun-bronzed countenance, her head tilted to one side. "But if I mustn't come this far, then we won't be able to meet here again," she murmured. "I'll miss this place."

Jim took her hand as they strolled together to the place between the oaks. "It will soon be too cold for lovemaking outdoors anyway, hussy," he chuckled. "In the spring, you can leave the child with Rosita and steal away again like before. I promise never to try to stop you."

They sat side by side upon the earth. Bryony wrapped her slender arms about Jim's neck. "It's not too cold today, is it, Jim?" she whispered, nibbling his ear with seductive languor. Jim stared at her with gleaming blue eyes.

"It's cold enough," he drawled. "But don't worry, little tenderfoot, I'll keep you warm," he assured her and, laughing, pushed her down upon the grass. He kissed her so forcefully that his lips bruised her mouth. His hands deftly removed her denim jacket and slipped inside her red shirt. He cupped her breasts, all the while kissing her with rough, demanding, loving kisses that left her breathless and weak. Fire engulfed her at his touch. Passion flamed in her limbs, sending sparks of ecstasy through her body.

I'll never get enough of him, she thought dizzily as every part of her throbbed in wild response to his demands. *I'll want him till the end of my days, till the last breath leaves my body. I'll need him always.*

They made love in the valley, heedless of the gusting November wind, heedless of the jackrabbits and squirrels and the wild geese that squawked overhead. The world ebbed away, and there was only the two of them.

Much later, Bryony rode alone back to the ranch house. Jim had returned to his work branding mavericks on the range, and she had errands of her own to attend to. Glowing from the loving interlude with Jim, she enjoyed a luncheon of chicken enchiladas and fruit, then went to her writing desk in the parlor and composed several letters. The first was to the Scott family in San Jose, California, and the second to Dr. Charles Brady of San Francisco. Dr. Brady, along with Tom and Martha Scott, had befriended Bryony on her journey to Arizona months ago. They had been her traveling companions on the stagecoach, and their friendship had endured beyond the trip west. When Bryony and Jim had honeymooned in San Francisco, the travelers had staged a reunion, greeting each other with heartfelt affection. Dr. Brady and the Scotts had been shocked to find that Bryony had married the gunfighter she had sworn to hate, the same man who had killed her father, but they had listened to her story with growing respect for Texas Jim Logan. They had ended up shaking his hand, convinced that Bryony's heart had not misled her. When the time had come for all the friends to part, Martha Scott had grasped her hand and whispered that Bryony had chosen wisely. "He loves you," Martha had said simply, smoothing her brown hair behind her ear with a work-roughened hand. "He will make you happy." And Dr. Brady had kissed her cheek, then turned his portly form toward Jim, admonishing the gunfighter to take good care of "our Bryony." Jim, with unusual seriousness, had vowed to do just that.

Now, Bryony was delighted to be sending them all word of her pregnancy. She could imagine the excitement of little Hannah and Billy Scott when they heard the news, and she knew Martha would share in her joy. Tom would give a shout of approval, and Dr. Brady, Bryony guessed, would blink rapidly to keep the happy tears from flowing down his kindly face.

When the letters were ready to be dispatched, Bryony placed them in the pocket of her riding skirt.

She rose and walked out to the porch. It was quiet today on the ranch. All the cowhands were busy on the range, and the corrals were empty. The wind flayed the dust into little dancing whirlwinds. As far as the eye could see, green and gold grasses carpeted the earth. Bryony heard Shadow whinny in his stall; she smiled to herself as she headed toward the stable, wondering if the stallion sensed that they were to ride out again so soon. She wanted to post her letters in Fort Worth this afternoon, and also to purchase some new, more loose-fitting apparel. Every garment she owned was beginning to pinch her waist now that her belly was expanding. A shopping expedition was definitely in order.

As she neared the stable, she heard a horse approaching and turned her head to see Danny riding hard across the prairie, waving his hat at her. His mustang came to a halt twenty paces from her, and Danny jumped from the saddle.

"Howdy, Bryony!" he greeted her. "Where are you off to?"

"Town. I have some errands there. Can I get you anything while I'm there?"

"Nope. I'm goin' there myself." Dan wiped his flushed, perspiring face with the sleeve of his plaid shirt. His chaps smacked against his long legs as he walked beside her toward the stable, leading the dusty mustang. "I've got supplies to buy at the feedstore. And I need to buy me a brand new lariat. He glanced at her and smiled. "Why don't we drive in together? I'm going to hitch up the wagon as soon as I tend to Windy here, and we can be off in no time."

Bryony paused and stared at him. A suspicion entered her mind at his deliberately casual tone. "Danny," she said slowly, clasping his arm. "Did Jim send you back here today—to keep an eye on me?" she demanded.

"What?" Danny turned an innocent face upon her, but Bryony saw the laughter glinting in his blue eyes, so like his older brother's. "Heck, Bryony, what makes you think that? I told you, I have some purchases to make in town and—"

"I don't believe you." She watched his face. "I told Jim this morning that I might ride into Fort Worth today. He knew of my plans. And I think he sent you here to accompany me." Bryony struggled against the anger flickering within her. She faced Danny squarely, intent on learning the truth. "Am I right?" she queried, her mouth set tightly. "Tell me."

Danny put an arm across her shoulders. "I reckon," he admitted with a grin. "He just asked me to drive you into town, that's all. He's worried about you, Bryony. It's a long ride to Fort Worth and—"

"And I've made that ride nearly every week since we've been married!" she flashed. Rage swept through her from head to toe. It was bad enough that Jim sought to prevent her from riding Shadow to town, but this subterfuge with Danny infuriated her even more. Jim didn't even respect her enough to be honest with her. No, instead he worked out this little scheme with Danny, both of them no doubt laughing behind her back at how easily she would be duped. Her hands trembled, and she clenched them tightly into small, hard fists.

"How dare he treat me like a child when I am about to be a mother myself!" she cried, flinching away from Danny's friendly embrace. "And you—you're no better!"

"Aw, Bryony!" Danny shook his head, chuckling. "It's no big deal. There's no sense in getting all riled up just because—" He broke off in alarm as she spun away from him and ran toward the stable. "Where are you goin'?" he yelled.

"To town!" she shouted back over her shoulder,

and ignoring his pounding footsteps behind her, she flew directly to Shadow's stall. In very little time she had the horse saddled and ready to ride, despite Danny's vociferous protests.

"I'm going to town anyway, damn it!" he finally exploded as she brushed past him, leading the glistening stallion. "Come on, Bryony, just keep me company in the wagon! Don't be such a stubborn little jackass!"

Bryony gritted her teeth. With the help of a corral post she mounted Shadow, then sent her brother-in-law a smoldering look. Her face was set with the determined look he had come to know. Danny realized in exasperation that, short of hog-tying her, there was nothing he could do now to prevent Bryony from riding to town.

"Tell my husband I'll see him at dinnertime!" she called grimly as she wheeled Shadow away from the ranch. *"Adios, mi hermano!"*

She felt Danny's eyes upon her as she and the stallion galloped off toward Fort Worth, but she did not look back. The chill November wind whipped back her ribbon-tied hair as she rode and slapped resoundingly at her burning cheeks. She urged Shadow faster, letting the scenery blur as the once-wild stallion raced the wind. Anger coursed through her, washing away every other emotion and thought. Like a ravine in the path of a flood, she was soon overtaken by the torrent, her mind consumed with the passion of rage.

How dare he treat me this way! she stormed inwardly, leaning low over Shadow's billowing mane. *I explained to him how I felt about being confined, guarded, pampered! I'm not an invalid! This ruse with Danny proves he didn't listen to a word I said! He is still the same arrogant, stubborn man I knew in Arizona, the one who thought he knew best for me!* Her thoughts whirled on and on, growing as she dwelled on Jim's high-handed and conceited behavior, his determination to master her. During that tumultuous ride, as she and Shadow flashed past the yucca and mesquite and wild verbena, thundering toward town, the tall gunfighter with the chestnut hair and vivid blue eyes with whom she had made love only hours before took on all the aspects of a tyrant to her, and every part of her being strained with rebellion against him. Instead of dissipating, her anger had intensified by the time she reached the outskirts of Fort Worth. In her blind wrath, she failed to check the stallion's pace as he roared up the main street of the bustling town.

When the wagon drawn by two geldings and laden with lumber and feed sacks turned abruptly into her path from a side lane, Bryony yanked desperately on Shadow's reins. A cry of fear sprang to her lips. But it was too late. The black stallion was already crashing into the horses and heavy wagon, rearing in alarm at the collision. The impact shattered the boards of the wagon, sending its grizzled driver flying into the dust. And the slender girl atop the great stallion was thrown clear across the street, her scream of terror piercing the afternoon air, echoing horribly a full moment after she lay crumpled and unmoving upon the wooden board-walk.

CHAPTER FOUR

JIM LOGAN bounded up the knobbed pine stairway to Doc Webster's office in three swift strides. Without bothering to pause on the outside platform overlooking the street below, he flung open the door with a violence that sent it banging into the wall beyond. He surged forward, his face a ghastly white beneath the sun-bronzed facade.

"Where is she?" he demanded hoarsely as the tall, spare form of the physician emerged from a room on the far side of the office. Doc Webster shut the door behind him. "In there?" Jim didn't wait for an answer, but strode toward the closed door. The doctor held up a hand.

"Wait, son," he said with the calm, resigned air of a man who has seen death too often to be unnerved by any mere man, even a famed gunfighter. "Your wife is sleeping now. I gave her laudanum drops to ease the pain."

"How is she?" Jim's piercing eyes searched Doc Webster's face. His body was rigid with tension. "Is it bad? Will she . . . will she be all right? Tell me, damn it!"

"Please sit down."

Doc Webster moved across the small, orderly office to the chair behind his oak desk. He folded his long, thin frame into it. Then he sighed, raising his gray head to gaze at the man who stood motionless in the center of the room, seeming to fill it with his size and the intensity of his emotion. Jim Logan hadn't shifted a muscle. His lean, handsome features were harshly set, his fists clenched tightly at his sides. In his hard cobalt eyes the doctor saw incredible strain. A wave of pity crossed Sam Webster's face. Then, with an effort, he blotted out this pity, smoothing away all emotion. In its place he clamped the calm, steady mask he wore like armor every day in his dealings with patients and anxious family members.

"Your wife will be just fine," he said quietly, watching the relief flood the gunfighter's countenance. "She has some broken ribs, a sprained wrist, and some cuts and bruises, but nothing life-threatening, to be sure. She's a hardy girl. And lucky, too. She sustained no permanent or scarring injuries."

At these words, Jim sank into the chair beside the window. "Thank the Lord," he whispered, burying his face in his hands. "Doc, I thought for a while there..." He broke off, struggling for self-control. The relief sweeping through him was dizzying. From the moment Danny had come tearing to the northern range with the news that Bryony had been hurt in town, a terrible fear had possessed him. He'd had the awful feeling that he would never see Bryony again, never hold her in his arms and know the gentle love that only she could give him. A vision had sprung into his head of what his life would be without her: dry, barren, without color or texture. Savage pain had ripped through him, and he'd ridden like hellfire for town without even waiting to hear Danny's explanation of what had happened. Something about a wagon and that damned black stallion.

He'd spurred Pecos as he never had before, desperate to reach Bryony's side, terrified he might be too late. Now, learning that her injuries were not serious, he felt as though someone had handed him his life again, bringing the world sharply back into focus. He took a deep breath, steadying himself. Then he came to his feet, strong again and determined. The thought of his beautiful young wife lying hurt in the next room made his heart twist painfully. He had to see her. He moved swiftly toward the opposite door.

"I'm going in, Doc," he stated curtly. "I want to see for myself that she and the baby..." His hand froze on the doorknob as he stopped in midsentence. He wheeled suddenly to face the physician again. "The baby!" he exclaimed. His words rang in the quiet room. "You didn't mention the baby! Is... is the baby all right?"

In his anxiety for Bryony, every other thought had been driven from his head, but now he remembered the precious life she bore within her, and his previous alarm returned. A new, horrible fear knifed through him as he watched Doc Webster's pallid face. Jim felt his body grow cold. "Damn it, man, tell me about the baby!" he ordered, as terror locked him in its icy grip. "Now!"

Doc Webster didn't speak for a moment. He ran a hand through his wiry, iron-gray hair, then picked up a writing pen on his desk and began to fiddle with it. He didn't meet Jim Logan's eyes.

"I couldn't save the baby, son." He spoke flatly, softly, like someone remarking that the rain has ended. "Your wife miscarried. The fall brought it on. There was nothing I could do."

Through the open window near the desk, the sounds of the town intruded upon the room. A dog barked in the street, wagon wheels creaked, and a horse whinnied loudly as a whip cracked in the air. Men shouted greetings to one another, a woman laughed, and the wind moaned softly as it blew tumbleweeds in the dust. Texas Jim Logan stood like a statue in the small, neat office as the sounds of the living drifted about him.

Doc Webster's voice came to him from afar. "I'm sorry, son."

Jim gave no indication that he had heard the physician's words. He remained motionless, frozen by the shock of a loss he was unprepared to withstand. It took a full minute for the impact to strike him, and when it did, the room swam before his eyes. He rocked on his feet and grasped the oak desk for support. Tears scorched the back of his eyelids as the pain ricocheted through him. *No. No. It couldn't be true.* He shook his head, trying to clear his brain, trying to rid himself of this awful thing that had happened. Yet, dragging his eyes to Doc Webster's face, he knew that it was true. He saw the sympathy in the physician's pale eyes, saw the weariness of a man accustomed to announcing tragedies. A second wave of agony rushed over him, and he spun away so that the doctor could not read his naked face. After a moment, the physician cleared his throat and spoke again. There was now a slight bracing note in his tone.

"There now, son, it's not as bad as it might be. Sure, the baby's gone, and I'm powerful sorry about that. I know how it feels to lose an expected child—especially the first one. My wife and I went through it, too. It hurts like hell. And I know that what I'm saying now doesn't mean much to you, the pain being so fresh and all, but I can tell you that it will pass. The important thing, the thing you have to remember, is that you still have your wife. She's going to be just dandy in a week or two. You and she can go ahead and have all the kids you want. Everything's going to turn out fine." He waited, watching the other man's face. He knew damn well his words brought little comfort at this moment of loss, but it was the best he could offer. Time, and another pregnancy, would be the only true cure for what ailed Texas Jim Logan right now.

His words echoed slowly in Jim's mind. *The baby's gone. The baby's gone.* Pain spread through his insides, hot and burning. He thought of the little wooden horse he'd been whittling every night this past week, his child's first toy. Every shaving had been made painstakingly and with love. Then he thought of the maple cradle that he'd carried down from the attic only two nights ago. It was the same cradle he had slept in as a baby, and Danny, too. Their father had carved it with his own hands nearly thirty years before and had proudly painted the Triple Star brand upon the crest. It was a treasure from the past that Jim had anticipated passing on to his own firstborn son or daughter, his father's grandchild. His throat tightened as he remembered all his plans for this child, his excitement and joy. When he at last turned toward the doctor, his shoulders sagged beneath the weight of his sorrow.

"My wife." The words somehow crept from his numbed lips. "I want to see her."

Doc Webster nodded. "This way, then. But don't disturb her. She took the news pretty bad herself, and it's better that she sleep awhile."

Jim followed him into the adjoining room, where the doctor normally conducted examinations, but which also served as a temporary sickroom for emergency situations. It was small and tidy, like the office, with a wooden floor and wood-paneled walls. The strong odor of antiseptic permeated the air. Along two of the walls were long oak bureaus whose deep drawers contained medical instruments. Upon the bureaus sat a variety of vials, bottles, gauze bandages, and other medical equipment. Against the wall on the right was a cot, flanked by a high-backed chair. It was this cot that drew Jim's immediate, exclusive attention.

He reached it in two strides. Bryony lay between stiff white sheets, sleeping. She looked pale and ill. Her left wrist was wrapped in bandages. Her lovely face was scratched and bruised. Her skin was nearly as white as the sheet she lay upon. In contrast, her black hair, which flowed like ink across the pillow, looked darker than ever. Jim's heart wrenched as he stared down at her. His chest was tight with grief. She looked so fragile, so small. Her delicate beauty stirred him as never before. He knelt beside her, gently cupping her slender unhurt hand between his. The sweep of her eyelashes against her cheeks made his heart ache. He remembered the feel of her against him, beneath him, so soft and so yielding. His lovely, loving Bryony. If only he could spare her this agony. He would do anything, anything at all if he could remove this pain from her. He would gladly bear the entire burden if that was possible. But it wasn't. When she awoke, she would be assaulted by the same terrible grief that engulfed him. In addition to her physical hurts, she would have to suffer the torment of heartbreaking loss, and there was nothing he could do for her. Nothing but be there, to comfort her and love her. Together, with their combined strength and their love, they would somehow manage to get through this ordeal. But he knew it wouldn't be easy for either one of them. This was a pain they would both carry for a long time.

Jim's mouth was grim. He tightened his fingers around Bryony's hand. He would be there when her eyes opened. He would tell her he loved her, that he would always love her. It was the least he could do. It was all he could do.

Doc Webster's voice broke the silence. "Mr. Logan..." he began softly. "Why don't you wait outside? I'll pour you a drink. I expect you need one, son."

"No." Jim didn't even glance away from Bryony's pale face. "I'll stay with her."

"She'll probably sleep awhile longer." The doctor gently took Bryony's hand from Jim. Holding her wrist, he checked her pulse, then lowered her hand upon the cot. He felt her brow. "Come on, son, she'll be just fine. Have yourself a shot of whiskey now, because you'll be plenty busy when she comes to and needs you near her."

Jim hesitated. Maybe the doctor was right. He could use a drink right now. Then he'd come back and wait for Bryony to come around.

He got stiffly to his feet and followed the doctor from the room. As he passed through the door, his gaze fell upon a pile of bloodied clothing in the corner of the examining room. It was Bryony's clothing. Fresh pain shot through him. He used every ounce of self-control he possessed to keep the nausea from choking him. Bolting through the door, he realized how badly he needed a drink.

He was finishing his whiskey when footsteps came pounding up the outer stairs and the door to the office flew open. Danny rushed in, disheveled and breathless.

"I got here as soon as I could!" The boy wiped his flushed face with his bandana. His eyes were wide and frantic, his sombrero askew. "I brought the wagon. It's packed with bedding. How . . . how is she?"

Jim turned to his brother. He straightened his shoulders, forcing himself to speak the necessary words. "Bryony will be fine, Danny. Her injuries aren't serious." He went on wearily, unable to hide his pain. "But she lost the baby."

Dan Logan blinked. Shock struck him, bringing pain into his young, handsome face. "Damn!" he muttered under his breath, and he came quickly forward to grasp Jim's shoulder. "I'm . . . sorry, Jim. Sorry as I can be."

Jim nodded. He felt control slowly returning. Shock and grief over the loss of the baby had rocked him to his core, but now he felt strength seeping back. He needed to be strong. He couldn't fall apart. It was his responsibility to help Bryony endure this tragedy.

He glanced at Doc Webster, who had moved to his desk and begun writing in a note pad. "Doc, when Bryony comes to, will it be safe to move her? My brother brought a wagon, and I'd like to take her home."

"I've packed it with pillows and blankets," Danny put in quickly as the doctor pursed his lips in consideration. "We'll be real careful with her."

The physician nodded. "I reckon that will be fine. She'll do better in her own house. But I'll come by to check on her tomorrow."

Jim paced to the window and stood gazing out unseeingly. He felt as though a mountain rested upon his shoulders. It seemed strange that only a few hours ago he and Bryony had lain together in the valley, joyful in their love and in their plans for the future. Now, everything had changed. All because of one damn-awful accident...

"Danny." He spoke suddenly, turning on his heel to face his brother. "What exactly happened this afternoon? All I know is that you rode out to the range and said that someone had come from town with news that Bryony was hurt. Something about a wagon and that black stallion of hers. How did it happen? Weren't you supposed to drive her into town?"

Danny sank into a chair and removed his dusty gray sombrero. He turned it over in his hands. "Yep, Jim. I was." He sighed. "I tried to persuade her to go with me. Honest, I did. But she saw through our plan and guessed that you sent me to keep an eye on her." He crushed his hat between his fingers in frustration.

"You know how Bryony gets when she's riled. Damn, she was mad as a hornet. Saddled her horse and galloped off before I could spit." He went on talking, unaware that his brother's shoulders had suddenly stiffened, that his blue eyes had grown keen and alert. Dan was hanging his head in dismay, staring at his mangled hat. "I was going to follow her, but she was gone so fast, I knew I couldn't catch her, especially if I took the wagon. Jim, I just didn't see the sense in trying to chase her all the way into town. So I did some chores in the barn, repaired that corral fence, and was just about to get some grub when Hank Miller came barreling up the trail and hollered to me that Bryony had been hurt in town. He said she rode in like thunder and crashed straight into Hal Lindsey's feed wagon."

"She was thrown clear across the street," Doc Webster put in quietly, glancing up from his paperwork. He shook his head. "Lindsey was knocked out for a few minutes, but came to without more than a bump on his head. He went home swearing about his wagon bein' busted up. The horses got scratched up, too, but none of them were badly hurt. Your wife, though, had a nasty fall, son. She hit the boardwalk real hard."

Jim had listened to all this intently, a strange dark fury slowly descending upon his taut face. Suddenly, he moved with quick, catlike strides across the room. He grabbed Danny by the arms and lifted him from his chair. His strong fingers bit into the boy's flesh. He spoke with slow, deadly calm. "Did you say Bryony wouldn't let you drive her to town? She rode off alone, angry?"

Danny stared into his brother's intense blue eyes, taken aback by the rage he read there. Misgiving made him hesitate, but Jim shook him ruthlessly. "Answer me, Danny!"

"Yeah, but..."

"And then, riding 'like thunder,' she rammed into Lindsey's wagon? She caused the accident?"

"I...I reckon so..." Danny stammered, trying in vain to shake loose of his brother's powerful grip. "Damn it, Jim, let me go. Are you loco?" he exploded, and then broke off as his brother released him abruptly and spun away on his heel to the window once more. "Jim?" he queried, moving closer. "For Pete's sake, what the hell are you..."

Jim whirled back upon him, a vicious expression upon his lean countenance. Danny had never seen him look like that before. He froze, staring at him as though seeing an apparition. The doctor, too, had risen from his desk in alarm.

"*She* did this," Jim whispered savagely, his tone low and trembling with wrath. "*She* killed our baby!"

"Jim, no! It was an accident!" Danny cried, but his brother's eyes narrowed.

"It was no accident!" he flashed. "It was Bryony's doing! All because of her damned temper, her pride! If she had let you drive her into town instead of riding off like a madwoman, none of this would have happened!" His hands clenched into fists at his side, and a look of such murderous rage shone in his eyes that Danny took a step backward. Jim continued grimly. "She killed our child, all right. That damned, independent spirit of hers got out of control once too often. I warned her, I tried to protect her, to protect them both, but she wouldn't listen to me!" His voice rang furiously in the quiet office. Then it grew strangely soft, steely. "I'll never forgive her," he muttered. A mask of granite seemed to shut down suddenly over his hard features. He pulled his sombrero low over his eyes. "I need a drink," he rasped, then strode suddenly toward the door.

"But, son, your wife will be coming around soon!"

Doc Webster stared after him in dismay. "Wait and talk to her. Take her home. You'll feel better about all this once you sit down with the little lady and..."

His voice trailed off as a low moan sounded from the adjoining room. Even as the doctor spoke, Bryony was awakening. Jim Logan paused with his hand on the doorknob. He listened a moment to the soft, pained cry. Then his body seemed to tense. His hand gripped the doorknob with frightening strength. He yanked the door wide, then left the office without a backward glance.

Danny and the physician stared at each other as Jim's boots stamped swiftly down the outer stairs. In the silence that followed, they both heard the soft moan repeat itself in the adjoining room. Danny moistened his lips with his tongue.

"I'll ... I'll get him back," he said after a moment, though his voice lacked conviction. "I'll talk sense into him. In the meantime, you take care of her, Doc. Tell her ... tell her ... damn it, I don't know what to tell her. Just say we'll be there to bring her home real soon." Without waiting for an answer, he was gone, his boots thumping down the stairs as his brother's had only moments before.

Doc Webster passed a hand across his tired brow. He turned to the sickroom door, thinking of the beautiful, grieving young girl lying hurt within. What the hell was he going to say to her? He took a deep breath as he opened the door. Then he fixed upon his face the smooth, professional mask that hid from all the world the pity and pain in his heart. He only hoped it would be strong enough, secure enough, to hide the truth from Bryony Logan. He had a grim suspicion that a greater ordeal lay before her than the loss of her child. He hoped he was wrong. He hoped that Jim Logan would calm himself soon and soften his anger, that he would see the futility of his bitter rage. But remembering the hard, ruthless expression in the gunfighter's eyes, doubt creased his narrow brow.

Sam Webster's heart was heavy as he entered the sickroom. He spoke heartily to the girl with the huge, stricken eyes who gazed up at him from the white sheets of the cot.

"There, now, Mrs. Logan, there's nothing to fret about. Everything is going to be fine. Just fine."

The words clogged like dust in the doctor's mouth.

CHAPTER FIVE

THROUGH THE open window of her bedroom, Bryony listened to the dwindling shouts of the cowhands as they returned from the range and disappeared into the barn and the bunkhouse. Intent on their supper, they joked and sang and swore, unaware of the woman who lay silently upon her bed in the upper floor of the ranch house, her eyes turned to the vibrant beauty of the sunset outside. Hawks cried shrilly as they circled through the blood-red sky. The fiery orange ball sank slowly into the horizon, and the crimson stain upon the heavens gradually gave way to softer hues. Ribbons of orange and violet and mauve billowed into the sky of palest lilac. The dry gold prairie shimmered below. It rolled endlessly away in every direction, glinting, glittering, alive beneath the panoramic sky. Gold met lavender and palest pinkest rose at the distant horizon, blending into a blur of color softer than a dream, as gentle and beautiful as dawn or a rainbow. The prairie went on forever. The sunset reigned in splendor for long and priceless moments, at last giving way in dying agony to the dusk, but the prairie, that endless golden sea, remained forever. It lost its luster as the glow of sunset fled, and one could almost see it darkening, settling into readiness for night, but it rolled on, with the timeless strength and endurance that is, was, and always will be, the land.

Bryony watched until the delicate pastels of the susnset sky faded into the soft gray-lavender of dusk. The evening breeze began to rustle the blue curtains at the open window and put a chill in the darkening room. Shadows crept up the walls. A floorboard creaked somewhere in the silent ranch house, and a sudden gust of wind sent the bedroom curtains flying out into the room. Bryony shivered in her bed. She turned her face from the twilight sky and let the tears pour unchecked down her pale cheeks.

She had been home for nearly two hours now. In that time she had been disturbed only once. Rosita had stolen in quietly to ask if she wanted anything: some tea, a pillow, anything. Bryony had shaken her head, too heartsick and weak even to reply, and the plump, pretty housekeeper had padded quickly from the room, her dark, braided head bent in sorrow. Bryony had shut her eyes tightly to keep the tears back. She had known that once she started to cry, she would not be able to stop. So she had fought the onslaught of weeping that threatened to consume her, fought the racking sobs that were only a gasp away. She had lain in the huge, feather-soft bed, surrounded by plump pillows and satin coverlets and empty dreams, and wondered why Jim didn't come to her. Her heart was so heavy within her chest that every breath was painful. She thought of the baby now lost to her and writhed in silent agony. She thought of the husband who had been so cold and quiet during the ride home on that dreadful wagon and wailed in silent grief for the pain she knew he was undergoing.

Bryony understood how Jim must be feeling over losing this baby; she knew how much he had wanted this child. Her own sorrow was overwhelming. In her pain, she wanted to reach out to him, to hold him and comfort him. She knew it was not his way to openly show his feelings, so his silence during the ride home hadn't surprised her at all. But ever since he and Danny had carried her up to the bedroom and left her to Rosita's ministrations, she had been waiting for Jim to return alone, to open his heart to her and gather her into his arms. He hadn't come. Bruised and aching from her injuries and wracked by an inner grief that hurt far worse than any physical pain, she had waited, yearning for him. She wanted to lighten his burden of grief with an outpouring of love. She wanted to feel his strong arms wrapped around her, sharing this loss as they had shared their joy. Yet sunset came and went, and the first star burned in the charcoal sky before a quiet knock sounded on the door.

"Come in." Bryony turned her tear-streaked face expectantly, but it was only Rosita who entered, bearing a tray.

"I've brought your supper, señora." The house-keeper spoke in the hushed tones one uses when conversing with the very ill. "*El doctor* said you could have soup and bread and fruit. I will help you to eat."

Bryony didn't even glance at the tray. She wiped the tears from her cheeks with the back of her hand. "Rosita, where is Jim?" she whispered, her green eyes enormous in her white, pinched face.

Rosita bit her lip. She set the tray down upon the nightstand beside the bed and busied herself turning up the oil lamp. Soft light shone into the darkened room. It made Bryony's eyes appear even more darkly luminous as they stared fixedly at Rosita.

"The señor is downstairs in his study," Rosita replied, not meeting Bryony's gaze. She lifted a linen napkin and shook it out for her mistress.

"I want to see him." Bryony pushed the napkin

aside. She put her hand upon the housekeeper's arm as the dark-skinned woman reached for the bowl of soup to serve her. "No, Rosita! I don't want any supper. Take it away!" The tears began to flow again, rolling uncontrollably down Bryony's cheeks. All of her anguish poured out at last. "I want my husband!" she gasped, covering her face with trembling hands. "I need him! Why hasn't he come to me?"

The housekeeper hesitated. She shook her head. "He is upset, señora. He has locked himself in his study and refuses to come out. I am certain that soon, though, he will open the door and then..."

"Please, bring him to me!" Bryony's voice was shrill and desperate. She couldn't understand why Jim was staying away, grieving alone downstairs instead of sitting beside her. She needed him! Then an idea occurred to her. Perhaps Jim thought she was too ill to be disturbed. Yes, that must be it. She tried to compose herself as she lifted her face to Rosita again, wiping away the tears with the lace-edged handkerchief the woman handed to her.

"Listen, Rosita," she whispered. "Tell him I'm all right. I am strong enough to see him. Tell him I *must* see him!"

"Señora, I do not know if he will listen to me. Señor Danny has been trying to convince him to come out for many minutes, and still..."

"Please!" Bryony's glistening eyes gazed pleadingly into Rosita's. Her bandaged hand lifted a moment and then fluttered down upon the bedsheets once again in a gesture of despair. "I need him!" Her voice throbbed. "Tell him that. Convince him to come to me."

Rosita was silent a moment, staring into Bryony's tormented face. Then she nodded, slowly. "*Sí, señora.* I will bring him." There was strong determination in her voice. Leaving the tray upon the nightstand, she moved

purposefully across the vast room, her back straight and
stiff. "He will be by your side soon, señora. *Muy pronto.*"
She closed the door quickly behind her.

Bryony sank back against her pillow, drained and
weak. She waited, her heart heavy with grief. The minutes dragged by. Outside the window, the sky was now
black, sprinkled with stars. The house and the grounds
were very quiet. From somewhere in the distance she
heard the faint high call of a mockingbird.

"Señora." Rosita had pushed open the door and
stood upon the threshold with her head bowed. "I tried.
The señor did not even answer me."

Bryony stared at her in shock.

"Be patient." Rosita cleared her throat. "Perhaps
mañana, the señor will—"

"No." Bryony pushed the sheets away with her
good hand. She sat up with an effort. "Help me, Rosita.
I'm going to talk to him."

"No!" In alarm, the housekeeper rushed to her side,
trying to push the wincing girl back upon the pillows.
"You mustn't exert yourself, señora! *El doctor* said..."

"Damn the doctor." Bryony slowly swung her legs
over the side of the bed. Each movement sent waves of
pain rippling through her sore body. Her bandaged rib
cage throbbed as she stood, grasping Rosita's arm for
support. But there was no arguing with the determined
light in her jade-green eyes. "I'm going down to Jim."

Wearing nothing but the thin silk nightgown Rosita
had helped her don when she had first come home from
town, Bryony moved toward the door. With Rosita's
help, she made her painstaking way across the lamplit
room. A cool breeze from the open window sent the
diaphanous, pale-rose gown blowing about her legs and
hips, and lifted her dark mane of hair from her neck.
Bryony shivered and bit her lip against the pain that
enveloped her. She blinked back the tears that stung

her eyes, concentrating only on Jim, on her need to reach and comfort him.

When Danny Logan saw the two women making their slow way toward the head of the staircase, he swore aloud and pounded up the steps in a flash. "Bryony, what are you *doing?*" he demanded, slipping an arm around her for support. "You ought to be in bed, honey, not walking around. Let me help you back to your room."

She shook her head, speaking through pain-clenched teeth. "Take me to Jim. I . . . won't go back to bed until I've . . . seen him."

Danny stared at Rosita in dismay. A long and telling look passed between them. Then he addressed Bryony again.

"Honey, look, I'll do what I can to get Jim to come out of his study. I'll send him up to you just as soon as I can, but in the meantime . . ."

"In the meantime he needs . . . me and I need him . . . and I'm going down there now," Bryony gasped, and put a hand upon the banister.

"Damn." Helplessly, Danny realized he had no choice but to lend her his support as she began her slow descent toward the bottom of the stairs.

When they reached the study, Bryony glanced at the closed heavy oak door. She slipped her arm from Danny's shoulders and leaned against the wood-paneled wall. "Leave . . . me," she implored.

"Hell, no!" Danny exploded, and he pounded his fist upon the door. "Jim, you damned bastard, open this door. Bryony's here! She wants to see you pronto!"

There was no answer from within the room. Rosita muttered something unintelligible in Spanish. Bryony clung weakly to the wall.

"Jim!" Danny roared in fury. "Open this damned door!"

Still there was silence. Bryony gathered her strength.

"Jim." Her voice sounded soft and faint after Danny's yelling. She swayed slightly with the effort that every word now cost her. "Please, open the door. I must... speak to... you."

To her relief, she heard the latch click and the door swung open.

Jim stood before her. Behind him, the study was dark, the writing desk, windows, and draperies all merely silhouettes in the blackness. She could barely make out Jim's face, but she saw that his features were harsh and set, that his blue eyes were narrowed. She also saw that he had been drinking.

"Jim. We must... talk."

She was aware that Rosita and Danny were standing behind her and, with great effort, turned her head toward them. "Leave us," she whispered.

"No!" Jim's voice sliced through the air. "Take her back to bed."

"I won't go! I... must talk to... you..."

"It'll wait until morning then. Doc Webster's orders were for you to stay in bed at least twenty-four hours. Damn it, can't you for once in your life do what you're told?"

She was unprepared for the fury in his voice, in his rigid body. Shocked, she stared into his eyes. "Jim, I only want to help you. Losing the baby was terrible for both of us. We should be together now. We need..."

Suddenly, she felt the last shreds of her strength ebbing. She clawed at the wall, trying to stay upright, but her knees buckled beneath her. She fell forward, crying out in despair. Jim caught her before she reached the floor, sweeping her into his strong arms as Danny and Rosita darted forward.

"Damn it, she belongs in bed!" he lashed out, and

after one swift glance at Bryony's chalk-white face and closed eyes, he strode with her in his arms to the staircase.

Danny touched Rosita's arm as she started after them. "No," he said quietly, watching his brother bear the exhausted girl up the winding steps. "Leave them be. Perhaps alone they will be able to work this out. It's up to Bryony now."

Slowly, Rosita nodded, saying a silent prayer that Danny would be right, that, between them, Bryony and Jim would settle their problems tonight.

Jim carried Bryony to the bedroom they shared and set her down upon the brass bed. She opened her eyes and gazed up at him, pain and fatigue etched upon her face. "Jim!" she whispered and lifted her arms to him.

He stayed where he was. Bryony's eyes widened in surprise. She lowered her arms and stared at him in bewilderment. "Darling, what is it?" she cried, shocked again by his coldness. She had already concluded that his earlier aloof behavior on the wagon returning from town had been due to grief and pain and tension, and his longtime habit of concealing his true emotions with a steely facade. But now, seeing the way his hands were clenched into fists and the icy glint in his cobalt eyes, she knew that it was more than grief, more than a matter of locking away his emotions. Something was wrong, terribly wrong. Her heart lurched inside her chest as though someone had kicked it. She struggled weakly to sit up on the bed.

"Jim, what is it?" she said again, her voice trembling. "Why, you . . . you're angry with me!"

His face was taut. He spoke roughly. "We won't talk tonight, Bryony. Tomorrow will be soon enough."

"No! No. I must . . . know now what is . . . wrong." Suddenly, tears burned Bryony's eyes again. Her face crumpled. "Jim, I feel so awful about the baby! I . . . I need you to hold me! Please, just put your arms around me and—Jim!"

She watched in horror as he turned on his heel and strode toward the door. She couldn't believe this was really happening.

"Jim, what is it?" she cried in an agonized voice that stopped him in his tracks and made him wheel to confront her. "I don't understand why you're punishing . . . me!"

"Don't you?"

He stepped closer, his powerful frame rigid and shaking with rage, and suddenly Bryony was frightened. She stared at this man whom she had married as though gazing at a stranger. He was no longer her tender, loving Jim, but was once again the cold, merciless gunfighter she had first known and feared. A knot of terror tightened inside her, constricting her throat. She cowered against the pillows as he closed in upon her, towering over her at the side of the bed.

"Don't you understand, little tenderfoot?" he mocked. He reached down suddenly and hauled her up so that she was at eye level with him upon the bed, his fingers biting into her arms. Bryony caught her breath, her eyes widening. Her breasts rose and fell rapidly beneath the sheer silk of her nightgown. Her black, tumbling hair brushed his strong hands as they gripped her. "Then let me explain! I could kill you for what you did today! You lost your temper and rode off into town like a fool and caused that damned accident! You almost got yourself killed! And you did kill the child within you by your stupid, willful actions!" His eyes glittered with rage. He was wild with fury. "It's you fault, Bryony!" he shouted. "You're to blame for this tragedy!"

She gasped as the impact of his words struck her. "No! No!" she cried, turning her head from side to side as if to ward off his wrath. "How can you say that? Jim, I never meant to ... harm the baby ... I only wanted to show you that you weren't my ... master ..."

"Your master!" He stared at her incredulously. A muscle pulsed in his jaw as he took in the import of her words. *"Your master!"*

Suddenly, with a snarl, he flung her away from him in disgust, and she tumbled upon the bed. His face was dark as thunder. For a moment he stared down at her, his breath coming hard. Then a brutal laugh rang from his lips. "You have a master all right, my prideful little tenderfoot. But it isn't me. That stubborn, pig-headed streak in you rules you more than I or any man ever could. You are a slave to your own damned independent spirit! It bade you risk your own life and that of your baby in its service, and you obeyed! You sacrificed your unborn child—and my love—with your blind obedience. I hope you're satisfied, you proud, stupid little bitch! I hope your *master* was worth it!" His words flayed her more cruelly than a physical assault. Bryony lifted her head to gaze at him in torment.

"Please, Jim! For ... forgive me!" She sobbed brokenly, shattered by his furious accusations. Everything he said was true. She couldn't deny it. It was her own pride that had caused her to lose the baby. Dear Heaven, her own stupid, ignorant pride! Tears streamed down her face. Her skin was ashen. She wept like a tortured animal. "I know I am to blame," she cried. "You are ... right." She shut her eyes as heaving sobs wracked her. Her words were almost inaudible. "But ... I never intended to hurt myself ... or the baby! Surely you ... know that! I can't bear the pain! Oh, Jim, please! Forgive me!" She stared at him desperately, lifting her arms once again in supplication. "Come to me! I beg you to forgive what I've done ... to hold me just for a little while! I need you!"

There was no response. Bryony dropped her arms and stared at him. Her heart wrenched in despair.

Jim was coldly surveying her. Gone was the ungovernable fury, the violence. Only harshness remained upon his features and in his rigid stance. She felt the blood draining from her face.

Jim spoke softly, calmly, yet she heard the bitterness in his voice. His words chilled her to her very core.

"I'll never forgive you, Bryony. I don't reckon I can."

She gasped, and her hand flew to her throat. His eyes pierced hers like icy shards. "You've defied me once too often," he drawled grimly. "And this time, what you did can't be made right." He shook his head and seemed about to say more, then, instead, he turned abruptly away from her and walked toward the door. "That's all."

She couldn't speak. She wanted to call him back, to plead with him, but her mouth was frozen and the words wouldn't come. She watched him open the door.

"Jim!" She was trembling, more from shock than from the sharp November wind now whipping through the room. "Where ... where are you going?" she whispered.

He glanced back at her. For a moment, gazing at her small, delicate figure upon the bed, her green eyes huge and glimmering upon him, he seemed to hesitate. Warring emotions showed in his face for just an instant and then, so swiftly that Bryony afterward wondered if she had imagined them, vanished. He stepped through the door without answering and slammed it shut behind him.

Bryony sat in stunned agony upon the bed. Her silken gown and her hair fluttered around her as the wind roared through the room, but she could only stare wide-eyed at the bedroom door, oblivious of the chill, of the night, of the pain tearing through her body.

She had lost everything. Everything. Her husband and her child. What was she going to do?

"He'll get over it." She mouthed the words silently as tears rolled down her cheeks. "He'll ... forgive me ... tomorrow."

Yet, the hollowness inside her belied the words, and she collapsed upon the bed as hopelessness suddenly engulfed her. Lying with her face buried in the pillow, her hair spread wildly about, she wept. Her sobs shook her slender form, sending currents of pain through her broken ribs and causing her wrist to throb with fire, yet she couldn't stop as wave upon wave of grief crashed in upon her, drowning her, consuming her.

She was bereft and alone. Her world had erupted around her, leaving only devastation. She lay upon the huge bed, a broken, heartsick figure, mumbling a desperate prayer that morning would never come.

CHAPTER SIX

"IT LOOKS like we're in for a blizzard!" Danny announced, turning away from the parlor window to grin at Bryony. "I'd better add some more wood to this fire or you'll freeze your pretty little toes off, honey!"

She smiled at him and glanced out the window at the lacy snowflakes hurtling down from the sky to veil the land in glistening white velvet. "Yes, please do," she replied, trying to inject some vitality into her voice despite the heavy pain that gripped her heart like pincers. "My bones are chilled already. I'm glad I put up that stew for supper tonight. It will be wonderfully hot and steamy."

"It sure smells good." Danny inhaled deeply, then bent down to toss another log onto the blazing fire in the stone hearth. "I'm as hungry as a horse." Straightening, he turned back to Bryony. "You look mighty pretty tonight," he told her. "I like your hair trussed up that way."

Bryony couldn't help laughing at this description of her coiffure. She had taken special pains with her toilette tonight, hoping to perk up her spirits by looking her best. For weeks after the accident, she had had little

73

energy or inclination to fuss with her appearance, being too miserable to care. She had lain in bed silently or wandered, wan and alone, through the enormous ranch house, too caught up in her pain and guilt and sense of loss to give a thought to what she wore or how she dressed her hair. Tonight, though, a sudden surge of energy had possessed her.

She had ridden Shadow this afternoon for the first time since the miscarriage, and the exercise had invigorated her. Something about the frosty December air whipping at her glowing cheeks and the headlong, dizzying pace of the stallion across the hardened earth had made her feel alive once more. Suddenly, she was weary of being weak and unhappy. She wanted to resume her life. And that meant facing up to Jim, trying once again to break through the barrier he had so determinedly erected between them.

Ever since that awful night when he had confronted her with his fury, she had been sick with grief, too devastated even to try to fight the cold indifference with which he'd been treating her. Now, though, she felt ready to deal with the situation. With her womanly instinct, she had wanted to be beautiful for him, to appear so soft and alluring that he would be drawn to her despite all resistance. Then, after having softened his defenses, she would be able to talk quietly with him, to convince him through reason and gentle persuasion that it was time to heal and forgive, time to pick up the threads of their love and begin again.

She had luxuriated in a rose-scented bath and lathered her hair with fragrant suds. After drying herself briskly with a thick towel until her creamy skin glowed like a luminous pearl, she had donned a high-necked white blouse with lace trim at the throat and wrists, and a soft gray wool skirt, with gray silk stockings upon her shapely legs and elegant black slippers adorning her feet. She added the gold locket that had belonged to her mother and swept up her thick, lustrous black hair in a French twist that allowed a few soft strands to wisp about her face. Delicate touches of perfume completed her toilette. She had smiled at her reflection in the mirror above her ivory dressing table, pleased with the results of her efforts. She knew she looked soft and desirable without appearing blatantly seductive. She sensed that Jim would draw away from any obvious attempt to seduce him and that a subtle approach would stand a better chance of piercing his bitterness and anger.

Now, seated upon the rose-and-white brocaded sofa, the fire burning cozily in the stone hearth, she laughed at Danny's comment about her trussed-up hair. "If you ever tire of ranching, Danny, consider becoming a poet," she suggested, her green eyes sparkling. "You have a remarkably romantic mode of expression."

Her brother-in-law grinned at her and came to plop down beside her on the sofa. "Oh, come on, Bryony, you know what I mean," he protested. "I may not say it right, but I just want to tell you that you look real nice. If that damned fool brother of mine doesn't take one look at you and get down on his knees to beg your forgiveness, I'll eat my saddle!"

"No." She took his hands earnestly in hers and gazed into his vivid blue eyes, so like his brother's and yet so different. There was never a reflection of ruthless violence in Danny's eyes, or of hostility to anyone. He was a frank, open, easygoing soul. "Don't think that Jim must apologize to me," she said. "He has been hurt, dreadfully hurt, and he is very angry. And he is right, you know. The accident *was* my fault. I must bear the blame for the miscarriage."

As he tried to object, she shook her head, tears sparkling on her eyelashes. "No, don't argue, Danny. I see my shortcomings clearly. My temper ran away with me; I behaved with stupid, careless pride. It is something I will have to live with for all of my days." She bent her head to hide the tears that had escaped and now ran slowly down her cheeks. She brushed them away. Then she squared her shoulders and glanced up, taking a deep breath. "I don't expect Jim to apologize for his anger. I just want his forgiveness. I want us to resume our marriage, to love each other once again. I'm going to try to reach out to him and to win him back."

"I'm sure behind you, Bryony," Danny muttered, moved by his sister-in-law's quiet determination. He put his arms around her and hugged her tightly to his chest. "You're the best thing that ever happened to Jim, honey. If only he'd wake up and remember that!"

It felt good to be held again. Bryony hadn't been touched by her husband in weeks. She leaned her head upon Danny's shoulder and closed her eyes, clinging to his lean young strength, comforted by his concern.

A cool, steel-edged voice shattered the peaceful moment.

"Don't let me interrupt!" Jim drawled from the parlor doorway, and Bryony and Danny separated in a flash. They both stared at the tall, muscular figure in black who watched them with such ominous calm.

Silence fell in the parlor, and only the pop and crackle of the logs could be heard.

Bryony's lips parted as she stared at him. In his black shirt and trousers, dark bandana and boots, Jim looked as deadly and forbidding as she had ever seen him. His eyes were cold as icicles; his mouth a tight, thin line. The black shirt outlined the powerful muscles in his chest and arms, reminding her of his overwhelming physical strength. Wide shoulders tapered to a lean torso, with a flat, hard stomach and narrow hips. His thighs beneath the dark trousers were muscular and strong. As always, he wore his Colt .45 Frontier low on his hip, held in place by a gunbelt with a gleaming silver belt buckle.

"I reckon you don't mind if I join you?" He broke the silence with a mocking edge in his voice. "Or maybe you two would rather be alone?" There was a dangerous gleam in his blue eyes as they pierced first Danny's startled countenance and then Bryony's.

Bryony found her voice at last. "No, Jim, don't be silly!" she cried, her tone a shade too shrill. She fought to regain her composure and rose quickly from the sofa. She moved gracefully toward him. "Come in, please. May I . . . may I pour you a drink?"

She paused before him, gazing up at him with wide, brilliant eyes. Her hands reached out to take his.

Jim stared down at her. He noted the delicate loveliness of her high-boned features, her emerald-dark eyes, her silken porcelain skin, and her mouth so soft and alluring he could barely tear his gaze from it. Her raven-black hair looked as soft and lustrous as velvet. The dainty, white lace blouse and gray wool skirt she wore emphasized her slender, yet sensuously curved figure, making him grit his teeth. For just a moment—one wild, passion-flamed moment—he wanted to seize her in his arms and kiss her, to feel her soft body molded to his, melting beneath the onslaught of his desire. Then, with cruel wrenching pain, his desire was replaced by the memory of what she had done, of what she had cost him. Cold rage replaced the yearning of an instant before as he remembered that along with her beauty, his wife possessed some most undesirable qualities. Her wild, headstrong nature had hurt him indelibly, a fact he was unable to either forgive or forget. As she reached for his hands, he jerked them away, flashing her a contemptuous glance. He stepped around her and walked with long, purposeful strides to the cherry-wood liquor cabinet near the far wall.

"I'll get it myself." He removed a half-filled whiskey bottle and a wide glass. "Drink, Danny?" he inquired without turning.

"No."

"What about you?" Now Jim did turn his head, glancing at Bryony with that hard, ruthless gaze that stabbed at her heart. "Do you want something?"

"No."

Standing alone near the parlor doorway, she watched as he poured the amber liquid into his glass. Misery descended upon her. She wanted so desperately to be loved again. She couldn't go on like this. His rejection of her greeting cut her to the core, yet she pushed away the frustration that welled within her, reminding herself that patience was necessary. Jim's hostility would not be overcome in a moment, or an hour, or a day. She could not afford to lose hope, nor to lose her temper. The stakes were too high. She fought back the tears that burned her eyelids, and walked back to the sofa, standing uncertainly beside it. Jim ignored her, lounging against the mantelpiece with his whiskey in hand.

The uncomfortable silence in the parlor grew. Bryony twisted her hands together, wishing the knot of tension in her stomach would go away.

"I found nearly a dozen strays today," Danny offered in a tone of forced joviality. "Rounded them up and got 'em branded pronto. I'd run into Duke Crenshaw over by the south range. He'd spotted them on his land and pointed 'em out to me. Said he knew they weren't his because his herd's been grazing far to the north. Right neighborly of old Duke, I thought."

Jim tossed down the remainder of his drink. He spoke curtly. "He's just staying clean of trouble. That's all, little brother. He doesn't want us to accuse him of branding mavericks."

"Oh, I don't know about that. Duke's always been

a decent hombre. I remember the time—"

"I'm not interested in discussing Duke Crenshaw."
Jim's eyes had narrowed. He put his empty glass on the
mantelpiece with a clatter.

"When is supper on?" he demanded, turning back
to Bryony. There was no warmth or affection to be found
anywhere in his demeanor, only that cold, deliberate
indifference. She felt like a servant who is held in dislike,
but tolerated for lack of a replacement.

"Soon, I expect." She forced herself to speak qui-
etly. Patience, she reminded herself yet again. Patience.
But despair and resentment tore at her. "I'll go and help
Rosita."

"I reckon that's a good idea."

It was obvious he could not even bear to have her
in the room. His steely tone flayed at her. She walked
swiftly across the parlor, conscious of both men's eyes
upon her. Her gray wool skirt rustled about her legs;
her slippers whispered against the oaken floor. Nobody
breathed until she had departed.

Then Danny rounded upon his brother furiously.
"What the hell do you mean, treating her like that?" he
demanded, his face suffused with an angry flush. "Instead of feeling sorry for yourself, you ought to think
about what *she's* gone through these past weeks! Damn
it, man, if you acted any more coldly toward her, she'd
be buried in ice! Bryony's your wife, damn it! Or have
you forgotten?"

"You apparently have, little brother!" Jim returned
grimly. "That was a mighty cozy embrace you two had
going when I came in. Seemed to me you'd forgotten
the lady was a married woman!"

"Oh, come on." Danny shook his head. "That was
nothin', and you know it! I was just trying to make her
feel better. She's lower than a worm right now, thanks
to you. I'll tell you something, Jim. If *I* was married to

Bryony, I'd sure treat her different than you do lately!"

"Well, you're not married to her." Jim's eyes glinted like shards of blue steel. He pinned his brother with their piercing intensity. "And I reckon you'd better not forget that fact, little brother. Savvy?"

"Sure. You don't want her, but you don't want anyone else to have her. Is that it?" Danny taunted.

Jim's next movement was so violent and sudden that it caught Danny completely by surprise. He crossed the distance between them in a lightning flash, seizing his brother's collar with one hand, twisting his arm with the other. He hauled the boy to his feet. "Mind your own business, Danny!" he warned, his voice a low, savage hiss. "This is between me and my wife. You keep out of it, and keep away from her!"

Danny struggled, but could not break free of that vicious hold. He swore as Jim's fingers tightened their grasp on his twisted arm. "Damn your low-down hide!" he gasped, and both brothers' eyes met in a long, searing glare.

Then, as suddenly as he had attacked, Jim loosened his grip and released Danny's arm. He took a deep, ragged breath. Without speaking, he returned to the liquor cabinet and poured himself another drink.

Shaken, Danny could do nothing but stare at him for a moment. Fury and shock coursed through him. Jim had never treated him like this before, never. Even when they'd been kids, his older brother had always looked out for him, showing him the gentle, warm side of his nature that he hid from everyone else. Jim had fought like hell with their old man, finally running off and joining the Yankees upon the outbreak of the War between the States, but up until the moment he left home, he'd never said a cruel or bitter word to his adoring younger brother or raised a hand against him. Losing the baby must have scarred him more deeply than

Danny had realized. He was a changed man. Danny
had hoped that if he could jar him out of his pain, it
might somehow ease the rift between Jim and Bryony.
Now he feared he'd only widened it.

His face was gray and discouraged as he walked
slowly past his brother toward the dining room. Jim's
voice, tight and low, made him pause as he reached the
door.

"Danny. I'm sorry."

The younger man stared at him. He didn't know
what to say. At last he shook his head, weariness
weighting his shoulders. "Yeah," he muttered slowly,
"I reckon you are." He passed on into the dining room,
taking his place silently at the long oak table.

Dinner was a tense, strained affair with little conversation, and afterward Jim locked himself into his
study. Lately, he'd been spending more and more evenings at the saloon in Fort Worth, not returning to the
ranch until the wee hours of the morning. When he did
arrive home, he went straight to the small guest bedroom in the east wing of the ranch house, the one far-
thest from the master bedroom. But tonight, the snow
kept him at home all evening.

His presence in the locked study afforded Bryony
little comfort. Though Danny kept her company in the
parlor for a while, trying to maintain a flow of cheerful
conversation, Bryony could no longer keep her despair
at bay. She excused herself early and went up to her
room, sitting for hours at the window, staring out at the
snow. Silent sobs shook her. She wondered if it would
not be better to go away and forget this house she had
grown to love and this man who no longer cared for
her. She fought the impulse to seek Jim out yet again,
for she couldn't bear to be rejected any more tonight.
The pain in her heart was like a wound that had been
repeatedly rubbed raw, and she did not think she could

endure to have it bruised once again.

The next morning, however, she squared her shoulders and prepared to try again. Failure was not acceptable to Bryony. Her spirit rebelled at the idea of giving up. Especially in this case, when she yearned so deeply for victory. She would win Jim back if it took every ounce of determination she possessed. She would prove to him that love was stronger, deeper, and more enduring than hate.

Errands in town drew her to mount Shadow in the late afternoon. The ranch hands had commented that a norther was blowing in from the hills. They guessed it would strike the territory full force that night. Bryony had never experienced one of these ferocious Texas storms. She cast a speculative look at the deceptively calm, gray sky as she set off for Forth Worth, noting the black clouds gathered in the north. Glistening snow carpeted the prairie, and as Shadow galloped with huge strides across the open land, Bryony felt as though she and the great black stallion were the only living creatures on earth. A pale sun glimmered as Bryony pushed aside her troubles and let the snowy December landscape envelop her in a glittering white world.

It didn't take her long to complete her errands, and she was soon walking briskly away from the general store, her parcels in her arms. When an all-too-familiar voice shrilly called her name, she groaned inwardly. Turning, she managed a wan smile for Mary Prescott, who bustled up the street with a simpering grin upon her red-cheeked face.

"My dear, how on earth are you feeling?" Mrs. Prescott demanded, too loudly for Bryony's comfort as several passersby glanced at them on the wooden boardwalk. They made an odd pair: the slender, raven-haired young beauty in the blue velvet cloak and the stout, loud-voiced matron whose plumed hat waved in the breeze as they stood together outside the milliner's. "I heard about that terrible accident and all," Mrs. Prescott gushed, her mouth working with the speed acquired of long practice as she dove into the subject of Bryony's troubles. "I'm so sorry for your loss, and for all the problems you've been having of late," she babbled. A knowing look entered her eyes. "Men! I know just how they can be!" Then she gave Bryony a shrewd, appraising look, studying the girl from head to toe. "But I must say, you look wonderful. A little thin, of course, but my dear, after all you've been through, I'd expect you to be a bit haggard. I mean..."

"Yes, and thank you, Mrs. Prescott, for your concern," Bryony interrupted her. "Tell me, ma'am," she continued, smoothly shifting the subject away from herself, "how is your committee faring?"

"The Fort Worth Grand Society will hold its first general meeting on the third of January!" Mrs. Prescott proudly announced. "We expect a splendid turnout! I do hope," she intoned, fixing her dark, close-set eyes upon Bryony, "that you will attend!"

"Oh, I'll make every effort!" Bryony promised. She shifted the packages in her arms. "Now, if you'll excuse me, I must load these purchases in my pack and head home. Jim and Danny will be looking for their supper soon."

"Yes, certainly." Mary Prescott nodded, her eyes bright and shiny as plums. She put a detaining hand on Bryony's arm. "But I want you to know, child, that should you ever feel the need for some sound advice—motherly advice, if you will—feel free to call on me. You're not the first woman to have problems with her man—oh, no, we've all gone through it at some time, and I'm certain that your Texas's fascination with that saloon singer is no more serious than those ditties she warbles. Why, if I was you—"

"*What did you say?*" Bryony stared at her in shocked disbelief. Her heart froze in her chest. "What . . . what are you talking about, Mrs. Prescott?"

The woman blinked rapidly. "Well, surely you know. Word is that your husband has been spending a great deal of time in the saloon these past weeks and—"

"What does that have to do with a saloon singer?" Bryony demanded. Her green eyes bored into the older woman's dark ones with such fierceness that the matron actually took a step backward. Suddenly, Bryony Logan no longer looked like the bewitching, innocent young lady who had hosted the Triple Star gala with such charm and grace. She looked . . . dangerous. Like silk over steel. Her lovely young face was taut. Her eyes glittered. She held her parcels with one arm and with the other reached out to grip Mary Prescott's elbow with surprising strength. "Tell me what you're talking about, ma'am!" she commanded.

Mrs. Prescott uneasily complied. "Well, you see, I thought you *knew*. A new girl started working at the Tin Hat a few weeks ago. Her name is Ruby Lee. She's a blond hussy, rather pretty in a cheap, vulgar way. I've seen her at Wade Cooper's general store once or twice." The stout woman sniffed disdainfully. "I don't go in for gossip, of course, but Berta Crenshaw told me that all the ranch hands at the Bar Y are in love with her. They say she sings bawdy songs, dances with the men, and"— here she shuddered in revulsion—"heaven only knows what else!"

"What has that to do with Jim?" Bryony's chest was tight. She could feel the pounding of her heart like an Indian war drum as she listened to Mary Prescott's recitation. The woman's words echoed in her mind. *Men! I know just how they can be!* The implication filled her with horror, and she listened to the matron with growing dread.

"Well, child, it's plain as a pumpkin! Though I'm not one to care for gossip, as I've already said, the word is that your Texas has been spending more and more evenings—and sometimes days—at the Tin Hat ever since she came to town, and apparently . . . well, my dear, the interest is mutual!"

Bryony released the woman as though repelled. She fought to control the trembling that suddenly shook her, and drew herself up straight and proud. "I am certain you are very much mistaken," she said in a stiff, low tone. The urge to shriek and rail at this abominable woman was strong, but she quelled it, forcing herself to appear calm and unruffled, even amused. "Lots of men spend time at the saloon, Mrs. Prescott. And Jim likes to drink and gamble as much as any other cowboy!" Bryony managed a small laugh. "Apparently the gossip-mongers of Fort Worth have tongues as large as the outdoors and imaginations to rival any Pecos Bill tall tale. It is really quite absurd. My husband has no interest in some vulgar dance-hall hussy. I am fully aware of the time he spends in the saloon, time he needs to relax from the rigors of running our ranch. And Ruby Lee has nothing whatsoever to do with it!" She gave Mary Prescott a tight-lipped smile. "In the future, ma'am, you would do well to question the opinions of gossips and fools who run to you with their tales. Those who have nothing better to occupy their minds than the habits of their neighbors are usually feeble-brained and lacking in sense, and their words are not to be trusted. Good day."

Mary Prescott flushed. She puffed out her enormous bosom. "My dear Mrs. Logan! I am only trying to help you. It seemed to me that you could benefit from some mature advice."

"You are very kind." Bryony's eyes pierced hers with blazing green intensity. "I hope, ma'am, that one day I might be able to repay you for your service."

With these words, she turned away abruptly and headed toward her horse. She felt, rather than saw, Mrs. Prescott's penetrating gaze following her, but did not turn to glance at the woman. Instead, she stuffed her parcels into her saddle pack, secured them, and mounted in one smooth motion. Then she rode for home at a hard gallop.

This time she did not even notice the wintry white beauty of her surroundings. She didn't even notice that the wind had picked up, that it now howled through the lonely yuccas and barren cacti and sent her heavy blue cloak billowing around her slender frame.

All about her, the land seemed to have awakened from some frozen slumber. The fine frost upon the ground fairly crackled beneath Shadow's hooves, and snow blew up from the earth in little whirling dervishes whipped by the wind until they spun and danced around her. The sky had grown darker. Charcoal clouds moved overhead, yet they still did not obscure the pale sun. Light glittered hard and silvery upon the snow-crowned prairie. The effect was coldly, starkly beautiful, a crystal world draped in snow. But Bryony did not see any of it—the breathtaking expanses of snow, which blanketed the prairie and rolling hills as far as the eye could see, the pair of eagles whose wings beat the sky above as they swooped toward the shelter of their eyries, the strange white light which sparkled on the waiting land. Her mind was consumed by a whirlwind of thoughts, all crashing and colliding within her head until her temples throbbed and the pounding filled her ears. But by the time she reached the Triple Star, she had made up her mind. She knew what she was going to do.

CHAPTER SEVEN

BRYONY WAITED until darkness cloaked the ranch house and everyone had gone to bed. There was a bitter wind rattling the windows. An icy draft crept along the floorboards like a stealthy cat, making her shiver as she glided barefoot across the huge bedroom and eased open the oak door leading to the hallway. Her pale-green satin nightgown flowed about her in a shimmering cloud as she swept lightly along the carpeted corridor. Her inky hair cascaded loosely about her shoulders, and her eyes glowed a brilliant emerald in her pale, oval face. She could feel her heart pounding as she made her way in the darkness. At last she reached the door she sought, and she put her hand to the brass knob. Anxiety pricked her like a thousand tiny spears embedding themselves in her heart.

She took a deep breath to steady herself as she began to twist the knob. This was going to work. It was going to be wonderful. Jim would not be able to steel himself against her.

She did not for a minute believe the ugly implications Mary Prescott had made today in town. Jim loved her, despite his anger and resentment. He would not

betray her with another woman. He could not. Ruby
Lee, whoever or whatever she was, meant nothing to
him. This she knew even as she had galloped home
from Fort Worth, her mind spinning in turmoil. Yet, the
story of Ruby Lee, the *idea* of it, spurred Bryony to
abandon her slow, patient approach, to take action immediately to win back her husband. She had decided
that if love and tenderness and patience alone did not
work, she would use another weapon, a more potent
one: passion. By kindling Jim's passion, she hoped to
once more ignite his love. So she had taken a tray in
her room tonight and dined alone, pondering her battle
plan. After her meal, while the sun was sinking and the
twilight fell over the vast, snow-laden prairie, she had
poured perfumed French bath oil into her brass tub and
luxuriated in the deliciously scented water. She emerged
dripping wet and promptly enfolded herself in a thick
towel, then wrapped another turban-style around her
streaming hair. She had sat down before her dressing
table, removed the towel from her hair, and brushed
the long, flowing curls until they shone like glistening
black satin. Her eyes reflected in the mirror were luminous with excitement as she contemplated the night
ahead. Gently, she had touched the silver-framed photograph of Jim and herself on their honeymoon, confident
that within a very short time they would be joyously
together again. After removing the towel from her body,
she had slipped into the pale-green nightgown of
powder-soft satin, and with her hair drifting behind her
in a mantle of sleek ebony, she was ready to implement
her plan.

Standing now at the door of the room in which her
husband slept, she felt excitement pulse through her.
Every inch of her body tingled with anticipation. As she
touched the cold brass knob, she wondered if Jim was
asleep already. So much the better, she thought with a

small, secret smile. She would slide into the bed beside him before he knew she was there and entwine her perfumed arms about his neck, greeting him with a flaming kiss. He would not send her away. He could not. Tonight he would be hers...

The door opened soundlessly. Bryony stepped inside.

Jim was not in bed. He was standing by the window smoking a thin cigar. He was stripped to the waist. His bronzed muscles shone in the lamplight as he raised the cigar to his mouth. He looked as darkly handsome as she had ever seen him, with his chestnut hair tumbling across his brow and his eyes glinting silver-blue as he gazed out at the windswept night. His tall, hard-muscled form and rugged features tore at her heart, causing her blood to heat as she watched him. Desire ached within.

She closed the door with movements slow and careful. Barefoot, she slid forward, her nightgown rustling. The noise of the wind drowned out all sound within the small room, and she reached him before he was aware of her presence. He stabbed the butt of the cigar into a clay bowl on the windowsill. The muscles of his body rippled as he leaned forward. When he straightened, Bryony placed a slender hand upon his arm.

She had forgotten for a moment who, or rather what, her husband was. In his profession, speed of reaction was essential to survival and danger was ever present. Instinctively, Jim reacted to her unexpected touch. He spun about and seized her, slamming her against the wall. The next instant, as he recognized her, the violence fled his features. His body relaxed, and his powerful hands ceased their bruising grip against the tender flesh of her arms. Yet he held her still, staring down into her startled, upturned face with narrowed eyes.

"What the hell are you doing here?" he demanded, his jaw tightening. "I might have killed you before I realized it was you!"

"It is my house. I have a right to be in any room I please." Bryony, though at first alarmed by his violence, now smiled into his glinting eyes. He was very close to her, his body pinning her against the wall. She knew by his sudden intake of breath that he had just become aware of her perfume. "I wanted to see you. I miss you, Jim."

He stared at her for a long moment. In that time, he was aware of everything about her. He could see her creamy, rose-tipped breasts through the sheer satin gown, could feel them pressed against his naked chest as he held her. Her silken hair was a midnight cloud, her high-boned features as delicate and beautiful as fine china. Her luscious scent tormented him. Her eyes, bottomless emerald pools, held him spellbound. He felt his muscles tense as he looked at the soft, tempting pinkness of her mouth. He wanted her. Damn, how he wanted her!

Bryony slipped her arms free of him. She raised them and wrapped them around his neck. Gently, determinedly, she pulled his head down to hers and swayed against him. Her lips covered his, rejoicing in the feel of his mouth against hers. Desire leapt into her eyes as she kissed him with all the passion and ardor she possessed. Her limbs melted against him. Their bodies locked together like sword and sheath. Fire engulfed them as though they were of molten steel.

Jim responded to her kiss with an intensity that thrilled her. His mouth sought hers desperately, and he plunged his hard tongue past her lips. Strong arms enclosed her like iron bars as she pressed close against him. Bryony felt a burning heat slide over her, up and down her arms, her breasts, her thighs. An inferno engulfed her. Jim's hands moved roughly, hungrily over her as though he could not get enough of her. His hard, demanding touch sent ribbons of flame through her body, and when his lips scorched the pulse at her throat, making it leap and quiver, she shuddered in his arms. Her hands clung to the powerful rippling muscles of his naked back as he tangled his hands in her hair and conquered her lips with his. Ecstasy and triumph swept through her as she felt the power of his unrelenting passion. He was hers. He wanted her. His desire was as vibrant and alive as ever. She would drive him mad, and he would forget his anger, his bitterness, his pain, and know only the need to be one they both shared.

For long moments they were wild with passion, both of them trembling with urges too long suppressed, and then, suddenly, as Bryony's hands worked to unfasten his breeches, longing to feel the length of him throbbing inside her, the spell abruptly shattered. Jim froze, his entire body stiffening with rage, and he jerked away from her as though she were a rattlesnake coiled to strike. He thrust her from him with such roughness that she stumbled against the wall, her hair swirling like black velvet about her shoulders.

"You damned little bitch!" Jim rasped, his chest heaving as he tried to jam all the passion back inside. "You dirty, scheming vixen! Get the hell out of here!"

Undaunted, Bryony swept the hair from her eyes with one hand and straightened to face him, stepping away from the wall. She moved closer, her face flushed and glowing with desire. "You don't want that, Jim! And neither do I! You love me still! Don't fight that love, just love me. There is no reason not to! We are husband and wife!"

"I don't want you!" His raw voice split the air. "Can't you understand that? I don't want you!"

"I don't believe that." Bryony's chin lifted as she

met his furious stare. Her own eyes sparkled like emeralds set afire. "You've shown just now that you *do* want me. That kiss was no lie!" Her lips curved upward as she stepped deliberately toward him. Her nude beauty beneath the flowing gown was provocatively revealed, and she glided forward with sultry assurance. "Admit it, my darling. You want us to be together. You want to make love to me. Just as I want to make love to you." Her hands slid sensuously upward over his broad, gleaming chest, lightly brushing and caressing the thick brown hair matted there. "Jim," she whispered, pressing close against him, "love me."

His eyes darkened to cobalt. There was a sudden, sharp intake of breath. Then every muscle in his body tensed. He moved with lightning speed, grasping Bryony's fingers from his chest, imprisoning her wrists in iron hands.

"I don't love you," his voice grated between clenched teeth. "Damn you, I don't want you anymore! But you don't seem to care about that!" His eyes flashed dangerously. "You come in here and throw yourself at me like a common whore. You think that by seducing me you can erase everything else. Well, you're wrong!" He shook her, his fingers biting into her flesh. His face was harsh as he stared down at her. "There's one thing you were right about, though, my bewitching little tenderfoot," he drawled grimly. "I do still desire you. The way an animal desires its mate. Not from any feelings of love—no, you killed those when you killed our child. My desire stems solely from lust. You're a damnably beautiful woman, Bryony. I can't deny that."

She began to struggle as she saw the cold darkness in his eyes. Fear and anger sprouted suddenly within her. "Let me go!" she ordered, trying in vain to break free of his powerful grasp. "I don't want you that way! I want your love!"

"You came here, little tenderfoot. You came looking for me, trying to catch me like a mouse in a trap. Well, you've got me. Only I reckon the mouse and the cat have switched places. It seems you're the one who's caught." His mouth curled. There was a mocking, deadly glint in his vivid blue eyes. "You're here, and you're my wife, and I'm going to give you what you came for."

"No!" Bryony kicked out at him as he suddenly dragged her backward toward his bed. She wrenched her arms in an attempt to free herself of his ruthless grip, but her struggles had no effect. He threw her down upon the mattress and straddled her, pinning her arms above her head with one hand. His other hand slid inside the bodice of her nightgown and cupped her breast.

His voice was harsh, savage. "This is what you wanted, isn't it, Bryony? Or did you expect roses and moonlight?"

He didn't wait for an answer. His lips crushed down upon hers, smothering any response. She bucked beneath him, twisting her head, but he held her tighter and forced her lips apart with his tongue. His body held her captive while he plundered her mouth. His kiss was hard and hungry, bruising her lips as she writhed helplessly beneath him. His fingers massaged the taut nipple of her breast with rough expertise. Bryony fought to escape him, but he was too strong, and as his loins pressed her into the softness of the bed and his hands stroked her ruthlessly, she cried out in anguished protest.

Jim ignored her. His fingers found the top of her bodice and ripped it downward, rending the satin gown in two. He gazed down at her exposed and trembling form beneath him, raking the length of her.

"No! Damn you, no!" Bryony cried, so loudly that he released her aching wrists from the uncomfortable hold above her head and clamped his free hand over her mouth. He regarded her through dark, angry eyes.

"Quiet, little tenderfoot! We don't want Danny interrupting us, do we?" he drawled harshly. "If necessary I'll gag you. I don't reckon you'd like that."

Bryony's green eyes burned with hatred, and something else—horror.

This was a mockery of what they had once shared. All of her beautiful memories with Jim were being destroyed. He knew she yearned for tenderness, for passion born of love, and instead he was humiliating her, turning something that should have been beautiful between them into an ugly act of revenge.

She twisted once more beneath him, her arms flailing against him. It was no use. He held her easily, helplessly, like a tiger who has captured a bird. She lay still. She was breathing hard, and her face was wet with tears. Her black hair tumbled damp and tangled across the sheets. Jim removed his hand from her lips, watching her intently. Her mouth was red and bruised from the ferocity of his kisses. There was a film of sweat upon her brow. He could feel her body quiver uncontrollably beneath him. Yet it was her eyes that held him arrested, their jade depths reflecting an anguish that penetrated to her very core. He saw it and knew that, at last, she understood.

"I don't love you, Bryony. I don't give a damn about you!" His cold blue gaze bored into her. There was no mercy, no pity in his eyes. His features were as hard as the frozen prairie. "I reckon now you see that. Don't you?"

She stared back at him, wracked by a suffering that went far deeper than any physical hurt. The knowledge that he could use and humiliate her in this way bombarded her with pain. Yes, she understood. He had proven to her the extent of his hate. There was no longer room for love or compassion, or even pity, in Jim Logan's heart. Only hate. He could not have done this to her otherwise. A sob choked in her throat. Jim dug his fingers into her shoulder, shaking her as she lay under him.

"Answer me, Bryony!" he ordered. "Do you understand?"

"Yes. Yes!" she gasped as she closed her eyes against his cold-blooded expression, no longer able to bear the callous disregard she read in his face. Tears squeezed from beneath her lashes and streamed down her cheeks. "You don't want me... don't love me. I understand, damn you! What more do you want?"

"Nothing more. That's all."

With these words, he let her go. His hands released her. He withdrew his weight from her and stepped back from the bed. Then he walked away.

For a moment, Bryony was too stunned to move. She sat up slowly, her arms and shoulders aching. She stared at Jim swiftly fastening the buttons of a blue linen shirt across his chest and tucking the ends of it into his trousers. She watched in dazed silence as he sat down on a small carved chair and began to pull on his boots. It was over. Over. She was numb with pain, her heart as heavy as though it were bound with iron chains. Then, abruptly, her strength returned as rage rushed through her, crowding aside everything else.

"You... you despicable bastard!" Bryony hissed, her hands clenched into tight little fists as she jumped off the bed and dove at him. "I'll kill you!"

Jim caught her as she tried to strike him and thrust her backward onto the bed once more. Ignoring her, he reached for his worn gray sombrero and pulled it low over his eyes. Then he slung his gun belt over his shoulder and turned toward the door.

"Don't you dare leave!" Bryony gasped. She darted

forward again to block his path, heedless of her naked-
ness, of the tears pouring down her cheeks. Blind rage
consumed her. She glared at him like some wild, attacking she-cat. "We're not finished yet, Jim Logan! I've
a few things to say to you..."

"I'm not interested." With one hand, he pushed
her aside and was out the door before she had recovered
her balance. Bryony scrambled after him, incensed nearly
to madness.

She was too late. From the top of the staircase she
heard the front door slam. He was gone. Gone! Her
cheeks were flaming with fury. Her fist slammed into
the top of the banister. Livid, uncontrollable wrath bub-
bled inside her as she stood alone in the cold, darkened
hallway. She turned and ran to her bedroom and began
to pull on some clothes. Her fingers shook as she fastened the buttons of a white cambric shirt and stuffed
its ends into a black wool riding skirt, then shrugged
quickly into the tight-fitting red velvet jacket with small
jet buttons down the front. She pulled a brush through
her hair and swept it back from her face with a red velvet
ribbon, all the while her brain seething with murderous
frenzy, recalling the despicable way Jim Logan had used
her tonight. Did he really think she would let him get
away with it? Did he think she would let him humiliate
her like that, abuse her love for him, and then leave as
though it didn't matter at all? Bryony's lips tightened.
She tugged on her boots with vicious strength and then
strode swiftly to the chest of drawers where she kept
her derringer. She dropped it into the pocket of her
riding skirt and turned toward the door.

The house was still quiet. Apparently Danny and
Rosita had not heard any commotion. So much the better. If they awoke, they might try to prevent her from
riding out tonight after Jim, and she did not want to be
delayed by arguments. Downstairs, in the hall, she lifted

her heavy blue velvet cloak from the hook near the front door and donned it, drawing the hood closely about her face. Then she thrust her hands into warm leather gloves. An instant later, the double oak doors were open and she was running toward the stable, a savage wind ripping at her garments and flaying her face.

She bent her head against the freezing gusts. *We're not finished yet, Texas Jim Logan!* she thought venomously, and yanked open the stable door. *Not by a long shot!*

Minutes later she was riding off into the bitter, windswept night, a small, lone figure on a dark horse, plunging through the moonlit snow filled with single-minded, deadly purpose.

CHAPTER EIGHT

THE TIN Hat Saloon boasted few patrons on this wild December night. Most of its usual clientele had chosen to huddle in their homes with blanket and hearthfire instead of braving the savage gale and plummeting temperatures outdoors. A handful of drifters and railwaymen were scattered throughout the gaudy crimson-and-gold-papered saloon, leaning their elbows on the bar as they gulped whiskey and surveyed the bored dance-hall girls. The girls looked cold in their skimpy, tight-fitting gowns, all of which were decorated with an assortment of sequins and feathers and glittery rhinestones. Big Jake, the huge, red-bearded bartender and owner of the place, kept a watchful eye on the slate-eyed gambler in the corner who had suggested a poker game to two drifters in ragged garb. He hoped the two could afford to pay up when they lost, because he didn't want any fighting in here tonight. Big Jake's back was hurting him again, and he wasn't in a humor to break up anything or spend the whole evening cleaning up the aftermath of a brawl. His attention shifted from the poker players when the doors to the saloon swung open and a girl he had never seen before swept in, looking half-frozen and more than a little battered by the gathering storm. She took a second to glance about the room and then hurried toward him, her step sure and quick upon the crimson carpet.

Big Jake stared at her curiously. She didn't look like a saloon girl, that was sure. She was a beauty, but in a ladylike way. Beneath her hood he caught a glimpse of black hair. Her eyes were green. There was something at once delicate and wild about her, something that held his attention and made him smile hopefully as she approached him. Maybe this would be his lucky night. Maybe the norther had blown in this pretty little filly just to warm his bed tonight.

"I'm looking for Texas Jim Logan. Where is he?" the girl demanded. Big Jake hid the quick disappointment in his gut. Now he knew who this girl must be. Everyone knew Texas had a wife. Big Jake had never met her, but then he seldom met women outside the saloon, and a nice married lady from the East wouldn't have much reason to set foot inside the Tin Hat. But this had to be her, no doubt about it. Word had it she was a beauty, and this girl sure was that. Too bad, he thought, his olive-brown eyes appraising her up close with warm approval. There wasn't a chance in the world he would fool around with Texas Jim Logan's woman. Even if she was interested, which, from the look of things, she wasn't. She seemed wholly concerned with the gunfighter's whereabouts, and that was the one thing Big Jake wasn't about to tell her.

"Who?" he asked gruffly. He began to polish the shiny black surface of the bar with a cloth. "I reckon I didn't catch the name, ma'am."

"Texas Jim Logan." Bryony spoke through clenched teeth, her smouldering eyes fixed on the hulking bartender's round, fleshy features. "Tell me where he is."

Big Jake shook his head. "Nobody here by that

name. Just look around, ma'am."

There was no perceptible movement, yet somehow Big Jake suddenly found himself staring into the barrel of a trim little pearl-handled derringer. The girl held it steadily in her gloved hand. "No more stalling," she said evenly. "His horse is hitched up outside. Now, are you going to tell me where he is, or do I blow a hole in you? There's a man in Arizona Territory buried with a bullet in him bearing my name. I'm not against making it two. So talk!"

Big Jake gaped at her in astonishment. He tugged at his black string tie, which suddenly felt tight about his perspiring neck. "Well, I'll be damned!" he muttered and shook his head. He had a hunch this little filly meant what she said. Feisty little thing, wasn't she? Short-tempered, too. Then, as Bryony cocked the safety of the gun in warning, he muttered hurriedly, "All right, lady, all right. He's upstairs in Ruby's room. Third door on the left." He exhaled slowly as Bryony clicked the safety once more into place and backed toward the stairs. She kept her eye on him as she moved quickly up the narrow steps, as alert and keen to everything around her as any lawman stalking a desperado. Big Jake would have given a lot to see what happened when she found her man. Reluctantly, he turned his attention back to the poker game, his brows drawn together. He had a feeling, one way or the other, that there would be gunplay before this night was over.

Bryony crept down the hallway of the second floor of the saloon as softly as a rabbit. She didn't pause outside the third door on the left, or knock; she just shoved it open with a violent bang and sprang forward into the room. With the derringer leveled, she stared at the two startled occupants.

Jim was sitting on the edge of a wide, pink-canopied featherbed, his hat pushed back on his dark head. His blue shirt was unbuttoned to the waist, his arms wrapped around the girl who sat half-naked on his lap. Ruby Lee. Bryony scrutinized her swiftly as rage mounted. The saloon girl had thick, silver-blond hair, a pointed nose, and full, scarlet lips, with cheeks rouged to hide a pallid complexion. She had enormous, lily-white breasts, which spilled almost completely out of the skimpy red negligee that adorned her body. Apart from this flimsy garment, she was naked, except for the heavy perfume that must have covered every inch of her voluptuous form. A smirking giggle had died on her lips as the door had burst open, and now, as she stared at the blue-cloaked girl on the threshold, the girl who so furiously brandished a gun, she gave a squeal of panic.

"Aaaaah," she shrieked and clung to Jim like a crazed octopus. "Honey, *do* somethin'."

He pushed her off his lap and rose slowly, regarding Bryony through smoke-blue eyes. "What the hell are you doing here? Are you loco?"

"Yes." Bryony aimed the gun at Ruby Lee. "Out!" she snapped. "Now!"

"Hon-eeee!" the girl whined, clutching at Jim's arm. "Are you goin' t'let her get away with this? How dare she point that awful thing at me? Why don't you..."

Bryony clicked the safety free, and the sound seemed to echo in the small bedchamber. Ruby Lee's mouth dropped open, and she stared in terror at the girl near the door.

"You have two seconds. Go!"

Ruby Lee bolted toward the hallway, her flimsy negligee drifting behind her. Bryony slammed the door after she'd departed, never turning her eyes from Jim. He was lounging before her, dark anger suffusing his features, yet there was no fear on his countenance. Just wrath. *Good*, Bryony thought with vicious satisfaction.

Then we're even. It will be a fair match.

"Are you finished, Bryony?" Jim's voice, as hard as bullets, cut the air between them. "Have you made a big enough fool out of yourself? What the hell do you think you're doing?"

"You warned me once that the next time I took up a gun against you, you would kill me," Bryony said, holding the gun steadily, aiming it now directly at his chest. "Are you game to try?"

"I sure as hell ought to!" he growled, clenching his fists. "You deserve it, pulling a stunt like this."

"You asked what I was doing here. I'm asking you the same question."

"Isn't it obvious?" he drawled, hooking his thumbs in his trouser pockets. He appeared relaxed now, totally at ease. Almost, but not quite, pleasant. "You're an intelligent woman, Bryony. You ought to be able to figure out for yourself exactly what Ruby and I were doing here."

Up until this moment, Bryony had maintained rigid control over her emotions, refusing to feel pain or betrayal or grief. Only anger had she drawn on and fed, using it to get her through this ordeal. Now, though, pain burst through her once more and shook her to her very depths. Her voice trembled as she cried out, "No! I don't believe you!"

His lips curled in a mocking smile. "You don't belong here, Bryony. Go home."

"Home?" Her voice rose dangerously. "What home? You mean that ranch house back there that you brought me to after we were married? The one where you promised to love me forever, to be my true and faithful husband until the end of our days? Is that the home you mean?"

He turned away from her. "Get out."

"Not until I'm finished with you. I want to know

something." She bit her lip to keep it from quivering and tightened her grip on the gun. "Is that woman your lover?" Her voice was low and filled with suppressed emotion. "Tell me the truth, damn you—if you have any decency left in you. Have you . . . made love to her?"

Jim glanced at her. There was no emotion visible on his face, but his eyes touched her like icicles.

"Yes."

Her vision blurred with sudden tears. She blinked rapidly, aware that she could no longer see Jim. A feeling as dry and cold as death rustled through her, and she drew in her breath sharply. The stench of Ruby Lee's cheap perfume lingered in the air.

"You bastard," she breathed.

A muscle throbbed in Jim's jaw, and he swung impatiently forward. "I reckon I've had about enough of this," he remarked, his broad frame bearing down upon her. "Give me that damned gun, Bryony, and get the hell out of here."

"No! Stand back or I'll shoot!" she cried shrilly, retreating as she again raised the pistol to chest level. "I will shoot, Jim, I swear it!"

He never broke stride. His long legs bore him swiftly across the room, and he seized her gun hand, twisting the weapon away. Bryony gave a sob and threw herself upon him, her fists pummeling his chest and shoulders. He caught her, hooking an arm around her waist and staring down into her tear-bright eyes.

"You had your chance for revenge," he muttered, giving her a hard shake. "You couldn't take it." His tone was brutal. "But don't worry, Bryony. You've already hurt me far more than mere bullets could. You took away the child I wanted more than anything, and you destroyed my love for you with your stupid, reckless pride. There's not much more you can do to me, or I to you, so let's just call it a night. Leave me to my drunken pleasures, and you go home to your nice soft, comfortable bed. All right?"

"I could have forgiven you." Bryony's voice was an agonized whisper, her face very close to his. "I could have forgiven you anything, even this. Even Ruby Lee, even the vile way you treated me tonight. If you had but asked me, I would have forgiven you, because I loved you that much. But you"—she trembled in his arms, her entire body aquiver with fury and pain—"you cannot forgive me for being me. I asked your forgiveness when I acted out of blind, foolish anger, when I made that horrible, tragic mistake! I begged for your forgiveness! But no! The mighty Texas Jim Logan does not know how to open his heart and forgive anyone! You couldn't forgive your father all those years, and then he died before you had the opportunity to make it up to him. And now you cannot forgive me. I wonder," she went on, her pale face awash with tears, her reddened eyes staring up at him, aware of his arms tight around her waist, "I wonder if you will forgive me in ten or twenty or forty years, when our love has been wasted and our lives have been ripped apart. Is that when you will finally find the courage to forgive, when it is too late?" She struggled suddenly to free herself of him, and he let her go. He watched in silence as she hurled herself toward the door, her heavy cloak swirling around her.

"There's one more thing, *Texas*."

Her use of his nickname made him stare at her with sudden penetrating intensity. Bryony never called him Texas. That was the name of his other self, the gunfighter feared and dreaded throughout the West. Lawmen and desperadoes knew him by that handle, but ever since the first time they had made love, Bryony had called him Jim. It had always been a welcome sound from her lips, a tribute to her belief in him, in the man he really was, and not the cold-blooded legend. Now, hearing her address him as Texas, he paused, a sudden stillness coming over him.

"I'll always love Jim Logan. Always." She met his gaze, her green eyes swimming with tears and an aura of dignity enwrapping her, despite her distress. "The only problem," Bryony concluded softly, "is that I don't know where he's gone."

Her gaze lingered on his face for one final moment, as if memorizing every detail, and then she whirled and yanked open the door. She ran from the room without glancing back, but Jim heard her footsteps echoing down the hall until all sound was lost except the muffled din of the saloon below.

He stood where he was, a thousand thoughts crashing in his head. Her words echoed in his brain. *Forgiveness. Love. Courage.* He saw her face, vivid as life. The courage to forgive? Isn't that what she had said?

No! His boots thumped the wooden floor as he strode back and forth, emotions churning inside him. He couldn't forgive, not this time. *Which time then?* A persistent voice rang out amid the confusion. *Which time?* Certainly not the time he had fought with his father and run off to join the Union Army. Bryony was right about that. That feud had lasted years, too many years. By the time he'd found the courage to try to patch things up, his father was dead; his mother, too. Then he'd turned the anger on himself. He'd refused to return to the Triple Star, unable to overcome his own stubbornness and pride, unable to forgive *himself.* It was Bryony who had helped him come to terms with himself and his past, Bryony who had taught him to begin again. She had forgiven him for killing her father. She had loved him, comforted him, helped him realize that by accepting his birthright, the Triple Star, and returning to the ranch his father had wanted him to own, he was establishing a link with the past, forging a bond of forgiveness with his parents despite their death. Bryony knew how to forgive. It had come naturally with her love. But he? Did he know how to forgive? Did he?

He tried to hold on to the anger, to the bitterness and hate. They were all he had been feeling lately, all he had allowed himself to feel. But he felt them slipping from him, slipping away. *I'll always love Jim Logan. The only problem is that I don't know where he's gone . . . where he's gone . . . where he's gone . . .* He stopped pacing and suddenly saw her delicate face glistening with tears, heard her voice calling him Texas. Something deep inside him started to hurt.

As if from a distance came Ruby Lee's high, faintly Southern drawl.

"I heard every word, Texas. I was listening outside the door."

Slowly, he focused on her thin, painted face staring so curiously at him.

"I just don't understand, honey," Ruby remarked. "Why'd you tell that little bitch-wife of yours that we've been bedding down together? You know damn well we never have—not once. Not," she went on, grinning and snaking her arms around his neck, "that I haven't wanted to. But you've never let me show you how good I am at pleasing a man." She gave her thick, silver-blond hair a toss, slanting a seductive glance up at him. "I am good, Texas, I truly am. I'd make you forget all about that green-eyed girl. Want me to show you how?"

Jim disengaged her arms from his neck and walked away from her. He pushed aside the frilly curtains at the window and gazed out into the night.

He couldn't make out one damned thing out there. The blackness was as thick as mud. But he could hear plenty. The wind screamed and whistled, shaking the window, filling his eardrums. He heard a crash as shutters from one of the shops on Main Street blew loose and smashed into the boardwalk below. He thought of Bryony out there fighting the wind, crouched on her stallion's back with the gale battering at her slender frame, and sudden apprehension sliced through him. He wheeled about and paced the room again.

Why should I care? he asked himself angrily. *Why the hell should I give a damn?* He had done everything in his power to hurt her these past weeks, especially tonight. He had tried above all else to show her that he didn't love her anymore, didn't want her or care about her. And finally, tonight, he had succeeded. He had convinced her. Only... He shut his eyes, trying to blot out the memory of her anguished face when he had humiliated her in his room back at the ranch. He tried to shut out the way she had looked tonight in this room when she had called him Texas and told him that Jim Logan was gone. He tried to blot out the fact that he loved her still...

What have I done? What the hell have I done?

A voice inside him screamed questions, and his brain tried to answer them. But it was his heart that told him the truth, destroying the hateful illusions he had tried so hard to maintain all these weeks since the miscarriage. He loved her still. Damn it, he loved her still!

What have I done?

He groped for the bitterness, for the fury that had kept him going, but it had slipped away from him and he couldn't retrieve it. Love pounded at him, flailing him from every side as his mind replayed a hundred images of Bryony, and it seemed that her fragile beauty and joyous soul filled his being until he could no longer bear it.

He pulled his hat low over his eyes and swung toward the door. As he shrugged his broad shoulders into his buckskin jacket, Ruby Lee clung to him, pleading.

"Honey, don't go! It's plum awful out there! Stay with me till the mornin'. Honey? Honey!"

But Jim was already gone, pounding down the stairs and through the saloon, out into the wild, shrieking night. It wasn't until he had begun to untether Pecos that he realized he still held Bryony's pearl-handled derringer in his hand. He stared at it, suddenly struck once more by that strange stab of premonitory fear. An instant later, after pocketing the gun, he vaulted into the saddle and sent Pecos thundering toward home.

It had begun to rain by the time he reached the Triple Star, an icy, sleeting downpour driven harder by the wind. Soaked and nearly frozen, he led Pecos into the stable, both of them shivering and numb to the bone. Wiping the rain from his eyes, Jim glanced toward Shadow's stall, expecting to see the giant black stallion housed there, but the stall was empty.

He stared and swiped at his eyes again, disbelieving. The stallion wasn't there. Throat constricted, he ran up and down the aisles, scanning every stall. There was no sign of the horse.

"Bryony!" Panic tore through him. The next moment he was sprinting for the house, assaulted by wind and sleet. He burst through the front doors and bolted up the stairs two at a time. "Bryony!" he yelled again, his voice raw.

She wasn't in the master bedroom or in the room he'd been using these past weeks. Danny heard him tearing through the house and appeared, rubbing his eyes. Irritation was plain on the younger Logan's face as he caught up with his brother in the darkened parlor.

"What the hell...?"

"Have you seen Bryony?" Jim shook him, getting chill water all over his brother's bare arms and shoulders. "Answer me, quick!"

"Bryony? No. Not since she turned in early and

said she'd take supper in her room. I reckon she's asleep right now, or at least she *was* until you started this ruckus..."

"Get dressed. Round up the men. We've got to start a search."

Danny gaped at him. "What the hell are you talking about?"

"Bryony's gone!" Jim slammed his fist into the mantelpiece, shattering a glass figurine. "We had a fight. She followed me to town, and I sent her home. Now I come back, and Shadow's not in his stall and she's not here and that means..." He broke off. The two brothers stared at each other in dawning anguish.

"She's out there—in *this?*" Danny gasped.

"She's either hurt or lost or..." Jim's voice cracked. His face was gray as dust. "Get going!" he ordered, wheeling toward the door. "I want every man in this ranch out searching for her. No one sleeps until she's found!"

He disappeared into the roaring darkness, and Danny, gripped by horrible fear, bolted up the stairs in search of his clothes.

Three hours later, there was still no sign of her. Jim sat atop Pecos on a low ridge, trying to see past the driving rain, peering frantically into the raging, wind-tossed night. The norther had broken full force, engulfing the prairie in violent upheaval as the wind screamed and tore at the cacti, hurling rocks and branches and saplings every which way. Jim's feet were numb, his hands in their leather gloves felt frozen, and his face was blistered raw. He saw other riders approaching, heads and shoulders bent. He dug his heels into Pecos's flanks, pushing the exhausted animal farther.

"Any sign?" he shouted, but Dusty Slade and Pike Owens both shook their heads.

"Boss?" Dusty leaned forward, ducking his face

from a sudden freezing gust. "This just ain't no use! We can't see a thing!"

"It's too damn dark—and wet!" Pike put in, huddling deep within his plaid wool coat and scarf. "I think we oughta wait till tomorrow when the rain lets up and this damned wind—"

"No one quits until my wife is found!" Jim grabbed Pike by the neck and nearly pulled him from his saddle. "You savvy, you lazy, whipped-dog coward! You keep searching until you find her, or I'll kill you! All of you! Now move!"

The men rode off, stiff and frozen in their saddles, and Jim turned Pecos with desperate savagery. He scanned the ice-crusted prairie, filled with more terror than he'd known in a lifetime.

Four hours later he could barely stay upright. It was nearly sunup, but there had been no slackening in the rain or the gale. Weary and sick, Jim rode doggedly on, drenched and frozen, his eyelashes fringed with ice. He had ridden the trail from Fort Worth to the Triple Star nearly half a dozen times, he had staggered down from his horse to search on foot, he had shouted and called until his throat ached. The thought that Bryony might be just around the bend, or lying beyond the next rock, or beside that battered tree kept him going, for in his mind's eye was the terrible picture of her lying hurt and helpless nearby. He couldn't quit. Not till he found her. And, he kept telling himself savagely, desperately, he was going to find her.

At dawn, the rain had tapered to a drizzle and Jim acted on a hunch. He headed Pecos toward the clearing in the valley where he and Bryony had spent so many secret, glorious hours making love. Their rendezvous, she called it, the special place they both loved so well. Through the faint gray light of morning, he espied the two barren oak trees, now slicked with ice, and his heart began to hammer. Maybe . . . maybe through some kind of miracle, some crazy chance, he would find her here in this place. Maybe . . . maybe . . .

He dismounted and stumbled forward, his head turning stiffly from side to side, scanning the country-side. All was bleak, wet, frozen. There wasn't a living creature in sight.

Jim groaned in despair and sank down between the two trees. He buried his face in his arms as the wind whistled all about him, buffeting his beaten frame. Where was she? Where could she possibly be? He felt as though his insides had been ripped out, torn asunder. Every muscle in his body ached. He could barely move, yet he knew he had to go on. He couldn't give up. He had to find her.

He lurched to his feet, one hand braced against an oak tree. He closed his eyes and saw Bryony's face, flooded with tears, as she had looked last night in Ruby's room. "I'll always love Jim Logan," she had whispered, and the words knifed through his heart. "The only problem is, I don't know where he's gone."

"Bryony!" he roared in agony, his arms thrown wide. "Where have *you* gone? Where? Where?"

But his words were captured by the wind and flung far away, and there was no voice to answer him.

CHAPTER NINE

THERE WAS great excitement as the Cheyenne war party hurtled into their camp in the midst of the ferocious norther enveloping the plains. Joy at the successful return of the braves with so many stolen horses was accompanied by relief that the warriors had survived the storm, and also, as several Cheyenne braved the freezing blasts of the wind and the driving wetness of the sleet to greet their returning brothers, there was curiosity and an undercurrent of tension regarding the captive brought in by the warrior band. Swift-as-an-Elk dragged the near-frozen woman down from his pony and pushed her toward his tipi, pleased by the accolade his accomplishment drew from the men who greeted him. It did not surprise him that a good part of their admiration centered on the horse the woman had been riding when overtaken, for few of the Cheyenne, acknowledged for their horse mastery as they were, had ever seen a stallion as sleek and magnificent as the steed that had belonged to the prisoner. This was a prize indeed. And the woman? Well, that would be for Swift-as-an-Elk to decide. Since he was the one who had caught her and borne her back to camp upon his pony, she was his to enslave or kill as he wished. Once he had an opportunity to see her, to judge, he would determine her fate.

Bryony cried out as the Indian lifted the flap of his tipi and shoved her inside. She went sprawling upon the barren earth, only inches from the circle of a banked campfire, her cheek scraped by a stone. Her sodden cloak tangled beneath her as she fell, encumbering her further. Yet as swiftly as she could, she rolled sideways, lifting her head to peer up at the tall, war-painted brave who stood over her.

The Cheyenne was a terrifying figure in his buffalo robe and feathered headdress, his coppery face streaked with bright red paint. Through dark, intense eyes he studied the white woman who lay upon the floor of his tipi, watching her with a sternness that did nothing to allay the obvious terror in the captive's face.

Bryony crawled to her knees, dragging her cloak around her in a feeble attempt to find warmth. She flinched apprehensively as the warrior suddenly hunkered down beside her; then she saw that he was kindling a fire. She caught her breath on a sob, watching in dread silence as he set previously gathered bark ablaze within the circle of his campfire. As hot tongues of flame licked upward, she inched closer, trying to warm her shivering limbs. She kept a wary gaze upon the Indian, desperately trying to fight the panic that had assailed her from the first moment the war party had swooped down upon her on the trail. It had all happened so quickly. She had been stunned to suddenly find herself set upon by a galloping horde, snatched from her mount, carried off through the night by the shrieking, fiercely painted band of nearly a dozen Indians. Yet here she was. Drenched and half-frozen, exhausted nearly to a stupor, she found herself alone in the tipi with this tall, silent brave, who watched her every movement as though waiting for an excuse to kill her. Bryony tried to be calm, tried to think. Through the pounding of her heart, she wondered if he would kill her, rape her, or torture her. Terror struck deep and hard. She stared at him, searching for a glimpse of human kindness in that harsh, angular face so fiercely painted and adorned, yet all she could see was dislike.

Suddenly, the Indian reached out an arm and yanked her close, nearly into his lap. Bryony tried to wrench away, but he held her, one hand twisting brutally in her hair.

"No! Please!" she cried breathlessly, the panic bubbling anew inside her, but she ceased struggling, sensing that to continue would intensify the danger. She saw that the Indian was studying her face in the light of the fire, his gaze keen and hard upon her. She waited, fear pounding through her in painful, crashing blows that shook every nerve in her body. Golden light touched her skin, illuminated the delicate line of her profile, the tilt of her chin, and the wide-set, brilliant eyes that stared so apprehensively at her captor.

A long, painful moment passed. Bryony was aware of the leather and tobacco smell of the tipi, of the odor of burning wood, of the Indian's pent-up anger and tension as he intently raked every plane and angle of her face. Something flickered in his dark eyes, something Bryony did not comprehend, and then, suddenly, he clambered to his feet, hauling her with him. He muttered something and stared down at her again, turning her chin this way and that. He lifted a strand of her wet, streaming hair and crushed it between his fingers. Then his lips compressed into a tight line. Without further hesitation, he pushed her out of the tipi, into the raging whirlwind of the storm, and Bryony staggered backward from the force of the wind. He grabbed her again, strong arms keeping her upright despite the buffeting of the wind, and he began dragging her toward the center of the camp, past rows and rows of tipis, until they reached the largest tipi of all, a structure made up of perhaps twenty buffalo hides sewn together and stretched upon intricately twined poles. The Indian spoke, shouting words she could not understand into the roaring night, and then she heard a faint reply from within the giant tipi. The flap was lifted, and she found herself once again pushed inside, sheltered from the icy, merciless wind.

This tipi was far roomier than the other and was heavily decorated with quills and beaded designs. There were weapons neatly stacked along one of the walls; above them hung a huge circular rawhide shield with feathers and geometric markings painted upon it. There were several large buffalo pouches, a magnificent beaded and feathered headdress, and piles of animal skins and robes, all adorned with quillwork and beads and feathers. Bryony had only a quick glance about the dwelling, but her impression was that this was the abode of a powerful man, probably a chief. Then she felt herself thrust roughly forward toward the center of the tipi, where a fire blazed. Sitting on the far side of it, facing east, was an Indian of indeterminate age whose weathered visage bespoke many seasons in the sun, yet whose piercing black eyes were as keen as any knife blade. She stared at his proud, strong-boned face, swiftly noting the deep-set eyes and prominent nose, the thin, harsh lips set firmly above a granite chin. He was seated cross-legged upon a bearskin rug before the fire, a buffalo robe wrapped about his stooped shoulders and his two thick braids bound with rawhide thongs. The brave who had brought her stood aside, arms folded, and spoke rapidly in his native tongue. Bryony waited, her hair streaming into her face, her bones frozen nearly to numbness.

What was happening? Why had she been brought

here to this lodge? Were they going to kill her now, or on the morrow, with the entire tribe watching? She was too exhausted to fight, even to think. Cold, horrible dread soaked her as thoroughly as had the sleet, and she knew of no way in which to save herself from whatever savagery was planned. She closed her eyes a moment, and Jim's image filled her mind. How she longed for him in this crisis! Only to be with him now in their own bed, safe, his arms around her. How had she come to this? How had they lost the security and happiness they'd once shared and thought would last forever? A silent sob shook her. Then came a new sound, wrenching her from her reverie.

"White woman. Come closer."

The Indian chief was speaking, and to her amazement, the words were in English. Bryony's eyes flew open. She stared at his coppery, imposing countenance, and slowly, warily obeyed.

The chief rose as she approached him, and reached out a gnarled hand. He turned her head from side to side, studying her as intently as the other Indian had done. She heard him mutter in his own language, but whether his words were mild or angry she could not tell. But when she met his eyes, she saw deep emotion betrayed in them, and what could only be a tear hovered on his brown cheek.

"Who . . . are . . . you?" he asked in a tone approaching awe, and Bryony swallowed hard before replying.

"I am Bryony Logan." She struggled to keep her voice steady and calm, remembering that Jim had told her often that the Indians valued courage in adversity as they also valued truth. If she was to plead and sob, they would despise her and probably show no mercy, but if she could maintain a brave facade and impress them with her dignity, perhaps there was a chance she would be treated with some measure of sympathy. "I

... I can see that you are a great chief. May I ... may I know your name, as you know mine?"

"I am called Two Bears, by the *Tsistsistas*, my people." He stared hard at the girl before him. "The white man calls us Cheyenne." His scrutiny was unsettling to her, for she had the feeling that he could see deep within her soul. Yet Bryony forced herself to meet his penetrating eyes. She sensed that her fate hinged upon this man and his judgment, so despite her fatigue and coldness, despite the fear pulsating through her blood, she stood straight before him and kept her gaze fixed upon his dark, unfathomable face. "Tell me, Bri-on-nee Logan, how it is that the war party of Swift-as-an-Elk came upon you this night?"

"I was ... returning from the town of Fort Worth to the home of my husband when the ... war party of your men came upon me and ... brought me to this camp." Bryony hugged her arms around herself to keep from trembling as the cold and wet continued to penetrate her icy flesh. "I ... I made no fight against your people, Chief Two Bears. I am no enemy to the Cheyenne or to anyone under the sun." She didn't add that even if she had had time to defend herself, which she hadn't, she would have been unable to do so since Jim had confiscated her gun in town. She could only hope that this imperial chief of the Cheyenne would decide that she was innocent of any offense against his people and show her mercy. Otherwise ... A tremor passed through her. She didn't want to think of the alternative.

He turned away from her abruptly and spoke in his own language to the other Indian. The brave replied swiftly, and Two Bears nodded. Silence fell in the firelit tipi. Then, with a rustling of his heavy buffalo robe, the chief swung back to address her. "Swift-as-an-Elk has done well to bring you to me. Now you return with him to his tipi. I will think upon your coming."

He lifted his hand in dismissal and turned away, but Bryony, spurred by an impulse, reached out to touch his arm. Swift-as-an-Elk jumped forward and seized her in a savage grip, snarling something in her ear, and Two Bears crossed his arms upon his chest, frowning.

Bryony cried out uncontrollably at the Indian's brutal grasp, but she did not try to break free. One of Swift-as-an-Elk's sinewy arms was clamped across her neck, pinning her back to his chest, and the other ensnared her arm in a viciously painful hold, rendering her helpless. "I . . . I am sorry . . . Two Bears . . . if I commited an offense," she stuttered, gritting her teeth against the pain and trying desperately to regain lost ground. "Forgive my . . . rudeness. I . . . I did not wish to offend you. But . . . please, I only wished to ask you a question."

There was a pause, during which Two Bears studied her in silence. Then he signaled to Swift-as-an-Elk, who released her as suddenly as he had attacked. "What is your question?" the chief asked, still regarding her with a disapproving frown.

"I wish to know . . . what you are going to do . . . what is to become of me . . ." Bryony rubbed her arm where the Cheyenne brave had gripped her. "I—"

"Silence!" Two Bears barked at her in a gravelly voice. His frown deepened. "If you are going to stay with the People, you must learn patience and respect, white woman! Do not speak again unless you are so instructed. Otherwise, your fate will not be happy. Now go."

Swift-as-an-Elk gripped her arm, and she found herself dragged outside once more. By the time they reached the brave's tipi, Bryony was shaking violently. Swift-as-an-Elk flung her to the ground and bent over her with a rawhide rope he took from a pocket of the tipi. As he began to bind her wrists behind her back,

Bryony cried out in protest and attempted to shrink away, but he seized her ruthlessly.

"No! Please, don't do this...don't..."

"Silence, white woman!"

She was so astonished to hear him speak English that she ceased struggling and stared up at him in amazement. The Indian sent her a scathing glance. "So you thought I could not speak your language? Did you think I learned nothing while living on the white man's reservation? I learned much—much that is useless and stupid and hateful. I do not like the ways of the white man, and I do not like to speak his language." Bryony waited for him to continue, her heart hammering. She tried to move her wrists, but the rope chafed her flesh. Swift-as-an-Elk raised her to a sitting position, then turned away and began to remove his feathered war bonnet and buffalo robe, revealing a supple, sinewy physique encased in deerskin shirt, leggings, and breechclout. Watching him, Bryony couldn't help being aware of something magnetically masculine about him. He was a strong and powerful warrior, a man of few words and quick actions. Her own feminine vulnerability seemed suddenly heightened, and apprehension quivered anew within her heart. Yet, after that one unexpected outburst, he seemed to have forgotten her presence.

"Please...Swift-as-an-Elk." Though afraid to draw attention to herself, she nevertheless could not refrain from speaking out against the taut ropes that so painfully bound her. "Do not leave me tied this way! I cannot escape. The storm is too wild, and the night too cold. There is nowhere to go."

He leveled a narrow-eyed look at her. "It is not your escape I fear. I do not wish to have my own tomahawk split my skull while I sleep," he returned. Bryony shook her head.

"I wouldn't..."

"The word of a white man—or woman—is worth less than all the dust of the prairie," he interrupted, and the glance of hatred he shot her quelled any further attempts at persuasion. He turned his attention to removing his rawhide-soled moccasins, and Bryony's heart sank. Shoulders hunched and teeth chattering, she watched him lift a buffalo robe from a pile near the rear of the tipi. To her surprise, he brought it to her and, unclasping her sodden cloak and tossing it aside, wrapped the heavy animal fur around her shaking form. She was grateful for the warmth that suddenly shrouded her, more enveloping than any comfort she had yet received from the small fire. She burrowed her chin deep into the thickness of the buffalo skin and closed her eyes in relief.

"Thank you, Swift-as-an-Elk."

He merely grunted in response, then moved with agile grace to his bedding. Stretching out upon a blanket, he pulled another buffalo robe over himself. He shut his eyes.

Bryony huddled in exhausted silence, her mind crashing with questions and fears, yet weariness dragged at every bone in her body and weighted her eyelids so that she could barely see straight ahead of her. In the shadowy glow of the firelight, the tipi with all of its alien trappings, weapons, and utensils filled her with fear, and the Indian sleeping so near to her did nothing to allay her terror. Her head sank down upon her knees, and tears slipped down her cheeks. She must have made some sound, a small, choked sob, for Swift-as-an-Elk's eyes opened abruptly, and he lifted himself on one elbow to stare at her. "Go to sleep, white woman. Tomorrow will be time enough to face what is before you."

His words chilled her. "What... what will happen tomorrow?" Bryony whispered, watching his lean, coppery countenance through frightened eyes. To her dismay, the Indian merely shrugged and rested his head down once more.

"That is now for Two Bears to decide," he replied and closed his eyes again.

Bryony stared at his sleeping form. Dread rolled through her. Gruesome imaginings filled her brain, and she bit her lip hard to keep from screaming aloud. She remembered the chief's creased, wind-weathered face and jutting jaw, and saw once more those black, deepset eyes filled with emotion she could not comprehend. Was it hatred or compassion she had read in their piercing depths? The tear upon his cheek—what had caused it? She could only guess blindly at any of it. Soon her exhaustion overcame even anxiety and she sagged sideways, lying upon her side, curled into a ball, her knees drawn up for warmth. The robe only half covered her slender form, yet with her bound hands, she was helpless to straighten it. She lay in a half sleep, riddled with fears and questions. Yet one image kept reappearing in her mind. *Jim.* Every time she closed her eyes she saw his rugged, darkly handsome features, felt the burning of his cobalt eyes upon her, almost smelled the clean, manly, leather-and-pine scent of him. Did he know yet that she was gone? Had he even returned to the ranch, or was he still in the Tin Hat, wrapped in Ruby Lee's arms? *Jim, find me! Save me from this nightmare, and whatever ordeal faces me tomorrow!* she pleaded in silent torment, but a part of her wondered if he would even pause when he found her gone, if he would even care . . . She fell into an aching slumber.

Swift-as-an-Elk waited until her breathing was even and steady. Then he rose from his bed and crept forward, a dark, shadowy figure in the windswept night. He leaned over the sleeping woman, watching her face. The firelight flickered gently over her delicate features. Swift-as-an-Elk noted the extreme whiteness of her skin compared to her midnight-black hair and the dark-fringed lashes that swept her cheeks. She was a thing of beauty. Her limbs were lithe and gracefully formed, her breasts full and generous beneath her white woman's garments. He compressed his lips together, fighting the primitive urges within him. As he had told the captive, it was now for Two Bears to decide. He drew the buffalo skin fully across her sleeping form and saw her snuggle into the warmth of the heavy covering, burrowing like a trapped animal into the only source of comfort she could find. Swift-as-an-Elk watched her a moment longer and then returned to his own bed. With firm resolve, he pushed all thoughts of this disturbingly beautiful captive from his mind.

CHAPTER TEN

MORNING CAME all too quickly for Bryony, and she found herself hustled out of the tipi by Swift-as-an-Elk shortly after dawn. The worst of the norther had passed, and though the gray sky still drizzled rain and wind moaned across the wet, frozen prairie, the temperature had risen again, and she found that the buffalo robe still wrapped about her shoulders protected her from what remained of the December chill. Swift-as-an-Elk had slashed her bonds and now drew her along by the arm, ignoring her weary stumbling across the melting patches of ice on the hard ground below.

"Where are you taking me?" Bryony asked breathlessly, shrinking into her robe as the sharp glances of Indians they passed grazed her. But the Cheyenne brave made no answer, and she was forced to speculate in silent trepidation as they walked swiftly through the Indian camp.

The camp consisted of perhaps thirty tipis clustered in rows within a large circle. Smoke streamed from the openings in the lodge poles, and the smell of cooking meat and woodsmoke drifted in the air. Bryony saw ponies grazing forlornly, their heads bowed, and some

127

children, bundled in heavy robes, played near tanning racks covered with buffalo hides. As she gazed around at the awakening camp, Bryony thought of her own ranchhouse back on the Triple Star. By now, Rosita would be cooking breakfast in the kitchen: scrambled eggs with tomatoes and green peppers, buttery biscuits dripping with jam, steak, and hot, steaming coffee. The coffee's tantalizing aroma would fill the parlor and the hall, drifting through the cozy, hearth-warmed ranchhouse where only yesterday Bryony had been safe. The coziness of her own home, the luxury and warmth of her bedroom, with its plump pillows and huge brass bed, the wardrobe, consisting of rows and rows of elegant silks and wools and linens all waiting to catch her eye and her fancy, struck her forcibly now as she was dragged, in her damp and crumpled clothes, through the gray, frightening starkness of the Indian camp. Tears stung her eyes. She wished, how she wished, that she could go back to yesterday, that she could be safe once more, that she could be *home.* The Triple Star, and Jim, seemed a thousand miles away. This encampment was a different world, a harsh and barbaric setting where she was at the mercy of hostile strangers, as alien to them as they would be at a Fort Worth social. She shivered as Swift-as-an-Elk guided her through the camp, but her trembling was not due to the cold.

At last they reached a tipi beautifully decorated with porcupine quills arranged in intricate geometric designs. It was here that they paused, and Swift-as-an-Elk called out for permission to enter.

The flap of the tipi was lifted by an old, wizened woman whose hair hung in thin braids to her shoulders. Her skin was wrinkled and the color of burnt coffee, and her eyes were narrow slits of darkness between puffy brown pouches. She stared intently at Bryony as

Swift-as-an-Elk addressed her in the language of the Cheyenne.

The old woman nodded when the brave had finished, and gestured to Bryony to enter the tipi. Swift-as-an-Elk turned to her. "This is my *na'go'*, my mother. She is called Antelope Woman. Go with her now, and she will make you ready."

"Ready for what?"

"For your meeting with Two Bears," he replied and gave her a push. "Go! I will wait here to be certain you do my *na'go'* no harm."

She started to protest indignantly that harming an old woman was the last thing she would do, but stopped short when she saw that he had already turned his back to her and was staring out over the camp, observing the morning activities of his people. Bryony glanced at Antelope Woman. Again, the ancient Indian beckoned her to enter, and this time, she obeyed.

A short time later she emerged from the tipi in a transformed state. Antelope Woman had fed her soup and chokecherry cakes, helped her to wash in a wooden bowl of icy water, and dressed her in a deerskin dress that reached well below her knees, accompanied by leggings and beaded moccasins with thick rawhide soles. Bryony's rippling mass of hair had been smoothed with a porcupine-quill brush and tightly wound into twin braids, which fell nearly to her waist, and tied with dyed strips of rawhide. Swift-as-an Elk's buffalo robe draped her slender shoulders. Though she had no mirror to see her reflection, Bryony realized that she probably looked as close to an Indian as was possible with her white skin and green eyes.

Swift-as-an-Elk gazed intently at her when she reappeared outside the tipi, then he nodded and smiled to his mother. Antelope Woman, who spoke no English, but who had treated Bryony with silent kindness all the while, spoke softly and then, still smiling, stroked Bryony's arm. The girl gave her a grateful smile and pressed the old woman's hand.

"Thank you, Antelope Woman, *na'go'* of Swift-as-an-Elk," she said. Then she glanced upward at the tall, dark-visaged brave. "Please thank your mother for her kindness to me. I do not know the proper words."

He translated for her, and the old woman smiled and nodded again. Swift-as-an-Elk took Bryony's arm.

"Come now. Two Bears is waiting."

With a quick, backward glance at the ancient woman, who watched her depart, Bryony found herself borne along once again toward the large tipi in the center of the camp. As they neared it, her apprehension increased. Despite the kindness of Antelope Woman, she was still an enemy in the camp of the Cheyenne. Though Swift-as-an-Elk had not harmed her thus far, she knew that if his chief ordered it, he would kill her in an instant. Her heart thudded with the speed of rifle fire as she and her captor entered the tipi of Two Bears. She saw the chief seated once more upon the bearskin rug before the fire. On his right sat a wiry, sharp-faced Indian with feathers stuck in his braids and a wolfskin enwrapping his narrow shoulders. This Indian's shrewd gaze raked her as she stood before him, and she felt cold pinpricks of fear up and down her spine. With an effort she tore her eyes from his hawklike face and looked instead at Two Bears.

"Sit beside me, white woman," the chief ordered with a motion of his gnarled hand. "And you, Swift-as-an-Elk, join us as we smoke the pipe and seek guidance from *Heammawihio*, the Wise One Above."

Bryony remained silent as they passed among each other a long-stemmed wooden pipe, each man smoking briefly before handing it to the next. Anxious as she was, she jumped when Two Bears broke the silence and turned to her with an expectant air.

"So, little Rider-in-the-Storm. What have you to say on this morning? I can see that you are a woman of many thoughts. Tell me what it is you are thinking."

Bryony moistened her lips. She glanced from Swift-as-an-Elk's stern countenance to the harsh, narrow face of the Indian beside the chief and, finally, rested her gaze upon the proud, majestic form of Two Bears. His deep-set eyes bored into hers, yet there was no malice or dislike in his gaze, only a piercing intensity, a keen effort to study her strength and character. Here was her judge. Here was the man who would rule upon her fate at the hands of this Indian band. Here was the one she must impress with her courage, her truthfulness, her inner strength.

"Two Bears, this morning I am thinking many things," Bryony said. Her green eyes never wavered from his stare. "I am thinking that I am grateful for the kindness Swift-as-an-Elk and his *na'go'*, Antelope Woman, have shown me. I am grateful, too, that you are treating me with such courtesy. I am also wondering, as you would wonder if you were in my place, a captive among strangers, what will be my fate—and what I might do to insure that it is a happy one." Bryony paused, uncertain whether to continue. She hoped the chief's command of English was sufficient to enable him to understand what she said, but she could not guess how many of her words he actually comprehended, nor how much of her speech he must grasp intuitively. The third Indian, the one whose name she did not know, had made a growling sound at her words, and she prayed she had not said anything offensive. Her palms were slippery with sweat as she sat before Two Bears' camp-fire. She glanced quickly at Swift-as-an-Elk for help, but he returned her look without expression. With fear knot-

ting and reknotting inside her, she turned back to Two
Bears. His dark, unfathomable eyes were still riveted
upon her face.

"I . . . I am sure you know that I would like to return
to my husband . . . to my home." She couldn't help the
little catch in her voice, though she struggled against
any further sign of weakness. She tried not to think of
Jim, knowing that if she did, she would begin to weep
with the desperate yearning within her. "If I had your
permission, Two Bears, I could go immediately. I could
leave your camp and go back to my husband and my
home and never trouble you again. I . . . I beg you with
all the respect due a great chief and a wise leader, please,
let me go!" Bryony felt all her self-control slipping away
as the emotions cascading inside her started to pour out.
In horror, she realized what was happening and pressed
her icy hands to her cheeks, fighting once more to retain
the calm facade she needed to confront her captors.
"May I," she began, drawing a deep, ragged breath,
"may I know what *you* are thinking this morning, Two
Bears?"

Something that might have been approval flickered
momentarily in the chief's eyes. He nodded slowly. "You
are a brave and strong woman, Rider-in-the-Storm. I am
thinking that I would like to see you join our band,
instead of seeing you staked out upon the prairie when
we leave this place today."

Bryony couldn't help the tremor that passed through
her at his words. She felt herself paling. Staked out! She
had heard of this method of dealing with prisoners and
enemies. The Indians would leave a person bound with
rawhide ropes that dried and shrunk to greater tightness
in the sun. The prisoner was left, staked upon the earth,
to die of starvation, thirst, and the elements, unless a
wild animal came upon him first. Every muscle in her
body quivered at this prospect, and she had to swallow

hard to force back the nausea rising in her throat. Two Bears handed the wooden pipe to the Indian beside him and spoke again.

"This is my wish, Many Eagle Feathers. This white woman will join our band and become one of the *Tsistsistas*. As the chief medicine man of the *oktouna*, do you know of any reason why she should not stay among us?"

"The *maiyunahu'ta* has offered me no vision of this white woman," the sharp-featured Indian replied with a certain reluctance. "Yet," he added quickly, "she has only just come upon us." His jaw tightened as he fixed his small, hawklike eyes upon the pale, rigidly silent girl sitting near him. "But I will tell you what is in my heart, Two Bears. My heart wishes to see her die! Even though you have had her clothed in the garments of our people today, it is plain to see that she is not one of us. She is a white woman! And though she looks much like Singing Deer, your daughter, whose *tasoom* has traveled in death to *Heammawihio*, we must remember that she is not Singing Deer. She has white woman's flesh and eyes like the river! She is the daughter of those who killed your daughter! Kill her, and ease your grief! Avenge the death of Singing Deer and She-Who-Knows-Truth and Little Star and all those others who were murdered by our enemies! This is the path I advise you to follow! Kill her, and know the honor of revenge!"

"No!" Bryony cried out despite herself, and all eyes turned to her. She could no longer contain her panic. "Two Bears, you are a wise and reasonable man," she implored, her hands clasped in a supplicant's pose. "My death would do nothing to bring back the life of Singing Deer or anyone else! *I* have done nothing to you or any of your people—"

"Silence!" the old chief ordered, frowning as he had the previous night when she had made her impetuous outburst. "You know nothing of our ways, white woman, and you have no voice in matters of the *oktouna*. Do not speak again! Swift-as-an-Elk, you have heard my wish and the opinion of Many Eagle Feathers. Tell me now, what do you think should be the fate of your captive, this woman that you found in the storm and brought as prisoner to our camp?"

Swift-as-an-Elk folded his arms across his powerful chest and spoke directly to the chief, glancing neither at Bryony nor the medicine man. "I know that your decision will be the wisest one among us all, Two Bears," he said. "But since you wish to know the feeling in *my* heart, I will tell you that I believe we should keep this white woman, this Rider-in-the-Storm, and teach her to be one of the People. We will claim her from the white man's world and show her the ways of the *Tsistsistas*. Let that be an answer for the death of Singing Deer, a revenge better suited to our purpose. As the white man on the reservation has tried to teach us his ways, many of them evil and hateful to us, let us teach this white woman the rightness of the path we follow, that she may learn of the strength and wisdom of our people. That is my answer to you."

Silence followed, a silence in which Bryony felt her heart would burst with the thunder of its beating. She hardly dared move or breathe as she waited for the verdict of Two Bears. When the chief began to speak, she closed her eyes, praying that she would hear words of mercy.

"The captive white woman, known from this time on as Rider-in-the-Storm, will stay among us and learn our ways, and we will make her into one of our own, a daughter of the *Tsistsistas*, a member of our *oktouna* warrior band, and someday, a wife to one of our braves. She shall live in the tipi of Antelope Woman, and the *na'go'* of Swift-as-an-Elk and the other women of our camp will teach her all that she must know. And when a man wishes to take Rider-in-the-Storm for his bride, he will come to me with his offerings, and I will judge his worthiness."

Many Eagle Feathers leaned forward at this pronouncement, and it seemed to Bryony that his cruel eyes stabbed at her in the dimness of the tipi. But Two Bears merely drew upon his wooden pipe and ignored the medicine man's displeasure. "I have spoken," he said in a tone of finality. "And so it will be."

Bryony's breath came out in a rush of relief, but even as she gave thanks for this favorable judgment, her heart ached with pain beyond words. It was true, her life had been spared, but her destiny was not what she desired. Her only wish was to be reunited with Jim, to live with him again in joy and love. Now she despaired of ever seeing him again. Though she was to become one of the tribe, she was still a prisoner of the camp. Would she ever see Jim again? Or Danny or the Triple Star? Would her husband, who had proven his indifference to her, even care if she never returned? She tried to hide the tears that blurred her eyes as Swift-as-an-Elk raised her to her feet.

"I will take you once again to the tipi of my *na'go'*," he said. "There is much to be done, and you have much to learn."

She read no hint of triumph or pleasure in his handsome, coppery face, no sign that he was glad of Two Bears' decision. Bryony turned back as the warrior led her to the flap of the tipi.

"Th . . . thank you, Two Bears," she said quietly, her gaze meeting the chief's. If Two Bears noticed the torment in those huge, vivid eyes, he gave no indication of it; instead, he nodded and lifted a hand in parting.

"We will speak again, Rider-in-the-Storm. When the time is right, there is much I will say to you."

She was then taken from the tipi, with little chance to ponder these words. Her heart was heavy and filled with despair as Swift-as-an-Elk drew her forward once more into the gray drizzle of the morning.

CHAPTER ELEVEN

A LONE figure moved across the prairie as the pale January sun dipped lower in the sky. Slender and graceful despite the heavy buffalo robe she wore over her buckskin garments, the woman peered this way and that about the ground as she made her way slowly east, her arms burdened by a hefty pile of twigs and bark. Once she paused and then moved quickly across the frozen earth, stooping to add a new twig to her bundle. Then, with a glance at the setting sun, she rose once more and set off with small, gliding steps toward the tipis clustered beyond a small rise.

Bryony had been with the Cheyenne band nearly three weeks now. She was accustomed to the routine of the Indian camp and was quickly learning to do all that Antelope Woman and the others taught her. Since the camp was on the move, headed toward the Staked Plains, the *Llano Estacado*, there were many tasks to occupy her hands and mind. Each day she and Antelope Woman would dismantle their tipi and load it, along with all the accompanying poles, furnishings, and utensils, onto a travois, which was drawn behind their poies as they followed the band farther west, up into the

vast, barren desert that was the high plains. When the
destination for the evening's camp was reached, the
women of each household were responsible for erecting
their tipis once more, unpacking the belongings, gathering wood for their fires, and cooking the meals for
their husbands and children. Bryony soon learned that
while the sons-in-law provided the food, the married
daughters brought the meat to their mothers' tipis for
cooking and then carried it back to their own lodge to
eat. Antelope Woman, though, had no other living
children besides Swift-as-an-Elk, so he was their only
guest at each and every meal. He treated Bryony to
stern silence most of the time and conversed in his
own language with his mother. Bryony, though of
necessity picking up bits and pieces of the Cheyenne
tongue, could not generally follow their rapid exchanges
and, more often than not, consumed her meals in silence, with downcast eyes hiding thoughts that were
far, far away.

Every waking thought not concerned with a task
at hand was centered on Jim. She missed him with an
almost physical despair, wanting to be near him so badly
she ached. Though the Indians had accepted her in their
midst, she still felt a foreigner, an enemy, and uneasiness pricked her often at odd moments when she walked
alone past a little group of braves or a knot of women
with their heads together. Antelope Woman had intro-
duced her to many of the older women of the band, and
several of the young, and though they willingly showed
her how to use her stone maul to drive tipi pegs into
the hard ground or break up her firewood, and how to
thicken soup with sun-dried, pulverized Indian turnips
or prickly pear fruit, she sensed a certain resentment
among them, an aloofness, and this added to her iso-
lation. Now, as she walked back to the camp with her
pile of firewood, she smiled tentatively at a woman called

Gray Dove, who was also returning with arms laden, but the large-boned, sullen-faced woman merely gave a grunt of acknowledgment before disappearing into her own tipi.

"Rider-in-the-Storm." She turned at the sound of her Indian name and saw Two Bears approaching her, attired in rich, highly decorated buckskin garments as befitted a chief, his two braids bobbing upon his shoulders as a wolfskin cloak shrouded his tall, thin form. "Bring your firewood to Antelope Woman and then come to my tipi. I have words to speak with you, and this is a fitting time."

"Yes, Two Bears." Bryony stared after him, watching as the chief moved with long strides through the camp. She hadn't spoken with him since the morning when he had decided to spare her life and keep her with the tribe. She wondered now, with more than a little trepidation, what he wanted to speak to her about. She was assailed by a sudden fear that he might have changed his mind and decided that she did not belong among his people, but she pushed aside this thought as she entered her own tipi, reassuring herself that Two Bears did not seem the kind of man to doubt his own decisions, nor to change them upon a whim, and that certainly he could not have heard any complaints about her from Antelope Woman or even Swift-as-an-Elk. Antelope Woman, grateful to have someone to share the burden of her chores, praised her hard work, and Swift-as-an-Elk had found no cause to rebuke her. But still . . . a nagging worry clouded her eyes as she informed the old Cheyenne woman of her meeting with the chief, and when she left the tipi to head for Two Bears' lodging, apprehension slowed her footsteps.

When she entered the tall, stoop-shouldered chief's tipi, Bryony noticed, as she had on her first night in the camp, that it was much larger and even more richly decorated than the others she had seen. Graceful, beaded designs were worked upon the many buffalo skins which made up the lodging, and intricate quillwork adorned all of the animal skins and robes piled in the corner. Her attention was drawn by the huge rawhide shield set in a place of honor among a stack of weapons, and she could visualize the chief in battle, his shield raised up high as he shouted his war cry. Then, her gaze fell upon the magnificent beaded headdress with its cascade of painted feathers. Yes, attired in this, with his shield and other ceremonial articles of war, Two Bears would truly be an imposing figure.

At his command, she seated herself opposite him. There was no campfire burning in the center of the tipi today. The lodging was dark and quiet. Sitting before the chief, watching his stoic face, Bryony felt some of her nervousness ebb. She had learned a little about Two Bears and this band of perhaps seventy or eighty Cheyenne in the weeks of her captivity, and it seemed to her that he was a wise and good-hearted man, one whom she could trust to adhere to his word. He was a member of the council of forty-four peace chiefs who governed the entire Cheyenne nation, and as such had been elected to his position by virtue of his even temper and kindly, sensible disposition. As a Cheyenne peace chief, he was considered a father to every member of the tribe, and the welfare of each man and woman was a matter of his concern. The war policies of the *Tsistsistas* were determined by the chiefs of the various warrior societies, but a chief of the council of forty-four held the highest authority in the tribe and was respected by even the most honored warrior. Studying Two Bears as she waited for him to speak, Bryony realized that he was well-suited for this position of trust. There was strength in his face, but also kindliness and wisdom, and Bryony felt herself relaxing somewhat, dismissing her earlier worries. She unclenched her hands and clasped them loosely in her lap as Two Bears glanced at her and smiled.

"I hear many good things about you, Rider-in-the-Storm. You have done well since coming among us."

"Thank you, Two Bears." To her surprise, his praise brought a flush of pleasure to her cheeks. She hadn't realized how important his approval was to her until he had expressed it. "I am trying to learn the ways of the *Tsistsistas*. Antelope Woman is a good teacher."

He nodded. "She tells me of your hard work. That is good." His keen, black eyes studied her a moment before he went on. "When you first came here, Rider-in-the-Storm, Many Eagle Feathers and Swift-as-an-Elk talked with me about your coming and about my *na'ts*, Singing Deer. Do you remember?"

"Yes."

"Have you learned about the death of Singing Deer? Do you know what happened at the place the white man calls Stone Creek?"

Bryony knew. After persistent questioning, Swift-as-an-Elk had revealed to her a little of the tragic story. Ten years ago, a peaceful Cheyenne camp only thirty miles from Fort Wyeth had been massacred by white soldiers. Despite the fact that an American flag flew over the chief's tipi as a symbol of loyalty to the U.S., despite the fact that Two Bears was at the time considering signing a treaty with the government and had camped at the spot with permission and approval from the authorities, men, women, and children had been brutally mutilated and slain without reason or provocation. Two Bears had seen his daughter, a girl of only sixteen summers, killed before his eyes, along with his wife and countless others. Somehow, he had managed to escape, one of only a few who survived the massacre. Swift-as-an-Elk and perhaps a dozen other braves had been on a hunting expedition at the time and returned later to find the horrible carnage left by the white man. From Swift-as-an-Elk's fierce expression when he finally related the story, Bryony had realized that it was something none of the Indians would ever forget. She herself had been unable to keep from gasping aloud at the inhumanity of the soldiers, especially when she heard that Swift-as-an-Elk's pregnant young wife had been one of those butchered. Her own recent pregnancy and the loss of the baby caused her to place her hands involuntarily over her own stomach when she heard of Little Star's slaughter. Thinking of all this now, she raised her eyes to Two Bears and nodded solemnly.

"Yes, I know about Stone Creek. It was a terrible thing that the white soldiers did."

"There have been many killings such as this. Black Kettle, my brother, escaped a massacre much like this at the place called Sand Creek, when Colonel Chivington's soldiers attacked a peaceful camp. The next time, when General Custer sent his men against an innocent village on the Washita River, Black Kettle did not escape. At least one hundred of my people died with him then." Two Bears lifted his hand in a gesture of sadness.

"The white man has no mercy upon us, Rider-in-the-Storm. He kills our buffalo, steals our land, and kills our women and children. Then he tries to put us upon the reservations, to make us live like white men and give up the old ways." He shook his head slowly. "We, this band of which you are now a part, have lived on the reservation. We fought to avenge the deaths at Stone Creek, but in the end, the council of forty-four saw only more death for our people, and we agreed to go to the reservation, in the land the white man calls Indian Territory. But we could not stay there." His black eyes shone in his sun-browned face like fiery coals. He raised his fist and shook it. "I learned many things in that place. I learned to speak in the white man's tongue so that I might talk to him of our troubles and our needs. But he did not listen." He leaned forward, powerful and intent as he spoke to the girl before him. "I learned, Rider-in-the-Storm, that our people can never be happy in houses of wood and logs. I learned that, besides giving up our land, our homes, and our ways of life, the white man wanted us to give up our braids, to cut our hair so that we might look more like him. I learned that we were not meant to live upon the reservation, that we will never again do as the white man tells us to do. We will never go back! Swift-as-an-Elk is warrior chief of the *oktouna*, and I am one of the forty-four tribal chiefs. We decided to leave that place with as many of our people as wanted to follow, and to live upon the land of our people in our own way and to never return to the reservation." He leaned back and took a deep breath suddenly, his eyes narrowing upon her. "Do you wonder, Rider-in-the-Storm, why I tell you all this today?"

Bryony nodded, touched by his story. The cruelty of her own race had never seemed so heightened as it did now, seen from the perspective of this Cheyenne leader. "Why, Two Bears?" she asked softly.

"Because you are one of us now, and you should know what is in our hearts. You should know why we make war against the white man, and why we will die before we give in to him again. We are only a small band of a great and once-powerful tribe, but we are true to our ways. You must learn to be true to them, too."

Bryony stared at him a moment, then glanced down at her clasped hands. She fought to contain the tears that pricked her eyelids, but they escaped and trailed slowly down her cheeks. She heard the old Indian speak in a tone of quiet concern.

"What is it, Rider-in-the-Storm? Tell me now what troubles your heart."

"Surely you...must know," Bryony whispered,

lifting her head to gaze at him. A long, silent moment passed, during which the twigs in the fire popped and crackled, and then Two Bears gestured to her to move closer. As she edged nearer to him, he took her hand and held it between his gnarled brown ones.

"Yes, I know," he went on. "You want to return to your husband, your home. But it can never be."

"Why not?" she cried, tears slipping unheeded down her face as she stared at him. "You can understand how awful it is to be separated from someone you love, to be a stranger among those whose ways are different from yours! I am not Cheyenne! I am a white woman, and I want to go home!"

"No. I have spoken."

"It isn't fair!" She wrenched her hand away and used it to dash the tears from her eyes. "I did nothing! I was attacked by Swift-as-an-Elk and his war party simply because I was riding at the same time and place that he was..."

"Why were you out that night in the storm?" Two Bears asked suddenly, interrupting her diatribe. "Does the husband of a white woman permit her to ride about at night alone—in the middle of a storm as fierce as that one? It seems strange."

Bryony clamped her lips together. She tried to keep her tone even, but defensiveness crept in nevertheless. "That is not the point. Why I was riding does not matter. What matters—"

"Why, Rider-in-the-Storm?" Two Bears would not allow her to change the subject. His keen-eyed gaze was fixed steadily upon her, and Bryony felt her own will weakening beneath his insistence.

"All right, I will tell you," she cried. "My... my husband and I had argued in town. I was riding home. He stayed behind. That... that is all there is to say."

"You were not happy with this husband?" the chief inquired.

"No. Yes! I mean, I was very happy! I love my husband, Two Bears!" Her cheeks were flushed now, her eyes sparkling with tears. "I want to return to him more than anything in the world!"

"Does your husband want you back, Rider-in-the-Storm?"

"Yes." Bryony lowered her eyes, praying what she said was indeed the truth. She held her breath, wondering if Two Bears would relent and agree to let her go after all. When he responded after a lengthy pause, her heart began to race with a wild, surging hope.

"I do not wish you to be unhappy, Rider-in-the-Storm. This is not only because you remind me of my *na'ts*, Singing Deer. It is because I see much that is brave and good in you." He smiled and patted her shoulder with one weathered hand. "I will make a treaty with you. You will stay among my people until six full moons have come and gone in the great sky. When the days are long and full of sun, in the time you call summer, I will ask you again if you wish to stay or to go. If your heart is still full of this husband and this home from where you came, I will take you there myself with a party of our warriors. We will watch, though, and see what your husband has been about while you were gone. If he was true to you, and kept you as his wife in his heart, and wants you back with him again, you may go to him. If not"—he studied her carefully—"if not, you will return with us to our camp and become a true daughter of the *Tsistsistas*, never speaking again of this husband or this other home."

Bryony caught her breath, startled by this plan. She had hoped that Two Bears would release her outright, and her disappointment was sharp, but at least, she realized, he had not totally rejected her pleas. This proposal offered a chance, a hope for the future. But . . . six months! She swallowed hard, trying to ignore the painful ache in her chest. Slowly, she lifted her head and met the chief's black, piercing stare.

"Do you accept this treaty, Rider-in-the-Storm?" he asked in his solemn, gravelly voice. Bryony moistened her lips.

"Yes, Two Bears." She noticed that her hands were trembling and clutched them together in her lap. "I . . . I accept your treaty."

He nodded. "In the months to come, you must do your part. You must do all that our women do, all that I would expect of my own daughter. You must not speak of your husband or your home, or seek permission to leave. When the long days come and the time is near for the Renewal of the Sacred Arrows, I will ask of your decision, and then we will see."

"I know what my answer will be." Bryony looked at him with quiet conviction. "My heart will never be swayed."

"There is your husband to think of," the chief replied, getting slowly to his feet. Bryony, too, rose and faced him. "He may have taken another woman by then. He may no longer hold you in his heart as you hold him."

Bryony's pale cheeks seemed to grow more pinched. "No," she whispered, shaking her head. "No. He . . . he will be true. He will not forget me."

Two Bears' strong-boned, stern face softened as he regarded her. "We will see," he said again and, to her surprise, held out his hand. She clasped it and felt the warmth and strength of him seeming to flow through her. He smiled down at her.

"Go to your supper, Rider-in-the-Storm. Time will

answer all the questions in your heart. For now, be happy, little daughter."

A strange rush of feeling surged through her at his words, at the kindliness in his sun-browned face. She couldn't speak for the lump in her throat, but merely nodded quickly, then turned and ran from the tipi. Outside, she collided with a tall, hard-muscled figure.

"Swift-as-an-Elk!" she cried, recognizing his fierce, coppery face. "I . . . I am sorry."

He frowned down at her. "What is it, Rider-in-the-Storm? You act like a rabbit pursued by the fox." He took her arm and drew her along with him toward Antelope Woman's tipi. "Come to the cook-fire now and tell me why you were running away from the tipi of Two Bears."

As they walked and, later, as she and Antelope Woman served the deer-stew, turnips, and pemmican made from chokecherries mixed with dried, pounded buffalo meat, she told him of her conversation with the chief, explaining in excitement that she must wait six months before receiving permission to leave the camp. Swift-as-an-Elk listened, a scowl upon his handsome, angular face. When Bryony finished, her eyes shining in anticipation, he took a bite of the deer meat and chewed it in silence. His buffalo horn spoon then clattered into the wooden bowl.

"What makes you think that this husband of yours will wait six months for your return without taking another wife?" he asked, regarding her through narrowed eyes. "I think he will grow tired of waiting. You will find him with another, and then you will come back to our camp."

"No!" Bryony leaned forward. "That will not happen! You . . . you will see, Swift-as-an-Elk!"

"We will both see, Rider-in-the-Storm," he replied

in an even tone. Something in his voice made her stare at him, and she could not look away. His black, glinting eyes held her, speaking to her without words. She felt a flush steal across her cheeks. Antelope Woman, glancing from one to the other, got slowly to her feet and left the tipi. Bryony tore her gaze away at last.

"I... must clean away these things," she began, reaching for his empty bowl, but he caught her hand in his as she did so. His touch was warm and strong around her delicate fingers. Once more her gaze jumped to his face.

"Ah, Rider-in-the-Storm!" he breathed, then pulled her close to him. He stared down into the startled countenance of the beautiful ebony-haired girl before him, his eyes noting her rosy, half-parted lips, her creamy skin, the rapid rise and fall of her breasts beneath the deerskin blouse. "Sometimes I am sorry I brought you to Two Bears that first night," he said softly. "I should have taken you then as my own. It was my right. You would have been mine, and—"

"No!" She struggled to free herself of him, but his sinewy arms were like steel bands around her. "Swift-as-an-Elk, let me go!" She was frightened, and it showed in her tremulous voice, in the widening of her glowing green eyes. "I... I am not your captive any longer; I am one of the People now!"

"You are beautiful," he murmured, and before she could move, he had tilted her head up and lowered his mouth, and he was kissing her, a long, savouring kiss, a kiss oblivious of her vehement resistance. Filled with dismay, Bryony twisted and turned, trying to break loose, but the Cheyenne held her close. When he at last lifted his head, he saw that there were tears in her eyes and her cheeks were flushed with anger.

"Let me go!" she cried and, with a final push, she managed to free herself. She stumbled to her feet and ran to the opposite side of the tipi, her face buried in her hands. From his position by the fire, Swift-as-an-Elk could hear her sobs.

He rose with lithe grace and strode forward. His hands touched her shoulders. "Rider-in-the-Storm, do not cry."

"Leave me alone!" She whirled to face him. Her lovely face was wet with tears. "You . . . you do not understand! I have a husband—I love him! I want no other man!"

"Six months." He spoke softly. "That is a long time to be without a man."

"I will wait for him—forever, if necessary!" she flashed. She flinched as he grasped her arms and pulled her near once more.

"What . . . why do you look like that?" he demanded suddenly, noting the scared expression that darted into her eyes, the way her body tensed in resistance to him. "Do not fear, my Rider-in-the-Storm. I will not force myself upon you. It is not the way of the *Tsistsistas*." He wiped away one tear with his finger and smiled. "But I will wait for you. If you still choose to leave our camp when the summer moon has come, I will ride with Two Bears to find your husband, and I will see if he has been worthy of your love. If he has not"—and Swift-as-an-Elk's eyes lit with determination as he spoke these words—"then I will be your husband when you return to our camp. I, and no other! Remember!"

He touched her hair then, a light touch that sent a shiver up and down Bryony's spine. Then he turned quickly and left the tipi.

Bryony stood in shock for a moment, her mind whirling in confusion. Swift-as-an-Elk's kiss, and his unveiled feelings, had stunned her, for throughout the weeks of her captivity she had thought only of Jim and had not noticed that this strong and powerful warrior was attracted to her. Now she felt a strange sinking sensation in her stomach. She liked Swift-as-an-Elk, and she respected him. He was a handsome man, strong and bold and keen of mind, and there was kindness in him as well as strength, but he was not Jim. She knew, as she had always known, that there would never be another love in her heart like the love she had for the tall, steel-eyed gunfighter who had once touched her with such tenderness and passion, who had held her in his arms and kissed her in such a way that the world spun away and there was only the two of them, blazing, glowing, shimmering with their love. She would like to have the friendship of Swift-as-an-Elk; she would like to have his admiration and respect, but not his love. There was only one man in the world whose love she cherished and desired above everything else. But he was far away. And worse, he might no longer give a damn. She gave a ragged cry of despair, then broke off as Antelope Woman came into the tipi. The old woman came forward, slowly, wearily, until she stood looking up into Bryony's tormented face. Her weathered flesh crinkled into a smile.

"Do not weep, my child." She spoke in the Cheyenne tongue, but Bryony understood. "As the winds of time blow across the land, all creatures must find their path. You will be shown your path; it will be written in the sand and dust, and whispered in the breeze. You will know."

Bryony gulped. She swept away the rest of her tears with the back of her hand and leaned down to embrace the Indian woman. Two pairs of arms reached out and tightened. Bryony laid her head against the Cheyenne's shoulder. "I hope so, Antelope Woman. I hope it will be . . . the path I desire."

"It will be the path that you are meant to follow," the old woman whispered. And she closed her eyes, nodding silently to herself.

That night, as Bryony lay in the tipi, wrapped in her buffalo robes against the bitter chill of the winter night, she wrestled with the doubts that beset her. She told herself that deep down Jim still loved her, that he would be true to her, and that when she returned to him in six months, he would want her back. But the memory of their final parting was burned indelibly in her mind. Thinking of the way he had used her that horrid night and of the cold, callous expression upon his face brought tears to her eyes. Remembering the sight of Ruby Lee upon his lap in the Tin Hat and his words when he had admitted that he and the saloon girl had been lovers made her weep wretchedly upon the floor of the tipi. What if Jim married that vulgar girl in her absence? Or someone else? Or what if he merely dallied from one woman to the next? He wouldn't want her back. He had made it clear the night she had followed him to town that he didn't give a damn about her. How could she even think he would still claim her as his wife, still want her to return? It was hopeless.

Her tears fell rapidly as the painful memories besieged her. Yet, somewhere deep inside, an ember of hope still flickered, refusing to be quenched. Though despair engulfed her, a small, stubborn part struggled to stay alive, to believe and hope.

"We will see," she whispered into the darkness of the tipi as deepest night shrouded the prairie. "In six more months, we will see."

Sleep claimed her at last, but it brought her no peace. She found herself tumbling through an unending series of garish nightmares: images of Jim kissing Ruby Lee, fondling her, carrying her through the entrance doors of the Triple Star ranch house. She heard their laughter—horrible, evil laughter—and woke to the sound of her own sobs. After that, she did not try to sleep again.

CHAPTER TWELVE

"FRANK! FRANK! Open the door! Texas Jim Logan jest rode into town!"

Willie Joe Chester pounded his small, hairy fist against Ruby Lee's door. It seemed an eternity until it opened, and he hopped up and down on one foot, bursting with an impatience born of a longtime hatred. At last the door creaked open. The thin, wiry young cowboy with the dark moustache and unshaven jaw grinned wolfishly up at his older brother.

At thirty-five, Frank Chester was ten years older than Willie Joe and at least forty pounds heavier. Not that there was an ounce of fat on his six-foot, two-hundred-pound frame. He was all muscle, brawny and wide, with shoulders like small mountains and a hair-shrouded barrel chest. Right now, his chest was bare as he stood on the opposite side of the door, one beefy arm around the silver-haired saloon girl's waist, holding her tight against his side. His olive-brown eyes flicked over Willie Joe, scowling to match the downward line of his mouth.

"What's all this damned ruckus, Willie Joe?" he growled. "Me and this little honey were just gettin' to know one another."

"You'll have plenty of time for that!" the younger Chester spat. "Get your shirt on, Frank! Do you want to settle this score with Logan or not?"

Frank's face grew taut. "You know I do."

"Well, then, what are you waiting for? Damn, I'll wager anythin' Logan'll stop in downstairs for a drink. We can take him there—both of us together. C'mon, Frank, what do ya say?"

"I say come in outta the damned hallway and we'll talk while I get dressed." Frank released Ruby Lee, who was listening wide-eyed to the discussion, and grabbed Willie Joe's grimy collar. He yanked his brother into the room.

"What's all this about Texas Jim Logan?" Ruby Lee gasped as Frank began pulling on his plaid shirt and soiled boots and Willie Joe leered at her with his small, feral eyes. Although she was accustomed to being ogled and fondled by all manner of men, Ruby Lee found herself shuddering as she glanced at the dirty, unshaven Willie Joe. Something in the shine of his dark, close-set eyes made her walk to the wardrobe and shrug into a cherry-colored dressing gown; the sheer material did little to conceal her skimpy black negligee, but it somehow made her feel more comfortable under Willie Joe Chester's eager scrutiny. "Why are you-all out to get Texas?"

"You know him?" Frank rounded on the girl suddenly. She took a step backward.

"A little." Her pointed chin came up. "He used to come here sometimes. He was real friendly. A gentleman, too—not like *some.*" She eyed Willie Joe with contempt. "He ain't been around, though, since that little bitch-wife of his disappeared some months back. He still comes in to the saloon, but he don't say more'n two words to me or any of the other girls downstairs." She shook her thick, silver-blond hair, and it fell across her thin shoulders. Her voice had a high, plaintive note, which fell gratingly upon the men's ears. "It's a real shame, too, a real shame. A good-looking man like that just cries out for a woman's lovin', and—"

"I'll tell you what he cries out for, honey!" Willie Joe interrupted, grabbing her elbow and jerking her toward him. "He cries out for killin'! And that's what me and my brother are goin' to do today!"

"You two?" Ruby Lee pushed him away with a scornful laugh and put her hands on her hips. "It'll take more than a couple of low-down drifters to kill Texas Jim Logan! He's faster with a gun than any man you ever saw. Half of Fort Worth saw him kill three cowboys last week who shot up the feedstore and tried to rape a woman customer. I don't think you and your big brother will scare Texas much."

Willie Joe's small eyes began to glitter. He swung his arm and struck the saloon girl across the face, knocking her backwards onto the pink-canopied bed. "You shut your mouth, bitch!" he hissed. "Frank and I can handle Texas Jim Logan. Don't you worry!"

Ruby Lee put a hand to her jaw and staggered to her feet. "You low-down snake!" she cried and started to charge toward him, her long, pointed nails ready to claw, but Frank Chester grabbed her from behind and pulled her in close to his burly form.

"Now, hold on a minute, Ruby Lee," he growled, giving her a shake. "You'd better calm down, honey, or Willie Joe and I might really get mad. Then you'd have yourself a peck of trouble."

The girl caught her breath. Willie Joe was nothing but a filthy weasel, but this man was more like a bear: big, dangerous, and mean. Frank Chester's beefy face was clean-shaven, unlike his brother's, but there was a vicious line to his square jaw, a hard gleam in his eyes that warned her that he was capable of just about anything. Fear rounded her pale-blue eyes, and beneath her heavy rouge, her face blanched.

"I...I sure don't want no trouble," she stuttered in her high, shrill drawl. "I didn't mean nothin', mister. I just wanted to tell you that Texas Jim Logan ain't a man to take on lightly. That's all."

"Don't you worry about Texas Jim Logan." Frank stared down at her, his thick lips curled unpleasantly. "We know just what kind of a killer he is."

"Hey, did she say somethin' about Logan's wife disappearin'?" Willie Joe scratched his beard-stubbled face as he paced the confines of the small room. "Now that's real interestin'. I met that little filly, Frank. She was a beauty, a true beauty. Prettiest thing you ever saw, all dressed up in a yellow gown, with ribbons in that long black hair of hers." He glanced suddenly at Ruby Lee. "How'd she disappear, honey-bitch?"

"I don't know." The girl's voice was sullen, and she turned away with a swish of her silk dressing gown. "Nobody knows."

Willie Joe stopped his pacing and chortled suddenly. "I bet Logan feels real bad about losin' her. I would, if I was him. Too bad, eh, Frank?"

His brother didn't even glance at him. He was checking his gun and tightening his gun belt around his hips. "Yeah, Willie Joe, it's too bad. Now let's quit talkin' and get downstairs. I want to be ready for Logan when he shows up."

"If he shows up!" Ruby Lee interjected and then retreated behind her bed as both men glared at her. Her hands slid nervously to her throat as the Chesters sent her long, frowning looks, but they made no move to come toward her. Instead, they stalked to the door, slamming it behind them.

When she was alone once again, Ruby Lee breathed deeply and then darted to her dressing-table mirror to examine the bruise inflicted by Willie Joe. Silently, she damned all men, and herself for putting up with them.

Texas Jim Logan saw Willie Joe and Frank Chester as soon as he entered the Tin Hat saloon. Habitually, his keen gaze always raked any room he entered for sign of an enemy, noting and appraising each occupant with swift, sharp-eyed judgment. Today was no exception, and he spotted the brothers who were his longtime enemies immediately, but without any change of expression. His long legs strode forward to the bar, where Big Jake poured him a shot of whiskey. The massive, red-bearded bartender noted that Logan didn't turn his back for an instant on the dust-bitten pair in the corner, yet the gunfighter's demeanor was as cool and careless as ever.

"You know those cowboys, Texas?" Big Jake inquired as he pushed the glass toward Jim. "They're buffalo hunters, so they said. Just riding through."

"I know them." Jim raised his glass and drank slowly. "Watch your step around them, pardner. They're mean as they come."

"I'll remember that," Big Jake muttered, then moved on down the bar to serve some hands from the Double Q.

Jim lounged back on his stool, keeping an eye on the Chesters even as his thoughts drifted elsewhere. Seeing Willie Joe brought back searing memories. The last time Jim had seen that mangy horse thief, he'd been accosting Bryony at the Triple Star fiesta. That night still stood out vividly in Jim's brain: the black October sky ablaze with stars, the gaily-colored swinging lanterns, the dancing and merriment and feasting. And central to it all was Bryony, beautiful and fragile and resplendent in her pale-yellow gown, her creamy shoulders exposed, her black hair silken and lustrous in the moonlight. He would never forget the way her eyes had glowed when she had danced in the courtyard, dipping and swaying and lifting her arms to the sky. Or the way her lovely face had shone when she had told him that she was carrying their child.

Jim cursed as pain ripped through him like a knife thrust. He downed the rest of his whiskey and forced his thoughts to other things.

It was March now, and the spring roundup would be starting soon. He and Danny would be working night and day, getting the cattle ready for the drive to market. *Good*, he thought, taking another sip of his whiskey. *The harder I work, the less time I'll have to think. To remember.* His strong hand tightened around his glass as the ever-present pain within him swelled with even greater intensity.

Each day was a living hell to Jim Logan now. He missed Bryony with every muscle and fiber of his being, wanting her so badly his heart screamed out in agony. But it was a silent agony. On the surface he was the same: cool, controlled, dangerous; yet beneath, there were layers and layers of pain that had no means or hope of being assuaged.

For weeks after Bryony's disappearance, Jim had searched for her, refusing to give up. He had ridden to all the towns within fifty square miles of the Triple Star, questioning, demanding, combing the countryside. But there had never been a single sign of the beautiful young wife he had so cruelly sent riding into the windstorm that icy December night. What had happened to her? What in hell had befallen Bryony when she'd left the Tin Hat, riding astride the big black stallion? Not knowing her fate tortured him as much as missing her did. He kept telling himself that if she'd had an accident and fallen, he'd have found her. He'd searched every damn inch of the trail and environs, hadn't he? That left only two possibilities. She might have left on her own, convinced that their marriage was over. But to ride off into the night just like that? Without packing her clothes and possessions, without a farewell to anyone? She had the temper for it, he reminded himself grimly, over and over. In one of her rages Bryony was capable of all manner of wild, impulsive acts. But there had been no sign of her in any of the nearby towns. And ... Jim couldn't put his finger on it, but he had the feeling that Bryony hadn't left voluntarily. She hadn't been in a rage when she'd fled the Tin Hat. She'd been sad, hurt, despairing, but not in the grips of fury. That left only one answer, and it was the one that terrified him most. She'd been kidnapped. By Indians, or desperadoes, or whomever had happened to come across a lone woman riding in the storm, unarmed and helpless to defend herself.

The suspicion that she was in the hands of savage captors—hurt, possibly raped, possibly killed—filled him with indescribable agony. For the first month he had been unable to sleep or eat, always pacing and restless and close to exploding. He'd ridden out for days on end, searching and praying, hoping to come across something that would help him track her down, but Texas was a vast, sprawling state, and deep down he knew that his quest was hopeless. *Bryony!* he had screamed in silent, grief-stricken wails that reverberated through his soul. *Come back to me! Bryony!*

But she hadn't come back. And he had been forced to go on living, trudging through a life that was now devoid of all happiness and all laughter. The Triple Star seemed shrouded in a permanent mist of gloom that afflicted all of them: Jim, Danny, Rosita, even the ranch hands. The bright flower who had filled their lives with her beauty and vibrancy and joy was gone, and in her stead there remained only desolation.

"Hey, Logan." The crude voice of Willie Joe Chester intruded on his reverie, and Jim started, damning himself for having forgotten about the Chesters for even an instant. With snakes like that in town, he had to be on guard every minute.

Now he glanced coolly toward the small table where Frank and Willie Joe sat. Jim pulled his dark sombrero lower over his eyes and stood up. He threw money on the bar to cover his drink and strode nonchalantly over to the Chesters' table.

"You have something you want to say to me, Chester?" His cool blue eyes glinted beneath the rim of his sombrero. They impaled Willie Joe like icy blades.

"Yeah." The stubble-faced cowboy grinned up at him. "How's that purty wife of yours?"

Frank Chester gave a snort of laughter and raised the bottle of whiskey in his huge fist to his lips. He drank greedily, his eyes pinned to Jim Logan's face.

Jim stiffened at Willie Joe's words and the tension ran through his body like a whipcord, tightening each sinewy muscle of his powerful, six-foot-four-inch frame. His voice, when he spoke, was deceptively soft, almost silky.

"You thinking to die today, Chester?" Jim drawled. "I sure hope your brother here has the cash for a funeral."

Willie Joe spread his hands innocently. "Hell, Logan, I'm just bein' sociable. I remember that little filly of yours real well. Boy, what I wouldn't do to have myself a little woman sweet as that."

"Come on, now, Willie Joe," Frank put in, giving his brother a nudge. "You remember what we heard from that little girl upstairs? Logan's wife done disappeared. He hasn't seen hide nor hair of her in months. I reckon that's a real sore subject with him. I'll wager he thinks it's kinda rude of you to bring it up."

For just an instant, Jim met the older Chester's eyes. He read the malice there, the vicious pleasure he took in wounding, and it was all the gunfighter needed.

Before the other man had time to blink, Jim's fist shot through the air and connected sickeningly with the side of Frank's face. Chester crashed backward into the crimson-and-gold papered wall.

"Whooee!" Willie Joe let out an earsplitting shriek as he leaped across the table in a flying tackle aimed at Jim's shoulders, but the gunfighter deftly sidestepped, leaving Willie Joe to collapse upon the floor. By that time, Frank had heaved himself to his feet and closed in upon Jim with a ham-sized right fist. Though Jim blocked the punch, he had no time to dodge Willie Joe's clutching hands, which dragged him down to the floor. The filthy cowboy hit him as he went down in a crash. Frank's boot caught his ribs as he landed on his side, and Jim groaned as pain exploded inside him. He rolled sideways, however, and staggered to his feet before either of his opponents could prevent him. Half crouching, he faced them, his big fists doubled, and when Willie Joe darted forward, aiming a blow at Jim's hard, flat belly, the gunfighter stopped him cold with a smashing left, which sent the other man reeling sideways, right into a chair. Jim didn't wait for Frank to advance. He leaped forward and dealt the thickly built Chester brother a battering blow to the chin. Blood spurted from Frank's mouth, but he kept his feet and connected a solid jab at Jim's already sore ribs. Again, Willie Joe dove at the gunfighter, and this time, knocked off balance and still recovering from the assault on his ribs, Jim tumbled to the floor with Willie Joe atop him. He heard Big Jake bellowing for them to break it up, then felt the crunch of Willie Joe's fist against his eye. From the corner of his good eye, Jim saw Frank's boot lift, aiming for his jaw, but the kick never connected. Instead, Frank's foot disappeared, followed immediately by a tremendous crash and the splintering of glass, and Jim heard Danny's voice exclaim in breathless fury, "Let's even it up a little, boys! Then we'll see if you low-down snakes know how to fight!"

The next instant, Jim hurled the thin, wiry form of Willie Joe from atop him and sprang to his feet. He saw Frank Chester straightening up from a pile of broken glass on the bar and realized that Danny had thrown the other man halfway across the room.

"Thanks, pardner," he said with a grim smile as he swung toward the hulking Frank. "I don't know where you came from, but I'm glad you showed up. I'd be obliged if you'd keep that pesky rat, Willie Joe, occupied for a spell. I want the pleasure of dealing with this hombre all to myself."

"Sure, brother!" Danny grinned and stepped toward the half-stunned Willie Joe. "I reckon I can handle this cowboy without mussin' up my hair."

Jim faced Frank Chester with savage anticipation. All of his pent-up tension went into the struggle that followed. Each staggering blow he dealt was a strike not only against the man he fought, but also against his own helplessness to find Bryony. Filled with anger and frustration, his fists pounded his opponent like hammerheads as he gave vent to his roiling emotions. Though Frank Chester fought with the aggressive power of a wild bull, a vicious snarl curling his thick lips, Jim was a formidable match for him. Tall and broad-shouldered, with chest and arm muscles like sculpted iron, the gunfighter drove his punches home with ruthless power, wearing away at the endurance of his adversary until Frank sagged to the floor, unable to lift his head. Jim wiped his own bloody mouth with the sleeve of his shirt and, panting, glanced across the saloon to where Danny had knocked Willie Joe Chester cold and was standing triumphantly over the cowboy's prone form.

"Nice work, little brother." Jim was breathing hard, as was Danny. He grinned at the younger man. "Let's get these two outside. I think they've overstayed their welcome in this town."

"Good... idea." Leaning down, Danny slung Willie Joe's limp body over his shoulder. "I don't reckon they'll trouble folks here again—not for a long while."

After tossing a wad of money to Big Jake to cover the shambles they had made of the saloon, Jim dragged Frank Chester outside to his horse.

"Is this one yours?" he demanded as the groaning man stared blearily at a big roan. "And that mustang belongs to your no-good brother? Fine." He gave the staggering Frank a shove toward the horse while Danny deposited Willie Joe, still unconscious, sideways across the mustang's saddle. "Now ride. I don't want to see your ugly hides around here again. I told Willie Joe once that I'd send him to hell if he ever showed his face in these parts again. He should consider himself damned lucky this time that I didn't shoot him down like the rattlesnake he is. You, too, Chester." Jim's rugged features were harsh and cold in the March light as he surveyed the beaten man before him through glittering steel-blue eyes. "Next time, you won't get another chance."

Frank Chester shook his head as if trying to clear his brain. His face was bruised and gray, his lips swollen, and the knuckles of both big hands were caked with dried blood. "Next time, we'll kill you... Logan. Same as... you killed... Tommy. We never... forgot."

Jim's lips tightened. "Ride." He spoke in a hard tone that left no room for further conversation. Frank Chester stumbled and staggered, but finally managed to get into his saddle. Leaning low over the horse, grasping the reins of his brother's mustang in his fist, he spurred the roan forward, followed by the other horse bearing Willie Joe.

"You'll pay, Logan," he muttered as the horse gathered speed heading away from town. "You'll be sorry."

Jim heard these final words without comment. The Chester brothers were savage, stubborn fools. They'd never have the brains, courage, or strength to kill him, but they'd probably never stop trying. He shook his head and dismissed them from his mind. He clapped Danny on the shoulder and the two started walking toward their own horses.

Later, after they had cleaned up and changed their bloodstained, torn garments, the two brothers shared a quiet meal. Rosita had clucked and shaken her head as she tended to their cuts and bruises, but they merely grinned at her scoldings and ate in companionable silence.

Since Bryony's disappearance, all the strain between Jim and Danny had evaporated. They had needed each other in the time that had followed, they had needed each other's strength and support, and the deep-rooted love that had never really died between them. Danny missed the slender, beautiful girl almost as much as Jim did. The friendship that had grown between him and his brother's wife was deep and abiding, filled with admiration. When she had disappeared that night, Danny had been frantic. And in the days that followed, his heart mourned the loss while horrible fear about what had become of her possessed him.

Only one good thing had happened since the night Bryony disappeared. Jim had come to him the following day, consumed with anguish. He had confessed that he had wronged Bryony, treated her cruelly, and told Danny that he would beg her forgiveness if only he could find her again. Danny had enfolded his brother in a rib-crunching embrace and assured him that they would find her, but to his dismay, his words had proved false. There had never been a single sign of what had befallen Bryony Logan.

After dinner, Jim and Danny retired to the parlor to share a bottle of whiskey. A fire blazed cheerfully in the stone hearth as Jim leaned his massive shoulders against the mantel. Danny, watching him from the white-and-rose brocaded sofa their mother had cherished, recognized from his thoughtful, frowning countenance that he was thinking once again of Bryony.

"I miss her, too, Jim," he said quietly, glancing down at his hands. "Remember how she used to sit right there before the fire at night, her eyes all dreamy, and then she'd turn to us and smile in that way she had? I . . . I never met a woman as beautiful as her. Or as sweet."

Jim's features darkened with pain. "Don't . . . Danny," he said hoarsely.

"Why not?" Danny's blue gaze was direct, yet gentle. "You've got to face up to it, Jim. All of it—the memories, the feelings. It's the only way you'll ever be able to get on with your life."

"Get on with my life?" Jim repeated, running a hand through his thick chestnut hair. "What life? There's nothing left that's worth a damn. Not without Bryony."

Danny felt a catch in his throat, but forced himself to speak the words. "You've got to face the facts, Jim. She's gone. We'll never see her again. And . . . you've got to go on living."

"Shut up!" Jim wheeled angrily toward him. "Don't say another word." He paced rapidly to the cherry-wood liquor cabinet and refilled his glass from the half-empty bottle. He swallowed the contents in one long gulp. Then he turned back to his brother, his face filled with an unspeakable anguish. "I need her, Danny! I need

Bryony! There will never be another woman for me."

Danny stood up and moved toward him. His face reflected a deep sorrow, which stood out touchingly on his youthful features. "I...I don't mean to hurt you, Jim," he faltered, laying one hand on his brother's powerful arm. "But I think you've got to accept that she's gone. I don't mean you have to do it right this minute, or tomorrow. But...start thinking about it...start to get over her, start to forget. Damn it, Jim, it's been three months. If...if Bryony was still alive, if she could get back to us or wanted to get back to us, she would! Don't you see that?"

Jim shook off his arm. He faced Danny eye to eye, but there was no anger in him now, only quiet desperation. "I see it, Danny. I know. But...I can't give up. I love her too much to ever forget."

"I loved her, too." Danny had tears in his vivid blue eyes. "But Bryony's gone now. Much as it hurts, we've both got to accept that."

Jim stared at him wordlessly. His pain was too great to express, even to Danny, and after a moment, he turned on his heel and went into his study. He slouched into the carved chair behind his writing desk and lit one of his thin Mexican cigars, but he left it smoking in a clay bowl as his thoughts overtook him.

"It's my fault," he muttered bitterly in the darkness of the simple room. "If I hadn't treated her the way I did and then ridden off to the Tin Hat, Bryony would never have been out in that damned norther. She'd have been home, safe and warm and dry. She'd be here now. And I'd have had the chance to tell her what a jackass I've been, to beg her to forgive me." Self-hate surged through him. How could he have been so cruel to her all those weeks after the miscarriage? He must have been loco. Now he would give up everything he owned just to hold her in his arms once again, to hear her speak his name in that soft, loving way she had. Her bitter words during that last night in the Tin Hat, and the way she had called him Texas, were branded forever in his brain, but if he could only hear her whisper his name gently once more, feel the velvet of her lips against his, he would strive for the rest of his life to make her happy and to prove himself worthy of her love.

Memories of Bryony floated all about him as he sat alone in the darkened study. He almost imagined he could feel the satiny brush of her midnight hair against his jaw, and the lovely, small-boned face glowed before him with all the delicate beauty he remembered. A light waft of her perfume touched his nostrils, and his hands tightened on the carved arms of his chair. He longed for her, with his heart and with his soul. His loins cried out for the softness of her body, for the graceful curves and smooth silken skin he had once known so intimately. But most of all, he missed her smile: that soft, enchanting smile she gave him when he entered a room, or glanced at her across the dinner table, or when she held her arms out in their bed, inviting him to come to her. Her smile and her laughter, those were the things he loved best about Bryony. They were as much a part of her as her beauty, for they symbolized her great joy in life, her spirit and vitality. How could he go on without her? She had brought so much splendor and love and joy to his life. Now, all that remained seemed bleak and forlorn. *Bryony! Come back to me!*

But the night was still and empty. Bryony was not there to heed his words or to read the torment in his heart. And in the deepest hours of the night Jim fell asleep in the hard-backed chair with images of his vanished wife lurking all about him, haunting him, mocking him with the fact that she was gone. Gone, gone...

CHAPTER THIRTEEN

SPRING CAME gently to the high plains.

The Cheyenne band headed by Two Bears had spent the winter upon the *Llano Estacado*, camped on the vast, frozen land over which Indians had roamed for centuries. When the breezes of spring began to waft across the plains, carrying with them the scent of buffalo, the warriors of the *oktouna* readied themselves for the hunt, and under the sharp eye of Swift-as-an-Elk, they set out in large groups to find and kill the buffalo. When they returned with a good kill, there was much feasting and celebration. The women were constantly busy sun-drying and cooking and storing the meat. Using their fleshers and drawblades, they tanned the hides, then mixed a compound of liver, brains, soapweed, and grease to rub into the skins; after that the hides were soaked overnight and then softened by laborious use of a rawhide rope or buffalo shoulder blade. The result was a soft, tanned hide, suitable for constructing a tipi or for making into garments. The Cheyenne women loved to decorate the skins with quills and beads and feathers. It was not only a skill, but an art. Rider-in-the-Storm, under the tutelage of Antelope Woman, was fast becoming proficient at

169

not only the tanning of the buffalo hide, but the adornment as well. The girl who had once been silent and forlorn worked vigorously through the long winter and into the spring; when the days began to lengthen and the earth to ripen once more beneath the golden sun, her energy reached new heights. She blossomed, even as the desert flowers bloomed upon the plains, and her dainty, graceful steps became as light as the song of the morning birds.

"Do you always sing as you do your work, Rider-in-the-Storm?" Two Bears' voice broke into the soft humming of the girl before him one fine afternoon in May. They were far out upon the prairie, alone; in the distance they could see other women, scattered here and there upon the endless, rolling land, gathering their roots and seeds. Two Bears had approached her so silently that Bryony, intent upon her chore, had not even noticed. Now, she glanced up in surprise, a happy smile wreathing her sun-kissed face as she gazed at the proud, stoop-shouldered man who had grown so dear to her.

"Yes, Two Bears, when my heart is glad," she replied, and her eyes glowed like green flames in the sunshine. Using her dibble, a short digging stick with a knob at one end, she worked loose some roots from the earth, then put them into her pile.

"Why is your heart glad today, Rider-in-the-Storm?"

"Why should it not be?" The girl laughed, and her long, black braids swung as she got to her feet, brushing the earth from her fringed deerskin skirt. "The sun shines like a golden halo, the sky is bluer than the sea, and the winds are warm upon my cheek and much softer than a feather." She whirled happily, still clutching a handful of red turnips and thistle stalks. The weathered face of Two Bears crinkled into a smile as he surveyed her obvious happiness.

"I think there is another reason," he said when she

had turned to him once again, her cheeks flushed with her soft, rosy lips parted in laughter. "I think your heart is light because you feel that soon it will be time for you to return to your husband."

Bryony's head flew up, and she stared at him in sudden solemnity. "Yes," she breathed after a moment. "Yes, Two Bears, you are right. Each day and each night brings me closer to him. The long days of summer are nearly upon us. And then it will be time for me to go home."

The Cheyenne chief nodded, his eyes dark and sad. Bryony reached out quickly for his hand and clasped it in her own. "Oh, Two Bears, do not think that it will be easy for me to leave you. I . . . I have grown to love you. You have been a true father to me, in a way that my own father never was."

The chief smiled at her words and drew her near. He embraced her, his long arms wrapping themselves around Bryony's slender frame. With her head upon his shoulder, Bryony spoke in a voice that shook with emotion.

"I . . . I am so grateful to you for all you have done for me. You are so kind, so good and gentle. My heart grieves that I must leave you, for a part of me will always belong here with you. Yet, my place is with my husband."

"Is it duty that makes you wish to return, my *na'ts?*" Two Bears frowned at her, his hands resting upon her shoulders as she gazed up at his face. "Or do you truly wish to leave me and Swift-as-an-Elk, and all of us who think of you as one of the People?"

"It is not duty that sends me back to him," Bryony whispered, her green eyes wide and earnest in the sunlight. "It is love, Two Bears, only love. I must go to him or live forever in pain. I need him."

The chief's eyes closed for a moment. "So," he said

very quietly. "Then that is the way it must be."

"Two Bears, I wish there was a way we could all be together," Bryony burst out, leaning against him once more and resting her head upon his shoulder. "I love you, too, and Antelope Woman and..."

"Swift-as-an-Elk?" The chief had hoped that the handsome warrior would find the path to Rider-in-the-Storm's heart and, thereby, keep her with them. Now, he listened carefully to her reply.

"Yes. I love Swift-as-an-Elk. But as a friend or a brother. Not in the same way I love my husband. For me there will only be Jim, and no other man. That is the way it must be."

Two Bears smiled as she echoed his words. His heart was heavy, and yet, he had already guessed what her answer would be. "The decision is yours to make, Rider-in-the-Storm," he acknowledged. "But it is not yet time to go. Perhaps Swift-as-an-Elk will change your mind in the time that remains."

"No." Bryony smiled through her tears. "No, my *nihu'*, he will not change my mind."

As she spoke the Cheyenne word for *father*, Two Bears caught his breath. He stared down at her, his wise black eyes alight with joyous emotion.

"It is the first time you have called me by that name, little *na'ts*," he said in wonder, and Bryony nodded, her eyes bright with tears.

"It is what I feel in my heart," she responded, and lifting his hand, she raised it to her lips and kissed it. "Even when I am far away from you, I will carry my love for you in my heart. You will be my *nihu'* always, and I will be your *na'ts*."

They embraced then, and love flowed between them like a gentle river.

The days grew longer, and hotter, and the winds that had once fanned Bryony's face with feathery softness now whistled with blistering force across the parched land. The heat was fierce, drying out the grass that had been so abundant in the spring and enveloping the plains in a searing inferno from which there was no escape.

Overhead, the summer sun was a circle of flames, and its scorching heat laid waste to the fruits of spring, withering the wildflowers, drying out the roots and seeds, baking the land brown. Watering holes evaporated, and the water supply the Cheyenne so carefully hoarded in their *histaiwitsts* disappeared little by little with no opportunity for replenishment. The sky above burned so blue it was almost purple, and it seemed to glare down upon the wasted, windswept prairie.

Then, in July, a thunderstorm crashed across the prairie, sending lightning bolts shooting jagged flames across the dusky sky, and thunder boomed like cannon fire all through the night. Many Eagle Feathers sent thanks to *Heammawihio*, the Wise One Above, who had sent the great Thunderbird to save them, and there was great joy and relief among all the Cheyenne. Immediately afterward, preparations began for the Renewal of the Sacred Arrows; Bryony knew that the time had come for her to leave.

Two Bears sent for her one starlit evening, and they talked until the fire in his tipi had burned low. They agreed to start out upon the half-moon, so that Two Bears, who would accompany her upon the journey east, would have time to return to the band before the ceremony of the Sacred Arrows, the Cheyenne's most important ritual, was underway. A part of Bryony wished that she might be present for this most revered, four-day ceremony, which involved the treasured fox-skin bundle of four Sacred Arrows, and yet, the rest of her spirit soared at the prospect of finally returning to Jim. She began to dream of him every night, dreams of hap-

piness and love as he held his arms out to her in glad-
ness. She floated through her final days in the camp as
one upon a cloud, her heart filled with a strong and
heady excitement.

It was a relatively small band that set out upon the
half-moon. Two Bears rode his speckled mustang, and
Swift-as-an-Elk sat astride Shadow, the magnificent black
stallion that had once belonged to Bryony. She missed
the horse that had carried her so often and so swiftly,
yet she did not begrudge him to Swift-as-an-Elk, so
happy was she to be going home, and she sat her frisky
spotted pony with grace to equal any Cheyenne. Six
other warriors accompanied them upon the journey, all
of them dressed in full war regalia, complete with painted
faces, feathered bonnets, and shields. Swift-as-an-Elk
was by far the fiercest-looking of all the men as he sat
tall and proud in the saddle, his strong shoulders
squared. Despite his war paint and magnificent war
bonnet, and despite his harsh visage, he no longer
frightened Bryony. The look and ways of the Cheyenne
were no longer alien and terrifying to her. She herself
was part of them, one of the People, and she was quite
at home among them. Yet she was leaving these people
whom she had grown to love, leaving the way of life
that had given her a sense of serenity, a oneness with
the universe; she was leaving all because of one man—
one man who possessed her heart, her spirit, and her
blood, whose touch would ignite a thousand sparks
within her. Jim Logan. Her husband, for better or for
worse, now and forever. The only man she would ever
love.

They camped the second night near Palo Duro
Canyon on a flat stretch of land by the riverbed. When
Bryony had cleared away the supper things and all was
quiet upon the plains, the little group sat about the

campfire, the men smoking and the lone woman staring absorbedly into the flames.

"What is it, Rider-in-the-Storm?" Two Bears was watching her intently. "Why do you look so sad?"

"I was thinking of Antelope Woman, *nihu'*," she replied, her hands clasped before her. "It grieved me to part from her. I will miss her sorely."

Two Bears nodded, but did not speak the words that hovered on his tongue. Rider-in-the-Storm already knew that he would miss her. It would do no good to remind her of his sadness, for he knew that nothing on earth would change her mind. He would lose her before many days were out, and it was doubtful that they would ever see each other again. He glanced at Swift-as-an-Elk. The warrior, too, was staring at the dark-haired woman, his keen eyes sharp and piercing, as if he would drink in now her alluring beauty so that he would re-member it for all his days when she was gone. Two Bears knew that the tall, sinewy brave had loved no woman since Little Star. Now, when he would have given his heart, it was not wanted.

Two Bears sighed. Perhaps he had been wrong to make this bargain with Rider-in-the-Storm. If he had not, she would still be at the camp with the rest of the band. She would have accepted her fate and perhaps even allowed herself to feel love for Swift-as-an-Elk, the kind of love a woman feels for a man. She would have had no choice. But this way... All her feelings for this husband had been kept alive by the hope that she would return to him after the arranged time. She was full of determination. And it was too late now to break the treaty. That was the white man's way. Whatever the cost, Two Bears kept his word.

Bryony rose gracefully to her feet. "I will gather more wood for the fire," she said, gesturing toward the grove of willows and cottonwoods near the riverbank. Two Bears nodded his approval, guessing that in truth she wished to be alone with her thoughts, to think upon the past and the future without the eyes of others upon her. For a moment, their gazes met and silent understanding passed between them. A smile of infinite sweetness curved the tender line of Bryony's lips and as she passed him, she bent and kissed him quickly upon his coppery cheek. Then she was gone, her slim figure melting into the trees.

Swift-as-an-Elk scowled after her, his handsome features darkening. After several moments, impatience seemed to completely overtake him and he, too, came to his feet. His dark gaze locked with that of Two Bears. He needed no permission to leave the camp, yet he sensed Two Bears thought it useless to follow her. Useless, was it? He would see. At any rate, there was something he wanted to say to her. He was returning that black horse to her. He wanted her to have the beast— as a gift. She would be grateful, Swift-as-an-Elk knew. But grateful enough to stay with him, to accept him as her husband and the *Tsistsistas* as her people? He sighed to himself and strode determinedly toward the willows. He would see.

The other Indians hid their smiles, waiting until Swift-as-an-Elk had disappeared. Then they shook their heads, smiling among themselves at the suffering of their love-lost brother, while Two Bears shook his head and sighed.

Bryony leaned against a willow tree, watching the twilight steal across the sky. The river was low, a mere trickle, yet it made a pleasant, gurgling sound as she stood beside it, filling her with a sense of peace, a calmness that was a welcome relief from the turbulence of the past few days.

She was caught in the chasm between two worlds. Behind her lay the Cheyenne camp, which had been home to her for many months now. There were people there whom she cared for and loved. Antelope Woman had wept upon their parting and presented Bryony with a beautiful, blue blanket, delicately woven, that had been passed down to her from her own mother, and her mother's mother before her. Even Gray Dove, who had once barely spoken to her, and Many Eagle Feathers, who had initially wanted her killed, had bidden her kind farewells, with friendship and respect replacing their earlier hostility. Bryony had found a strange kind of happiness among the Cheyenne. Life at the camp was orderly and set. It was filled with the rhythm of nature, of the great land upon which the Indian wandered. Bryony, whose longing for freedom and adventure had first led her to abandon her staid life in St. Louis, had reveled in being close to the land, in finding sustenance from the roots of the earth. She had learned to appreciate the buffalo, not in the way the hated white buffalo hunters did, slaughtering the beasts en masse and trading the hides for huge profits, but as the Indian did, because it provided food, clothing, and shelter, and supported the entire Indian way of life. She had learned much from Two Bears and his people. And she had found quiet contentment among them. But now she was returning to the home she had left behind, and though it was what she had been longing for all these months, she felt an almost fearful excitement about what would happen when she returned.

Certainly they all believed she was dead. They would be stunned when they saw her, and then... Danny would be thrilled, she knew, and Rosita...dear Rosita, she would probably smile so widely her cheeks would ache. And Jim? Bryony clenched her fingers in tight fists. Would Jim be glad to see her, or would he stare at her with those cool, steel-blue eyes and tell her she could go right back where she had come from because he didn't give a damn? She shuddered inside, praying that this separation would have reawakened his love and given him time to put the bitterness behind him. Oh, if only she knew that he would welcome her with joy and sweep her into his arms! If only she could be sure of that!

Suddenly, she straightened her shoulders. She thought of her own overwhelming love for Jim, of the tenderness and passion smoldering inside her. And she knew that she would make him come to his senses somehow, even if he hadn't already. Despite all that had gone between them in the past, she would never give up. She would win back his love, she would woo him with every feminine wile at her disposal. *Jim Logan, watch out,* she thought with determination. Her chin lifted proudly. *I will take you by storm. I will conquer all your defenses. By the time I'm finished, you won't know what hit you.* And she laughed softly to herself, filled with a sudden exultation as she imagined what it would be like to lie with him again, to feel the power of his arms around her and the hard pressure of his body against hers. She ached to kiss his mouth, to see the light of love gleaming again in his vivid eyes. "Oh, Jim," she whispered, as warmth spiraled through her. "I love you so. I will bring back the love I know is in your heart, and find the gentle man beneath the anger. I will make you happy again, and you will be mine. Nothing will ever come between us again."

Lost in her thoughts, she leaned against the tree. Eagerness for the completion of the journey surged through her.

She had no warning of what happened next. There was no sound, no movement, no premonition of danger.

But suddenly a hand clamped roughly over her mouth and she was grabbed from behind. She felt herself held in a vicious grip that pinched her arms and bit into her cheeks. She gave a scream, which was muffled by the hand across her lips, and felt the powerful arms tighten cruelly. Then she was lifted clear off her feet and spun around by the man who held her.

"Whooee, Frank, just what I been wantin'!" A wiry, unshaven man leaned toward her, his grimy face lit with wicked delight. The unclean stench of him made Bryony nearly choke, but the unseen man who held her so ruthlessly did not lessen his grip. "I ain't had myself an Indian squaw in quite a whiles," the man before her gloated. His tone was hushed, for all its triumph, and he licked his lips as he surveyed the captured girl's heaving breasts and curved hips. "This is goin' to be a helluva party!"

Terrified, Bryony fought to free herself from the man who imprisoned her, his heavy hand still clamped tight across her mouth, but she could not break free. Whoever held her was too big, too strong. She kicked at him with her moccasined feet, but he only grunted and twisted her arm more painfully behind her.

"Looks like this one's a real fighter," he chuckled, but the slim man facing Bryony suddenly started as though someone had jolted him.

"What the..." He leaned closer, putting one hand upon the girl's slender jaw and turning her face up to his. "Frank, damnation, I can't believe it!" he gasped excitedly. "This here's no Indian squaw! This here is that black-haired wife of Texas Jim Logan!"

Bryony stared at him, recognition hitting her in the same instant. Willie Joe Chester! The man who had shown up the night of the party—Jim's enemy!

"Are you sure?" Her captor sounded incredulous.

"Damn straight I'm sure. Look at those green eyes.

Pretty as emeralds. No Injun squaw has eyes like that. Besides, I couldn't ever forget this little filly, not in a million years."

"So, Logan's wife has been with Injuns all this time. Whatta you know? Say, do you think the boys are 'bout ready over there? Maybe we should lend a hand."

Just then, Frank Chester spotted a tall Indian emerging through the trees. "Willie Joe, there, behind you! Get him!"

Willie Joe Chester spun around, his six-shooter drawn. He saw Swift-as-an-Elk step through the trees. The Indian took in the scene before him in an instant: Rider-in-the-Storm imprisoned in the stranger's burly arms, the second, dirt-bitten white man beside her. He sprang forward, his hand going for his knife. But he had no chance. Willie Joe Chester's gun spat fire, and Swift-as-an-Elk hurtled down into the dust, blood gushing from his chest.

Bryony stared in horror. She screamed and screamed, but the sound was trapped in her throat. With renewed fervor she struggled in the stranger's grasp, but the sound of gunfire at the campsite made her freeze in sudden terror. Willie Joe sprinted forward, his gun still smoking, and leaped over Swift-as-an-Elk's lifeless form. He disappeared through the willows.

"Wal, now, Miz Logan. It'll all be over soon." Frank Chester's deep, growling voice spoke in her ear. "All those Injuns'll be dead before you know it, and we can hear all about how you happen to be travelin' with them. Good thing we came along, ain't it? Willie Joe and the boys and me been buffalo huntin'. Spotted Injun tracks this morning and figured we'd kill ourselves a couple of red devils. Indian ponies bring a good price in California. That's where we're headed. And now, you get to come along."

Bryony's green eyes were huge with terror. She couldn't tear her gaze from Swift-as-an-Elk's bloodied corpse. But as gunfire continued to boom from the campsite, desperation gave her unaccustomed strength. She bit down viciously on Frank Chester's hand. He cried out and withdrew it, and in the next instant, she pushed at him with all her might. Suddenly, she was free and running across the clearing, her feet flying upon the grassy earth. She heard Frank's panting pursuit behind her, but never glanced back. All she could think of was Two Bears, and the frantic fear in her heart spurred her onward. She burst upon the campsite just as the last shot echoed across the air. The sight before her made her knees buckle and sent all the color draining from her face.

All the Indians lay dead, blood running in crimson streams from their bodies. They had never had a chance, for the ambush had been swift and brutal, the white men attacking from behind with their buffalo guns and six-shooters. She cried out in anguish as she beheld their massacred bodies, watching the stain of blood flow across the bright feathers and war shields, blotting out the bold designs of the wearers' buckskin garments.

"Two Bears!" Her voice cracked with grief as she darted forward toward the fallen form of the old chief. There were tears streaming down her cheeks, and her heart felt as though it was bursting with her anguish. But Willie Joe Chester stepped suddenly into her path and shoved her away from the chief, his filthy, moustached visage filled with contempt. Behind him, a half-dozen armed men moved forward, eyeing her curiously.

"So, you ain't just been captured by Injuns. You been livin' with 'em. Consortin' with 'em. You're no better than they are!" Willie Joe spat.

Quick as lightning, Bryony stooped to the prone

form of Big Wolf and yanked his knife from the sheath at his hip. The next instant she was on her feet, raising her arm for the plunge. Her eyes flashed emerald fire. "I'll kill you, you no-good, murdering *snake!*" she screamed. "I'll kill all of you!" She lunged toward Willie Joe, but he ducked aside and, lifting his booted foot, kicked her in the stomach. Bryony doubled over, all the breath knocked out of her. Through the breathless suffering of the next few seconds, she felt Frank Chester grab her once again, jerking her upright. With a crow of triumph, Willie Joe snatched the knife from her fingers.

"Wal, now, little Injun-lover, I reckon it's this old redskin you were so upset over," he drawled, stepping over Big Wolf to stand beside the body of Two Bears. The knife glinted in his hand. "I think I'm gonna scalp this red devil, so as you and me have a little memento of this occasion. Ain't that a good idea, boys?"

He grinned up at the seedy-looking men surrounding him. All of them wore eager, bloodthirsty expressions.

"No!" Again, Bryony felt her knees buckling beneath her. She stared from the knife in Willie Joe's hand to Two Bears, his stoop-shouldered form covered with blood. "Don't! Don't! Haven't you done enough! Don't touch him!" she pleaded.

But Willie Joe bent over the dead chief, the knife gripped firmly in his grimy hand. "Watch this, Injun-lover," he chortled and put the blade to Two Bears' scalp.

"*No!*" Bryony's scream reverberated through the campsite, echoing horribly in the gathering dusk. Nausea choked her, and her blood had turned to ice. She fought frantically to rid herself of Frank Chester's restraining hands, desperate to stop Willie Joe. The horrible events of the past minutes seemed like a nightmare, but they were true, savagely, gruesomely true. All of the Cheyenne braves were dead, including Swift-as-an-Elk, and . . . Two Bears. Her *nihu'*.

"Stop!" she screamed over and over. "Please stop!" She closed her eyes against the grisly sight as waves of faintness passed over her. But the darkness grew stronger, blotting out everything else, and she felt herself swaying in Frank Chester's arms.

"Two Bears! My . . . *nihu'*!" she gasped finally, then gave herself up to the blackness descending over her. She sought refuge in the enveloping darkness, hiding from the terror of the present by plunging into that velvet sea. Deeper and deeper she went, grateful for the smothering dark, grateful for the blessed peace of unconsciousness, until she reached the bottom of the sea and the blackness was all around her and she knew she would never, ever face the light again.

CHAPTER FOURTEEN

BRYONY AWOKE to a world of pain. First, there were the sounds—roaring, rushing all around her. Her ears were filled with it, and pain exploded inside her head. She felt as though she was bursting through a wall of water. Then she was free, breathing again, and her lungs sucked in air. But the pain didn't go away. Her head ached. Her eyes ached; light pricked them. Where had the darkness gone? Reluctantly, she forced her eyelids open. Daylight stung her. She cried out and shut her eyes again, rolling over. Her hands, weighted like rocks, managed to lift enough to cover her eyes. She became aware of hard ground beneath her. Her body felt stiff and sore. She tried to sink again, to sink into that lovely black nothingness, but it didn't happen. The aching, the pain, the noises, and the light continued to intrude. She heard voices.

"Maybe she's finally coming out of it." The first voice was low and gravelly. It was not far away. "It's about time. I'm getting tired of dragging her along without her doing anythin' to make it worth the trouble."

"You never did have any patience, Willie Joe." The second voice was deeper, stronger. "I reckon you'll change your tune when she comes around and starts flashing those pretty green eyes at you." The voice laughed. "I'm mighty anxious for her to wake up myself. This is goin' to be a real interestin' trip home."

What were they saying? What did it mean? She tried to think, but it hurt too much. She gave in to the pain then, moaning as it enveloped her again and blocked out everything else. Then she felt a hand upon her shoulder, turning her. She tried to shrink away, but her body didn't respond. She felt as stiff as hardened clay. She wanted to keep her eyes closed, shutting out everything, but against her will, they opened once again.

"Willie Joe, she's awake!" It was the second voice again, and it held a note of excitement. "Well, well, little honey. We've been waiting for you. Feeling better?"

The man who stared down at her was big and beefy, with deep-set brown eyes, a rugged nose, and thick, well-formed lips. His jaw was square and strong, his neck and chest enormous beneath his blue-and-yellow plaid shirt and blue bandana. He was grinning slightly, his eyes holding a gleam she didn't quite like or understand. Before she could protest or speak, he placed a big hand under her shoulders and lifted her to a sitting position. The world swam as dizziness washed over her in sickening waves. He grabbed her and held on tight as her slim body slumped against him.

"Whoa, darlin', hang on there," he chuckled. "I reckon you need to sit a spell and get your bearings. We don't want you passing out again, now do we?"

Suddenly, another face joined his above hers. This one was smaller, thinner, and dirtier. Unshaven stubble clung to a narrow chin, and small, dark eyes peered eagerly into hers.

"Howdy, little lady. I sure am glad to see you wakin' up. For a while there, we thought you were going to sleep forever."

She stared at them, feeling as though they were miles away. "Where ... where am I?" Her voice was small and weak. It took all her strength just to speak the words.

The two men grinned. "You're in our camp. 'Bout ten miles from them dead Injuns," the smaller one answered her.

She struggled to take in his statement. Injuns. Indians? Frightened, she stared about her. There was no one else around. Daybreak was just spilling through the clouds, bathing the world in weak yellow light. She saw that they were on a seemingly endless plain, dotted with short grass, wild flowers, and an occasional cactus. A campfire was blazing a few feet away, and there was the smell of coffee. In a daze, she glanced downward, becoming aware of the deerskin Indian garments she wore, of the loosened braids, which dangled nearly to her waist. She pulled her gaze back to the faces of the two men before her. She stared hard at them, trying to think, trying to clear the blankness from her head. Fear rippled through her.

"Am ... am I an Indian?"

They burst out laughing. "No, honey, you sure as hell ain't," the big man assured her. "You've got the prettiest green eyes I ever saw, and white skin beneath all that sun and grime. You're no more an Indian than I am!"

She moistened her lips with her tongue. Her mouth felt horribly dry. Using all her strength to keep the panic from overwhelming her, she forced herself to speak calmly. "Who ... are you?" she whispered.

Now the two men stared at each other. The big one turned back to her slowly. "Don't you remember? Here, look at Willie Joe. Remember him?"

She stared at the lean, filthy cowboy who leaned toward her. She shuddered in revulsion, but could not recall ever having seen his face before. "N...no. I...I don't remember..."

"How 'bout the Injuns? The Cheyenne. You remember them?" the big man questioned.

She shook her head. In her mind, she was searching, searching for images, memories, but her mind was like a huge, empty cavern, filled only with impenetrable blackness. Suddenly, terror gripped her, and she turned wide, brilliant green eyes upon the two men leaning over her. She clutched at the big one's hand, holding onto it as though clinging to life itself.

"Please," she gasped, trembling all over as the horrible fear mounted inside her. "Please help me! Tell me—who am I? I...I don't even know my name!"

Silence rocked the campsite after this announcement. All she could do was stare pleadingly at the two men, desperate for answers, as panic shook her every bone. She was trembling uncontrollably, her body quivering with icy terror. Her pounding heart sent a pulse-beat of alarm through her slender form, and she felt as though she would splinter into a million tiny fragments if she didn't hear the answer to her question.

"Why, you're—" The smaller one, Willie Joe, started to speak, but the second man, the one whose hand she held, jabbed an elbow into his ribs and took over.

"Don't you fret now, little darlin'," he said, and there was something changed in his tone. It was kinder now than it had been before. His face wore an almost benevolent smile, and he no longer appeared to be laughing at her. "We'll give you all the answers you want."

"Just...just tell me my name!" she cried, staring imploringly up at him.

He gazed down at her, taking in her long, black hair, which had come loose from the braids of the night before, her lovely, delicate face filled with terror, those beautiful eyes that sparkled like emeralds, and noting also the swell of her breasts beneath her soiled deerskin blouse. He sucked in his breath at the sheer beauty of this woman, despite her exhausted, bedraggled appearance. Excitement surged through him as he gave her the answer she sought from him.

"Your name, honey, is Katharine Chester," he said slowly, deliberately, watching her face with shrewd, gleaming eyes. "And I'm proud to tell you that you're my wife."

His wife! She stared at him while something inside her stomach turned over with a lurch. His wife! "Katharine Chester?" she repeated blankly.

He nodded. The smaller man, Willie Joe, chuckled suddenly. "Yeah. Yeah, that's right, little lady. You're his wife. This here is Frank Chester, and I'm his brother, Willie Joe. We're your family, girl."

She stared from one to the other of them, praying that some remnant of this would sound familiar, that something about them would trigger a memory in her brain. But she couldn't recall ever having seen either of them before. A sob rose in her throat, and before she could stop herself, she was weeping, with hot tears pouring down her dirt-streaked face.

"I...I don't remember anything!" she gasped. Horrible fear filled every part of her as the blankness enclosed her like prison walls. "I...don't know you... either one of you!" she cried.

Frank Chester smiled down at her. "It's all right, honey," he said softly. "You had a real bad experience, bein' captured by those Injuns and all. It's no wonder you can't remember anything. But don't worry. I'll explain everything. And me and Willie Joe will take good care of you. You're goin' to be just fine."

She sat upon the hard ground, weeping, unable to stop. Weariness and pain dragged at her body and made her head throb. But no memories came. She was aware that the men were rising, moving away, talking. But she couldn't stop crying long enough to hear what they said. She just sat there, cold with terror, her brain screaming for answers. But there was only emptiness, a dark, lonely emptiness that rose up all around her and invaded her and filled her with despair.

Why couldn't she remember? What was wrong with her? What should she do?

The tears kept flowing. Her cheeks and hair were damp. Her muscles ached from sobbing, and her eyes were swollen almost shut. She wanted to scream, to run. But that was insane. She couldn't escape from herself, or from the terrifying blackness that engulfed her mind. What was she going to do?

Remember! she willed herself with every ounce of strength that remained. *Remember, remember!*

But she could not remember. Her mind was a stone wall, smooth, blank, impenetrable. She could not remember a single thing.

Who am I? she wailed silently, as the sobs came harder. A tiny, insidious voice within her replied: *Katharine Chester. Your name is Katharine Chester.*

But the words stirred nothing inside, and her tears flowed faster.

Katharine Chester? she asked herself. *Katharine Chester?*

CHAPTER FIFTEEN

THEY RODE for six days before stopping at Cougar Junction to buy supplies and spend the night at the dirty little town's run-down hotel. Cougar Junction seemed as if it had been stuck haphazardly in the middle of the endless sun-scorched prairie.

At first, Bryony could only blink as her eyes took in the sad cluster of ramshackle buildings, the thin, droop-tailed dog prowling the single dusty street. Her eyes focused slowly as she shielded them from the sun with one raised hand. Yes, it was a town. A small, pitiful, grimy place, but still a town. It seemed forever since she had seen another human being besides Frank and Willie Joe Chester, and her eyes ached with the effort of staring at the old Mexican huddled on the hotel stoop in his faded serape and the dark-bearded drunkard who staggered out of the saloon. But her heartbeat quickened at the thought of a decent meal, and a real bed, and a solid roof over her head throughout the night. She followed Frank's lead in heading toward the hotel with a feeling closer to eager anticipation than anything she had experienced in days.

Bryony was only vaguely aware of the long, bone-grinding days she had spent in the saddle. Though her body throbbed with fatigue, her mind was in far worse shape. Dazed and frightened, she did as Frank instructed her, riding the pinto pony he set her on for hours on end, drinking from his canteen without even tasting the water, cooking jackrabbit and biscuits and coffee over the campfire at night with automatic movements. She slept beside him on the hard ground, with only a blanket between her and the prairie, grateful he didn't pay much attention to her. She was still in a state of shock over the loss of her memory and still trying to overcome the terror gripping her. Confusion whirled through her head, making her temples continually ache. She ate little and spoke hardly at all. For the most part, Frank and Willie Joe had ignored her, spending all their time riding, eating, and sleeping. She was glad. She didn't want anyone to talk to her. Exhausted and filled with fear, she wanted only to be left alone.

By the time they reached the hotel in Cougar Junction it was nearly seven o'clock. A two-story frame building with shuttered windows and clapboard roof, the hotel looked older than the hills, and was badly in need of paint, but Bryony was too tired to care. She followed Frank inside, ignoring the rat which scurried past her as she crossed the creaking porch. Though the sun had gone down, heat still permeated every inch of the dingy, plank-floored hotel. The small lobby contained only a desk for the elderly clerk, and a solitary bench. The dining room beyond had four tables, hard-backed chairs, and a sideboard crammed with chipped plates and saucers. Flies buzzed over the remains of someone's dinner. The smell of fried food lingered in the air. There was a faded painting of a vase filled with roses upon the wall at the base of the stairway. Bryony glanced at it as she passed into the dining room with Frank, but though she would have stayed a moment to gaze at the painting, Frank's hand pushed at the small of her back.

"C'mon, Katharine, I'm just about starved. Let's get us some grub."

She walked on, her shoulders drooping as she sat beside him in one of the hard-backed chairs.

After the meal, Frank led her to the stairs. This time she didn't even glance at the painting as she held tightly to the railing and climbed the narrow steps to their room. She felt ill. Her dinner of greasy steak and refried beans stuck like mud to her stomach. Her head throbbed. She barely had the strength to put one foot before the other. At the landing, she tripped over a loose floorboard and stumbled. Beside her, Frank chuckled and gripped her arm, keeping her upright.

"Careful, honey. Don't go hurtin' yourself now. Not tonight. We got real special plans for this evening, you and me, don't we?"

His laughter boomed through the dim hallway, echoing down the stairs. She flinched, wondering if the wispy-haired, bespectacled clerk at the desk below had heard his remark. Her feet dragged as Frank steered her to the door of their hotel room.

"Frank!" Willie Joe's furious voice made her glance back in his direction even as Frank did. The lean, dark-haired cowboy in the grime-splattered shirt, which had once been blue denim but was now little better than a greasy rag, was standing behind them at another doorway, the key to his room in his hand. His enraged expression and darkly lit eyes made Bryony's nerves stiffen with alarm. There was something about her brother-in-law that always disturbed her. The way he looked at her made her feel dirty, and when he happened to touch her, while helping her to dismount or handing her a metal cup to fill with coffee at the campfire, her entire body seemed to shrink in revulsion. Now, his harsh voice was raw and barely controlled, the undercurrent of violence she always sensed in him roiling to the surface.

"We gotta talk, Frank! This ain't fair!"

"Shut up, Willie Joe!" Frank sent him a warning frown. "Don't you say another word!"

"But you've got no right to—"

Frank swung toward him like an enraged bear. One blow from his huge fist sent Willie Joe slamming backward into the wall. Bryony gasped as she watched him stagger. She had no idea why they were fighting or what had infuriated Willie Joe, but the violence distressed her. She clung to the wall, watching helplessly as Frank towered over his brother.

"I told you to shut up!" Frank growled. His voice changed to a low hiss, so low that Bryony could not hear what he said. "Do you want to ruin everything, you damned fool? I can't go sharing her with you! She thinks she's my wife! You'll just have to wait!"

"It ain't fair, Frank!" Willie Joe tasted blood on his lip as he came away from the wall. He, too, kept his voice lowered, but there was no mistaking the ferocious outrage charging through him as he glared at his brother. "I want her, too, and I've got every bit as much right to her as you do..."

"You'll have your turn." Frank's broad face suddenly creased into a grin. He clapped a hand on Willie Joe's arm, giving him a shake. "Hell, Willie Joe, this little joke won't last forever. I'll turn her over to you eventually, and you can do whatever you damn well want with her. But for now, think about Logan." He leaned closer, his olive eyes alight with pleasure. "Think about how we've fixed him good: capturing his wife, making her think she's married to me. It's perfect, boy, it's right perfect! Someday ol' Texas Jim Logan will find out about this. It'll kill him, Willie Joe, it'll sure kill him.

Down the line, when we've finished with her, we can kill the girl or sell her to some bawdy house in Frisco, or whatever the hell you want. But right now, let's just let her think she's my proper wife. Let's jest play it out a while longer."

Willie Joe's gaze traveled past his brother to the girl leaning against the wall, watching them. He licked his lips. He hated waiting, but what Frank said did make sense. Damn it. His eyes narrowed as he thought of how neatly this revenge on Texas Jim Logan had fallen upon them. It was the dandiest revenge anyone could imagine on that low-down gunslinger who'd killed Tommy. He was soothed thinking of Logan's wife being at their mercy and believing she was married to Frank. He studied her, his blood warming with the urge to master her. Look at her now. She wasn't near as uppity these days as she had been that night at her ranch. No, now she seemed scared all the time. Quiet too. He smiled slowly to himself. Yep, she was paying. And Logan, too. So why spoil things? Like Frank said, his time would come. He would wait. And then . . . he'd make her sorry she'd ever ordered him off the Triple Star. He'd make her sorry she'd looked at him that night like he was nothing, a piece of cow dung she could kick aside without thought. He nodded slowly.

"All right, Frank. I'll wait." He gingerly touched his bruised chin. "But I sure as hell wish I'd thought of the notion instead of you. I'd like this a hell of a lot better if *I* was the one who was s'posed to be her husband!"

Frank chuckled. "You'll have your chance to lay hands on her, Willie Joe—don't you worry none—but not yet."

He winked and turned back to Bryony. "Why don't you head over to the saloon and find yourself one of them ripe, painted women to spend the night with?"

he called over his shoulder as he sauntered down the hall toward his "wife." He grinned at the slender girl who watched him approach with such trepidation. "Don't look so worried, Katharine," he admonished her with a hearty pat on the back, which nearly sent her sprawling. "Me and Willie Joe got everything settled jest fine. He won't be bothering us one little whit tonight."

"What was he angry about?" she asked softly, her expression still worried.

Frank shrugged impatiently. "Nothin' you need to fret about," he replied. "He just needs to find himself a good woman, that's all."

He laughed shortly, and Bryony realized that in his mind the subject was now closed. She followed him inside the dingy little bedroom, eyeing the bleak, dark interior through a mist of fatigue. The floor was bare, the pine bureau chipped and scarred, the dust-streaked mirror tilted crookedly on the wall of peeling, faded green paper. She glanced longingly at the big bed with the patched quilt. How she ached to sleep, to lie perfectly still for hours on end. Her back was stiff, her leg muscles throbbed, and her bottom was painfully saddlesore.

Frank and Willie Joe had driven her and the horses to their limit, traveling close to forty miles a day for the past six days. This was the first time they had stopped at a town in all that time, and this place, Cougar Junction, was little more than a single street lined by half a dozen wooden storefronts, a saloon, and this shabby two-story hotel with its facade of peeling lime-green paint and shuttered windows. She yearned for a bath. Her deerskin garments were filthy and damp with perspiration. The hot, airless room added to her discomfort. Frank immediately went to the shutters and flung them wide, while she sank down upon the bed, her shoulders sagging.

"May I... order a bath?" she asked as he came to stand before her, a strange, unsettling light in his eyes. "I feel so hot and sticky."

Frank cocked his head to one side. "Well, honey," he drawled, "I'm about as impatient as a rooster in the chicken coop, but"—he grinned—"but I reckon I can wait for you to get all cleaned up and sweet-smelling. After all, you're my darlin' little bride, ain't you? Tell you what: I'll go tell that clerk to get some kind of a tub and water up here pronto, and I'll run down to the store for some new duds for you while he's doin' it. I'm mighty tired of seeing you in that Injun garb. Too bad those Cheyenne destroyed the rest of your clothes when they attacked us that night. But I'll buy you a couple of things to last you till we get home to California. Then I'll be right back to watch you take that bath, honey, and then"—he placed his hands on her shoulders—"then we'll get on with our honeymoon, sweetheart. It's been too long since I had a chance to claim my husbandly rights."

He leaned down suddenly and planted his lips to hers, giving her a long, greasy kiss that tasted of stale tobacco. Bryony cringed, her body stiffening as he lifted her off the bed and pressed her close against him. Revulsion rushed through her, but she fought the urge to wriggle away, remaining still but rigid in his arms. After a moment, he drew back and regarded her, a grim glint in his olive-brown eyes.

"That's not good enough, Katharine," he growled. "You're stiff as a dead critter. You ain't much fun that way, honey."

"I... I'm sorry," she whispered, her green eyes bright with dismay. "But..."

"But what?"

"I ... I don't remember you," she moaned, as tears of misery fell upon her cheeks. "I feel like you're a ... a stranger."

"I ain't no stranger," he rasped. "I'm your husband!" He scowled down at her, his hands tightening on her arms. "I've told you a dozen times: I met you in El Paso. You were teaching school there. You were plumb crazy about me, and we got hitched right away. I was taking you back home to San Diego when them Injuns attacked our camp and carried you off. But I got you back, didn't I? Me and Willie Joe and some of our buffalo huntin' pards tracked you down and killed those redskins who stole you. Then our pards set out for Hide Town, and we headed this way toward home. You're safe now, Katharine. You've got to get that through your head. I'm your husband and I'll protect you. But you can't go denying me what I got a right to have. We're hitched, all legal and upright. And you told me you loved me lots of times. Why, honey, you couldn't wait to tie the knot! So just relax, and we'll both enjoy ourselves a whole lot better."

He wrapped his arms around her and his face nuzzled close. She trembled, unable to stop the tears of confusion and dismay that continued to slip down her cheeks. "My b ... bath," she whispered, still rigid in his arms. "First I ... I want to have my bath."

Frank swore. His hands gripped her shoulders so tightly she cried out in pain. Then he released her. "All right." His voice was menacing. "You'll get your bath, honey. And then, when you're all clean and sweet-smelling, I'll get what I want."

He stalked from the room, slamming the door behind him. Bryony watched him go in silent misery. When she was alone, she dropped down upon the bed, sobbing. What was she going to do? What could she do?

She didn't want him to touch her, or to kiss her, or to put his filthy paws on her. She just wanted to be left alone. But he was her husband! He had every right! *I must have loved him once*, she told herself, her slender shoulders shaking as she wept. *But why? How? How could I ever have loved such a brutal bear of a man?* More than ever she longed for a thread of insight into her past, but all she could summon forth was darkness.

A knock on the door made her glance up. It was probably a maid with her bath water. If she hurried, maybe she could finish her bath before Frank returned. Maybe she could go right to sleep and he wouldn't bother to wake her. . . . It was worth a try.

By the time Frank Chester returned to the hotel, Bryony had washed all the grime and sweat from her body and cleansed her hair with a thick lather of soap. She had rubbed herself dry with a thin, torn towel provided by the hotel and smoothed her thick mass of coal-black hair with her fingers until it fell in damp waves to her waist. She was lying in the lumpy bed when Frank entered the room. The bedside lamp was low, and starlight beamed in through the shutters, touching the slender figure huddled beneath the sheets. Bryony lay trembling, her eyes tightly shut. *Please, leave me alone,* she prayed. *Please, let me have some time to get used to all this.* Her heart hammered painfully. Tension coursed through her, whitening the knuckles of the slender hand clenched beneath her chin.

Frank stared at her. His face was flushed with the liquor he'd consumed in the past hour. He had stopped at the saloon to drink and gamble away some of his buffalo-hide profits after buying Bryony some riding clothes. Swaggering slightly, he moved forward so that he stood beside the bed, gazing down upon the girl who lay silently there.

What a beauty she was. Willie Joe had been right.

He'd never met any woman like her. Her black hair looked so dark and lustrous in the starlight. He longed to twine his fingers through it. Her skin was smooth and fair, her features delicate. Her lips had felt so soft beneath his earlier tonight. And she tasted sweet. Like honey. He dropped the bundle of clothes he'd bought for her on the floor and swiftly unbuttoned his shirt. His whole body quivered with excitement and anticipation. It would be a pleasure to couple with Jim Logan's wife tonight. A double pleasure, for not only would he be exercising a pungent revenge on his old enemy, he'd also be enjoying one of the most bewitching women he'd ever seen. Frank's breathing was heavy as he finally shed the last of his garments and lurched around to the other side of the bed. The mattress springs creaked beneath his weight as he lowered himself. He slid closer to the sleeping girl beside him and reached out brawny arms to grasp her.

Bryony stiffened as he touched her. She was naked beneath the sheets, having had no clean garments to don after her bath. Her flesh shrank beneath Frank Chester's hands, and she gave a little cry of despair. He turned her to face him, then sat up, looming over her like a great, hairy-chested giant. His hands yanked the protective sheets away, and he gazed eagerly down at her glistening naked form.

"I been waitin' a long time for this," he muttered, his eyes wildly, lustfully aglow. The smell of liquor mixed with stale tobacco on his breath made her gasp in revulsion, but he did not allow her to draw away or to cover herself. "I been watchin' you every day. Wanting you. You're a temptin' woman, Katharine. You're my woman. And I mean to have you!"

She lay still but for the rapid rise and fall of her creamy breasts. Frank's big hand slid down the white column of her throat and across her shoulders, finally resting upon one rosy nipple. He sucked in his breath. "Ah, you're soft, ain't you, Katharine? Jest like silk." He raised her slowly, staring down into her pale face. "Kiss me," he ordered softly, holding her before him. "A real kiss, not like the one before. Kiss me the way a woman kisses her man."

She didn't want to. *She didn't want to.* But he was her husband.

Trembling, she leaned forward and put her mouth to his. His face was moist and warm. He sucked greedily at her lips. She forced herself to kiss him, choking back the revulsion that filled her as he forced her lips apart and plunged his tongue inside her mouth. His hands pressed her to him, crushing her breasts against his barrel chest so tightly that she could feel his heart hammering against her own. He continued to kiss her with greedy delight, all the while holding her slim frame hard against him. Finally, he let her go and chuckled as she put a shaking hand to her mouth.

"That's better, Katharine," he said softly. "That's much better."

Suddenly, he shifted so that she was lying beneath him on the bed. His hands groped for her breasts, squeezing them with rough fervor. His eyes shone into hers as passion lit his beefy face. He crushed her against the groaning springs of the mattress, and his hard manhood pressed against her.

"Frank . . . no!" Bryony tried to push him aside, frightened by this sudden, rough ferocity. Her body squirmed helplessly beneath his as she began to struggle. "Stop . . . please . . . you're hurting me. Please stop. Frank, I . . . I don't want to . . . I'm not ready . . ."

"Shut up." He twisted a hand through her hair, pinning her with his heavy body. "I don't take no back talk from the woman I married!" he growled. Grunting, he spread her thighs with his own legs. He entered her without any further preliminaries, shoving deep inside her despite her cry of pain.

"You just relax, Katharine, honey, and you and me will get along just fine," he whispered hoarsely as he pushed deeper and deeper. A grin spread across his passion-darkened features, lighting his shining eyes. "Oh, yeah, honey, we'll be just fine."

Bryony squeezed her eyes shut as he buried his face in her hair. Sobs clogged her throat. She felt as though he was ripping out her insides, tearing her apart. She wanted to scream, to die. But it was no use. She couldn't fight him, and she didn't even have the right to do so. They were married. This was her duty. *I must have loved him once*, she told herself desperately as his huge body thrust savagely down upon her slender frame. *If only I could remember!*

It seemed impossible that she had ever loved this coarse, brutal man. Or that he had ever loved her. He was hurting her, and he didn't even care. She wept aloud, her bones nearly crushed beneath him. Somehow, she knew this was all wrong, that this savage, animal coupling was not at all the way it ought to be. It ought to be beautiful and dizzying and overwhelming. . . . A vague memory stirred within her—more a feeling than a memory. Her body recalled how it felt to be touched with tenderness, to be set aflame with desire. Not like this. But once—she could have sworn it—once she had known something totally different, she had known rapture and delight in the arms of a man. . . . She shuddered as the memory both warmed and taunted her, tantalizing in its mystery. Was that man Frank? Was that how it had been between them before she'd lost her memory, before the Indians had taken her?

When Frank had finished with her and lay snoring at her side, she wept softly into her pillow. Her body was sore from his rough handling, and she knew there would be bruises come morning. She trembled in despair. She felt alone, adrift, as if she were at the mercy of her husband instead of under his protection. *I must try*, she told herself, gritting her teeth as night's shadows filled the tiny room. *I must try to love him again, to recapture what we once had. It is my duty. I owe it to him!*

But her misery remained. There seemed no hope for happiness in the long, empty days ahead. A lingering sorrow filled her. She yearned for something, something she could not name. But her soul hungered for it, crying out in that hot July night, seeking a solace she did not understand the need for, but without which she was lost.

CHAPTER SIXTEEN

SOMETHING WOKE Jim Logan in the dark of night. He leaped upright in his bed, cold sweat soaking his powerful body. His face was ashen, his vivid blue eyes staring wildly. What was it? What was it that had wakened him, tearing him from the depths of sleep and filling him with such horror?

His racing heartbeat slowed to a steady drumming as he gazed around the tiny bedroom in the east wing of the ranch house, where he'd slept all these months. He'd never had the heart to return to the master bedroom, where he'd spent so many glorious nights with Bryony. No, this small, plain room suited him far better. His gaze traveled to the bedroll and saddle pack bundled on the floor in the corner. Everything was set for the morning. Now all he had to do was wait till dawn.

But the panic that had jarred him from sleep lingered, jangling his nerve endings like acid-tipped darts. Uneasiness gripped him, and he couldn't shake it off. An odd, creeping feeling prickled his flesh. Swearing, he slid from the bed and went to the window, staring out into the gloom of night. Stars filled the sky by the thousands, but they cast a mere silvery shadow upon the vast blackness of the Texas prairie. The night air was still and heavy. Even at this time, the July heat was sweltering, but that wasn't what had made him awaken in a sweat. What then? What?

An image of Bryony swam into his mind, and he closed his eyes, rocking slightly before the window. Bryony! Where are you? Do you need me tonight? He had the horrible feeling that she did, somewhere, and his stomach tightened in helpless despair. He tried to tell himself that it was only his foolish imagination, that Bryony was probably dead and beyond anyone's help, but that strange, haunting mood persisted, pricking his skin with cold, clammy horror.

He had to get out of here. Now. There was no way he'd be able to sleep again tonight, so why not set off immediately instead of waiting for sun up? Something inside him called for action, demanded that he *move*. He dressed in swift, practiced silence, excited suddenly about the mission ahead of him. It was only two days since he'd received the letter from Tomas, requesting his help down in Mexico. Jim had jumped at the chance to get away.

Don Tomas Felipe Diego y Ramones was an amigo from his gunfighting days, the son of a wealthy Mexican family, who was having trouble with bandits raiding the Diego y Ramones ranching empire, even setting fire to the hacienda. Tomas had asked Jim for help, and without hesitation, Jim had sent back word that he would come. He was all set to leave in the morning, but now he found he could no longer wait. He would leave tonight, with a note to Danny explaining that he had decided to start his journey in the relative cool of nighttime, a note that would spare them both the necessity of saying good-bye.

He had no qualms about leaving Danny. The kid was doing a damn good job with the Triple Star and would manage just fine without him. Besides, he had a feeling that by the time he got back, whenever the hell that might be, Danny would have taken himself a wife. He seemed smitten as a honeybee by Duke Crenshaw's visiting niece, a coquettish little blonde by the name of Rebecca Canaby, and would probably propose to her before the girl went back East to school at the end of the summer. Jim was glad for him. He wanted Danny to be happy, to have a woman he could love and care for, but it was still hard for him to see Danny and Rebecca sitting together on the front-porch swing, hands clasped tightly together, for the sight of their young love and newly awakening passion stabbed at his own heart with all the pain of a love that is forever lost.

He wanted and needed to get away, so Tomas's letter had come at exactly the right time, giving him an excuse to leave the monotonous routine of ranch life and to set out on his own once more, a solitary, unencumbered man. Danny had not wanted him to go. Jim had read that in his brother's eyes, but the younger man had not spoken a word in opposition when Jim had stated that he would indeed go to Mexico to aid his old friend.

Jim sighed as he scrawled a few lines to his brother and then folded the paper in two. Danny was a good kid. Jim would miss him. But the time had come for Jim to leave the Triple Star, for there was nothing now to anchor him to this place—no wife, no children, nothing to make the handsome, sprawling ranch house into a real home.

He picked up his bedroll and saddle pack and headed into the hallway, but something stopped him as he reached the stairs. He turned abruptly and stole silently down the corridor to the master bedroom he had once shared with his wife. He hadn't entered the room in months, though Rosita cleaned and dusted it every day. All was exactly as it had been in the days

when Bryony was here, yet it was all different. The scent
of her perfume was missing from the air, and the sparkle
that followed her everywhere no longer illuminated this
room. He stared about him, his chest so tight with grief
that his breath came in short, painful rasps. Longing
filled him, a longing to see her again, to hold her, to
make love to her here upon their bed as he had done
so many times before. But that would never be. She was
gone. Dead, probably. He knew he would never see her
again.

Jim Logan struggled for long minutes with his grief.
It was a burden he had carried with him for the past
seven months, ever since the night of Bryony's disappearance. It had not grown any easier with the passage
of time, but instead had weighed even heavier upon his
heart. In the months that he had endured without her,
he had grown even more silent and alone than he had
ever been before. Laughter was a thing of the past,
happiness only a distant memory. Jim Logan moved
through his life with outward strength, but inwardly,
pain wracked him. He missed Bryony more in this moment than at any other. And he knew from experience
that tomorrow the torment would be even worse than
it was today.

That's why he had to get away. This house, as
much as this room, held too many memories. Maybe
when he was alone out on the range again, with only
the stars and the cactus and the campfire, he would be
able to forget just a little, to ease the terrible pain. And
he'd be busy in Mexico, laying his life on the line to
help Tomas against those bandits. That ought to shift
his mind away from his loss. With any luck, he'd get
killed and end this misery forever. With a grim smile,
Jim Logan turned toward the door.

His gaze fell then upon something that glinted in
the darkness—a picture frame of silver resting atop the

dressing table. He walked toward it, and his fingers grasped the gleaming frame. He stared hard at the man and woman photographed there, smiling faces captured by the camera forever. The lump in his throat tightened. His honeymoon with Bryony in San Francisco seemed so real, so recent, yet it had taken place more than a year ago. They'd been so happy then, so certain that nothing would ever again interfere with their love. His knuckles whitened as he gripped the frame, almost overcome by his emotions. For an instant he wanted to hurl the photograph across the room, to rip it to shreds and shatter the glass that protected it from dust and light, but instead, he clutched it to his heart and stood for a while with eyes shut to hold back the threatening tears. Then he hunkered down beside his pack and carefully placed the photograph among his belongings. When he rose again, shoulders straightened, Jim did not glance about the room another time, but headed straight for the door. He left the note for Danny on the mantelpiece in the parlor and strode from the house without one backward glance.

He felt better somehow when he was in the saddle, galloping Pecos beneath the stars. The night swirled about him, a gaping dark hole into which he charged to answer some desperate inner call. Its black, ponderous silence engulfed him, swallowing him as he dug his heels into Pecos's sides, and he felt the wind sting his face. There was no sound but the howling rush of air in his ears, and his own labored breathing. The glitter of stars overhead swam in his vision as he leaned low over the stallion's neck.

The urgency that had taken possession of him in his bed, rousing him from sleep, came upon him again, but this time, he was able to respond to it, urging Pecos to an ever faster pace, until man and horse fairly flew across the shadowed prairie, flashing past the sagebrush and mesquite like dark fleeting shadows of the night. He was racing, not away from something, but *toward* something. He didn't know what it was. But something was drawing him, calling him, compelling him to ride. He felt the pull of some unknown magnet drawing him closer and succumbed to it with a strange relief. Leaning low, almost as one with his horse, he gave the bay stallion his head. A wild need filled him, drove him. Whatever called him, he would answer. Whatever awaited him, he would face. It was his destiny that beckoned, and he rode hard and fast to meet it, his body throbbing with urgency, and an odd excitement whirling through his head.

CHAPTER SEVENTEEN

HAVING WOLFED down a slab of beef and four fried eggs before the woman called Katharine Chester had even set the coffeepot on the table, Willie Joe eased back in his chair, his thumbs hooked in the pockets of his worn denim pants. He leered at the silent young woman who refilled his empty cup and set the dented pot before him on the rough pine table, watching her move about the kitchen as she fixed breakfast for his brother. Frank had not yet appeared this morning. Willie Joe licked his thin lips, appreciative of this brief time alone with Bryony Logan.

"You cook up a damned fine breakfast, honey," he declared in his raspy voice, which made every comment he uttered sound like a sneer. "This old place sure feels a lot more like home now that you're here to clean it up a bit and, uh, brighten up the view." His small, dirt-brown eyes lit with approval as he surveyed her slender yet sensuously curved figure, clad in a pale lilac dress of soft muslin. The gown had an edging of white lace at the sleeves and around the scooped neckline and a white sash that tied in a floppy bow in the back. It emphasized her tiny waist and full breasts, sending a jolt of desire through Willie Joe's blood. To his annoyance, she made no answer to his remark and kept her back turned to him as she worked at the stove. Quiet as a cat, he eased himself off the chair and crept up behind her. Thin, rope-muscled arms snaked suddenly about her neck, pulling her tightly up against him. Willie Joe's breath was warm in her ear.

"Yep, you sure are a pleasin' sight!" he snickered, nuzzling his lips against her neck. She tried to push him away, but he held her pinned against him.

"Let me go!" she gasped in revulsion, struggling to wriggle free of his enclosing arms. His mouth was wet upon her skin just below her earlobe, and a shudder of disgust shook her. "Don't touch me! Willie Joe! I said *don't!*" She kicked him with the heel of her foot, putting all her strength into the movement. He yelped and released her, stepping backward, and Bryony spun about to face him.

"You ... despicable toad!" she cried, her breasts heaving with agitation. Her ebony hair swirled around her flushed, fine-boned face. "Don't you ... don't you ever touch me again!"

"Don't you ever *kick* me again!" Willie Joe snarled as he lunged forward. He grabbed her wrists in a grip that sent waves of pain rushing through her arms. "I'll teach you to mind your manners, girl, if it's the last thing I do!" He shook her violently and steered her backward, dangerously close to the hot stove where the eggs and butter in the frypan had sizzled into a burnt brown mass. A savage light shone in his eyes, and his lips beneath the thin dark moustache twitched in cruel anticipation. Bryony cried out in sudden terror.

"What's going on, Willie Joe?"

Frank's deep voice cracked through the kitchen, and Willie Joe stopped in his tracks. He released Bryony's arms.

"Nothin', Frank, nothin' at all. Me and Katharine were just havin' a little chat."

Bryony was trembling from head to toe. She turned eyes that were still brilliant with fear toward Frank.

"You all right?" His gruff voice demanded an answer. Willie Joe was watching her intently, still standing close enough to ruffle her hair with his breath.

She nodded, mute and rigid before them.

"Good. Now, I don't want any more trouble between you. Willie Joe, quit botherin' Katharine. She's got plenty to do without having to take any of your lip. And Katharine"—Frank squeezed her shoulder with one heavy hand—"honey, don't pay no mind to Willie Joe. He's just an ornery cuss who needs to find himself a woman of his own."

"I'll tell you what I need," Willie Joe began, rounding on his brother with sudden intensity, but Frank cut him off.

"You need to head on over to Ben Forrester's place, pronto," he advised. "I'll meet you and the others there after I've had my chow—and a chance to talk with my darlin' little wife this fine autumn morn. Now get goin', Willie Joe, before I lose my patience with you!"

Bryony drew a deep breath after the younger Chester had departed. She went to the stove and began to scrape the burnt eggs from the bottom of the frypan.

Frank sat at the table and poured coffee into his tin cup, watching her work. They'd been home now in California for nearly four weeks, and she still hadn't fully recovered from the grueling journey across the desert. It had taken them two months to cross Texas, Arizona, and New Mexico in the broiling heat, riding hard as Indians for nearly ten hours a day. Three times she had fainted from the effects of sun and thirst, and sometimes he'd had to practically carry her off her horse. But she had never complained. She just did whatever

he told her to do and accepted the lot he handed her.
Yet he knew it had been pure hell for her. And part of
him, grudgingly, admired her for coming through it with
such pluck. Oh, she was thinner all right, thinner than
she had been when they'd first come across her at that
Cheyenne camp, and she looked about as weak as a
lamb. Yet, there was a strength in her, a refusal to buckle
under to everything that had happened to her, and Frank
had to confess that he liked that in her.

   She did look pretty this morning, he mused as she
brought him a plateful of freshly cooked eggs and beef.
Almost as pretty as she'd looked last night, lying under
him in his big double bed. He grinned to himself at the
memory. Too bad he didn't have time this morning.
He'd like to carry her up to that bed right now. But Ben
Forrester and the others would be waiting for him. Ben
had a plan to rob the bank in Santa Barbara, and Frank
wanted in on the job. It would mean some quick easy
money, and the risks were few. No, he didn't want to
miss out on this. With regret, he pushed aside his lustful
thoughts and turned his attention to his breakfast. He
attacked the meal before him with the same gusto he
would have otherwise turned loose upon his "wife."

   Bryony stood looking out the window while Frank
ate. It was the last day of September, and golden sunshine crowned the countryside of San Diego. The little
white house that belonged to Frank and Willie Joe was
nestled in a lush green valley, where orange and golden
poppies danced in the sea breezes and delicate violets
and pink-blossomed lupine dotted the hillsides in
breathtaking abundance. But she saw nothing of the
glorious spectacle nature offered her, not the chaparral-
covered mountains, nor the thickly clustered pine trees,
nor the flowering hillsides alive with bell sparrows and
yellow-billed magpies who chattered and sang from the
branches of tall oaks. She was reliving the moment when

Willie Joe had grabbed her from behind and pressed his lips against the flesh of her neck, when he had driven her relentlessly, purposefully closer to the hot stove. Her fingers curled around the thin muslin of her skirt, crushing it as her distress mounted. She whirled suddenly to address Frank.

"I . . . I'm afraid of Willie Joe!" she blurted.

Frank glanced up from his breakfast.

"He frightens me," she rushed on, before he could interrupt. "Frank, I want you to promise that you won't leave me alone with him. Ever. I don't know what would happen if he had a chance to . . . to . . ."

"Now, Katharine." Frank set down his metal cup and pushed back his chair. He went to her, placing his burly arms on her shoulders. "You just settle down, honey. Willie Joe won't hurt you. He's a little wild, and he seems a mite rude, I reckon, especially to a fine young woman like you with all your manners and ladylike ways, but he wouldn't harm a hair on your head." His smile was indulgent, patronizing, as if talking to a frantic child.

Bryony stared up at him. "What about this morning?" she demanded, her voice trembling. "He . . . he grabbed me, Frank. He . . . kissed me." Revulsion crossed her small, delicate face. "I know he's your brother and you don't like to hear badly of him, but he . . . he's lusting after me, I'm certain of it. And yet, I think he hates me, too. If you hadn't come in when you did, he would have . . ."

"I did come in, though, didn't I? And I took care of Willie Joe." Frank's hand, the size of a bear's paw, touched her hair, stroking its silken strands as he spoke. "You know I won't let anything happen to you, Katharine. So don't worry your pretty little head over Willie Joe."

"But . . ."

"I said don't worry about it!" Frank's voice lashed at her, and she recoiled instinctively. At the stricken expression on her face, something inside Frank Chester twisted uncomfortably.

"Look, honey, I'm sorry you were scared this morning," he said in a gentler tone, which surprised him almost as much as it did her. "I don't want you to be scared of nothin'. I'll take care of you. And I'll have a talk with Willie Joe 'bout steering clear of you from now on. All right?"

She nodded. Frank pulled her close against him, and he lowered his head to kiss her. As always, she was obedient in her response, but nothing more. There was no answering warmth in her lips, no hunger as they touched his, and her quivering as he enfolded her in his arms was due to distress and not passion. Frank fought a surge of disappointment. Just once he'd like her to react like she really loved him. The thought shocked him. He let her go and turned quickly away, striding toward the kitchen door.

"You rest easy now," he said, taking his gray stetson from the hook on the wall and setting it on his head. "I'll be back by suppertime and . . . and Willie Joe'll be with me all day."

"You'll talk with him this morning?" Her eyes still held that hint of fear.

Frank nodded. "Soon as I get to Forrester's."

He took one last look at her pinched, worried face before disappearing through the door. He *would* talk to Willie Joe, too! He'd make damned sure his ornery little brother stayed clear of his wife! *His wife?* A flush crept up Frank Chester's swarthy face as he stalked to the barn to get his horse. He must be loco to have these feelings! Lately there were times—too many times— when he forgot that this was all a hoax, that the dark-haired, green-eyed beauty he'd brought across the desert and mountains was not really his wife, but Jim Logan's. Sometimes, she stirred feelings in him that were unlike any he'd ever imagined. He wasn't sure he knew what was happening to him. And he sure as hell didn't like it. *Quit taking this all so serious,* he told himself as he saddled his big roan. *The girl ain't important, except as a means of getting revenge on Logan. She's just a tool. And you'd better get ready to turn her over to Willie Joe real soon, 'cause he's gettin' tired of waiting his turn.*

But the notion of giving up his sole claim on Jim Logan's woman filled him with regret. It was like having a winning hand at poker and being forced to fold your cards.

As he led the roan from the barn, he shot a regretful glance at the black stallion that had been among the Indian ponies they'd taken from the Cheyenne. That horse had reared and bucked like a mad creature when he or Willie Joe had tried to ride it. Once, Willie Joe had come close to shooting the damned beast. But Frank had stopped him, knowing the value of a fine piece of horseflesh. They could always sell the horse for a good price. But one of these days, Frank was determined to break in that stallion. Same as he had broken in Logan's woman. The sweetness of his revenge against the gunfighter who had killed his youngest brother gave him immense satisfaction, and he set his mind to pondering this instead of Bryony's fragile beauty and graceful charm. Thinking of Texas Jim Logan's outrage if he only knew the truth restored Frank's good humor, and he grinned to himself as he mounted the roan and kicked the animal into a gallop, heading east toward Ben Forrester's adobe homestead.

Bryony finished cleaning the kitchen in dreary silence. She herself had no appetite for breakfast, and she moved around the kitchen listlessly putting away the plates and saucers, wiping the old pine table with a damp cloth.

The two-month journey to California had taken its toll on her. Her strength and spirit were all but drained away. But it wasn't only the rigors of traveling across the stark, untamed wilderness in the scorching summer heat that had affected her. Her memory still had not returned, not even a whisper, and she felt more isolated and depressed than ever. It seemed to her that she was merely a shadow of a human being, like a walking skeleton without a soul. She had no past, no heartfelt links to anything or anyone. As far as she could tell the future before her loomed bleak and joyless.

Coming "home" to this ramshackle little house, with its broken porch steps and scarred, grimy adobe front, with the old, unpainted furniture and bare, dusty floors, she had hoped to find some sense of fulfillment. She had spent the past four weeks scouring and scrubbing and painting until the small, run-down little place looked as bright and shining as the jewel-blue sea that lapped at the coast in the distance. She had filled the house with the aromas of home cooking, and the scent of freshly picked flowers. She had sewn some pretty new curtains for the windows and made bright new slipovers for the creaking old sofa and the one decent upholstered chair. She regularly and vigorously washed all the clothes and dried them in the fresh, open air so that even Willie Joe's filthy garments rinsed clean, and she had even planted a garden in back of the house. But still . . . still, contentment eluded her. She was never comfortable with Frank and Willie Joe; she felt most at ease when she was alone during the days. Nighttime was the worst of all. She hated the moment when Frank shut their bedroom door and came toward her with his hands outstretched.

She knew she ought to feel something toward him, the sort of emotion a woman ought to feel for her husband, but something inside her heart was dead, buried away in an impenetrable coffin, and try as she might, she could not bring it to life or set it free from the vault that imprisoned it.

Having tidied the kitchen, she walked aimlessly through the little house. After all these weeks of cleaning, there was still much to do, but this morning she had no strength for it. The long journey and the hours she had spent making this house habitable had exhausted her. She turned away. Her gaze fell upon the window in the tiny sitting room, and through the soft blue curtains she had sewn so carefully, she saw at last the heartrending beauty of the day.

Golden sunlight cast a glow upon the distant mountains, and veiled their towering peaks in gilded splendor. Against the vivid blue of the sky, the emerald valley sparkled brightly. Orange poppies flamed on the hillsides like sparks of fire. Birds twittered from the branches of trees. Upon a distant rise, Bryony spied a doe and her fawn, poised like tawny statuary. She caught her breath, and then, in the next instant, they fled from view through a web of oaks. The breeze blowing up from the bay tantalized her with its salt-scent. Violets fluttered like a thousand tiny butterfly wings, beckoning her to run, to fly through that glorious carpet of blooms. Beyond them, beyond everything, including the chaparral and the pines, the majesty of the mountains and the perfume of the wildflowers, was the sea. It was there beyond the hills, waiting, calling, blue waves lapping against white rocks, singing a song of irresistible allure.

The impulse came to her then, with a swift, surging uplift of the spirit. She could no more resist it than she could resist the need to breathe. She would get away for a while, away from this house and the problems posed by Willie Joe. She would walk across the hills and find a quiet place to watch the sea. She would breathe in the salty, invigorating ocean air and watch the ships sail into San Diego Bay. The prospect excited her, and she darted through the front door like a young girl about to meet her lover. Happy anticipation filled her as she left the small adobe house behind and began to walk with long, graceful strides in the direction of the sea.

Jim Logan's shoulder throbbed dully as Pecos picked his way up the steep ravine. The fight down in Mexico had been both briefer and bloodier than even Jim had anticipated, leaving eight men dead and three others in a gruesome state. Jim had been fortunate only to have been wounded in the shoulder, a grazing shot that caused pain but did little damage to muscle or bone.

Tomas Ramones had been elated by the triumphant outcome and very grateful to Jim, who had arrived when the situation had been at its gravest and had somehow managed to elicit victory from the throes of defeat. Tomas had pleaded with Jim to stay on at the sprawling, beautiful hacienda for as long as he wished and at least until his shoulder was well healed, but Jim had grinned and shaken his head, unaccountably impatient to move on. So he had left Mexico yesterday, having rested only overnight from the rigors of battle. Now, scrambling up the ravine that led out of a canyon some fifteen miles from the Mexican border, Jim paid scant heed to the twinges in his shoulder.

He reached the crest of the ravine and halted Pecos to gaze about him, squinting his eyes against the brilliant gold glare of the September sun. He had no clear destination. He might head up to San Francisco or ride straight on up the coast to Oregon. A restlessness flowed through him like the currents of a strong river, and he felt he could not stop until he had followed it to its head or until the current had run its course.

Close by, his ears caught the distinctive, always seductive rush of the sea. Spurred by impulse and drawn by the tangy salt scent of the Pacific, which stung his nostrils with pungent freshness, he turned the bay stallion sharply toward the western coast.

They galloped across low, flower-carpeted hills as dazzling sunshine streamed down upon them. The breeze from the nearby bay cooled Jim's face. Reaching a rise of greater height than the others, he saw a spectacle that snatched his breath away. Below and just beyond a wide, emerald hill where violets and pink-blossomed mint danced in the sunlight, the sea of deepest indigo, frothing with silver-white foam, rolled in from the seemingly limitless breadth of the ocean and crashed upon the rocks and boulders of San Diego Bay. The ocean went on forever, or so it seemed to the human eye, a vast blue mass of unrivaled power and beauty, flowing inward to collide against the jutting rocks of the bay. Jim gazed in fascination at the magnificent indigo waters, calm against the backdrop of sapphire sky, and his glance wandered with pleasure to the inlet below, where white-capped waves slapped against the shore. Then his eye fell upon a figure seated far below him on the emerald hill that overlooked the bay. In the excitement of finding the sea, and in the sheer astonishment at its magnificence, he had not at first even noticed the small form, which sat among the flowers, skirts of pale lavender spread gracefully upon the soft green grass. Now, as he stared at her, something deep inside of him gave a strange lurch.

It was a woman, a young woman, of slender build and graceful carriage. Her hair was dark, and it cascaded in raven waves down her back as she sat looking out to the sea. There was something poignant about her as she sat upon the lush hillside, her face turned toward the bay. Her lilac skirts fluttered upon the grass, and her hands were held quite still in her lap. Her whole attention, her whole being, was focused upon the lapping blue waters below, and she was touchingly unaware of the lovely, dainty picture she presented against the backdrop of sun, mountain, and sky. But it wasn't only her beauty that held Jim Logan's gaze or that made his blood start to thunder in his ears. He leaned forward in the saddle, his hands suddenly damp, every muscle straining. His eyes were riveted upon her. From this distance, it was difficult to see, it was impossible to be certain, but...

"*Bryony!*"

His joyous shout rang across the hilltops, shattering the serene silence of the morning. At the same instant that he yelled, he dug his heels into Pecos's sides and sent the stallion flying across the ground.

The woman on the hill below turned at the sound of his shout, and when she saw him galloping headlong toward her across the velvety grass, she scrambled to her feet and stood facing him, an expression of surprise crossing her delicate features. Jim shouted again. "Bryony!" His heart thundered in wild joy as he bore down upon her, hardly able to believe the miracle before him, his amazement at finding her rivaled only by the frenzied rush of love that filled every part of him and sent a blazing fire surging through his blood.

But as he reached the bottom of the hill where she had been sitting and started Pecos up the incline, she turned and started to run in the opposite direction, her ebony hair lifting in the wind and tumbling around her shoulders. Holding onto her skirts, she fled across the hillside, darting as swiftly as she could down the far side of the hill, the side closest to the sea.

"Bryony, stop! It's me!" Jim roared in frantic desperation, spurring Pecos to a dangerously fast pace. But the lovely, slender girl in the pale lilac dress had disappeared, like an ethereal vision of man's dreams that vanishes in the merciless light of day.

CHAPTER EIGHTEEN

FEAR KNIFED through Jim as he raced Pecos up the incline. For an instant he doubted his own sanity, questioning that there had even been a girl sitting upon the hill, gazing out to sea. And that it had been Bryony. Hell, was he loco or what? When she disappeared from view, panic flooded through him and all his wild joy crashed about him like the breakers that shattered upon the rocks of the bay below. But as Pecos gained the top of the hill, Jim saw her again, running down to the sea itself, her skirts blowing wildly about her. It was Bryony, he was sure of it! But a new terror sliced through him as it appeared she might topple down upon the jagged boulders below, so headlong was her pace. He spurred the stallion after her in desperation.

"Stop!" he shouted, leaning low in the saddle, but his voice seemed only to speed her flight.

He caught her midway down the hill. He leaped from Pecos before the horse had fully halted, and overtook her after only three long strides. He grasped her arm, yanking her to a halt, then quickly grabbing hold of her other arm as well when he spun her to face him. She was gasping for breath, her face white with fear, and the huge, glimmering jade-green eyes he knew so well stared at him in complete panic.

"You!" His voice emerged as a hoarse whisper. "It . . . it *is* you!"

"Let me go!" She struggled frantically within his grasp, but was unable to break free. "Leave me alone!"

Piercing the shock of finding her, of gazing down once more upon that beautiful, beloved face, came the realization that she was trying to run away from him, trying to wrench away from him. Pain vibrated through his tall, broad-shouldered frame. So she hated him still. Feared him, even. His jaw tightened in self-condemnation for all he had ever done to cause this reaction from her, but he kept a firm grip on her arms, as though by releasing her for even an instant he might lose her all over again.

"Don't run away! Damn it, I won't let you run away! Not ever again!" He towered above her, staring as if hypnotized at her flowing ebony hair and creamy skin, hungering for the feel of her rosy lips upon his.

He had thought she was dead! He had thought he would never see her again! And now, here she was, in his arms, as enchanting, and fragile, and alive as ever. He pulled her up close against him, and his vivid blue eyes burned into hers. The next moment, his lips came down upon her mouth, capturing the warm velvet of it and kissing her with the violent, explosive fervor of long-tortured love.

Bryony struggled to break free of his steel-like arms, but found herself imprisoned by one whose strength was far greater than her own. Terror swelled in her. Her peaceful reverie upon the hillside had been shattered by this stranger's sudden shout and his equally sudden advance upon her. She hadn't been able to hear what he had been yelling as he rode his horse like the devil toward her, but she had been sufficiently frightened to flee as fast as she could. But he had caught her and held her in arms more like iron than flesh and blood, and as he stared down at her, devouring her with the intensity of those glinting, cobalt-blue eyes, she felt a ripple of some strange emotion flowing through her.

What did he want with her? Why had he pursued her? Frightened as she was, she couldn't help but be aware of how overwhelmingly handsome this tall, rugged stranger was. As she stared up at him through wide, brilliant eyes, noting his dusty, black sombrero pulled low over his brow and the way his jaw tightened as he looked at her, she felt her heart start to drum in quickened beats. When he kissed her, terror surged through her, but something else as well. His warm, hungering lips and the pressure of his hard-muscled form against her own body stirred a wondrous new emotion within her. Though she fought at first to break free of his powerful arms and tried to twist away from the onslaught of his lips, she soon found her resistance melting away like morning frost in the sunlight, and something inside her heart trembled with a rapturous awakening.

His mouth moved upon hers, bruising in its ferocity, yet oddly tender, tasting her lips with his own, sending a hot blue fire licking along her veins. Her head was bent backward under the force of that kiss. Dizziness washed over her. His hands still held her arms pinned to her sides, but his body had overpowered her and she felt the entire slender length of her own body crushed tightly against an iron-muscled physique that seemed afire with need.

He kissed her for what seemed like forever. She did not even realize when he stopped. Half-swooning, she was cradled in his arms, her head thrown back and her eyes closed. Slowly, slowly, the mad spinning inside her head eased. The blood beating in her ears subsided to a low rushing sound, and her pulsebeat ceased its wild racing. With great effort, Bryony opened her eyes.

He was leaning over her, staring down into her flushed, dazed face. The sun overhead hurt her eyes, and she blinked. His head bent suddenly to block its rays, filling her line of vision. She heard his voice, low and deep and very close to her.

"Little tenderfoot. Are you all right?"

Suddenly, she returned to her senses. She went rigid in his arms and began struggling to be free. This time he let her go.

"Don't touch me!" she cried, horror filling her as she realized what she had just done. "How d . . . dare you!"

He laughed. His features wore an exultant look, as though something wonderful had befallen him. She backed away from him as though from a madman.

"Who . . . who are you?" she whispered, as the wind lifted her midnight hair from her neck and sent it billowing into a dark mane about her.

At her words, the triumphant expression vanished from the stranger's face. He went absolutely still, his hands frozen at his sides. His voice conveyed his astonishment. "Who *am* I?" he repeated, and his face paled beneath its dark, sun-bronzed tan. "What do you mean who am I?"

She started backing away from him, all of her previous apprehension returning, but he advanced on her and gripped her shoulders. "Don't you know me?" he demanded, disbelief written upon his lean, handsome features. "Answer me!"

"N . . . no. I . . . I never saw you before!"

"What kind of game is this?" He was angry now, and he shook her by the shoulders. The perfume of wild flowers and the crash of the sea on the rocks below filled the air all around them, but there seemed no other human life in all the world as they stood together upon the sun-washed hill. "I'm not in the mood for any of your tricks, little tenderfoot," he drawled grimly, his blue eyes narrowing as they pierced hers. "So you can drop this game as quickly as you started it!"

She had never seen anyone look so deadly. Frank intimidated her with his huge bulk and gruff ways, and Willie Joe was mean and unsavory, but this man, this tall, powerfully built stranger with eyes like blue fire possessed a dangerous aura that made the Chesters seem like whining coyotes. He was dressed all in black, with a belt buckle wrought of silver and a gun belt containing two gleaming black six-shooters slung low on his lean hips. She could already bear witness to his tremendous strength, and his riding prowess, and she had a feeling he could handle those guns as well as he did his horse. There was a hardness in his eyes now, a cynical tautness in his face that had not been there a few moments ago, certainly not when he had kissed her. But there was no mistaking the change in his mood, for he looked as cold and dangerous now as a man who has been crossed once too often. She caught her breath, not understanding who he was or what he wanted from her.

"My . . . my husband would kill me if he knew what just happened between us!" she said quickly, filled with belated shame about what she had just done, what she had felt. "Please, let me go home and—"

"*Your husband!*" The stranger sucked in his breath. His hands tensed brutally on her shoulders, though she didn't think he even realized it.

"Frank . . ." she rushed on breathlessly, hoping he would leave her alone when he realized she was married. "Frank Chester. He . . . he has a terrible temper. He doesn't even like me to talk to any other men . . . Oh, what is it?"

A pallor had come over the stranger's features. He seemed suddenly to be carved from marble, or ice, so frozen and still did he become. Yet she sensed the incredible tension gripping his towering frame, felt the deadly rage pumping through him. She winced as his hands nearly crushed the bones of her shoulders; seeing her pain, he released her instantly. But he held her motionless with his eyes, which were riveted upon her face, examining her as if seeing her for the very first time.

"Who are you?" His voice was low, and it sounded strangely frightened. She swallowed hard before replying.

"My name is Katharine . . . Katharine Chester."

At the expression that crossed his features then she felt a shock wave of fear. She took a step backward. Overhead, valley quail squawked and circled, then dipped away, but the two people upon the hillside did not even glance toward them. They were staring as if mesmerized into each other's eyes.

"You don't know me?" the stranger continued after a moment, his deep voice deliberate and soft, as if kept under tight control.

She shook her head.

"They call me Texas." He stepped closer and searched the emerald depths of her eyes as he answered her. "Texas Jim Logan."

She moistened her lips. "What . . . what do you want with me?"

The tall, wide-shouldered cowboy let out his breath. She noticed that his hand was shaking as he pushed back his black sombrero. He seemed stunned, at a complete loss for words.

Bryony's brain whirled in puzzlement at the odd behavior of this man who had chased and captured her, kissed her, and now was stunned by the mention of her husband's name. She started to edge past him, toward the opposite side of the hill, the side that led toward her home, but he stopped her with his voice.

"Wait. Don't go!"

"I want to go home now." Suddenly, tears pricked her eyes. She held her hands out imploringly. "Please ...just let me go!"

He looked at her pleading face, filled with distress and bewilderment. He saw now what he had been too elated and overjoyed to notice earlier. There were hollow lines in that beautiful face, and dark smudges beneath the vivid green eyes. She was thin—thinner than he'd ever seen her before—and she was pale. But more than that, he saw something in her that made his heart twist with fear. She wore a haunted look, an expression of such desolation and anguish emanating from deep within her soul that it shook him to the depths of his being. Bryony—his strong, ravishing, brave Bryony— looked like a creature lost and cornered, hopeless, a woman pushed to the edge of all endurance. As she turned and began to run away from him across the green-carpeted hillside, he didn't move. But he watched her in stunned, devastated horror as she fled swiftly away from him toward whatever place was home.

Jim Logan stood for long minutes without moving. He didn't hear the rush of the sea below or see the lacy clouds drifting across the sapphire-domed sky. He didn't even notice the jackrabbit that peeked out from behind a clump of poppies and then skittered away. Nearby, Pecos grazed contentedly upon the short grass. But Jim stared at the tiny, retreating figure, which could barely be seen in the distance.

Shock had settled over him. It descended upon him like the icy waters of the Pacific, soaking him, numbing him. Standing in the sun, he shivered. He shook his head slowly. Amnesia? Was it possible that Bryony had amnesia? He swore savagely aloud. There had been no mistaking the real confusion he had seen in her. She hadn't known him, hadn't reacted at all even to his name. His blood curdled as he remembered what she had told him. Married to Frank Chester! *But how?* How had she fallen in with him? And what had he done to make her lose her memory and get her to marry him?

He didn't have a single answer. But he did know one thing: Frank Chester was a dead man.

Jim groaned suddenly. He wrestled with the notion of riding after Bryony, of grabbing her and telling her the truth. But something stopped him, just as it had stopped him from telling her a few moments ago, when she had been standing right before him. He recalled the expression upon her delicate, fine-boned face, that look of pain and bewilderment. He also remembered how fragile she had appeared, so haggard and worn. She was obviously weak and under terrible emotional strain.

What if he *had* told her the truth, that she was *his* wife, not Frank Chester's? What if he had told her that her name was Bryony Logan and she belonged to him? She might not have believed him. Worse, she might not have been able to deal with the facts. Fear of her reaction had forced him to keep silent, even though his instincts screamed at him to tell her, to take her away with him. Indecision tore at him. He had found Bryony at last, when his hope had all but disintegrated, but she didn't know him! She didn't even know her own name! A cool, slow agony spread through him as he pondered how deep her terror and loneliness must be. He didn't know a damned thing about amnesia, but he was afraid that if he said or did the wrong thing he might push Bryony over the brink and shatter her already fragile grip on life.

He longed to be able to talk to Doc Webster. That keen-minded, wise physician would surely have been able to advise him. Then he thought of Dr. Brady, Bryony's friend in San Francisco, who had shared the stagecoach with her when she had first come out West. *He* might know what to do. But Jim gave up this notion almost as soon as it entered his brain. Traveling back and forth to San Francisco, not matter how brutally he pushed Pecos, would require several days. And there was no way in hell he would let his wife spend one more night under Frank Chester's roof, or—and with this thought, Jim underwent a torturous agony—in his bed. No, he would get Bryony away from Chester today, even if he had to shoot every man in the county to do it.

The next idea that occurred to him was both practical and easy to accomplish. He mounted Pecos without any further hesitation and headed the horse away from the bay, toward the town. Answers he needed, and answers he would have. Ignoring the throbbing in his wounded shoulder, which had worsened after the vigorous activity of the morning, he concentrated on the situation at hand. The most important thing was Bryony's well-being. He had already sacrificed his own instincts for quick and direct action in order to spare her any further shock, and he would continue to do that if he had to in order to protect her. But somehow, someway, he would get her away from Chester before the sun had gone down on this day. That was a promise he made to himself and to the woman who, though she did not know it, had once been his wife.

CHAPTER NINETEEN

BRYONY TUGGED so hard upon the black strand in her hands that it snapped completely in two. She stared blankly down at the needle and dangling thread while Frank's socks in need of darning lay forgotten in a limp dark pile upon her lap. Her hands were shaking too badly to rethread the needle. She thrust it aside and stood up, the socks falling unnoticed to the parlor floor. She ran to the window, her lilac skirts rustling, and stared out at the hills beyond the valley. Her mind was in a whirl, with thoughts tumbling about frantically. Nothing made sense. She couldn't concentrate on her chores, or upon anything else. She kept thinking of that man, that stranger who had chased her up on the hill and kissed her with such passionate, overwhelming intensity. She had been able to think of nothing else since she had left him and returned home alone more than five hours ago.

She pressed her trembling hands to her cheeks. Her skin was flushed with the memory of that kiss. How could she have done such a thing? It was shameless! True, she had fought against him, trying to escape, but then, when he had held her fast and covered her lips with his, his body pressed so excitingly, intimately against the length of her, she had given in to him with sudden abandon, allowing the mad frenzy of her emotions and the delightful sensations he aroused in her body to overrule all the protestations of her outraged brain. How he had kissed her! Not at all like Frank, for whom she had never once been able to feel the slightest tremor of response. But this man, this Texas Jim Logan, had kissed her with such sweet, dizzying ferocity that he had stolen her breath away and robbed her of her senses. He had demanded a response, and she had given it, effortlessly, joyously, wrapped in a spiraling ecstasy that had swept her far beyond the reaches of the sea.

Texas Jim Logan. She repeated the name to herself, wonder filling her. Who was he? Why had he come after her and . . . and kissed her like that? Everything had happened so quickly and so confusingly that she could barely recall all that had been said between them. She knew only that he had awakened something in her that Frank had never once aroused, and it filled her with shame.

What sort of a woman was she to melt in the arms of a stranger and yet freeze when her own husband claimed her in their bed? She shook her head, praying she would never see Texas Jim Logan again. Maybe then she would forget what he had done to her, what he had stirred in the secret places of her soul. She shut her eyes, trying desperately to block the image of the tall, powerfully built stranger who had ridden into her life this morning and thrown her emotions into such raging turmoil. But she could almost feel the power of his arms encircling her, almost smell that clean, leather-and-pine scent that had tickled her nostrils when he had pulled her close and lowered his lean sun-bronzed face to hers.

Frank and Willie Joe rode into view suddenly, shattering her remembrances. She darted from the window, guilty and tense. Supper! The sun had moved across the valley, and it would be suppertime soon. She hadn't even thought about her preparations.

As soon as the men entered the adobe house Bryony knew that something was wrong. Frank was in a foul temper. He was yelling and cursing, while Willie Joe argued just as volubly. From the kitchen, where she was slicing peppers for chili enchiladas, she heard their loud voices. She stiffened uneasily. She hated it when Frank and Willie Joe argued. It usually resulted in some violence. And Frank was always so rough with her afterward.

"No, damn it, Willie Joe! No, I won't do it! Not with Logan in town!"

"Frank, we can take care of him when we're through with the job! You heard what Forrester said. They're riding out pronto, and if we want to go..."

"You expect me to leave her here with *him* in town? Everett said he saw Logan plain as day right outside the Horton House hotel. And if he knew she was here—"

"If Logan knew she was here, Frank, he'd be bustin' down that door right now!" Willie Joe exploded. "Come on, Frank, let's get our gear. Those boys are goin' to take in a pretty penny with this job, and there's no reason why we can't share in it. We'll jest..."

Bryony had crept to the door at the sound of the argument, and she caught some of their words. But it was the mention of Logan that made her heart start to hammer wildly. *If Logan knew she was here...* What did Willie Joe mean?

"Katharine!" She started guiltily at Frank's voice, realizing he had spotted her hovering behind the door.

"Frank, I...I heard you come in..." she stammered, but he cut her off and waved his arm at her.

"Come in here, Katharine. I've got to talk to you."

She put down the pepper and the knife on the wooden worktable and wiped her hands on her apron as she walked into the parlor. Frank was pacing nervously while Willie Joe fairly buzzed with suppressed excitement. She glanced uneasily from one to the other.

"Frank, what is going on?"

"Did you hear us talkin'?" he barked, wheeling upon her suddenly and grasping her arm. "Did you hear what we said? Answer me, Katharine!"

"No, I... I just heard Willie Joe say something about getting your gear. Frank, are you going away?"

He stared down at her, breathing heavily. Bryony didn't know why she had lied or why she didn't ask him openly about Logan. But some inner voice warned her to keep quiet about the conversation she had just heard.

"Yep, I reckon I am going away," he said at last, and Willie Joe let out a whoop. "But it's only for a few days. Willie Joe and I have some business to tend to. We'll be back as quick as we can." His shrewd eyes pierced hers. "But before we go, honey, I've got to warn you about something."

She grew very still. "What is it?"

"Whilst we were over at Forrester's, Jed Everett rode in from town and said he'd just seen a man named Logan that Willie Joe and I used to know." His fingers tightened on her arm, and he stared at her with fierce intensity. "Does that name mean anything to you at all, Katharine? Logan—Texas Jim Logan."

She shook her head, fearful that the pounding of her heart would give her away. The same instinct that had prompted her to deny overhearing the conversation kept her from revealing that she had met that very man today. What would Frank do if he knew that she had encountered Logan and fallen into his arms like a loose saloon woman? Cold fear swept through her, and again she shook her head. "N... no, Frank. I never heard that name before. Did I know him back in El Paso?"

Willie Joe smirked, and Frank glanced at him briefly before turning his attention back to Bryony. "He's one man you never want to meet up with, honey. I don't mean to scare you or nothin', but Texas Jim Logan is about the meanest hombre in the whole West. He's a gunfighter. You know what that is? A gun for hire. He kills for money, Katharine, and sometimes just for the fun of it. He hates me and Willie Joe something fierce. And we hate him. You see, darlin', Texas Jim Logan killed our brother."

She gasped, and he nodded in response to her horrified expression. "Yep. Our youngest brother, Tommy, was shot down in cold blood by Logan three years ago. Willie Joe and me swore to kill him. But he's a plumb dangerous man, and we ain't never been able to pull it off. But maybe, when we get back from this business we've got to tend to in, uh, Cedar Gap, we'll do our best to rid this world of Mister Texas Jim Logan."

"Damn straight!" Willie Joe swaggered forward. "This time we'll see that hombre crawl!"

Frank looked down into Bryony's pale face. "Are you scared, honey? Well, I'm sorry, but you had to know. If Logan knew my pretty little wife was hereabouts, he'd come after you for sure. I shudder to think what he'd do to you if he had the chance, just for spite. He's known to have raped women before, and I reckon he'd do it again. He's like an animal, honey; he don't care who he hurts or who he kills. Do you understand what I'm sayin'?"

Bryony felt the earth spinning beneath her feet, and she put a hand to her head to steady herself. What Frank had just told her filled her with horror, and she went cold from terror. "Frank, don't leave!" she begged suddenly, clutching at his shirt. "If that man is in town, he might... he might..."

"Sh, honey, don't you worry." Frank smoothed her

dark, tumbling hair back from her brow. He grinned down at her and spoke soothingly. "Logan doesn't know a thing about you bein' here. He doesn't even know Willie Joe and I live in these parts. You're safe, honey. You're completely safe."

"But..." She ought to tell him about this morning, she *had* to tell him, but she was too frightened of his reaction to do so. "But Frank..."

"Let's ride, Frank." Willie Joe rubbed his hands together and started toward his room. "Forrester said they're leavin' *pronto*. Let's go."

"Yeah, yeah." Frank still gazed down at Bryony. "Look, honey, the only reason I told you all this is so you'll take precautions. Stay inside the house while Willie Joe and I are gone. Don't go out, don't visit anyone or ride into town, or nothin'. Just lay low, and we'll be back before you know it. Then, if Logan's still hanging around in town, we'll take care of him once and for all."

He grabbed her, kissed her, and released her abruptly. She rubbed the wetness from her lips as he strode to their bedroom to pack his gear.

If Bryony's thoughts had been whirling before, now they were cast into a veritable frenzy. Icy terror rushed through her as she realized she had been alone with a cold-blooded killer, a ruthless gunman, and one who hated her husband at that! Now she understood the deadly expression that had come over Texas Jim Logan's face when she had mentioned Frank's name. Now she knew why he had seemed so dangerous, so harsh and cold when only a few moments before...

But for each answer to her earlier bewilderment, new questions arose. Texas Jim Logan hadn't hurt her, as Frank had warned he would do. He had kissed her. He hadn't prevented her from leaving, even though he knew she was married to Frank. He had let her go.

Frank's dire words didn't precisely fit what had happened today. And yet, it was plain that Texas Jim Logan was a dangerous man, that he hated Frank Chester, that he would make an implacable foe...

She was confused. She needed time and quietude to sort out this situation. But there was no opportunity for reflection; scarcely moments later, both Frank and Willie Joe barged from their separate rooms with their packs in tow and stamped to the door. Bryony followed them out onto the porch.

"You take care, honey." Frank loaded his saddle pack on his roan, which was hitched right in the yard. "I'll see you in a few days."

"Adios, Katharine." Willie Joe pinched her bottom as he sidled by, throwing a feral grin over his shoulder. "I'll be seein' you right soon."

Frank started to mount the roan, then glanced back at Bryony standing so still upon the porch. The breeze ruffled her dark hair and blew the skirts of her lilac gown. He started toward her, his face filled with regret.

"I'm gonna miss you tonight, honey," he announced. "I'll miss you real bad." He bounded onto the porch once more and put his arms around her. Then he leaned down and kissed her long and hard, his mouth assaulting her lips with rough enjoyment. He threw back his head and laughed when at last he released her.

"There's lots more where that came from, Katharine. You wait till I get back and I'll show you!" he promised. Then he clambered back to the roan and mounted, still chuckling. Willie Joe had already kicked his mustang forward, and as Frank joined him, they galloped off together in a gray whirlwind of dust.

Bryony watched them go, feeling a mixture of relief and dismay. She would have been even more unnerved if she had known that she was not the only person present watching the men and horses disappear over a distant ridge.

From his hiding place beyond a clump of oaks, Jim Logan had seen everything. A raging fury possessed him when he saw Frank Chester grab Bryony—*his* Bryony—and kiss her with such brutal pleasure. His hand had flashed downward to the Colt at his hip, and he had come perilously close to killing Chester in one blinding, furious instant. But the rigid self-control for which he was famous reasserted itself in time, clamping down upon his emotions.

He had to think of Bryony! What would it do to her to see the man she thought was her husband shot down before her eyes in an explosion of blood and bones? It might very well destroy her. He couldn't take the risk. No, Jim told himself as he gritted his teeth in frustration, he had to do this thing another way. He had to remember the advice of Doc Peese in town. Or else he might lose Bryony all over again—this time for good.

He waited as the Chester brothers rode away, reviewing again what Doc Peese had told him today when he'd ridden into town and sought out the local physician. His nurse, Norah Clark, had been taken aback by the towering, determined cowboy who had entered the office and demanded to see the doctor at once, but she had hurried to comply with his request. And afterward, she had offered quiet sympathy when Peese finished his analysis of the problem.

The doctor had never before treated a case of amnesia, but he had read of it in medical journals. He referred to one case in particular, a pianist, an Englishwoman by the name of Lana Rutherford, who had been blinded in a carriage accident that had also left her without her memory. The doctor asserted that this woman had even forgotten how to play the piano as a result of her memory loss, but gradually, through slow encouragement, she had not only learned to play despite her blindness, but had regained her memory completely. "Amnesia can be cured," Peese had informed him. "But it can be a slow, painstaking process. The patient must have time to come to terms with the trauma that caused the affliction. Sudden shocks and disturbances are to be avoided whenever possible. In the situation you describe, telling your wife the truth of her identity and the deception that has been practiced upon her could be disastrous. It could have serious consequences to her sanity in general and would probably do nothing to bring back her memory." Jim grimaced, remembering the doctor's grave words. "Whatever you do, Mr. Logan, don't tell her outright what has happened. You must wait for her to discover it herself. There is every possibility that, given time, she may do so."

So he had to wait. He had to be very careful. He couldn't risk pushing Bryony over the edge. But he was damned certain he wasn't going to let her remain with Frank Chester any longer. What he planned to do next would be a shock for her, and he prayed she could withstand it. He was counting on the inner strength she'd always possessed to see her through. It would have to. He had no choice but to get her far away from the Chesters, and quickly. Jim didn't know where Frank and Willie Joe were headed, but he had observed their bulging saddle packs with satisfaction. Their timely departure was a lucky break for him. He and Bryony would be long gone before the brothers returned from their trip. Jim knew how to lose himself so that no one could find him, and that was exactly what he intended to do.

He straightened from his crouching position as Bryony turned toward the house once more. He braced himself for what he had to do next. Then, moving swiftly and stealthily, he sprinted forward.

She never heard his approach. Her mind was so

consumed with her problems that when she felt herself grasped firmly from behind and held steadfast in iron hands, it came as a complete surprise.

She screamed. The sound echoed through the deserted valley, but a hand quickly covered her mouth.

"Quiet. If they ride back here, I'll kill them."

It was him! She gave a muffled cry as he pulled against him. She began to fight with all of her strength.

"It's no use," he said in a grim, hard tone as she flailed against his restraining arms. "You can't get away from me. Don't fight me, and you'll be fine. I won't hurt you."

She continued to kick and writhe, and he spun her around, releasing her as she faced him. The moment he let her go, she darted toward the house, prepared to slam the door in his face. But he was too swift for her, and he grabbed her before she had even reached the door. He shook her arms.

"Listen to me!" His cobalt eyes glinted in the fading afternoon light. "I won't hurt you! But like it or not, you're coming with me!"

"Why? Where?" she gasped, her skin whitening as she gazed up into his harsh, determined face.

"Far away from here. I'm sorry to tell you this, little tenderfoot, but you're being kidnapped!"

"No!" Panic twisted through her. She kicked out at him again, uselessly, since he held her at arm's length. "Let me go! You'll never get away with this!"

"I reckon I will," he drawled coolly. It was all he could do to feign calmness, to keep his own emotions under check in order to protect hers. "Now don't worry. I said I wouldn't hurt you, and I won't. But you're coming with me sure as night is going to fall. And I want to be far from here before sunup, so let's get moving."

He took a tight grip on her arm and began propelling her toward the barn. Fear pumped through

Bryony's heart. She tried to break away, but he held her fast, forcing her into the barn. He glanced suddenly at the tall, magnificent black stallion snorting in its stall. Holding her with one hand, he reached for a bridle with the other.

"You don't expect me to ride that wild beast, do you?" she cried in horror. "I . . . I can't! He throws Frank and Willie Joe whenever they try to ride him!"

Texas Jim Logan cast her a long look. "You're afraid of this horse? Well, you don't have to ride him tonight, but I'll bring him along anyway."

But when he started to slip the bridle over the stallion's head, Bryony saw her chance. She wrenched away and ran for the barn door. Cursing, Texas Tim Logan leaped after her. She wept in frustration as he grabbed her once again.

"I won't go with you!" she screamed, twisting futilely in his arms. "I'll fight you every step of the way! I'll run as soon as your back is turned!"

"So, you haven't lost *all* your spirit!" Logan muttered as he pulled her against him. "That's a good sign, little tenderfoot."

"What are you talking about?" she demanded, filled with desperation. "Why won't you just leave me alone?"

"I can't do that." He glanced about, his face grim. "I'm going to have to tie you up, I reckon. I'm sorry, but you don't leave me any choice. We've got to get out of here pronto, and you keep delaying things."

"No! I . . . I promise, I won't run away anymore! Don't do this!" She gasped as he lifted a rope from a bench. Texas Jim Logan's jaw tightened.

"Hold still."

She bit her lip in anguish as he tied her wrists behind her back, but was surprised that the knot, though firm, was by no means cruelly fastened. He let go of her then and turned his attention to the black stallion, saddling it and slipping the bridle over its proud, glossy head. Then he led the beast from the stall and took Bryony's arm once more, dragging her along with him.

His own horse, the bay she had seen earlier that morning on the hill, was hidden away in a clump of trees not far from the house. He untethered it, secured the black with a lead rope, then hoisted Bryony into the saddle, all in a matter of seconds. Then he vaulted into the saddle behind her, holding her upright with his hard-muscled arms.

Bryony gave a sob as he spurred the bay forward. She glanced frantically at the lovely, green-golden valley that had been her home, wondering if she would ever see it again. The sun would be setting soon, and nightfall would find her ... where? Somewhere out in the wilderness with this killer, this gunman who raped and murdered at will, who had already shown her the ruthlessness of which he was capable. Terror rose within her, and she trembled uncontrollably, remembering all of Frank's warning words.

She was agonizingly aware of Jim Logan's strong, muscular frame pressed against her back, of his arms hemming her in on either side as he gripped the reins. She shut her eyes tight, then opened them again quickly as dizziness made her sway in the saddle. The oaks and manzanitas whipped by, the wild flowers were a blur of color as the bay stallion galloped southward, straight toward the border of Mexico. To Bryony, helpless and terrified, it seemed she was riding straight into hell.

CHAPTER TWENTY

AFTER FOUR hours of hard riding, Jim Logan reined his stallion to a halt on a flat clearing beneath a rocky bluff. Bryony slumped in the saddle, weary beyond measure. She didn't even have the strength to glance around her to appraise her surroundings. When Jim dismounted and reached up to help her off the horse, she collapsed in his arms, her knees buckling. He tightened his hold about her waist to keep her from falling as her feet touched ground.

"Where are we?"

Her small, delicate face was whiter than chalk as she lifted frightened eyes to meet his cool blue gaze. Staring up at him now, she found it hard to believe that he was the same man who had kissed her with such tender, searing passion only this morning. He looked so cold now, so forbidding. There was no warmth in his lean, Texan face, only a hard impassivity. She trembled like a fragile flower in his arms.

"We're in Mexico. That's all you need to know. We're headed toward a place about four days' ride from here. Meantime, we'll camp here for the night and get an early start tomorrow."

He stared down at her with a kind of steely calm, his voice as steady and matter-of-fact as though they were polite acquaintances chancing to meet in town. His very casualness chilled her. He acted as though he kidnapped people every day of his life. She fought back an impulse to weep in helpless despair as she realized that none of this mattered to him. None of it. No doubt he would as soon kill her as take her along. What was it Frank had said? "He's known to have raped women before, and I reckon he'd do it again. He's like an animal, honey; he don't care who he hurts or who he kills."

She swallowed hard, trying to speak with a semblance of calm despite the apprehension coursing through her. "At least... at least have the decency to untie this rope," she began, meeting his piercing gaze with a bravado she was far from feeling. "Unless you are afraid I shall overpower you and get away."

He grinned at this, his handsome features lighting with amusement. For the first time, humanity warmed the cold planes of his face, making him look somehow younger and less remote. He put a hand under her chin, forcing her to meet his eyes. "Do you really think I'm afraid of you, little tenderfoot?" he asked softly. His lips curled upward in a sardonic, yet not ungentle smile. "You wound me."

"I'd like to wound you!" she cried suddenly, her eyes flashing in her pale face. "I'd like to put a bullet through your heart!"

"I reckon you would." The grin deepened. Texas Jim Logan turned her about and began working at the knot that bound her wrists. "But I don't expect you'll get the chance, *querida*."

"*Querida!*" she gasped. "How... how dare you call me that! I would never willingly associate with a man like you—not ever! I... I hate you! And I hate what you stand for!"

He slipped the rope from her wrists and spun her to face him once again. "What I stand for?" he asked quietly. There was no amusement in his face now. "What do you know about what I stand for?"

"My husband told me all about you! I know what you are! A gunfighter, a hired killer! You are a member of the most despicable breed of men!"

Something flickered in his face, something far from laughter. Something she had said had punctured that infuriatingly cool nonchalance, penetrated his calm, careless air of amusement. She was glad! The victory spurred her to forget all caution. She blazed on, glaring at him from beneath her tangled mane of hair. "So. You didn't think I was aware of your identity. Well, I am! I know, Mister Texas Jim Logan, that you killed my husband's brother. I know that you are the lowest kind of cruel, lawless scum! I know that—"

"I reckon that's about enough!" he growled, gripping her arm suddenly. The cold glint in his eyes sent a shaft of renewed fear straight to her heart. "I'm not the least bit interested in what you know or what you think you know! If I were you, lady, I'd save my breath and save my strength. You've got a lot of hard riding ahead of you, and tonight was only the beginning."

She caught her breath, terror rushing back as he towered above her, holding her arm in that unbreakable grip. She well remembered his strength, how effortlessly he had imprisoned her. And now, reading the fury that darkened his face and feeling anew her pathetic vulnerability, she cursed her own folly in baiting him. "I'm sorry," she breathed. "P . . . please, let me go. You're hurting my arm."

He released her abruptly. For a long moment, he stared into her pale, shaken face, his jaw tightening. Then he tipped his black hat lower over his eyes. "My apologies, ma'am," he drawled. "I reckon I got a mite carried away." With these words, he sketched her a bow she could only interpret as mockery and then turned away, directing his attention to tethering the horses and making camp.

Bryony watched him and rubbed her chafed wrists. She was filled with wonder at her own temerity. She had never dared speak in such a way to Frank, her own husband. Yet here she was, openly antagonizing Texas Jim Logan. She must be mad! In the future, she realized, drawing a deep breath, she had better watch her step. If she ever truly angered him, Logan would be unlikely to show her the smallest bit of mercy.

She passed a weary hand across her brow. After her brief, angry outburst, fatigue returned, seeping through her body. She sank upon a wide rock as she glanced about the clearing, wondering dully if there was any means by which she might escape her captor. Her spirits sank still further as she realized the futility of this hope. Sunset had long ago lavished the sky with its pastel palette, and now lavender dusk deepened over the mountaintops in the distance. It would be dark before long. She had no idea where she was. Somewhere in Mexico, at the base of a range of barren hills, which stuck up out of the desert floor like huge, swollen thumbs. Agave and ocotillo were everywhere. Red-rock boulders formed strange statues beneath the hills, and all was stark, forbidding, and wild. They were in the midst of a desolate land, far from any human habitation. A lizard watched her from a nearby rock. Eagles swooped overhead, and there was a furtive rustling from behind some bushes only a few feet away at the base of the bluff, a sound that made Bryony's skin prickle uneasily.

She left the rock and edged closer to Jim Logan, wondering if the unseen beast might be a mountain lion. Despair rose within her. Even if she could manage to steal Logan's horse, which way should she ride? She could get lost for days out here without ever meeting another human being. And without a weapon, she would be defenseless against snakes or cougars or any wild beast she might encounter. No, she realized in frustration so bitter it made her want to scream, she couldn't get away even if she had the means to ride off. She needed Jim Logan. Without his guidance and protection, she might never find her way back to civilization. But, she thought with a faint glimmer of hope, as soon as they passed near a town or a village, or saw one single human soul, she would try to get help and somehow escape. She would try to get away from Texas Jim Logan if it was the last thing she ever did.

A short time later she sat silently before a small campfire, chewing beef jerky and staring at the midnight-blue sky, which was ablaze with stars like millions of tiny candle flames. A cool breeze touched her bare arms, and she inched closer to the fire, shivering. Night rustled softly all round her, its quietude broken occasionally by the faraway mournful bark of a coyote. She felt Logan's gaze on her and slowly turned her head to meet it.

He sat just beyond the fire, his handsome face half in shadow. From beneath his black sombrero, she could just make out the outline of his strong, rugged features and the cobalt glint of his eyes. Yet his expression she could not determine. He was watching her, calmly, steadily, but with what thoughts? What lay hidden beneath that cool and arrogant exterior?

Bryony felt a tremor go through her. She pushed away the rest of the jerky and reached for a water canteen, drinking deeply. When she had set down the canteen once more, Logan's gaze still pierced her. She met it again, warily, a strange uneasy tension beginning to knot inside her.

At last, unable to endure the silence any longer,

she spoke. "What do you want with me?" she asked.

He made no answer.

Desperation drove her to press on. "The least you can do is explain to me why you've taken me from my home, my husband. I've done nothing to injure you."

He took a drag upon his thin cigar, then tossed it into the fire. "I have no intention of harming you. There's no need to be afraid."

"Then why am I here? I don't understand."

"I have a score to settle with Chester," he replied at last, grimly. "An old, deadly score. You're the means of settling it."

"The means of settling it." She stared down at her hands. "I might have known. Frank warned me you would do something like this. Before he left, he told me all about you. I guess I didn't want to believe it." Her eyes smoldered when she glanced up at him again. "It's not fair, you know! I've never harmed you!"

"And I don't intend to harm you."

"You have no principles," she muttered through clenched teeth. "No notion of what is decent or right or just. Or maybe you simply don't care about those things." Her lip trembled. "Maybe you don't care about anything."

He regarded her, his features cool. "You're wrong, little tenderfoot. I care a lot about some things."

"What?" she cried, rounding on him in contempt. "I'd like to know what!"

With lightning swiftness, he was on his feet then. He reached her side in two quick strides, yanking her up beside him. He loomed above her as they stood beneath the soft September sky, and it was as if they were the only living people in all the world. "You will, little tenderfoot," he promised huskily. "You'll know all about me before this is over."

"I d... don't want to know about you!" Bryony took a step backward, alarmingly aware of a change in the air between them. To her chagrin, Texas Jim Logan stepped closer. She quickly retreated another pace, but she trod upon a pebble and lost her footing. She would have fallen but for his arm, which swiftly encircled her waist. He pulled her close against him, so close she could feel the thunder of his heart. His hands felt warm and strong at her waist. The pressure of his fingers sent an odd excitement pulsing through her blood. Panic assailed her. "I don't want to know about you!" she cried again. "I... I want to go home!"

"Home? To Frank Chester?"

"Y... yes!"

"Why? Do you love him?" There was a new harshness in Logan's voice, a tension she didn't understand. His eyes were colder than mountain frost, and his fingers bit into her flesh. She cried out, and he loosened his grip, but did not let her go.

"Do you? Do you love him?" He pelted the question at her with relentless savagery.

"Yes!" She dropped her head to hide the telltale tears that sparkled on her lashes. "He... he's my husband. I... belong with him!" Tears of misery slipped down her cheeks. "Let me go!" she cried, overwhelmed by the emotions that suddenly crashed through her. "I can't think when you hold me like this! Let me go!"

She wrenched away and darted around to the opposite side of the campfire, covering her face with her hands. Jim Logan could hear her muffled weeping. Unbeknownst to her, he exerted a powerful control to bring his own roiling emotions under check. Slowly, steeling himself, he moved toward her. He spoke with deliberate calm, which cost him more than she could ever guess.

"I'm sorry." His voice was quiet in her ear. It had

a reassuring effect after the strange intensity of their last exchange. She felt his hand upon her shoulder, his touch light, yet strong. "I didn't mean to upset you."

Bryony struggled for self-control. She was grateful for the neckerchief he handed her and used it to wipe the tears from her cheeks. Jim Logan's presence so close to her had a disturbing effect. Though he no longer seemed angry or threatening, she was very aware of his nearness, of the powerful, driving masculinity that emanated from his tall and muscular frame. His breath rustled her hair. She fought against a strange trembling that threatened to overwhelm her. With great effort, she spoke. "How long do you . . . plan to keep me with you, Mr. Logan?"

"That all depends. A month. Maybe two." Logan's reply was casual. "I'll send a ransom note to Chester in a few weeks. Then we'll see what happens."

"What if he doesn't want me back? What if he won't pay the ransom?"

"What man wouldn't pay a king's ransom to get you back?" he said very softly. Struck by his words, and by something in his voice, she turned slowly to face him.

She regarded him in wonderment. In the pale starlight, she looked very delicate, very beautiful. Her coalblack hair fluttered in the evening breeze, its long, thick mass framing her fine-boned face. Her sensuous lips were parted. Eyes of dark, brilliant green glowed beneath long lashes, holding Jim Logan spellbound. The lilac dress she wore was now dusty and crumpled, but it still showed her slender, softly curved figure to fetching advantage. Yet she appeared oblivious of her beauty, oblivious of the powerful emotions she stirred in him, oblivious of everything but the man who stood tall and resolute before her. She took a long, deep breath, her gaze locked with his, while unspoken thoughts flowed between them. Then, slowly, her graceful hands lifted in a gesture of appeal.

"Please. Won't you let me go?" she whispered. "I only want to go home." Her eyes searched his. "I don't believe you are as awful as my husband claims. You . . . you have been decent to me, kinder than I had hoped. I believe there is some goodness in you. If this is true, I beg you to abandon this scheme of revenge and take me back to my home."

He pushed back his sombrero and regarded her for a long minute before speaking. "I reckon I can't do that, little tenderfoot," he said with awful finality. "I've got quite a stake in this myself. You're worth a lot to me, more than you know. From now on, we stay together until this thing is over. So you may as well accept the idea and make the best of it. You're stuck with me, like it or not."

All hope died within her as she heard this reply and gazed into those vivid blue eyes, so unyielding and cold. She had been wrong. There was no kindness in him, no decency. He was indeed everything Frank had said. She had been mistaken ever to have imagined otherwise. Frustration welled up within her, and she clenched her fists.

"I don't like it!" she cried, her voice trembling, for she could no longer control her anger. "And I don't like you to call me little tenderfoot!" Absurdly, her wrath centered on the least of his crimes. "If . . . if you're going to insist on making me your prisoner, the least you could do is to call me by my name. It's Katharine! Katharine Chester!"

Logan gave her a keen, hard look. Then he turned away, unstrapping his bedroll from the saddle pack. "It's time to turn in, little tenderfoot," he drawled.

"Ohhhh!" She screeched in frustration, but he merely tossed a second bedroll at her feet.

"Here. This one's for you. Unless you care to share mine tonight."

"No, I certainly do not!" She watched him in some apprehension after this remark, but he made no effort to approach her, appearing intent only upon arranging his sleeping comfort.

Bryony bit her lip, remembering all too well the dizzying, masterful way he had kissed her this morning upon the hill. She dragged her bedroll as far from his as was possible within the small clearing, then sat down upon it in some nervousness. The memories of his embrace, as well as her own shameless response to it, stirred her agitation until Logan could not help but notice. He sent her an appraising glance.

"Don't worry, I'm not going to rape you," he remarked. "Calm down. I like my women willing, *querida.* And besides, I promised not to hurt you, remember? Don't you believe me?"

"I want to believe you," she replied, fixing him with a wary look.

"Then get some sleep and forget all that hogwash Frank Chester told you about me." He faced her squarely and spoke with quiet reassurance. "Whatever else I am, and whatever else I do, attacking women is not one of my pastimes. So get some rest. You're going to need it."

Bryony found it difficult to doubt him when he looked at her that way, his handsome face no longer hardened with mockery. She almost thought she read compassion in his countenance, but realized she was being absurd. Nevertheless, her pulsebeat jumped as his gaze touched her and his strong, sensuously shaped lips curved upward in a slight smile.

"Good night, little tenderfoot," he said softly, and she felt a flush travel upward, heating her throat and cheeks. His voice had been almost a caress, arousing a strange fluttering within her.

"Good night," she answered, a shade too quickly. She averted her eyes and turned to her bedding, busying herself with arranging the blanket he had tossed to her. She peeped across at him as he settled his long form onto his own bedroll. To her relief, he did not even glance toward her.

Maybe he was speaking the truth. He *had* given his word not to harm her. She could only pray that he would hold to it. But she was besieged by doubts. After all, what was the value of a gunman's vow? Only a man of utter heartlessness could do what he was doing and be so calm and unemotional about it. Hadn't he taken her prisoner for no good reason? Hadn't he stolen her from her home and carried her off against her will, subjecting her to riding for hours with her hands tied behind her back, with the wind flailing her face, with no idea where she was headed or what was in store for her? She shivered in her bed, recalling his cool nonchalance. A man like Jim Logan was capable of anything. *Anything.* How could she trust such a man?

She couldn't. Yet, as she lay beneath the black Mexican sky, the cool night air fanning her cheek, she felt sleep coming upon her despite the jumble of emotions under which she labored. Her tense, weary body sank into relaxation almost against her will. It was odd indeed, she mused, struggling against eyelids that seemed suddenly weighted. At home every night with Frank she lay awake for hours, twisting and turning in her bed, yearning for something she could not define. Yet here in this desolate land, alone with this dangerous stranger, she felt herself succumbing to the sweet allure of slumber despite her efforts to think and plan and fret. She floated into dreaminess, feeling oddly light and free.

All of her troubles and all of the disturbing, conflicting emotions that tormented her receded. *Tomorrow*, she thought hazily, as the lovely soft cloud of sleep descended upon her. *Tomorrow I'll sort it all out. I'll find a way to escape. Tomorrow I will try to get away...*

She was deeply asleep when Jim Logan came and knelt beside her. He studied her face, in sleep as innocent and peaceful as a child's. He restained the impulse to stroke her cheek, to touch her glistening black hair. He longed to kiss her, but steeled himself against such a move. If she awoke, she would be terrified. He had to reassure her that he meant her no harm, that he would not force himself upon her. She had to learn to trust him again, and that trust was something he would have to earn. It would take time, Jim knew.

The sparkling, joyous Bryony he had married was locked away somewhere within this frightened, wary shell of a girl called Katharine Chester. It would not be easy to free her. Time and patience and self-restraint were required from him, and—damn it—he would abide by those requirements. Despite the fact that he wanted to enfold her in his arms and kiss away every fear in her soul, to swear his love for her and beg her forgiveness for all he had done in the past to hurt her, he would have to feign calm disinterest and keep himself at a good distance from her. Too many times tonight he had come close to losing his grip on his emotions. It had taken all of his self-restraint to keep from sweeping her into his arms and showering her with kisses, to keep from telling her that she was in truth *his* wife, *his* love, and that he would never let her go again. This was a harsh penance to pay for his sins, but he would pay it for Bryony's sake. And maybe, if he was damned lucky, she would remember him one day, and perhaps, if he was even luckier, she might find it in her heart to forgive.

Like a sentinel he stood over her far into the night.

He leaned against a boulder, smoking, as the stars swam above, his mind filled with memories of a girl who had once shone brighter than any moon or sun, whose spirit had flown like a fearless, graceful bird across the morning sky. Once he had cursed that spirit, cursed the defiant energy that had marked her as strongly as had her beauty and charm. He had cast her off because of it, sending her out into a night of storm from which she had never returned. He still didn't know all that had befallen her as a result of that night. He had no idea how she had fallen in with Frank and Willie Joe Chester, and now, he didn't care. He had her safe, under his protection once more. And he would see to it that no one harmed her again. But he wanted back the Bryony whom he had loved before, that brave and laughing girl. She had shown some little sign of spirit tonight, and he had been glad to see it, but it had been nothing to compare with the way she had once been. She was even afraid of Shadow, the horse so wild none had been able to ride him until she herself had gentled him and made him her own.

Jim's heart ached at the vast change in her. How he longed to see those emerald eyes spark with fire and to see that dainty chin lift in the old, infuriatingly defiant way! Once he would have crushed her spirit, for he had damned it like the fool he was, but now he wanted only to bring back his beautiful fiery girl, who had matched his pride with her own and who had forever conquered his heart. He would wait for her. He would give her time. And gradually, cautiously, he would offer her whatever tenderness she would take from a man who had stolen her from her "husband" and from her only remembered home.

CHAPTER TWENTY-ONE

MORNING FOUND Bryony in a far from tranquil state of mind. Under the pale-yellow glare of the desert sun, the world around her appeared harsh and frightening once more, and the man who packed and loaded up the horses with such deft efficiency appeared as intimidating as a sleek and deadly cougar. He had changed his clothing before she had awakened and was this morning garbed in a light-blue linen shirt of expensive cut and style, a shirt that appeared almost molded to his broad-shouldered, well-muscled physique. It was tucked snugly into the dark-blue trousers, which encased his lean hips and powerful thighs. A neckerchief of blue silk was loosely knotted about his neck, and the black hat, black boots, and silver-buckled gun belt that completed his attire gave him a cool, dangerous appearance as he prepared to ride out into the Mexican desert beneath the fiercely blazing morning sun.

Bryony watched him warily as he folded their bedrolls into two neat bundles and then secured them across the saddle of the black stallion. He had shaved somehow while she slept, and he appeared crisp and clean. His chestnut hair gleamed in the sunlight. He

261

was undeniably handsome. And in a hurry. He had not spoken to her at all yet, and he seemed intent on getting on with the journey as quickly as possible.

She, on the other hand, felt dirty and bedraggled as she sat upon a boulder in silence. Her gown of yesterday was filthy, and there was a rip in the skirt. Her hair fell in a tangled mass around her face. She felt unequal to another day of battling Texas Jim Logan. She recalled her angry outbursts of last evening with incredulity today, wondering at her own courage in clashing with him. Had she been mad, speaking to him so? What if he had grown angry? He was capable of anything, any kind of violence; that she knew from Frank. And yet, she remembered, shaking her head in wonderment, he *had* been angry. Still, he had not hurt her, nor even threatened her. All the same, she thought this morning, regarding his strong figure with distrust, one could never tell with a man like him. A man who killed for money, who raped and murdered at will...

"Let's ride." Texas Jim Logan turned from beside the bay stallion and held out his arm to her. He spoke curtly. "Come on. I'm in a hurry. You never know who could be breathing down our necks."

She rose from the rock and walked slowly toward him. "Do you mean Frank and Willie Joe?" An idea occurred to her. "Well, they will be back this morning. They'll come in search of me when they find me gone. And they're bound to know that you had something to do with my disappearance."

"I reckon so," he responded with a smile.

She clutched his sleeve. "Frank will be furious. He'll kill you if he catches up to us. Why don't you take me back before they come after us? He... he's a dangerous man, Texas. I wouldn't want to be in your boots if he finds that you've kidnapped me."

His handsome face broke into laughter. "So you

think I'm afraid of Frank Chester and that no-good brother of his? I'm much obliged." He tossed her up into the saddle with a grin. "It won't work, *querida*. I'm not taking you back. And as for that tall tale about the Chester boys coming home today, I doubt that very much. I saw them ride out yesterday, and their saddle packs were full. My guess is they won't be returning from their little trip for several days. By then we'll be long gone."

She bit her lip, cursing his perceptiveness. "Yes, but you said you're worried about our being followed. If it's not Frank and Willie Joe you're concerned about, then who?"

He shrugged and mounted behind her. "No one in particular. But I don't like to take chances. What if Frank does come back early for some reason? What if he's asked one of his pards to check up on you? Any number of things could happen. It's unlikely, but I prefer to cover all the odds. So, we're going to ride out early and keep to the hills. Later in the morning we'll stop for some chow. But first I want to get some miles between us and that pretty little valley back there that you call your home. So hang on to your hat, lady. We're going to ride!"

They left the campsite in a swirl of dust. Bryony had to admire the way he had erased all evidence of their presence there. He hadn't lied when he said he left nothing to chance. Jim Logan was thorough, swift, and cool-headed in all that he did. It made him a formidable foe. And this morning, faced with his keenness, energy, and strength, she cherished little hope of outwitting or persuading him. There seemed no hope of escaping from him today for he seemed unlikely to make any mistakes that would lead to her freedom.

They covered more than twenty miles that day, keeping, as Jim Logan had decided, close to the hills.

It was a hard, tedious ride, made monotonous by the constant cloud of dust kicked up by the horses' hooves, by the barrenness of the hills, and by the dull glare of the desert sun. Fortunately for Bryony, they made frequent stops allowing her to rest and eat. Logan's consideration surprised her, for though he said little, his actions gave every appearance of concern for her well-being. Bryony was unused to such solicitude. When she had ridden across the desert to California with Frank and Willie Joe they had given little thought to her comfort, ignoring the strains that their grueling pace wrought upon her. Yet, Jim Logan, for all his cool air of indifference, made certain that she had ample opportunity to rest, eat, and drink, and she often felt him watching her, as if studying the effects of the journey on her constitution. Some of her fear of him subsided. He baffled her, for she could not reconcile the hardened gunman who had kidnapped her for revenge with the man who took such care for her welfare. Yet, she could not help being grateful for his treatment. She found at least some of her fear easing as his attitude made it clear that he indeed intended her no physical harm.

She thought about him for a long time that night before falling off to sleep, her mind returning against her will to yesterday morning, when he had kissed her by the sea. That strange, unsettling warmth again spread through her with these memories, and she struggled to banish them from her mind. Yet, every time she had sat before him in the saddle, with his arms around her, the same unwanted, churning emotions were set spinning inside her, emotions she didn't understand and was ashamed to experience. It was a curiously pleasurable torment to sit so close to him upon the mighty bay stallion. After hours in the saddle, it was impossible not to lean back against him, and when she did she was keenly conscious of the hard muscles of his chest and

arms, of his strength and assurance in the saddle, of the
intimate pressure of his thighs as they touched hers
while they rode. All these stirred her in ways she found
delicious and new, heating her blood until it rushed in
her ears. She tried to hide her feelings from him, horrified by her own response. Never once in all their coupling had Frank evoked such sensations in her, yet this
stranger aroused them by his slightest touch or glance.
It was disturbing, and it filled her with wonder. Try as
she might, she could not shut him from her mind.

On the third day they stopped at a village for supplies. Her dress was by now in tatters, and Logan bought
her durable riding clothes: three cotton plaid shirts and
several pairs of blue denim pants made to fit a small
man or a boy of about sixteen. He kept her close by his
side as they perused the small Mexican general store.
In an amazingly short amount of time, the gunfighter
stocked up on a vast quantity of items: for her, a buckskin jacket, boots, and a small pearl-gray stetson, which
he set promptly on her head; a half-dozen neckerchiefs
of brightly colored silk, ammunition, foodstuffs, two
rifles, an assortment of knives, and two new canteens.
He bought a new saddle pack in which to store all this
gear, then moved down to the shelf where blankets were
stacked for inspection. Bryony aimlessly glanced at the
pile of woven blankets that the storekeeper brought forward to show them. The heavyset, swarthy shopkeeper
was spreading two or three upon his wooden counter
when her gaze happened to fall upon the one held in
his hand. It was beautifully woven and of intricate design. Bright blue, the color of sapphires, it was adorned
with yellow and red half-moons stitched in a distinctive
and particularly artistic pattern. She stared at it, mesmerized. That blanket! She recognized that blanket!

An image flashed in her mind, quick as lightning
across a stormy sky. She saw the face of an ancient

Indian woman, wizened and brown, her narrow eyes crinkled in a smile as she extended arms laden with a blanket exactly like this. The woman's face was at once crystal clear yet blurred at the edges, as though seen beneath water, and it stayed in Bryony's mind only an instant. Then a blinding light ripped through the girl's head, erasing the image, leaving behind total blackness. "Antelope Woman!" she cried, her eyes wide and fixed upon nothingness.

Jim Logan caught her as she swayed against the counter. "What is it? What's wrong?" he demanded, scanning her ashen countenance in alarm. Bryony shook her head from side to side, trembling all over.

"I don't know!" She turned back to the blanket, reaching out for it almost desperately. Señor Ramirez placed it in her hands. Nothing happened. No flash of recognition this time. It was merely a blanket, pretty and soft, little different from many others available in the store.

"Ah, la señora le gusta esta frazada. Muy bien." The shopkeeper beamed at her and nodded his head. *"Es bonita, sí, señora?"*

"Where did you get this blanket?" Logan addressed the shopkeeper curtly.

The man stroked his moustache as he thought for a moment. *"Sí, yo recuerdo!"* he exclaimed. *"Los cazadores.* The hunters of the buffalo. *Gringos.* They were here no more than a month ago, señor. They traded blankets and saddles for guns and food. *Hombres malos, señor, muy malos.* They talked of getting these blankets from *los indios muertos. Los indios Cheyenne, señor. Si, yo recuerdo en todo.*

"Dead Cheyenne," Logan repeated softly, then glanced at Bryony's pale face. She was still staring at the blanket. "Does this blanket mean something to you?"

She put her hand to her brow. Her temples

throbbed. Pain filled her head from ear to ear. "I don't know," she whispered. "For a moment, I thought..."

"You said something when you saw it. 'Antelope Woman.' Who is that?"

Tears filled her eyes. "I don't remember."

Logan withdrew some money from his pocket and placed the bills on the counter. "We'll take this blanket and two others," he told the shopkeeper. "And a bottle of tequila besides."

Moments later they took their leave of the shop, and he led her toward a small cantina at the end of the narrow street. It was nearly dark by now. Bryony felt exhausted, and her head still hurt. Yet an odd elation glimmered within. She had remembered something— someone from her past! Maybe everything would begin to come back now! She strained her mind, trying to recall the woman's face once more, but without success. Nevertheless, despite her throbbing head and crippling fatigue, the flickering hope within her continued to burn.

After a brief exchange with the Mexican couple who owned the cantina, Jim steered Bryony to the stairway and up to the second-floor landing. He opened a door leading into a tiny bedroom. "You look like hell," he told her, leading her toward the single narrow bed. "I want you to lie down and rest for a while."

"Where... where will you be?"

"Next door. There's another room adjoining this one. We'll sleep here tonight and get an early start tomorrow. I reckon we could both stand a hot meal and a real bed for once."

She nodded her agreement, then sank down upon the faded quilt that covered the small bed. The moment her head touched the pillow, she closed her eyes. The jarring pain in her temples eased. Through a swirling mist, she heard Logan's boots thump on the floor, heard the bedroom door open and close. The last thing she heard was a key turning in the lock outside. Then sleep overtook her completely.

She awoke to soft lantern light and the gentle sound of a woman's bustling skirts. She sat up, startled, only to find the stout and smiling Mexican woman Jim had spoken to downstairs pouring hot water from a steaming bucket into an old wooden tub.

"The señor asked me to get ready *su baño, señora*. And he left these for you to wear *esta noche*. Are you hungry? *El señor* has ordered *un banquete por su cena*. A true feast I have prepared for you this night!" While speaking, she laid out a delicate red lace blouse upon the bed and put beside it a full, flounced black skirt shot through with red and gold threads. Bryony stared at her in amazement. "In this, you will be *muy hermosa, señora. El señor* has chosen *muy bien*."

Bryony studied the lovely blouse and skirt, and the delicate red sandals the woman held in her hands. She glanced longingly at the steaming tub, the thick towels, and the inviting bar of soap. This was the time she ought to explain to this woman that *el señor* was not her husband, nor even her lover. She ought to tell this woman that he had kidnapped her and was holding her against her will, and to beg her for her help in escaping him. Yet the thought of the hot bath, the fresh, pretty clothes, and the *banquete* Texas Jim Logan had ordered and which, no doubt, awaited her below made her hesitate. She didn't want to get this woman or her husband in trouble with Logan. They might get hurt. She would wait until later. Perhaps there was someone else she might confide in, someone who could stand up to the gunfighter. Now, she smiled at the waiting woman and slid off the bed.

"*Gracias!*" she exclaimed, peeling off her tattered lilac gown and undergarments with fervent gratitude. "You are most kind, *señora!*"

It was wonderful to be clean again, to scrub the

trail dust from her skin and hair, and to soak in the healing warmth of the steaming tub. When she went to dress herself, she blushed to find that Texas had not only provided her with the blouse and skirt, but with lacy undergarments as well. There was also a variety of toiletries including a brush and comb and a small bottle of delicate lavender scent. Bryony had no idea how he had come by these treasures, but she could not resist them. Presently, she stood before the narrow mirror set above a rough-hewn pine chest of drawers and examined her appearance.

Gone was the pale, dirty, bedraggled creature who had followed Logan about the general store. Tonight she looked as fresh and beautiful as a Mexican wild flower, with the low-cut red lace blouse leaving her shoulders bare and accenting the generous swell of her bosom, and the tight-waisted black cotton skirt swirling gracefully about her lushly curved hips and long, slender legs. The lantern light caught the red and gold threads running through the skirt, making them flash and shimmer when she moved. The dark cotton cascaded to above her ankles, where the thin-strapped red sandals encased her slim feet. She had brushed her hair until it shone like lustrous black velvet. Unbound, it flowed like a loose dark cloak about her shoulders. Her face glowed for the first time in days, perhaps weeks, and there was a most becoming pink flush in her cheeks. The lovely eyes held a jade sparkle as she beheld herself, standing slender and erect before the mirror, watching her reflection as she lightly dabbed the lavender scent at her throat and beneath her earlobes, at her wrists and, finally, in the deep crevice between her breasts. She blushed at this and hurriedly thrust away the perfume bottle. She wasn't meeting a lover tonight! she reminded herself furiously. Jim Logan was her captor, a ruthless man hell-bent on revenge. That was his only interest in her, and she ought to thank heaven for it. Perfume indeed! With her small mouth set and her head high, she turned and went to the door.

She felt herself to be almost floating as she descended the candle-lit stairway to the cantina below. The air was soft and warm, filled with the pungent aroma of hearty food. Darkness enwrapped the cantina but for the candles that flickered here and there. She saw Texas Jim Logan immediately despite the dusk. He rose from the corner table as she appeared on the steps and watched her from beneath his black sombrero.

He, too, had bathed and changed his clothing. He was now dressed all in black, save for the silver buttons on his shirt and the handsomely wrought silver buckle he wore on his gun belt. His cobalt eyes gleamed as she approached him, and a smile tilted the corners of his lips.

"*Perfección, mi querida,*" he murmured, gazing down at her. Taking her hand, he kissed it.

She felt crimson color stain her cheeks. She removed her hand from his grasp. "Thank you for the clothes—and for ordering the bath. It was very thoughtful of you," she said stiffly.

He held the back of her chair as she seated herself beside him. Bryony was aware that his eyes were raking her with approval. She was suddenly very conscious of her sensuously bared shoulders, of the enticingly low-cut blouse beneath which her breasts rose and fell in rapid accompaniment to her heartbeat. To distract him, and to cover the moment, she spoke quickly. "I would like a glass of wine, if you please."

At a signal from Texas, a thin Mexican man hurried over and poured wine into deep goblets. His wife, the woman who had prepared Bryony's bath, served them from platters heaped with spicy roasted chicken, a thick, succulent soup, beef enchiladas, fruit, and rice, while a

boy sat cross-legged beneath the serving bar at the opposite end of the cantina, plucking the strings of a guitar.
The tune he produced with such seeming aimlessness
was melodic and sensuous, each note ringing with gentle
resonance in that dark and quiet room.

Bryony felt herself lured by an irresistible spell into
a kind of dreamy contentment as the aroma of food and
pungent wine lingered in the air, and the boy played
his guitar, and the candle flame danced in the dusk.
Texas Jim Logan watched her with those dark glinting
eyes, so close she had but to reach out to touch his sun-
bronzed cheek.

Of course, she did no such thing. But she stifled
an impulse to remove his hat and gaze full into that
lean, handsome face, to see the chestnut gleam of his
hair across his brow and know for certain the expression
in his keen and piercing eyes. Her anger had faded.
Whether it was the wine or the music or the intimate,
companionable silence they shared across the little table,
she felt relaxed and at peace with this tall, mysterious
stranger whom she knew not at all.

"Tell me about that Indian blanket." He broke the
silence at last as he pushed away his empty plate. He
put his hand over hers upon the table. "Why did you
react like that in the shop? I thought you were going to
faint."

Bryony's pulse, previously slowed to peaceful relaxation by the warm, drowsy atmosphere and the heavy
meal, now began to race as his strong hand covered
hers. She took a gulp of wine and then turned her eyes
to his face.

"I'm not sure." Something in his expression made
her continue more freely. "I remembered something, or
rather someone. It was an old Indian woman holding a
blanket like that. For an instant, I knew her. I remembered! I think her name was Antelope Woman. But

now"—she shook her head, filled with frustration—
"now, the memory is gone. I don't really know who she
is or why seeing that blanket had that effect on me."

"You have known many Indians, *querida?*"

She bit her lip, remembering that he didn't even
know about her captivity with the Cheyenne or her loss
of memory. He didn't know anything about her. "I...
I was imprisoned by Cheyenne Indians," she said quietly. "Frank and Willie Joe rescued me—they and some
buffalo hunters they knew. I...I don't remember anything about it though."

"Why don't you?" His tone was very casual. "I
reckon if the Cheyenne ever captured me, I'd remember
every single moment of it."

Bryony took a breath, deciding suddenly to tell him
the whole. There was something about him tonight,
something that banished the last vestiges of fear. He
had been so kind, so thoughtful, providing her with
these clothes, with this satisfying, delicious meal. His
expression now contained no mockery or indifference.
It was warm and concerned, and it tore at her heart-
strings. She found herself gripping his hand, respond-
ing to an impulse she could not resist.

"I don't remember," she told him. "I don't remember being captured, or rescued. I don't remember anything at all. When Frank found me, I didn't even know
my own name." She glanced down at the table and bit
her lip. "It is so hard to understand! Something about
my time with the Cheyenne must have been so terrible,
so frightening, that I...I wiped it from my mind. My
past is gone. All I know is that I awoke one morning
with Frank bending over me. And I didn't even know
him! I didn't remember my marriage or...or my husband or anything!"

It came out then, the entire story. She found it a
relief to express the anguish she had felt at not knowing

her identity, her astonishment at learning from Frank that he was her husband, that they had wed in El Paso shortly before her capture by the Cheyenne. She poured out the story to him, her expressive face reflecting all the turmoil she had undergone, her voice throbbing with the pain and uncertainty of these past months.

Texas Jim Logan was surprisingly easy to talk to. He listened in silence, his gaze fastened upon her, his hand holding hers with reassuring strength. When she had finished and leaned back in her chair, he spoke in a soft tone.

"You've had quite a time of it, little tenderfoot. I'm sorry." She stared up at him, tears glimmering upon her lashes. His understanding filled her with gratitude. "I have a hunch your memory will return," he continued. "I reckon you need time. And until then, no one will trouble you. Not Frank Chester, or Willie Joe, no one."

She caught her breath, realizing that somehow she had revealed much more than she had intended about the painful discomfort of her marriage to Frank. Had he guessed her feelings, her lack of love for the man who was her husband? She felt she had to be certain he understood. "Mr. Logan—Texas..." she began, meeting his gaze with quiet determination. "It... it is true that my marriage to Frank has not been easy. Because I don't remember him, I perhaps do not feel all that I should. But still"—she took a breath—"he is my husband. I owe him. He deserves my loyalty, my ... my devotion. It is only right that I return to my proper place with him. So I must try again to convince you to let me go back."

"Try all you like, *querida*. It won't do you any good."

She bit her lip. "Such revenge is unworthy of you," she said quietly.

"Unworthy? Of a gunman, a professional killer, a man of my infamous reputation?" He grinned at her and poured more wine into her goblet. "Let's talk of something else. Tell me about Willie Joe."

"Willie Joe?" Startled, she spilled some of the wine upon the table. "No, no, I definitely do *not* wish to talk about Willie Joe," she said with a shudder.

He nodded, sudden coldness darkening his midnight eyes. Her response told him all he needed to know about the younger Chester's treatment of Frank's "wife," and he added this knowledge to an already long list of scores to settle with the Chester brothers. If Bryony had happened to glance up at that moment, she would have been startled by the grim set of Jim Logan's mouth and by the murderous gleam in his eyes. But she was absorbed in blotting up the spilled wine and didn't notice.

They talked for some little while after that, and it wasn't until he had escorted her upstairs to the door of her room that she realized he had in all their conversation revealed nothing about himself. She searched his face as they stood together in the dusky corridor. What did she really know about him? She knew of his reputation and all those terrible things Frank had told her, but none of that fit with the man who had shown such consideration, even tenderness, for her tonight. Jim Logan was an enigma. A fascinating enigma. She tried to shake off the effects of the wine, which were making it difficult for her to remember clearly that she was married to another man, that her place was elsewhere. It had felt so right being with him tonight, talking to him. And the yearning inside her made her want to touch him, to trace her fingers over his lips, to slide them through his chestnut hair. She wanted to kiss him, she realized in shock, as he smiled down at her in the hallway. She wanted to be held fast in his arms and kissed the way he had kissed her on the hill by the sea. Horrified by her own wild thoughts, she fumbled with the knob of the door. He opened it for her and held it wide in silence. Bryony nearly darted into the room, rather like a fawn bolting danger.

"Good night," she said breathlessly, staring at him across the threshold, hoping he would leave before she completely fell apart and, at the same time, wishing he wouldn't. He gazed at her a long moment, his keen eyes studying every nuance of her unsettled expression. Then he took a step forward.

"No...no..." She held out her hands as if to ward him off, frightened of her own reaction if he should touch her, knowing she could not withstand him if he but placed his hand upon her arm. Texas Jim Logan halted instantly at her words, and something unreadable entered his eyes.

"Go away...please!"

"That's what you want?"

"Yes!"

He nodded slowly.

"Good night, then, *querida*," he drawled, and tipping his hat, he left her alone in the room.

Bryony heard the key turning in the lock before his footsteps retreated down the hall. Desperately, she reminded herself that she was his prisoner, that she ought to hate and fear him. But there was no fear in her heart. There was something else, something she could not bear to admit, much less explore. She dashed to the water basin the Mexican woman had left in the room and splashed cool water on her face and wrists, hoping this would quench the fire blazing in her blood. But it didn't help. She eventually lay upon her bed, seeking the sanctuary of sleep, but all she could do was think of Texas Jim Logan. He was branded upon her thoughts, searing and indelible. He left no space for anyone or anything else. She shut her eyes fast, and still his image remained, strong and handsome and rugged as the land of Mexico that they had traversed together these past days. Where would all this lead? she wondered in apprehension and dismay. And what would become of her foolish, wayward heart?

CHAPTER TWENTY-TWO

"I INSIST that you tell me where we're going."

Bryony stared about her in dismay at the wild and beautiful wilderness in which she found herself. It was two days since they had stopped at the cantina, two days of monotonous riding across the desert, deeper into Mexico. They had traveled nearly one hundred miles since leaving behind the hills of San Diego, and she could make out the majestic Sierras far in the distance. But this afternoon they had reached the foothills of another mountain range, one whose towering peaks loomed, she guessed, ten thousand feet above the desert floor. The sight of this imposing spectacle, silhouetted against the vivid jewel-blue sky, had filled her with renewed trepidation. Where on earth was Texas Jim Logan taking her? And what, exactly, did he plan to do with her once they got there? She couldn't help wondering if he was making his way toward some outlaws' den, where bandits and other gunmen would stare and laugh at her, ogling the soon-to-be-ransomed prisoner. She shuddered. His refusal to tell her anything on the subject added to her unease. But in a way she was grateful to have something to berate him for. It was easier, and safer, to be angry than to deal with her other feelings for him. These she forced aside and ignored with savage determination.

For the most part, she had found refuge from her confused emotions in silence. She had scarcely spoken ten words to him since they'd left behind the cantina and the little village. But today, the length and uncertainty of the journey was getting on her nerves, and she had begun questioning him about their destination. His close-mouthed handling of the subject both infuriated and unsettled her. Now, gazing about at the seemingly endless wilderness, surrounded by mountains whose jagged peaks seemed to touch the gleaming turquoise sky, she could no longer contain herself. Twisting in the saddle so that she could gaze up into Texas's face, she spoke with unaccustomed vehemence.

"Tell me where we are, where we're going. I demand that you give me an answer immediately!"

His arms tightened around her waist as he grinned down at her. "You demand?" His eyes glinted with amusement. "I don't think you're in a position to demand anything, little tenderfoot. Wait and see. We'll be there by sunset."

"*Where?*" She blazed, but he merely chuckled, then forced her to turn about in the saddle. With his arms holding her firmly, preventing her from turning to question him again, he guided the bay stallion up a rocky incline on the mountain path.

They had been following the same twisting path for nearly four hours, but suddenly they emerged upon a small plateau. At the end of this was a sheer drop to a steep canyon. Bryony gasped as she contemplated a descent down the canyon wall, but instead of attempting this, Texas unexpectedly turned Pecos eastward toward a clump of boulders. To Bryony's amazement, there was a trail hidden beyond the boulders, a narrow, chollastudded path, which could not readily be seen from the plateau. It was wide enough for only one horse to pass at a time, and the big black stallion, which for all this time had served to carry their supply packs, followed on the lead rope as they picked their way around the boulders and set off upon the hidden track. They followed this for half a mile before once more emerging upon the mountainside, this time nestled well within the mountain's protective walls, invisible from without. While Bryony gazed about in amazement, Jim rode on to higher ground, scaling the rugged terrain with the assurance of one who had been there before. After zigzagging and slashing a path that left the girl riding before him thoroughly confused, they emerged at length upon a wide, breathtaking slope where tall pine trees filled the air with their scent. Just as the sun began to melt in crimson fire over the desert to the west, Texas reined the bay to a halt upon the slope and bade Bryony to look before her.

A dizzying, magnificent panorama filled her vision. Blue-shadowed mountains rose up all around her, rugged and beautiful beyond measure. Wild flowers and creosote bushes and spindly boogum trees dotted the landscape. Squawking geese swarmed overhead, and there were deer poised on a distant bluff. Beneath the sky of gleaming turquoise, unmarred by the faintest cloud, the majesty of the vast wild country struck her forcibly with its splendor. And cupped serenely in the midst of all this mountainous glory was a small, square cabin built of mesquite logs, sheltered amidst a cluster of cool pine trees, with a tiny stream running downhill between mossy rocks just beyond. Bryony could only stare. After so much that had worn away at her soul, the sight of this exquisite mountain refuge was like a warm, healing balm that revitalized her flagging spirit. How could one gaze upon such magnificence and not feel a surge of joy, of hope? The rugged purple mountains commanded the eye, and the wildflowers and boogum trees delighted the senses, but it was the small mesquite cabin tucked cozily amidst all this rugged splendor that touched her heart. The cabin had the look of a *home*, of a warm and cozy shelter from every kind of adversity. Deep longing pierced her as she gazed at it. What a beautiful place, small and solid and strong, nestled within grand and wild country. She dared not move, or breathe, for she wanted the spell to last forever.

Jim's voice, gentle in her ear, held an unmistakable note of pride and pleasure. "That's it. How do you like the place?" As the fiery sunset stained the sky, spilling across the turquoise like paint upon a canvas, he waited in silence for her reaction.

She turned slowly in the saddle to face him. Her face was flushed and radiant against the changing colors of the sky. "It's spectacular!" she whispered. "It takes my breath away."

He nodded, then sent the horse into a trot once more. "I reckoned you'd like it. I've spent some time here before. It's a good place for laying low. No one can find it unless they come upon that hidden track back there. And unless they know it's there, and what to look for..." He let the sentence trail off as he reined up once more, this time directly in front of the cabin. He helped Bryony to dismount.

"There's a stove inside. I'll bring in our gear and the food supplies. You can get supper cooking pronto."

Still stunned by the beauty of this untamed mountain refuge, she nodded without really hearing him. She was busily drinking in the sight of those magnificent, pine-forested peaks, noticing the low gurgle of the stream, the rustle of the October wind as it rushed down through the trees and boulders. She caught a glimpse of a rough lean-to shelter for the horses behind the cabin; behind that ran the stream. The lofty precipice of the mountain jutted upward, like a huge, protective wall buttressing the rear of the cabin. It made access to the place from that direction nearly impossible.

She realized that the way they had come was the only approach to this spot. No one could ever find her here, not unless they knew exactly where they were headed. And knowing Texas, no one else in the world would. They were truly alone here. It was a two-day ride back to that village where they had dined in the cantina. Here, all was wilderness. And she was very much alone with this man who had brought her to this isolated spot.

She turned toward the cabin door, filled with unease, but Texas caught her arm and pulled her back before him. She lifted her chin, meeting his questioning look. He studied the delicate planes of her face.

"What's wrong?" One eyebrow lifted. "I thought you were pleased with the place. You won't find a more beautiful spot in all of Mexico."

"I don't doubt that." She faced him with as much composure as she could, trying to contain the thudding of her heart. "But it is so . . . isolated. So lonely. I didn't expect . . ."

"To be alone with me?" His expression was amused. "You've been alone with me all these days we've been riding. You ought to be used to it by now." He smiled down at her, one hand reaching out to touch the ebony hair, which cascaded down her shoulders and across her arms. "What are you afraid of, little tenderfoot?" he asked softly.

She stiffened and tried to wrench away from his grasp, but he held her tight, staring down into her up-turned face with a piercing look that, unless she was much mistaken, saw far more than she would have liked. For it was not him she feared, but herself. She didn't know if being here so close to him, so cut off from everything and everyone else, she would be able to fight back the unwanted feelings that had tormented her that evening in the cantina and which she had been trying to stifle ever since. Being so near to him now, with his hands upon her, made her tremble and ache. Something hot and fiery burned inside her. She sought to dampen the flames.

"I'm not afraid of anything," she snapped, staring defiantly back at him. "Certainly not of you."

"Glad to hear it." He pulled her closer and bent his face close to hers. His eyes, dark and molten as blue fire, burned into hers. "So if it isn't me that's made you jumpy as a calf about to be branded, what is it?" he inquired in his low, husky drawl.

She opened her mouth to answer him, but never found the chance. He kissed her, his lips covering hers, his hands tightening on her shoulders as he drew her close against him. Bryony gasped and tried to twist away. Then she felt herself swallowed up by a sweet ecstasy that overwhelmed her senses. He kissed her deeply, thoroughly, his mouth moving upon hers. As she gave herself up to that kiss, his strong hands slid over her shoulders and pressed against her neck, enwrapping her against his tall, iron-muscled frame. She lifted her arms about his neck and kissed him with trembling, desperate lips, sweet, flaming kisses that swept them both into a whirlwind of heady pleasure. She was drowning, drowning in the taste and scent and feel of him. And she never wanted to return to the surface. When his hand slid inside her plaid Western shirt and cupped her breast, she gave a moan of sheer delight. His thumb found her nipple and caressed it until the ache within her made her gasp and writhe in his arms. He scooped her up and began to carry her into the cabin, his mouth never leaving hers, but as they crossed the small wooden porch, some semblance of reason returned to her whirling mind. She tore her lips from his with an effort.

"No, Texas! No! We mustn't! Let me go!"

He didn't slacken his stride. He bore her through the small main room of the cabin and into the single bedroom at the rear. Bryony fought in his arms, but it was futile, for she had no chance against his strength. He set her down upon the bed and seized her when she tried to jump up. She found herself lying upon a faded patchwork quilt, imprisoned beneath him.

"No!" she cried again as he lowered his mouth toward hers. "I'm a married woman, Texas! This is wrong! Let me go!"

She saw his eyes of cobalt-blue flash dangerously in his lean face. There was no mistaking the need that drove him. She could feel the tension in his hard-muscled body as he pinned her beneath him, and she dared not move, fearing that the slightest tremor from her would drive him beyond the precarious control that was holding him in check. He was breathing rapidly, as rapidly as she, and his strong hands gripped her wrists with unconscious strength.

"This is not wrong, little tenderfoot!" he told her, staring down into her pale face. "I won't hurt you. But I'm not a blind man. I can see that you are as eager as I. You want this, *querida*. You want me to love you."

"No!"

"Yes."

She tried to twist away as his lips closed on hers once more. This time she resisted the fire that burst in her blood. A sob escaped her throat. "No!" she gasped, as he swore in frustration. "Stop. Please! I . . . don't want . . . this!"

He swore again, seeing the tears that slid now down

her cheeks. He let her go suddenly and straightened, standing over her as she lay upon the bed.

There was silence for a moment as they stared at each other. Slowly, she raised herself to a sitting position. Her breathing was ragged. She pressed her hands to her temples. "Leave me," she whispered, her eyes brimming with tears. "Go . . . away."

Texas Jim Logan drew a long breath. He opened his mouth to speak, then shut it again, clamping his lips tightly together. A grim, dark look came over his features. Without a word, he turned on his heel and left her alone in the room.

It was much later that Bryony emerged from the little bedroom. She had struggled long and hard to gain control of her riotous emotions. At last, she had managed to do so. She had spent the better part of an hour thinking of Frank, reminding herself of her duty to him, shaming herself into hating all that she felt for Texas Jim Logan. *It is animal lust, no more!* she told herself angrily. *To act upon it would be contemptible and weak. Ignore him. Forget him. Drive him from your mind.* She paced and wept and silently raged at herself for her own weakness, vowing to be strong. At last, calm again, she had dried her tears, combed her tousled hair with her hands, and tucked her shirt carefully into the top of her snug-fitting denim pants.

But the moment she stepped from the seclusion of the bedroom and saw him sitting at the square pine table in the kitchen, so rugged and strong, yet looking so forlorn, all of her careful resolution went flying out the window, sailing down the mountainside on the October wind.

The expression on his face, in that one brief moment before he saw her, tore at her heart in a way that nothing in her life ever had. He looked so sad, so alone, so filled with despair, that Bryony caught her breath in wonder. Then he glanced up abruptly, noting her presence like someone just startled from a melancholy daydream, and his face changed. He stood up, carefully polite and distant. He spoke in a cool, even tone.

"I reckon you're hungry. There's jerky and biscuits, and oranges left over from the village. And coffee to drink. Or maybe you'd rather have tequila?" She saw the opened bottle on the table before him and shook her head.

"Suit yourself." He picked up the bottle, turned away, and paced to the rough fireplace set against the west wall of the main room. He added fuel to the small blaze, his back to Bryony. "Go ahead and eat your supper. I won't bother you," he said dryly.

Silence hung between them like black thunderclouds before a storm. She tried not to think about what had happened a short while ago, about how she had felt, or how he had looked when she had come into the room just now. She turned her attention to her supper and forced herself to eat.

The cabin to which he had brought her consisted of only two rooms: this main room, which included the kitchen, and the little bedroom beyond. The kitchen had a stove and cupboards along one wall beside the window. There were two chairs flanking the square pine table and precious few other furnishings. A few battered iron utensils, an old tin drinking cup, and a broom were scattered here and there like ancient reminders of past habitation. A woven rug of orange and brown was stretched upon the planked wooden floor near the fireplace. A bench of dark wood sat beside the hearth. That was all. The entire dwelling was small, sparsely furnished, and as plain as could be. It was also extremely close quarters for a man and a woman to share when their feelings were running wild. As she cleaned up after the remains of her supper, she cast a wary glance at

Texas, but he was standing with his back to her, staring into the flames. As she watched, he lifted the bottle of tequila and took a long drink. She felt the muscles of her stomach bunch and tighten.

When all was tidied and the kitchen swept clean, she paced to the window at the front of the cabin. Darkness had fallen over the mountains, a heavy, midnight darkness unrelieved by star or moon. The night was silent, bursting with the fragrance of pine. Suddenly needing space and quiet away from the man who prowled the cabin, away from the tension quivering within these four walls, she went to the door, opened it, and stepped onto the porch.

The next sound was so loud it caused her to jump back into the doorway, a shriek upon her lips. Thunder crashed like an avalanche across the sky, rolling through the mountains with deafening force. Cold air rushed all around her. Rain began to plummet, pelting the earth, the cabin, the trees. Out of nowhere the storm hurtled across the mountain, as fierce and wild as the land itself.

Jim Logan seized her arm and pulled her back into the cabin, slamming the door shut. She was gasping, stunned by the sudden advent of the storm. "We'd better bolt up all the windows pronto," he warned. "Sounds like a bad one."

"Where did it come from?" Bryony followed him into the bedroom, where he fastened the wooden shutters upon the window there, forcing them closed despite the heaving wind that tried to send them rattling back against the wall. "It was so clear this afternoon, so lovely. At sunset there wasn't a cloud in the sky."

"Storms blow up quick in the mountains," he answered curtly, striding back into the main room of the cabin and securing the shutters there with quick precision. Then he tossed more fuel on the fire. "It's a good thing we're not still camping out tonight."

"Yes, a very good thing." She glanced quickly
around the cabin again, suddenly grateful for the snug
protection of the walls and the roof, for the blazing fire.
The temperature had dropped suddenly, and the October night felt chill. Rain pounded the windows, thunder crashed again, and she moved nearer to the glowing
orange flames. Jim Logan brought her a blanket and
wrapped it about her shoulders. It was the Indian blanket that had stirred her memory in the village. She looked
up at him.

"You were shivering," he said quietly. "Here, sit
down."

She huddled on the woven rug before the hearth,
watching the wild, shooting flames. Logan went to stand
beside the window, leaning his wide shoulders against
the wall. He had set down the bottle of tequila when
the storm began, and he did not reach for it again. Instead, he gazed in brooding silence at the girl who sat
upon the floor hugging her knees, her gaze fixed upon
the fire.

At last, Bryony could bear the silence no longer.
She raised her head to meet his eyes, and something in
her heart jolted madly at his expression. Beneath the
thick chestnut hair, which fell in careless waves across
his handsome brow, Texas Jim Logan wore a look of
longing, a look of utter sadness so poignant it stabbed
at her heart. His blue eyes, so vivid and keen, were now
dark as the night of storm that raged outside, dark and
filled with a haunted sorrow that his easy, careless mask
could no longer hide. His mouth was twisted in a grim
frown, and there was a shadow upon his bronzed features. He was a man beset by ghosts, consumed by a
sadness that went deep to his core. It was the same look
he had worn when she had unexpectedly emerged from
the bedroom earlier, surprising him, before he quickly
wiped it from his face. But now, he did not even seem

aware of the pain she read in his eyes. He stared at her, his hands clenched at his sides, while her eyes widened and something much more potent than any arrow pierced her heart.

Without even realizing what she did, she lifted her hand toward him. He was beside her in an instant, kneeling, her hand held tightly in his. "Oh, Texas," she whispered, a catch in her throat, for there was no mistaking the glow that had lit in his eyes when she had reached out for him.

"What are we to do?" she asked, cradling his hand against her cheek. "I can't bear to see you look so unhappy. Is it because of me?"

She could scarcely believe that this was true, but her heart pounded uncontrollably at the notion that she could have such an effect upon him. Bitter self-mockery showed upon his face. "Because of you?" He gave a short laugh."Yes, little tenderfoot. And no." He ran his hand through his hair in frustration. "How the hell can I explain? Listen." He turned her face up to his and addressed her with sudden intensity. "I've done things in my life that brought misery to others. Misery and pain, terrible pain. And especially to someone I loved more dearly than anything else. I've been a jackass, a fool, and a cruel one, to boot." His mouth twisted in cynical self-contempt. "I reckon now I'm getting my due. Whatever I'm feeling, whatever I'm suffering, it's my own fault. Not yours, not anyone else's. Do you understand? I sure as hell don't deserve your pity."

"There is goodness in you," she whispered, echoing the words she had told him the first night of her capture. "I don't care about what you've done in the past. And I don't believe those awful things Frank told me about you. I tried, but I can't. I see kindness, decency, even gentleness in you. That is why..."

"Why what?" he demanded when she broke off in

confusion. "Go on." He put a finger beneath her chin and tilted her head up so that she was forced to meet his eyes. His own indigo gaze was keen and probing. "Tell me what you were going to say."

She could not tear her gaze from his face. "I was going to say that that is why I love you," she said simply.

He drew in his breath sharply and pulled her to him, but she wriggled free, her hands on his chest. "No, Texas, this is madness. I can't allow it! I am married to Frank!"

"Damn Frank Chester to hell!" Fiercely, he pulled her to him, enclosing her in his arms. Her silken hair swirled about her, brushing his jaw with irresistible softness. "I'll make you forget Frank Chester, little tenderfoot! I'll make you forget you ever met him!" he vowed.

"Texas, no!" Desperately, she tried to reason with him, still held immobile in his arms. "I want you, it's true. Heaven forgive me, it's true. But it's wrong! We must fight this thing between us, we must ignore—"

"The hell we will," he growled, and before she could do or say anything further, he had crushed his mouth to hers in a kiss so fierce and powerful it drove all else from her mind. She was helpless beneath the flood tide of sensations that poured over her with that kiss, she felt herself caught up in an ocean of desire from which there was no retreat. His hands moved over her, caressing her, arousing her to a need as wild and demanding as his own. She lifted her arms to him and pulled him close, taking him to her without thought or reason, with only love. She slid her fingers through his thick, silken hair, then tore at the buttons of his shirt, tracing the bulging muscles in his upper chest.

"Texas, Texas," she moaned as he cupped her breasts and kneaded them until she was breathless and gasping with pleasure. He kissed her again, his lips burning her mouth, her eyelids, her throat. She was lost, lost in a world of scorching delight. She abandoned herself to the inferno.

Moments later, she and Texas were both naked upon the woven rug, the dancing flames from the hearth casting red-gold light upon their arching bodies. Wind roared at the windows, and thunder crashed throughout the mountain trees, but they heard none of it. Bryony felt herself held in iron arms, kissed by lips of fire, stroked by hands that were alternately tender and rough, until she felt she would die of need for him. His body covered hers, and she ran her hands up and down the length of him, hungrily touching and exploring him as she wrapped her legs around his and drew him to her. He bit her ear, kissed the pounding hollow at her throat, and tormented her breasts with his tongue and teeth until she cried out in breathless ecstasy. Texas poised above her, his dark-blue eyes glinting into hers, passion gripping his powerful frame and darkening his features.

"I love you more than life itself," he told her hoarsely, observing her wild fervor with deep satisfaction. "And now, once again, you are mine. From now until forever, little tenderfoot: *You are mine.*"

His words were a blur to her dazzled senses, but she caught their essence and knew he was branding her for his own. "Yes," she whispered, as the urgent ache within sent a shudder throughout her slender body. Her hair clung in damp tendrils to her flushed and radiant face, and she clung to his powerful frame as he entered her with a driving ferocity.

"Yes, Texas, I am yours," she gasped. "Only yours. And you are mine." Her lips parted, welcoming him, seeking him, and their bodies twined together, bound by need, by desire, and by love.

Rain slashed at the cabin all through the night. Lightning flashed in the inky sky, illuminating the buffeted trees, the mud-washed rock, the stream surging madly downhill like quicksilver. Thunder boomed again and again, rattling from crest to crest of the black-domed mountains. The night was wild with the storm. But the lovers in the cabin knew and cared not. Long into the savage night, they held and loved each other, unleashing all the passion each held locked within and discovering all the tenderness. At last, when a pearly pink dawn banished the last vestiges of rain from the pale sky, they slept, wrapped in each other's arms.

CHAPTER TWENTY-THREE

NOVEMBER CAME, bringing frosted nights and crisp, chill days, with the air whistling down the mountain, sharp as cut crystal. The wildlife took refuge in their nests and caves and all those nooks and crannies of the mountains, while the man and woman in the secluded mesquite cabin passed the days in simple, ever-growing joy.

The woman who called herself Katharine Chester ceased to think of her husband, Frank. He was part of her past, part of her forgotten life, and she could no more desire to return to him than she could desire a return to the fog of yesterday. Texas had brought her out of the fog: He had given her love and tenderness and a feeling of safety she had never felt under Frank Chester's roof. Whatever she may have once felt for Frank, whatever had spurred her to marry him in the first place, it had vanished with her memory and would never return. She didn't want to go back to him, and she didn't care now if she ever recovered her missing past. The present was all that mattered. These beautiful days in the cabin with Texas filled her with a happiness she hadn't thought possible. She blossomed, breaking free of her fears and worries. Like a flower choked by weeds that suddenly finds itself unfettered in a lovely, sun-kissed meadow, she bloomed and sprang to vibrant life. She was Texas's woman now, and she wanted nothing else.

The first week of December brought winds so fierce that Bryony and Jim were forced to stay inside the cabin for six unbroken days. When at last the violence subsided, Texas went hunting, for their food supplies had dwindled and Bryony wanted to cook deer or turkey stew to warm them after the bitter weather. He left early one morning, wearing both of his guns and carrying a rifle, promising to bring back a week's worth of game. He leaned down from the saddle to kiss her. She, on tiptoe, threw her arms around his neck. Laughing, he pulled her up into the saddle before him and kissed her long and thoroughly. It was quite a bit later that he finally released her. Breathless and flushed, she slid to the ground and blew him a kiss. The glow in her eyes matched the radiant aura in her cheeks as she watched him ride off down the mountainside.

An hour later, with the cabin swept clean and tidied, she decided to ride out herself. It was nearly a month since she had overcome her fear of the big black stallion Texas had brought along when he'd kidnapped her, and now she loved to ride the spirited animal, finding that his long, powerful stride and restless energy suited her riding abilities to perfection. She felt quite natural astride the glistening black horse and had grown fond of him during their explorations together. The stallion, in turn, always greeted her with excitement, even pleasure, and quickly obeyed her light-handed commands. To her surprise, he never once displayed with her the wild temper and rebellion he had shown whenever Frank or Willie Joe had tried to ride him.

Now she decided that he probably needed exercise as much as she did after being confined during the high

winds of the past week. Shortly after their arrival at the
cabin, Texas had enlarged the lean-to that served to
shelter the horses into a rough stable, completely enclosed against the elements. She led the black horse,
whom she'd named Midnight, out of this shelter into
the clear pale sunlight of the December morning and
mounted him from the porch. Then, cozily warm in the
thick buckskin jacket Texas had bought for her in the
Mexican village, her stetson set rakishly upon her dainty
head, she set off down the mountain trail amidst a clatter
of pebbles.

For a while she rode aimlessly, enjoying the chatter
of the birds, the cold, razor-sharp air, the sheer beauty
of the mountainous Mexican countryside. She often came
exploring alone like this when Texas went hunting, for
it gave her an exhilarating sense of freedom and she
loved to gaze at the splendors of the land. In her tight-
fitting denim pants, boots, and bright yellow Western
shirt, with a red neckerchief knotted at her throat, she
looked quite at home in her surroundings. Her black
hair had been pulled tightly back into a ponytail and
tied with a red ribbon, the stetson placed jauntily atop
this. The buckskin jacket completed the effect. She looked
competent and self-assured, quite different from the
confused and frightened woman who had kept house
for Frank and Willie Joe Chester in the California hills.
Indeed, the two men who spotted her from atop a stony
bluff less than one hundred feet from where she trotted
the stallion almost didn't recognize her.

She had taken the stallion on the same path that
had brought her to the cabin for the first time in October.
She was amused now to think that it had once as-
tounded her. It was an easy trail, really, once you knew
to ride beyond that clump of boulders. From the dizzying plateau overlooking the canyon, she surveyed the
glorious, pine-covered peaks that rose up to her left,

and gazed far out to where the distant Sierras were purple silhouettes against the azure sky. Then, she turned Midnight back toward home. More than two hours had passed since she'd set out, and Texas may have returned by now with their supper. She wanted to have plenty of time to simmer the stew, to bake biscuits and a berry pie. Texas didn't know it yet, but this was going to be a special dinner, for a special reason. Bryony had something important to tell him, and she couldn't wait to see his reaction.

She was carrying their child.

She laughed aloud with joy, ecstatic with the secret. Of course, it was far too early to be certain, but she had missed her monthly time and for the past two mornings she had felt distinctly queasy at the thought of food. And besides all that, she just had a *feeling* that it was true. Happiness surged through her. She was going to give birth to Texas's child, their child together, and it was the only thing she needed to make her life complete.

She was so engrossed in these happy reflections that she didn't notice the little knot of men skulking on the bluff above nor see that from behind the cover of a jutting gray rock they watched her disappear into the hidden pathway beyond the boulders.

She reached home in good time, only to discover that Texas had been there before her. He had left her a turkey, which he had plucked and butchered for her, and a note that said he would be back before suppertime with the rest of his day's game. She hung the buckskin jacket and her stetson on pegs beside the door, rolled up the sleeves of her yellow shirt, and washed her hands before turning to the business of setting the stew to boil.

While she was cutting strips of meat from the turkey, the blade of her knife broke cleanly away from the handle, clanging upon the bare wooden floor only inches from her booted foot. She retrieved it, frowning. She didn't know how to repair the knife, and it was useless in its present condition. It was also the only knife to be found in the sparsely equipped kitchen.

Then she remembered Texas's saddle pack. He had purchased an assortment of knives in that Mexican village when they had bought the Indian blanket and other supplies. She hurried to the corner beside the fireplace where he stowed his gear and knelt down beside the pack. Quickly, with an eye to the kettle boiling on the hearth and her mind racing with the preparations still to be made, she began to rummage through the biggest pouch.

But in the end, it wasn't a knife she found, it was a photograph. In surprise, she lifted it from the pack and placed it on her lap so that she might study it.

It was framed in silver. It showed a man and a woman, obviously very much in love. The man's arm was around the woman's shoulders as she smiled radiantly up at him. The man, as handsome and rugged as ever, was Texas Jim Logan. The woman was herself.

For how long she sat there, she was never to know. The shock was paralyzing. She could do nothing but look dumbly at that photograph, her eyes wide and staring, her mind a frozen blank. She blinked. She lifted it in hands that shook. The photograph slipped and clattered to the floor. With a gasp that was half sob, she retrieved it and stared again.

A photograph of her and Texas. *A photograph of her and Texas.* It could mean only one thing. They had not been strangers when they met on that hill. They had never been strangers—not as far as he was concerned. *He was a part of her past.* Texas Jim Logan, Frank, Willie Joe—they were all three part of her missing past.

She heard a noise at the door.

"Texas." Her voice was a hoarse whisper. Shock still held her in its grip, and she had not had opportunity to recover either her voice or her wits. "Texas..."

But it was not Texas she saw as she turned her stunned face to the door, still too shocked and shattered to frame a single question. It wasn't Texas at all.

It was Frank.

CHAPTER TWENTY-FOUR

VERY SLOWLY, Bryony set the photograph on the floor. She came to her feet. *"Frank."* It was a breath, a sob. She was staring in horror at the big man who hulked in the doorway, blocking the December sunlight.

Willie Joe charged past him through the door of the cabin, his eyes glittering. "What the hell kind of greeting is that for your husband and brother-in-law, Katharine?" he snarled. "Don't you have anythin' to say for yourself, girl?"

She looked from one of them to the other, while once again something died inside her. Then, as if from a distance, she heard other men's voices outside the cabin. Frank turned and barked an order.

"Forrester, you and the boys keep a sharp lookout! Logan could be back anytime. Wound him if you have to, but try to keep him alive for me and Willie Joe. Whatever you do, keep him away from this cabin until we're finished with my little wife."

The color had drained from Bryony's cheeks. Her heart had nearly stopped beating when she'd seen Frank. Now, as his ominous words took root in her mind, her heart started to slam against her chest in long, painful strokes.

"Frank, what are you doing here?" she cried. Her voice cracked on the words. She moistened her lips and tried again. "How . . . how did you find me?"

He strode toward her, his face black with rage. His muscles bunched beneath his heavy buckskin coat as he reached out for her. When he gripped her by the shoulders, his fingers dug deep into her flesh. "We followed you, honey, real easy and simple-like. Aren't you glad to see me?" His laugh was an ugly sound. He went on jeeringly, giving her a shake. "Where's the kiss for your husband who's searched high and low to save you from that no-good gunfighter who dragged you off? Come on, honey, don't hold back on me now. Show me how grateful you are to be rescued."

Willie Joe sidled closer and grabbed Bryony by the hair. "She don't look too eager, do she, Frank?" He yanked her to him as Frank released her shoulders. The younger Chester snickered when she cried out in pain. He tugged mercilessly upon her hair. "What's the matter, don't you want to be rescued from Texas Jim Logan, Katharine? Don't you want to see that murderin' son of a bitch get what's comin' to him?"

"Stop it! Let me go!" She shoved at Willie Joe with all her might and managed to break free. Breathing hard, she backed away from the two of them, panic bubbling within her as they closed in on either side. She was thinking quickly now, her mind racing with the threats they had made against Texas. They would kill him. There were too many of them for him to fight, and they would take him unawares when he returned. She had to get them away. She had to keep them from hurting him.

"Frank, listen to me," she began desperately, holding her hand out as if to ward off his advance. "I . . . I want you to take me away from this place. Now, right away! Please, just take me home. I'll go with you, I'll be a good wife to you. Let's just leave now."

He threw back his head and laughed, and the viciousness of that sound sent an icy chill coursing through her blood. "Honey, you must think I'm some kind of idiot or something. Do you think I want damaged goods? Do you think I want a woman who cheated on me, who was low-down enough to cheat with the man I hate most in the whole world?"

"I didn't cheat!" she lied, her wide green eyes fixed frantically on his face. "Frank, I swear to you I..."

"Liar!" With sudden, terrifying fury, he grabbed her and threw her backward against the wall. "Do you expect me to believe that? I saw you riding out today, free as a bird!" He was breathing hard, his eyes blazing in his swarthy face. "You're not a prisoner here, Katharine. You're sharing that one damned bed with Logan, aren't you? You looked happy as a meadowlark out there on that canyon rim, and you came back here—to Logan—without a care in the world." He raised his fist and struck her full in the face. "Cheating bitch! I ought to kill you *and* Logan, and let the buzzards pick what's left of you!"

Bryony screamed as the blow connected. Pain exploded in her jaw. Through a burst of white-hot, blinding stars, which danced across her vision, she tried vainly to block the next blow. Frank seized her arm and twisted it savagely behind her back. He yanked her away from the wall so that she was pinned with her back to his chest. Willie Joe faced her, his grimy face lit with malice.

"Don't worry none, Katharine. We're not goin' to kill you jest yet," he taunted. "We'll rough you up a bit, teach you a lesson, and then, why, you and me will have a chance for some fun, jest like I always wanted. *Then* we'll kill you, honey. So, relax, girl. You've got at least two, mebbe three hours left of living before we send you to hell right along with that no-good lover of yours."

"No . . . no!" She struggled to escape Frank's cruel grasp. Tears of pain streamed down her cheeks. As Willie Joe chuckled and raised his arm to strike her, she suddenly kicked out at him with her booted foot, aiming right at his groin. The blow sent him collapsing to the floor, a shriek of agony on his lips. Desperately, she stamped her foot down on Frank's, and for just an instant, his grip on her loosened. It was all she needed. She darted away and grabbed the first thing she could get her hands on. It was the poker that she and Texas used to stir the fire logs. She spun about, brandishing it, as both Frank and Willie Joe ran toward her.

"Get back! Back! I'll kill you if you take another step!" she screamed, and the two men checked.

"You'd better get out of here fast before Texas comes back and finds you. He'll kill you, both of you, and your filthy partners outside! And I won't lift a finger to stop him!"

Willie Joe's teeth gleamed at her as he drew his gun. "No, girl, that ain't how it's goin' to happen at all. We'll kill Logan and make you watch. We'll scalp him just like we scalped that old Injun you bawled over."

She stared at him, frozen, the poker falling from her hand. "What are you . . ." She shut her eyes as his words rang in her head. They echoed over and over, clanging through the empty hollows of darkness. *We'll scalp him . . . scalp him . . . just like that old Injun . . . we'll scalp him . . .*

Suddenly, blinding pain ripped through her. She shut her eyes, gasping at the agony. A series of images flashed across her mind in lightning succession: she and Texas together in the photograph, the Indian blanket they'd bought in the village, an old brown-skinned woman of the Cheyenne; and these were quickly followed by others, just as vivid: a tall warrior with red war paint streaked across his face; a chief with deep-set eyes and two dark braids; a bloodied campsite; butchered, broken bodies... and then back to the chief... the chief... Two Bears! *Two Bears!*

With a splintering force that made her drop the poker and clutch her temples in agony, her memory jolted back with savage clarity. "Two Bears!" she sobbed as tears spilled from her eyes.

Willie Joe kicked the poker aside, and Frank grabbed her arm. Bryony stared wildly at them.

"You killed him! My *nihu*. You killed him and took his scalp."

"So," Frank muttered, gazing down at her bone-white, ravaged countenance, "you finally remembered. It took long enough. I reckon you see the rest of it as well, don't you?"

Slowly, standing between them, her brain began to take in all that had happened since that awful event, and to understand its meaning. A deep horror engulfed her as she lifted her face to Frank's hard, olive eyes.

"It was a lie then—all of it, a lie." She shook her head dazedly. She felt as though she were groping her way through a tangled, overgrown jungle, searching in desperation for a clear path. Her mouth formed the words, but they emerged in a low, raspy whisper. "I was never married to you. You... you took me with deceit, as part of some horrible jest. You did it only to get your filthy revenge—on my husband, on Jim." The anger hit her then, rushing over her like a dam unleashed, drowning her in a sea of fury. "You damned filthy, lying pig!" she screamed, turning on him with clawing nails. "How could you... how could you?"

He knocked her aside easily, but not before her

nails drew blood on his face. Willie Joe jumped at her and threw an arm around her neck. Holding her pinned against him, he put his gun to her right temple, digging the barrel into her flesh. "That's enough out of you, girl. You try that again, and I'll put a bullet through your skull quicker than you can blink. You savvy?"

Gasping, still quivering with rage, she nodded. She didn't trust her voice enough to speak. She wanted to kill them, both of them, but she didn't know how.

Frank stood before her, an odd expression on his face. If she didn't know better, she might have thought it was a look of shame. But she did know better. She glared at him, her eyes sparkling with hate, her nails stabbing into her palms. If she only could, she would tear him apart.

Willie Joe's breath rustled in her ear as he gave a low, jeering chuckle. "We've got you now, don't we, my high-and-mighty Miz Logan, ma'am? We sure taught you and ol' Texas a lesson 'bout crossing the Chester brothers, didn't we?"

It was then that she remembered Jim, riding back at any moment, straight into the trap. Despair rose within her and she gave a choking cry. She had to do some-thing—something to warn Jim. But even as she finished the thought, it was too late. From outside the cabin came the deadly, unmistakable explosion of gunfire.

CHAPTER TWENTY-FIVE

JIM RODE home to the cabin in a state of high contentment. He had had a good day's hunting, and he was
returning to the woman he loved. He smiled to himself
as he pictured Bryony running out to greet him with
that upturned, lovely face, her eyes sparkling with the
special joy he always seemed to arouse in her. Yes,
things had turned out better than his highest expecta-
tions when he had first taken her from her California
home. Even though she hadn't regained her memory,
she had grown to love him once again, and he knew
that he had made her happy. She had regained the joyful
spirit he treasured, and each day she grew more beautiful and alive. These days and nights on the mountain
were among the best in his life. Part of him never wanted
them to end. Yet, he felt the day was coming when she
would be able to deal with the truth. Bryony trusted
him now. She was secure and content. If he told her
gently, Jim was convinced that she could accept her real
identity, and the awful deception that had been practiced on her by the Chesters. He felt certain she would
be relieved to learn that she was actually *his* wife and
that they had a home and a future awaiting them in

Texas. He'd been thinking about telling her for over a week, wondering each day if that might be the right time to tell her or if he should wait another week, another month. Prehaps tonight, when supper was done and the wind roared at the window and they sat together before the fire...

His thoughts broke off as Pecos suddenly lifted his head and twitched his ears. The stallion snorted. Jim put a hand to his mane.

"What is it, boy? Horses?"

There was really nothing to make him suspicious, aside from this tiny sign, and some sixth sense of danger that had grown as keen as a finely honed blade over the years. But he frowned and drew up just around the bend from the path leading to the cabin. Quickly tethering the bay to a mesquite, he went forward at a low, running crouch to survey the situation. His muscles were as tight as a drawn bowstring and all his concern was for Bryony. He drew his Colt and looked toward the cabin with an indrawn breath.

Tension quivered through his body like a whipcord as he saw the five horses hitched outside, the three men with guns drawn scanning the trail. Then, while part of his mind reacted in dread to the idea of Bryony being in danger, another, cooler part took note of and recognized two of the horses. He knew the mustang and the big roan belonged to the Chester brothers. And he knew as well that they must be inside with his wife.

Cold fury battled with white-hot fear as he summed up the scene. Then he heard Bryony scream inside the cabin. He couldn't make out the words she shrieked. An instant later, there was silence. He ran forward, keeping under cover as much as possible until he had no choice but to come out into the open. He was fifty feet from the men outside when he leaped into the trail, and all three swung toward him, guns blazing. But Jim's flashed fire in his hands and all three men dropped into the dust. He kept on running.

The door to the cabin burst wide, and the Chesters charged out. Willie Joe was holding Bryony fast against him, using her as a shield. Jim saw that the cowboy was holding a gun against her cheek.

"Logan, throw 'em down," Frank Chester boomed, sauntering across the porch. He had a six-shooter leveled at Jim's chest. "Don't try it. One move, and Willie Joe will blow a hole through the lady's face."

Jim's blood pounded in his ears. He was as still and deadly as a panther, his gaze boring into his enemies. He dared not glance at Bryony, dared not see the terror he knew must be reflected in her face. If he saw that, he knew it might push him over the edge, it might rob him of all reason and make him do something that might get both of them killed. So he kept his attention fixed on Frank and Willie Joe, his hands steady on the triggers of his guns, while he sought frantically for a way out of this mess. But Frank's voice barked at him again, an unmistakable note of derision marking it.

"Drop 'em, Logan! Now! Or I'll give Willie Joe the word. Her face is too pretty to blow to bits, ain't it? Well?"

Jim dared not hesitate further. He threw down his guns. Bryony gave a sob as Willie Joe shoved her across the porch. She landed in the dust at Jim's feet.

He bent swiftly and helped her to rise, his arms strong around her. Her small face was as white as parchment and streaked by tears. Her vivid eyes looked enormous and filled with horror as she clutched his arm. "Did they hurt you?" he demanded. "Are you all right?"

"Yes, but Jim, they mean to kill both of us! What are we going to do?"

He had no time to answer her, for Frank spoke again. He was surveying them from the edge of the porch, grinning. But for all his air of scorn, his complexion had a strange grayish pallor and there was an odd brightness in his olive eyes. "Well, Katharine, you see the trouble this hombre can land you in?" He gave a harsh laugh. "You should have stuck with me and Willie Joe, and you'd still be fine and dandy back in San Diego."

She straightened, clenching her fists. Her eyes were pools of emerald fire. "Don't you dare to call me Katharine!" she shot back venomously. "You're no better than a pile of buffalo dung—you and your filthy brother!" She gave her head a toss, and her proud, dainty chin came up in the way Jim remembered so well. "I'd rather be dead with my true husband than alive with you anytime!"

She heard Jim's indrawn breath beside her, and she turned to face him.

"You remember," he whispered hoarsely. "You *know*."

"Yes, I know." Bryony reached out to touch his cheek in a gesture of sadness, unable to tear her gaze from his stunned eyes. "I know, but it doesn't seem like it's going to do either of us any good, does it?"

Suddenly, Willie Joe bounded forward, his gun waving wildly. "You shut your mouth, you damned little bitch! You think we won't kill you because you're a woman? You think we'll let you back-talk us that way and get away with it? I'm gonna plug you right now and shut that damned mouth of yours. I'm gonna shoot you full of holes till there's nothing left for the buzzards to eat! And I'm gonna do it now!"

"Willie Joe! No!" Frank said sharply, half turning back toward his brother. "Hold on now . . ."

But the thin, wiry cowboy ignored him. Bryony's words had recalled her previous disdain the night he had appeared at the Triple Star gala, and her haughty contempt, then as now, heated to boiling the violence that always simmered in him. The killing that had already been done, the fighting in the cabin, Bryony's hot words—all these pushed him beyond the point of control. He raised the gun and pointed it straight at her heart. Still cursing her, he squeezed the trigger.

Two things happened simultaneously. Jim knocked Bryony to the ground, shielding her with his body, and Frank Chester darted in front of the gun, trying to grab it from his brother's hand. The bullet tore through his chest. Blood and bones splattered everywhere, staining the dust. Frank was blown into the air and off the porch, landing on his back in the rocky earth, his only sound a deep, heavy grunt.

In the stunned aftermath that followed, Jim dove for his own gun while Willie Joe backed away in confusion. His mouth gaped as he took in Frank's fallen form, the river of blood seeping across his chest, the gun still smoking in Willie Joe's own hands. Then, from the corner of his eye, he saw Jim grab the Colt and spring to his feet. Willie Joe's weapon veered toward him and roared again. But Jim's bullet struck first, shattering Willie Joe's brain as the shot went cleanly between his eyes. The thin cowboy's shot went wild, hitting a rock. He tumbled backward, dead the moment the bullet pierced his skull. Bryony, still lying in the dirt where Jim had knocked her, felt the bile rise in her throat as she beheld him, and she quickly looked away.

Then Jim was bending over her, helping her to her feet. He clasped her in his arms, holding her trembling form tight against him. "It's over, Bryony. It's all over. They'll never hurt you again."

She huddled against him, holding him as though she would never let go. "I can't believe you're safe.

We're both safe! It's a miracle." A shaky laugh came from her throat as she touched his cheek, his lips. "Oh, Jim..."

"*Katharine.*" They both heard the word and the agonized groan that followed it, and they turned in unison to stare at the bloodied form of Frank Chester.

"Frank?" Bryony had thought he was dead, but there was still a glimmer of life left in his huge body. She took a step closer, forcing back the nausea that threatened her at the sight and stench of his gaping wound. Jim moved beside her, his face grim.

It was obvious that Frank was dying. Bryony felt sickened looking at his tortured face, at the blood that still gushed from the pulpy gap in his chest. She took a few deep breaths to steady herself and then knelt at his side.

"Frank." She swallowed. "We're here with you."

She wondered what had happened to the hatred she had felt for him. It was gone. As she stared down at him, dying, helpless, in pain, she knew she ought to be feeling something. But she just felt empty. She had wanted him dead, yet she felt no pleasure at seeing him like this. Slowly, she remembered that he had been shot trying to stop Willie Joe from shooting her. He had taken the bullet that was meant for her. Wonderment spread through her. Numbly, she shook her head. "Why, Frank?" she whispered. "Why..."

His olive-brown eyes fixed themselves in desperation on her face. His hand moved limply at his side. "Katharine." His voice was a horrible wheeze. "I'm s...sorry...sorry..."

"Yes, Frank. It's all right." She put her hand over his. He clutched it for just a moment with the power of his old strength, and then his grip slackened. Bryony almost felt the life draining from his fingers. His hand dropped away. His face twitched once, there was another groan, and then he was gone, that hulking bear of a man who had used her, deceived her, and in the end, tried to save her. She made a strangled sound deep in her throat and closed her eyes, her head bent forward. Jim reached down and pulled her to her feet.

"Bryony, come away. There's nothing more to be done."

She allowed him to draw her away from Frank's body. They walked down the path until they reached a wide, smooth rock. Jim took off his buckskin jacket and put it on Bryony's shivering form. She seemed to be in shock. He wondered if she was going to faint.

The cool wind of the afternoon shook the branches of the trees and rustled the brush around them. A hawk called loudly overhead. Jim watched the pale, dark-haired woman in silence, wishing he could have spared her this ordeal. Just when she had grown strong again, and whole, she had to go through *this*. Damn those Chesters. Their deaths had not even partly compensated for all the pain they had caused her. Shooting was too quick and easy for what they deserved...

Bryony glanced up at him then. Her beautiful face wore a look of wonder. "You found me," she said slowly, as if seeing him for the very first time. "That day in San Diego on the hill. You came after me. Why?"

"Don't you know the answer to that?"

Her green eyes searched his face. "No. No, I can't understand. After all that happened between us, you came after me? You wanted me back?"

"I never stopped wanting you." He seized her arms. "Bryony, don't you know by now that I can't live without you?"

She shook her head, confused still by the sequence of events, trying to understand his reasoning. "You... you kidnapped me... I mean, took me away from Frank and Willie Joe to save me from them. Was that because you felt guilty about what they had done to me? Was it because you felt you owed it to me?"

"Bryony, stop it! Don't be a fool! When I saw you on that hill, it was the happiest moment of my life! Up until then, I thought you were dead. I had given up hope. Suddenly, a miracle was handed to me. I couldn't believe it. When I found out what had happened to you, that you had no memory of your past life, of me, or of anything, I was devastated. But I knew I had to get you away from the Chesters. I wanted only to spare you any more shocks, or I would have told you the truth right away! But a doctor in California warned me against it. He said your mind was already in a fragile state, and—"

She interrupted him, cutting across his explanation with sudden urgency. "But Jim, you didn't want me. You hated me. You said—"

"Don't!" he interrupted, pain shooting across his features. "Don't remind me of what I said. I know well enough what a jackass I was—a cruel, despicable jackass!" He grimaced, and his hands slid to her shoulders; he gripped them tightly. There was desperation in his voice.

"Bryony. You talked to me about forgiveness that last night we were together in the saloon. You were right. You always knew how to forgive, how to love. I didn't understand either one, not really. I found out that if you love someone, you accept them as they are, you treasure everything about them. I was wrong to want you to be different. All along, it's been your spirit and your courage I admire most, and there I was, trying to stamp it out! And now I know there's only one person here who needs to be forgiven. I don't deserve it, but I swear, Bryony, if you can bring yourself to forgive my pigheaded selfishness, I'll—"

"Hush." She put her fingers lightly to his lips. A smile brighter and more joyful than a pool of sunshine curved her lips. "Oh, Jim, there is nothing to forgive!"

"I'm damned if there isn't!" he retorted, a dark glint in his cobalt eyes. "Listen to me, Bryony..."

She pulled his head down and kissed him tenderly on the lips. Then she gazed at him with eyes that held only love. "Do I have to remind you? My memory has been mighty poor of late. Perhaps you have reason to beg my forgiveness, but I promise you, my one and only husband, I do not remember it."

"Bryony!" he began, a warning note in his voice, but she stopped him with a caress of her hand upon his cheek.

"No, my love. We will not speak of it. There is nothing to forgive. The past is gone—as good as forgotten. From now and forever, there will be only love between us. No more pain."

"I'm damned if I deserve you," he said huskily, crushing her to him in an embrace that squeezed her breath from her lungs, yet filled her with a quite delightful sensation. He kissed her soundly, then growled in her ear. "But now that I've got you back, you're stuck with me for good."

"That's a promise I'll hold you to," she murmured, lifting her mouth again for his kiss. And then, suddenly, on a rush of emotion, she cried out. "Oh, Jim, don't ever let me go!"

"I won't!" he vowed, his lips against hers. He kissed her with a violence that left no doubt of his determination. "I damned well won't!"

They might have been alone in a meadow of flowers for all the notice they took of their surroundings, of the death and mutilation farther up the path by the cabin. They clung to each other, filled with need, with the desperate realization that, against all odds, they had been given a second chance. And when sunset eventually brought its lavender bloom to the mighty peaks and painted the sky with pink and rose and gold, they stood in silhouette beneath the shadow of the mountain, wrapped in each other's arms and in a love that was far stronger, and far sweeter, than it had ever been before.

CHAPTER TWENTY-SIX

THERE WAS a three-quarter moon that night. It sailed high and bright over the mountains, spilling its cold white light upon the land and the waters, glittering the stream behind the cabin, frosting the pine trees in silvered mist, which rose up into the darkness like crystal smoke. Night creatures, visible in the beacon of this ghostly light, prowled the wild ridges and slopes of the mountains, seeking their prey. They skulked all about outside the mesquite walls of the cabin, but their presence did not disturb the man and woman within. These two were safe and snug from every danger, every care, and knew only the cocoon of blissful peace that they shared together before a glowing fire.

It had taken Jim several hours to bury the dead men and tend to their horses, and when at last he and Bryony had cleaned themselves of the dust of death, they had donned fresh clothing, warm against the December night, before sitting down to the hearty supper she had prepared. There was venison and turkey stew, hot biscuits dripping with honey, and a berry pie still steaming from the oven when she served it with strong, black coffee. They had much to talk about, and there was no more constraint between them as they told each other of all that was in their hearts and of all that they had feared and dreamed in the time of their separation.

Bryony recounted her capture by the Cheyenne and told of how the Chesters had massacred Swift-as-an-Elk, Two Bears, and the rest of the Indian party as they had been returning her to her home with Jim. She had time now to mourn Swift-as-an-Elk and Two Bears, to grieve for them with a pain sharper than any sword blade. Yet it was a healing pain. When she had regained her memory this afternoon, a dark burden in her heart had lifted, for all along she had grieved deep within, without knowing the cause. That pain had been all the more torturous because it was locked away in blackness, but now, she could grieve cleanly, openly, and it was a balm for the wound that had wounded her spirit. It was difficult for her to speak of her months with the Chesters, and Jim did not question her about that period. They both knew she had thought herself married to Frank, and Jim well realized what she had suffered because of that deception. He wanted only to spare her further distress.

He turned the subject to himself and described his own despair when he had lost her in the storm. On one note only did he bring up what had passed between them in the Tin Hat Saloon before her flight into the raging norther. He told her in no uncertain terms that he and Ruby Lee had never been lovers, that since meeting Bryony, there had never once been another woman for him. His comments to the contrary on that wild December night a year ago had been made to wound her, though they were without substance. Then he went on, relating for her all the anguish of those months searching for her, his initial hope that she would be found, and the subsequent agony of accepting the fact that she was probably dead. He omitted nothing up until the moment when he had spotted her on the hill over-looking the bay. At that point he gathered her in his arms and kissed her with every bit as much passion as he had that golden day, leaving no doubt in her mind about the power and intensity of his love.

For a while they sat before the fire, lost in each other's eyes, touching, caressing, savoring each precious moment together. Then Jim spoke, his mouth against Bryony's hair. "I'd like to go back to the Triple Star when we decide to leave here, little tenderfoot. I know Danny and Rosita would give just about anything in the world to have you back there again."

Bryony, who had been lying in his arms, now sat up and spoke with excitement, her cheeks glowing in the light of the fire. "How I miss them both! Oh, yes, we will certainly go back. As soon as we can pack up everything and set out. I love the cabin, Jim, but the Triple Star is our home."

He grinned at her. "I was hoping you'd feel that way. What do you think about sharing it? Before I left, Danny seemed pretty smitten by Duke Crenshaw's niece. I reckon by now he may have up and married her."

"Danny? Married?" It took her a moment to digest this startling news, and then delight showed in her delicate face. "Well, of course we will share the Triple Star with them! Your father left it to both of you! Tell me, this niece of Duke's. Is she nice? Is she pretty? Will she make Danny a good wife?"

Jim shrugged. "To tell you the truth, I was too miserable missing you to pay much notice. But I think old Dan did all right for himself." He went on, musingly. "You know, Bryony, it took me a long time to put down my roots at the Triple Star. But now that I have, I've grown pretty fond of the old place. Except it wasn't much of a home without you." Jim cupped her face in his hands. "I told you once that I would never let you go, that I would track you to the ends of the earth." He shook his head, his lean features rueful. "I didn't know at the time you would make me prove it, little tender-foot."

Bryony laughed. "Neither did I." Then her face sobered. "Jim, there is one thing I want to do when we go home to Texas... even before we go to the Triple Star." He raised an eyebrow, and she continued solemnly. "I want to find Two Bears' band. I must return to the Cheyenne and tell them what happened: that Swift-as-an-Elk died bravely trying to save me, that the others were murdered in their camp."

"They probably sent scouts, Bryony." Jim spoke gently. "They must have found the bodies and figured out what happened."

"Even so, I must go to them. Two Bears was a father to me, Jim, more so than Wesley Hill ever was. And Antelope Woman gave me that blanket—she was Swift-as-an-Elk's mother, and she treated me as she would her own daughter. It is my duty to seek them out, to ... to explain what happened, to pay homage, in a way, to those who died. I can't explain it, but it's something I feel I must do. If you don't want to come with me, then I will go myself and return to you at the Triple Star when I have done what I must do."

"Oh, no, you don't." His arms tightened around her. "You're not leaving me again. I'll go wherever you want, little tenderfoot, but you're not roaming halfway across the *Llano Estacado* without me."

"Well," she said consideringly, one finger tapping against her cheek. "I *could* manage it, of course, for the Cheyenne taught me all I need to know about survival upon the plains. And I know where to look for them..."

"Bryony," he said in a tone of warning, a dangerous glint entering his blue eyes. "Don't bait me. One more word, and I'll turn you over my knee."

"And," she continued, pretending not to hear this threat, though she couldn't hide the sparkle of mischief in her eyes, "if you're worried about meeting up with the Cheyenne, don't be, because I wouldn't let them harm you. I am a daughter of the *Tsistsistas*, and they would never hurt me or my companion. You'd be perfectly safe."

"Oh, I would, would I? It's a damn shame I can't say the same thing for you," Jim retorted. He seized her then, ignoring her outraged shriek and her attempt to break away. "That does it." Jim threw her down across his lap, giving her a resounding slap across the bottom. Bryony yelled again and struggled to get free, but he turned her over and pinned her to the floor, holding both her wrists in one of his strong hands. "For your information, *querida*, I am not worried about meeting up with the Cheyenne, and I just might offer them a few words of sympathy for having had to put up with my very troublesome and undeserving wife!"

"Troublesome! Undeserving!" She stopped trying to squirm free of him and lay still, staring up at him with mock indignation. "Just a little while ago, you told me you couldn't live without me, that I was the only woman you could ever love! And now you dare to call me troublesome and undeserving?"

He chuckled. "I don't want you getting a swelled head."

"And why not?" she retorted. "It will match my swelled belly."

"*What?*"

Stunned by this announcement, he released her. She sat up, a pleased smile lighting her lovely face. "You heard what I said," she murmured, pushing a lock of hair back from his brow. "I've been meaning to tell you all evening, but somehow I couldn't. Yes, my love, we are going to have a baby."

"How long have you known?" he demanded in wonder. "Why didn't you tell me before?"

"I've suspected it only for a few days. I'm not even certain yet," she admitted, but Jim cut her off, sweeping her into his arms.

"I am," he said firmly. A note of excitement throbbed in his voice. "It has to be true."

"I think so, too," she whispered, all her joy reflected in the emerald depths of her eyes. "Oh, Jim, I am carrying our child! And we're going to have this baby. It will be born at the Triple Star, where he or she belongs. We're going to have everything we always wanted—our home, our children, our life together!"

"All I ever wanted was you," he said huskily. "My little tenderfoot, my one and only love."

He swept her up then and carried her into the bedroom, and this time, unlike that first day in the cabin, she had no wish to stop him. She flung her arms around his neck and kissed him with all the tenderness in her woman's heart, and with a desire that no longer had to be stifled. He undressed her, and she him, and they held each other against the coldness of the night. Gently, he lowered her upon the bed. The warmth that flowed through her when he captured her lips in his own quickly ignited to flame. He stroked the mass of ebony hair that streamed down her naked back while he pressed his muscled length against her softly pliant limbs. Her slender body moved to the rhythm of his powerful one as her fingers caressed his rippling muscles and her heartbeat matched the wild thunder of his. Bryony moaned and clutched him to her with total abandon. His mouth aroused her nipples to stiff, hard peaks while his hands slid lower and sent a ripple of fire across her flesh. He took her to the crest of passion, filling her with a rapturous need that was answered only when he drove deep within her and thrust again and again, spiraling them both to a shattering explosion, which burst through them with white-hot fire. They were joined in a blazing union that left them breathless and spent. Afterward, they lay quietly together, for a little time, at peace.

"Jim." Bryony nestled closer within the circle of his arm, her hair brushing like silk across his chest. "Promise me something."

"Anything, *querida*."

"Never let us be driven apart again." Her voice quivered with ferocity as she turned and gazed up into his face. "I couldn't bear it. I need you too much."

"I swear to you," he told her, his blue eyes keen and vivid upon her. "We will be together for the rest of our days. Unless," he added, twining his fingers through the softness of her hair, "you decide that you want to leave me again, in which case I'll beat you soundly and..."

"Don't worry," she laughed, kissing his nose. "I won't."

They stared at each other as the moon sent thimbles of silver light in through the cracks of the shutters. Love and tenderness flowed between them. They had time now, time to be gentle, to cherish one another, and to say all the things they had left unsaid before. The future stretched before them, a future as vast and magnificent as the plains and mountains of the West. Together, they would conquer all the obstacles and sustain the precious beauty of the love they had almost lost, yet had found again with even greater richness than before. Together, they would fill each day and night with love.

EPILOGUE

HOT AUGUST sunlight shimmered through the Triple Star parlor, showering the room and all its occupants in a rich golden glow. Laughter rippled through the crowd, and there was the clink of glasses. Sweet wine quenched the thirst brought on by the broiling summer day. Through the open windows of the parlor came the fragrant and refreshing scent of Texas short grass, delicately laced with bluebonnets. The summer air was heavy, almost stifling. But the parlor, for all its August warmth, was a scene of celebration and frivolity. The deep baritone of Danny Logan filled the air as he improvised a comic song that oft repeated the words, "the littlest darling of Texas." Amidst much laughter and applause upon conclusion of this ditty, a small childish gurgle could be heard. Danny reached down and scooped the tiny child into his arms, lifting her high in the air. At his side, his wife, Rebecca, spoke with a smile.

"Oh, Danny! How foolishly she adores you! Now stop monopolizing the little dear and do put her down. Let's see if she'll walk to Bryony."

With a grin, Danny obeyed and set the child down upon her two tiny feet. Juliet Logan gazed at her mother, seated upon the floor only three feet away, her pale rose skirts disposed gracefully about her and her slender arms lifted in welcome.

"Come, Juliet. Walk to Mommy!" Bryony urged, a loving smile lighting her beautiful face. "Come, Juliet! I'll catch you, my darling!"

And the little girl, her raven hair threaded with pink ribbons, took one shaky step forward. Rosita gasped, and Danny shouted encouragement. Rebecca leaned forward, hands clasped.

Juliet tottered precariously and then, with a rush, put another foot forward. All in the blink of an eye she stumbled straight into Bryony's outstretched arms.

The pandemonium that greeted this accomplishment made the little girl gaze in bright-eyed wonder at the grown-ups surrounding her. She promptly buried her face in her mother's shoulder, but when she heard her father's voice above all the rest, she lifted her head and turned adoringly toward him.

Texas Jim Logan stood beside Rosita, his lean face lit by a grin. He had watched his daughter take these first steps with feelings of almost unbearable pride. Today, the tenth day of August, was Juliet's first birthday. How much joy she had brought to him and Bryony in that one short year! Glancing from her to her mother, he knew a pride and contentment beyond measure. He had all in life a man could want. For so many years he had been alone, riding from town to town, drifting, tracking, living a gunman's hard, lonely existence. Now he had a home, a family, a wife more lovely than the dawn, a daughter as sweet as the nectar of a peach. He didn't deserve them, he knew that sure as hell. But every day he did his best to make them happy, for Bryony and the little girl she had given him one year ago today were the treasures in his life, they *were* his life, and their simple presence filled his heart with all the joy a man could know.

"I propose a toast to my daughter!" he drawled, lifting his glass of wine high in the air. "To Juliet, child of Texas, daughter of the plains, princess of all the West!"

Bryony laughed at her husband's foolishness and hugged the little girl to her. She pressed her lips to the child's soft cheek, whispering something that made Juliet's exquisite midnight-blue eyes dance. Then she smiled up at Jim as he came forward and knelt beside the child.

"Now, I have a present for you—something from me and your mother," he told Juliet as she flung herself into his arms. He grinned and set her upon his broad shoulders. "Let's see what's waiting outside for my funny little cowgirl."

They all trooped outside, Rosita, Danny, Rebecca, and Bryony, as Jim led the way with the little girl high on his shoulders. Juliet laughed all the while and clutched delightedly at his thick chestnut hair. When he set her down upon the palomino pony inside the corral, everyone applauded. Bryony watched as Jim held his daughter atop the pony and proceeded to lead the animal about the corral. Her eyes shone with happiness as she gazed at the two of them, one so tall and strong, the other small and fragile. They were more dear to her than anything in this world.

Juliet, for all that she had inherited from Bryony's coal-black hair and delicate features, had her father's vivid blue eyes, and the same tough determination that characterized him. It was evident already in everything she did, and Bryony had to laugh whenever her own little daughter gazed up at her with just the look of hot-tempered wrath Jim produced when he was crossed. Of course, Juliet had also her mother's spirit and stubbornness, and her zest for life. She was a joyous little girl, fearless and filled with mischief. Watching her upon the pony, Jim's head bent close beside her dark one, Bryony felt a mist of tears veil her eyes momentarily as she thought about how lucky she was to have them. She had everything now, everything she had ever wanted. All the troubles she had known in her life, all the pain and sorrows, had all been worthwhile, because now she had them: Jim and Juliet, her two precious loves.

It was a beautiful, golden day, filled with the sweet laughter of a happy child. When it was over and darkness cloaked the prairie, Bryony tucked her daughter into the cool snugness of her bed. Night's shadows filled the nursery as she bent to kiss her child's cheek. She saw, with a smile, the little wooden horse Jim carved so long ago. It was clutched tight within Juliet's hand, as it always was when she slept. "I love you," Bryony whispered, smoothing the raven hair back from the girl's small, delicate brow. In her sleep, Juliet smiled and gave a tiny, baby sigh.

Bryony moved down the hall to the master bedroom. Soft lamplight lit the spacious chamber, reflecting upon the big brass bed, the silken coverlet, the silver-framed photograph resting on her dressing table near the open window. With a smile, she closed the bedroom door behind her, wondering where Jim could be. She had scarcely taken two steps into the lamplit room when she felt herself gripped by strong arms. Jim pulled her close to him, up against his naked chest. He was wearing nothing but his trousers, and his shoulders and sunbronzed torso gleamed dark copper in the golden light cast by the lamp. His voice sent thousands of shivers quivering up and down her spine.

"Do you have any idea how much I love you?" he

asked, kissing her deeply before she had time to reply. Bryony melted against him, her heart racing as it always did when he was near. Her lips met his with ardent delight, and she slid her slender hands up to his neck. Their kiss was long and deep and satisfying. When he lifted his head, Jim smiled down at her with his glinting blue eyes. His lips moved against her hair. "I have something for you, little tenderfoot. It's not as grand as the pony we gave to our daughter, but somehow, I reckon you'll like it all the same."

He pressed a small velvet box into her palm. "Oh, Jim, you didn't have to..." Bryony began, but broke off in astonishment as she opened the box and gazed in wonder at its contents. Diamond and jade stones winked up at her as she beheld a necklace of breathtaking beauty nestled upon a bed of velvet. Never before had she seen such an enchanting piece. She held it up with an exclamation of delight, marveling at the exquisite cut and brilliance of the gems, at the ornate yet delicate beauty of its design. Then she saw the earrings to match and she caught her breath. "They're... magnificent," she breathed, unable to tear her gaze from the lovely jewels.

"So are you, little tenderfoot." Jim spoke gently, catching her to him. "You, *querida*, are the jewel of my life."

Her jade-green eyes lifted to his. Their gazes held fast for several moments, then she clasped her arms around his neck. Remembering all they had been through, looking ahead to all they would share, she held him tight. "We're lucky, Jim, aren't we?" she whispered. "Very, very lucky."

"I reckon we are," he agreed, sweeping her into his arms. His eyes darkened to gleaming cobalt as he carried her toward the waiting brass bed. From outside the window came the sudden call of a dove flying home to nest. Bryony smiled in the cool, fragrant dusk.

"It's a pretty song, isn't it?" she murmured, and slid her fingers gently through her husband's hair. "A song for lovers, Jim. For us."

"Yes, Bryony." His arms tightened around her. "Always for us."

The night drifted slowly toward the dawn. The future awaited, and Bryony and Jim met it with joyous hearts, for they knew that theirs was a future of happiness—a destiny of love.